WATCHES II

THE ARMYBRATS

RICH KING

 FriesenPress

Suite 300 - 990 Fort St
Victoria, BC, V8V 3K2
Canada

www.friesenpress.com

ISBN
978-1-5255-7420-7 (Hardcover)
978-1-5255-7421-4 (Paperback)
978-1-5255-7422-1 (eBook)

Fiction, Horror

Distributed to the trade by The Ingram Book Company

Puddles of your blood will stain the beaches in splotches,
FOR I'M YOUR WORST NIGHTMARE,
WATCHES, WATCHES, WATCHES!

Every minute, the horrifying thoughts of the demented deliveryman, a.k.a. Stanley Watches Markesan—or whoever or whatever the thing was—continued to chip cells away from their minds. It gave them inexplicable feelings; feelings not found on any emoji flip board, feelings of trust being curtailed. Most importantly, they were unaware whom to depend on when their minds were boggled with fear.

The fear besieged all hope, hope that was like a single bubble in a vein, an embolization. The vicious cycle curtailed their better judgement like a cancerous tumor under chemical irradiation. One small cut could penetrate their hearts. Either end of the spectrum introduced possible death in this labyrinth of a Pac-Man ghost hunt.

Fear pressed heavily upon them, the fear of not knowing what was behind them, beside them, or in front of them—watching from beyond or within the shadows. It surrounded them. He lurked and waited. He waited and watched. *He watched from the dark, and he watched with his good eye, for he was . . . Watches, Watches, Watches.*

CHAPTER 1
THE CLEAN-UP

Smoke twirled between families gathered in the parking lot. Stretchers were lined up along one end of the lot. On them were bodies covered with sheets. Shadows outlined the humps in the fabric. They were being loaded into a couple of white vans that had two tiers, so they could be stacked tight and kept cool, six per truck. An ambulance and two paramedics were still on the scene. Firefighters were loading equipment into their trucks. The rest of the parking lot was empty—except for one lonely UPS truck. Most of the tourists had either gone home or to a bar to get plastered and forget the day's dealings.

Two men from the morgue were loading the bodies into the vans. They finished sliding one in, spun around for the next one, and then repeated the motion. It didn't take long to fill them. They would have to return with one of the vans to collect the last five bodies. After they finished loading, they left for the Iowa County Medical Examiner and Coroner's Office.

Back inside the House on the Rock Museum, it remained quiet. The power was out, and it was close to 2100 hours, so it was also dark except for emergency lighting in a few areas. A few police officers still swept areas with flashlights trying to locate any other possible survivors. It appeared as if a war had been staged there. Many priceless artifacts were riddled with bullet holes. The walkway carpeting was bloody and shredded, glass display cabinets were shattered, items were overturned, and the main entrances, including the catwalk as well as the room that never ended, otherwise known as the Infinity Room, were gone. Obliterated!

The police officers tossed objects aside as they searched through the wreckage. A few firemen worked alongside them. All the fires had been contained, but the smoke was still thick in some areas.

"Dodgeville Fire Department, call out," one firefighter said while checking through overturned artifacts and rubble. SWAT personnel exited as the firemen and police officers continued searching for signs of life.

Back in Verona, Wisconsin, the Emerson family had just returned from the House on the Rock and were dropping off their friends, Jake Carson and his son, Pete. The Emersons had taken them to the House on the Rock to get away from reality for a while. Unfortunately, all they had received was a reminder that no one was safe anywhere.

Mark Emerson, a police officer, put the car in park. The Emerson boys were in the car as well. Billy sat on the bench seat between his mom and dad, and Danny sat in the back seat next to Pete.

"Thank you for the fun time, Mr. Emerson," Pete said. Jake echoed his gratefulness.

"Well, it was supposed to be a fun, relaxing family time," Mark's wife, Mary, said.

Jake sighed. "Ah, Mary, even though things went a little haywire, I believe these boys still had a booming time. Though we have our differences about how things were resolved, I think we can all thank the Lord that we made it out of there alive."

Danny and Pete glanced at each other as Mark and Mary agreed.

As Jake stepped out, Mark spun around and grabbed Pete's arm. "Billy and Danny already got the talk, but I need your assurance that if you encounter this Mr. Fallway guy again, I'll be the first to know about it. I want to take a look at this guy's history. Don't get me wrong; you guys were the real heroes today. You really were. But you're just kids. I'm thankful you're all safe, including Wesley and his father and Robert and Barbara and Duffy. But you guys should have never been placed in a situation like this. I can't imagine my kids having to shoot at people to survive. I understand you might think Mr. Fallway was a hero today, but he's far from that. He endangered your lives by putting you on a pedestal before that insane freak. I fear he's made you guys a target. Therefore, I told Billy and Danny to use their better judgement when it comes to this Fallway character. Do you understand?"

Pete nodded. "Yes, sir."

"I'm not so sure you guys do. But in the event that he shows up, I expect at least the courtesy of informing me, so I can question him."

"Don't you mean 'interrogate'?" Billy asked.

"No," Mark replied. "I said 'question.'"

The boys laughed. Then Mark released Pete's arm, and he followed his father out of the car.

Jake ducked to peer in through the back door. "We'll have to do a cookout one of these days—brats, beer and dogs. Pete and I will probably be visiting my wife in the hospital here shortly, if not tonight then tomorrow. You kids have a good night, and thank you." He shut the door.

During the remainder of the ride, Mark listened to an AM station on the radio. There were a couple subdivisions in Verona, Wisconsin. The Carsons lived in East View Heights, and the Emersons lived in Cross-Country. Duffy Felter and his parents lived across from the same park that could be seen from both their houses. The Felters lived closer to the forest that wrapped up over the hill toward the high school. Some nice paths wove through the forest. One linked the neighborhood to the high school's backyard. The radio continued its broadcast as they drove across a bridge heading home.

Danny glanced down to see the water flowing. He had a brief flashback of when they came face to face with Watches for the first time under that bridge. He remembered the muddy monster that had attacked them a couple of times there. Those were some of the most outrageously freakish encounters. But he felt assured that Watches was gone. *He had to have been blown to bits from that grenade Pete launched at him,* Danny thought. *I'm sure of it.*

In the background, the radio announcer was discussing the catastrophe at the museum. "In today's news, a rather haunting shootout took place in Spring Green at the House on the Rock off Highway Twenty-three, just north of Dodgeville, Wisconsin. The shootout lasted over an hour, with the death toll currently at seventeen people and six injured. Authorities suspect a possible cartel; however, they're not certain at this time.

"Most museum goers are returning home at this hour. Some are looking for possible refunds due to their tours being cut dramatically short. Although, it's difficult to say if this was a dispute over drugs or an act of terrorism, seventeen members of the faction have been killed.

"Local authorities, including the Dodgeville Fire Department, are still sifting through the wreckage. Damages include, but are not limited to, the concession office, the main catwalk to the House on the Rock, the adjacent catwalk to the House on the Rock, and the Infinity Room, which was destroyed. Speculation at this time places the damages at roughly $14.7 million.

"One of the presumed suspects in today's shootout is Stanley Markesan, former UPS driver from Wausau, Wisconsin, and husband to Rosalyn Markesan. According to authorities, Stanley Markesan was placed in custody sometime in the late 1970s after putting his wife in a coma and severely injuring their son, who was twelve at the time.

"He is a wanted felon, and escaped fugitive, and authorities still have not recovered his body. His last known whereabouts was in the Infinity Room when it collapsed.

"Another suspect, Joe Johnson from Little Rapids, Wisconsin, may also have been in the Infinity Room when it collapsed."

Mark turned the volume down and glanced at Mary as they pulled into their driveway. The garage door opened, and they drove inside.

After Mark threw the shifter into park and killed the engine, the garage door closed slowly behind them, then stopped midway. Mark hit the button two more times to get it to close. As he waited for it to obey, he turned back to his sons. "What was the name of that guy you had a confrontation with in the Infinity Room?"

"Watches!" Danny cried.

"Ah, OK, Watches!" Mark bit his lower lip and sighed. "Don't you guys think I'll be letting this go. I'll be investigating this Mr. Fallway character too, mark my words!"

Billy smiled. "Your words are always marked, Dad!"

"How do you figure?" Mark asked.

"Isn't that your name?" Billy asked with a laugh. "Mark?"

"Ha ha," Mark said, unable to resist a smile despite the serious circumstances. "Very funny!"

CHAPTER 2
THE CHASE

Back in the museum, a few cops left the café and entered a larger room, their flashlight beams bouncing across the floors and walls. One of the cops swept his beam across a carousel. It was a phenomenal attribute to the tour, marking the halfway point. It held 220,000 lights and, when powered up, filled the room with the sounds of a vibrant orchestra. It was the most banging room in the House on the Rock. Now it was dark and quiet. However, when the cop's flashlight beam swept over the carousel, it revealed a bloody-faced figure snarling at him from one of the carriages.

"Oh my God!" the officer cried, swinging his flashlight back across the carousel to reexamine the carriage.

"What is it, Jack?" another officer asked.

"I swear I saw someone," the cop replied.

By that time, all three cops were standing in a row before the carousel, shining their flashlights across the assortment of horsemen, kinnaras, and maidens. They were searching for whatever had triggered Jack's outburst.

Meanwhile, outside in the parking lot, five bodies remained on stretchers, waiting for the guys from the morgue to return to pick them up.

Officer Darcy watched the SWAT team pull out, followed by the firetruck. Then he noticed the UPS truck chilling in the back of the lot. He shined his flashlight at the vehicle's license plate and signaled for another officer to join him as he advanced toward the truck.

Darcy grabbed his handheld radio. "House on the Rock, we have an 11-54, moving in for a closer look, over," he said, alerting dispatch about the suspicious vehicle.

A dark face in the driver's mirror wiggled as it looked in the rearview mirror. "No, no, no," a man grumbled. "Stay where you are." He didn't like the fact that the cops were closing in on the truck.

Suddenly, a box flipped out from the other side of the truck and landed in the grassy median between the police officers and the vehicle. Both cops stopped dead in their tracks and shined their flashlights at it. Suddenly, Officer Darcy grabbed his partner and tackled him to the ground. His brave act saved them both from the flames that ripped a couple of trees in half, knocking them over. The pavement buckled before the median, and the explosion lit up the entire lot. The stars in the night sky were consumed by bright fire and smoke. Then the UPS truck's lights snapped on, and it squealed out of the parking lot, heading for the far exit.

"What the hell was that?" asked Darcy's partner, Officer Penske.

"That, my friend, was a bomb!" Darcy said. "Quick, call it in. Let's go!"

Penske grabbed his radio from where it had fallen to the ground as they ran toward their squad cars and clicked the "talk" button. "This is Officer Penske at the House on the Rock. We have a 10-80 and are in pursuit of 11-54 toward Highway 23, over."

"That's affirmative," Dispatch replied. "Code 20, pursuit in progress Highway 23, House on the Rock. Any available units, please advise. Possible code 10 of 10-66." They were reaching out for any support from additional officers in the area, alerting them of a possible bomb threat.

Penske and Darcy got into their squad cars and tore out of the parking lot after the UPS truck, which turned south on Highway 23. Little did the young cops realize, they were about to embark on the greatest car chase of their lives.

The UPS truck took Highway 130 northwest of Dodgeville heading toward "The coolest place in the nation with the warmest hearts," Lone Rock, as it read on the community sign. Highway 130 was one of the windiest, head-bashing, twisty routes in the area.

Darcy got on his CB radio. "Attention all available units, this is Officer Darcy in pursuit of a possible suspect in a UPS truck heading northwest on Highway 130. Last known location was the House on the Rock, over."

Mark was kissing Mary in the garage when he heard the call over the CB radio. The boys had already gone inside.

"Oh no, Mark," she whimpered as he ran toward his car.

"That's one of my officers," Mark said as he flung the passenger door open and leaned in to retrieve the CB mic. "Officer Darcy, this is 315. Who's in the other squad car, over?"

"Oh, hi, Mark. I have Officer Penske behind me. We're in pursuit of a UPS truck that decided to use pyro against us in the parking lot at the museum, over."

"Please advise I'm on my way. Keep your distance, and shut your sirens off. Follow only. Do not pursue. How copy?"

"What's that, boss?" Darcy shouted through the static.

Mark shook his head; he couldn't make out a word Darcy said.

"What'd he say?" Penske asked. "Something about drive and follow?"

"That's what we're doing," Darcy replied. "Just keep up with me, Joe."

"Roger." Joe rolled his eyes as the CB's cord bounced over the console.

Mark clicked his garage door opener, and the garage door lifted partway and then stopped. Suddenly, he had a flashback of driving through his old garage door in Granite View, Wisconsin. The door had done the same damn thing to him in his old house in 1974. Back then he had ripped right through that sucker with his family car like a wrecking ball. He revved his engine and grabbed the shifter to drop the tranny into reverse, ready to repeat history.

"Don't you dare!" Mary hollered. She hit the button on the wall near the kitchen door, and the garage door finished opening.

He smiled and waved at her, waiting for the door to open fully. "Love you, honey," he mouthed just before his tires left thick patches of steaming rubber all the way from the garage onto the road.

"Michael James Anglekee, you stupid maniac!" she hollered.

The name she had just hollered was his real name. Her real name was Clarice Anglekee. In 1976, the beast named Stanley Markesan, a demented deliveryman, had driven a UPS truck through their home. At the time, Mike and Clarice utilized WITSEC (Witness Protection Program) to relocate to Verona, Wisconsin, under the aliases Mark and Mary Emerson with their sons, Billy and Danny. A handler by the name of Wayne Richards had helped make the move possible. He worked out of an office downtown above the floral shop owned by Barbara Felter, Duffy's mom.

While settling down in Verona, they started new jobs and made new friends, including Robert and Barbara Felter and Jake and Julie Carson. Each couple had a son—Duffy and Pete, respectively—who later became best friends with Billy and Danny. All four boys were later introduced to another boy, Wesley Fifer, whose grandfather, Gerald, owned a camp up north. The five boys were the prime target of Watches, a.k.a. Stanley Markesan. His steadfast retaliation against Officer Anglekee had moved on to the next generation. For years he had held a grudge over a domestic dispute gone viral.

Mike and Clarice's handler, Wayne Richards, underwent a series of attacks from the demented deliveryman as well. As his office crumbled around him, he had no choice but to fake his own death. Utilizing WITSEC (his own agency), he also relocated to Verona. There he became an investigator known as Ralph P. Fallway. He had taken an oath to protect the Anglekee family, and he felt duty-bound to honor it.

Without their parents' knowledge, Fallway had trained the Emerson boys and their friends in self-defense and tactical combat techniques. He also trained them in how to shoot. He trained them in things that most boys their age could only dream about. The five boys proved how lethal they had become at the hands of Mr. Fallway when their family vacation was torn apart at the House on the Rock by none other than Stanley "Watches" Markesan. Now the next chapter of their lives was slowly coming to light.

Mark soared down Highway 18/151 toward Dodgeville and then took Highway 23 north toward the House on the Rock in Spring Green. He had a solo flashing light on the roof of his car as he ripped the air apart. He didn't know what to expect from his young officers hunting the demon's truck. But when he heard mention of a UPS truck, the mere thought of Stanley still being alive churned his guts like butter as he tore more rubber from his tires, screaming down the highway.

Back on Highway 130, the two police officers continued to pursue the UPS truck. Contrary to Mark's orders, which they had been unable to understand, they kept their sirens on and maintained a high rate of speed. Their lights flickered, glaring through trees and across farmhouses.

Another box flipped out toward Officer Darcy's squad car and landed in the ditch. The explosion just across the road threw dirt, grass, and rocks behind him, jolting the rear end of his squad car. He dodged a power pole as it split apart and fell. Penske drove right through the flames but managed to stay on the hardtop, miraculously avoiding the pole as well.

"Whoa!" Darcy hollered across the radio. "You OK back there?"

"I'm great, Penske replied. "How are you?"

"You two nitwits stand down now!" Mark shouted over the radio. "Shut your damn sirens off, and just follow. Do not antagonize that driver. Do not use your sirens. Do you read?"

A burse of static came across the radio in each of their squad cars, but no words were transmitted. The cops just stared at their radios with crooked glares.

Moments later, they pulled up to the UPS truck. Penske remained at the rear; Darcy drove alongside the driver's side. "You must pull over immediately!" he said over the car's PA system.

The big dude in the driver's seat of the UPS truck smirked at the officer. Then he leaned back and threw a leg out the open door and kicked the passenger-side mirror off Darcy's car.

"Don't do that!" Darcy shouted. "That's criminal damage. Pull over. Pull over, or we will be forced to fire."

The big dude straightened himself out and pointed at the road ahead, which curved out of sight. Officer Darcy turned his steering wheel so that the nose of his squad car slammed into the side of the UPS truck and pinned it against the guardrail.

A skinny dude in the cargo bay jumped through the cab door and bumped a tattooed kid in the passenger seat. The tattooed kid glanced down at him after trying to lean out the door to shoot at Officer Penske, who slammed into the back of the truck. Together, he and Darcy pinned the box truck to the rail. Sparks flew up and over Penske's windshield. On the other side of the guardrail was no more road—no more earth. A cliff face dropped straight down. Treetops were swaying at the level of the road; that's how high they were.

Just then the truck's back door slid upward. A box flipped out and bounced into the middle of the road. A moment later, it lit up the sky, the guardrail, and rocks along the cliff face on the other side of the road. The exploding box sent pieces of the road in every direction, pushing a mushroom cloud upward. The road actually split apart and slid down the cliff.

The skinny guy stood in the truck's loading door and tossed boxes onto the hood of Penske's car. Before Penske realized it, five bombs were resting against his windshield. He did the noblest act possible: he swerved right and slammed his fender into the guardrail, sending four boxes over the ledge. However, one box refused to follow. It bounced off the driver's-side mirror and dribbled down the road. Penske stared at it as he drove past, his eyes bugging out as he stepped on the gas.

Dirt and grass blew beneath the guardrail as the four boxes blew upward and separated branches from trees. A section of the guardrail rippled inward and scraped across the road. The skinny guy's eyes widened as he stood in the doorway and covered his head. Fire sprayed through the door, and flames roared into the night sky as the last package obliterated the road behind Penske's squad car. The explosion launched his car into the back of the UPS truck, its grill slamming into the skinny guy's jaw. The bumper crippled the doorframe after sending the dude backwards through the truck. The driver and passenger glanced down at their unconscious partner.

When the squad car fell off the truck's rear bumper its front wheels bounced. Penske overcorrected and jerked into the guardrail a few times. Darcy continued to ram the truck into the guardrail.

"Idiot!" the truck driver said, reaching for his gun on the dash.

The skinny guy regained consciousness and returned to the crippled loading door as Penske slammed into the truck's rear bumper again. The skinny guy flew out the door onto the hood of Penske's patrol car. The man drew a 9 mm pistol and aimed it at Penske. The officer swerved against the guardrail as a few rounds flew through his windshield. The skinny guy was forced over the cliff along with another box, which followed the bloody-faced man. As he fell next to the box, he aimed his gun at the sky. The box ignited in midair. The force of the explosion threw the man's body sideways and dispersed him through the trees below. It also flipped Penske's squad car over, sending it skidding upside down along the guardrail.

Officer Darcy glanced in his rearview mirror at the brilliant explosion along the road. He could no longer see Penske's car. Smoke enveloped everything.

Penske screamed as his car slid along the rail. Luckily, the explosion had forced a tree to fall against the cliff. Branches bounced off the center of the road. The tree also happened to catch Penske's car, a branch smashing over his trunk. The tree rocked a bit as the car piled into it, coming to a stop with part of it hanging over the guardrail.

Darcy sighed with relief when he noticed Penske's squad car fall halfway over the guardrail with the other half of the car still resting on the tree. He could see the car's undercarriage as the guardrail stripped the siren from the roof, but he knew Penske was still alive.

Suddenly, bullet holes appeared in his hood. Darcy backed away from the driver's door and released the box truck from the guardrail. Just as he scooted in behind the truck, a tractor came around the corner. Another box flipped out of the truck, and Darcy swerved as it tipped off his sirens and flipped onto the road behind him. Dead center along the center line, the box rolled and flipped vertical. The blast engulfed the tractor. The farmer drove far off the road and away from the flames. He threw open his tractor door, tore off his John Deere hat as sweat beaded down his brow, and shook his fist at them until he noticed the cockeyed squad car teetering over the guardrail.

The farmer jumped back into his tractor and drove across the road, lifting his bucket as he did. He swiveled the tractor alongside the squad car. As the tree slid sideways, it pushed the squad car over the guardrail, but the farmer caught it with his bucket just in time, pulling it back onto the road.

"Officer down," Darcy said over his CB radio as he continued to pursue the truck. "I need emergency dispatch to my location."

"What the hell just happened?" Mark hollered, slamming his fist into the dashboard.

"Sorry, boss. Penske is sort of upside down at the moment."

"Do not push that UPS truck!" Mark said. "Stand down. Keep your speed down! Do not chase; just follow. Do you read? No sirens."

"Yes, Lincoln Charles, over," Darcy said. The term for "Loud and clear" was the police call similar to the military phonetic alphabet, Lima, Charlie.

"Darcy, I don't know who's in that truck," Mark said, "but whoever it is, do not lose them."

"Roger." Darcy turned his sirens off and then continued to follow the truck at a distance.

CHAPTER 3
PIANO MAN

Inside the House on the Rock, the cops gave up searching the carousel and walked away. Suddenly, a flash of light stunned all three of them, and they stopped dead in their tracks. The light flickered once again, and the room became an ear-screeching, arm-hair-bending nightmare. Power had been intermittently restored, and the carousel began picking up speed. Orchestra music echoed over the rafters and bounced off the ceiling. It started in slow motion and then picked up before stopping again as the power flickered. After a few flickers, it returned even louder. The cops spun around to watch the red carousel with 220,000 lights streaming in circles.

They were dumbfounded. Their flashlights at their waists, the three beams of light shined on the ground in front of them. The room remained dark for the purpose of entertainment from the 220,000 lights on the carousel. However, during a single rotation of the carousel, the bloody-faced demon reappeared. He was sitting in a carriage staring at them. It was Watches. All three cops advanced toward the carousel, their guns drawn. One cop swung wide left, another wide right, and one went up the center. The sound of the carousel was deafening.

"Sir, step down!" Officer Thompson ordered.

Watches' trench coat was half torn, his face bloody. His evil eyeball was visible, as was his black eye patch. Once again, he disappeared when the carousel spun him around the back side. The cops adjusted their aim as it rotated. This time the carriage returned without Watches.

"What the . . .?" Officer Jones asked.

The officer on the far right suddenly lost his nose and parts of his face as a throwing star flew through it. He bounced off a wall thirty feet behind him and fell to the floor with blood seeping into the red carpet around him. Officer Thompson ran to his aid, and Officer Jones took a knee, maintaining his aim on the carousel. It circled again, only this time Watches was standing on the edge facing them. A horse was slowly moving up and down before him. Officer Jones opened fire. The horse's neck split wide open, and a few lights sparked near Watches' waist as he twirled a rope over the side of the carousel.

"Sir, I will shoot you if you don't vacate the carousel!" Officer Jones shouted.

"Shit, he's dead, Tom!" Officer Thompson said.

Officer Jones glanced over at him and then shot two rounds at Watches. However, a rope cinched around his waist, and his body flew toward the railing along the carousel. Watches walked out from behind the carousel. He was no longer holding onto the other end of the rope. It was tied to the carousel, and Tom Jones's body was dragged through the railing like a noodle through a colander as he screamed in agony.

Officer Thompson stood up and aimed his gun at Watches. "Stop that, mister!"

Watches cackled. "Ha ha! You pathetic little pig. Watch him squirm. Ha ha."

"Mister, I order you—"

"You aren't ordering shit," Watches said, glaring.

Tom's body pulled the railing tight to one wall as the carousel continued to wind the rope. "Aaghh!" he yelled, but his scream was cut short as the rope cinched him in two, the carousel sparking along its undercarriage. The railing bounced forward, and pieces of Tom's body flapped on the ground as the carousel continued to drag him.

"You motherfucker!" Officer Thompson shouted, opening fire on Watches.

Watches ducked. A self-playing grand piano was playing on the ceiling above the officer. Watches pointed at it with a swift downward motion of his hand. As Officer Thompson continued shooting, the piano fell, consuming his body.

Watches stood up and brushed off his torn trench coat, cackling hideously. "Ha ha, piano man. Watches, Watches, Watches!"

On Highway 130, Officer Darcy continued following the UPS truck while avoiding box bombs.

Inside the truck, the driver, an older man with wrinkly skin, tattered clothing, and thin blond hair was at the wheel. The much younger, dark-haired, tattooed kid was now in the back tossing boxes out of the truck. A handheld device bleeped on the console, and Bonzo picked it up.

"Go for Bonzo," he said.

"Yo, numb nuts, where's the truck?"

"I'm in it, boss!"

"No shit!" Watches stood in the parking lot next to the crater in the asphalt and the fallen trees. "You picking me up or what?"

"Yes, boss, I'm just in the middle of a car chase right now. I'll have to call you back." He hung up and cranked the steering wheel as the road curved sharply ahead.

Officer Darcy slammed into the UPS truck's rear fender as he skidded around the curve. The truck lifted up on two wheels and sparked along the guardrail. Then it plunged sideways, rolling down a gradual embankment. The truck flipped and rolled, tossing up shrubs, grass, and frogs. Whatever was in its path, it tossed it, including the tattooed fellow consumed by boxes as he hit the ceiling, then the floor, as the truck continued down the incline.

As the truck continued to roll, Bonzo called Watches. "Hey, boss, slight problem!"

Watches was standing at the entrance of the House on the Rock. "You had one mission, you bonehead, one mission!"

"Oh crap!" Bonzo exclaimed as the Wisconsin River consumed the truck.

Officer Darcy's car spun in a semicircle against a cliff on the opposite side of the guardrail and blew a tire. The smashed fender exerted enough force to crimp the hood. It popped open, and smoke rolled out from underneath, crawling up the rock face. Darcy's body shook violently in the seat, only his lap belt holding him in. He sat there for a few seconds, blinking. "Ow," he said.

"Hello, Bonzo?" Watches shouted. "Crap, what?" He looked at the fat phone and checked to see if it was disconnected. He lowered the antenna and then raised it again. "I take it you're not picking me up, are you? D'oh!" he pressed a button with his index finger and headed back toward the House on the Rock.

Watches was walking back into the main lot when he noticed the five remaining bodies. He pranced around the crater in the asphalt from the explosive charge set off earlier and giggled. "Someone had fun." He unzipped one of the body bags. "Aww, poor Charlie! Sorry about this, buddy." He pulled the limp body onto the ground, then dragged it toward the brush.

CHAPTER 4
THE MORTUARY

One white van returned for the last five bodies. As its headlights turned into the entrance, they revealed potted flowers along each side of the drive. The flowerpots were like large kettles with holes scattered throughout and more flowers peeking through the holes. Other things were also peeking out, including reptilian critters that appeared to be ceramic dragon lizards crawling around the pots.

The van pulled up to the stretchers. The two morgue guys jumped out and loaded the first body. At one point, a body bag wiggled a bit. The two men didn't notice the movement as they loaded it into the van.

After loading all the bodies, they jumped back in the van, their headlights sweeping through the trees and shrubs as they turned to leave. The lights passed over poor Charlie's face as his body lay behind a stump, but he was concealed by undergrowth.

As the van drove out of the lot, the dragon lizards on the flowerpots cocked their heads and winked. One snapped at a fly. Their tails waved away from the kettles. Watches had brought life to the ceramics, and evil was definitely present.

On the way down Highway 23, a significant bump kicked the entire group of bodies upward. A grunt came from the back of the van. The driver, Paul, turned to his passenger. "Did you hear something, Joel?"

"I don't know!" Joel replied. "I hear strange things in this business daily!"

"Man, we've been at this for hours!"

"Yup, but at least we can go home after this."

They entered the mortuary's parking lot and backed up to a bay door, then jumped out to enter the mortuary.

Inside the van, a zipper on one of the body bags opened slightly, and fingers snaked out of the hole. Suddenly, the van doors opened, and the fingers slipped back inside the bag. The two men unloaded one body. They laid it on a cart, and Paul wheeled it into the building. Joel lit a cigarette and stood near the tail end of the truck, smoking.

Once again, the fingers wiggled out of the hole and slowly unzipped the bag. As he stood and smoked while staring into the empty mortuary hall, Watches emerged from the bag behind him. The van remained dark inside. Streetlamps in the distance created a silhouette of the devil as Watches made his way toward the front of the van, climbing over the console into the driver's seat.

Suddenly, Paul returned with an empty cart. He handed Joel a can of beer and smiled. "All I could find in the cooler were these two cold ones next to all the other 'cold ones.' I guess we'll have to make them last."

Joel exhaled cigarette smoke and sighed. "Ah, man, well, one beer is better than no beer. At least we can finish this workday with some taste, huh? Cheers, sir!" Their beer cans collided as they toasted the end of a nightmarish shift. Paul sat on the van's bumper and sipped his beer. Joel leaned against the van enjoying his beer and the remainder of his cigarette.

"So, Joel, whatcha ya think about the museum?" Paul asked as he watched Joel stomp out the butt of his cigarette.

"What a mess!" Joel stated as he kicked at remnants of tar and ash with his boot.

Paul took another swig of beer. "Ya think it has something to do with the cartel?"

"Nah, just some nutjob—or maybe a heist!"

Paul leaned back, and an empty body bag fell and rolled over top of him. He sat up straight and pulled it off, staring at it. "What the hell?"

As he jerked away from the body bag, the van's brake lights lit up the cinder-block wall behind them, casting their silhouettes across the loading dock. The van fired up, and the reverse lights came on. Paul shoved the empty body bag aside and dove off the van as Joel stepped away from it.

"What is this?" Joel asked. The reverse lights went out, and the van crept forward ten feet. Joel leaned forward to see a dark figure staring back at him from the side mirror. He walked toward the driver's door. "Hey, you! What's the big idea?" He and Paul were encapsulated by mystery, clutching their beer cans for dear life.

The van pulled away, racing to the far end of the lot. Joel retreated back near Paul. "I don't know what this bonehead is doing," Joel said, taking another sip of beer.

Suddenly, the van revved its engine. As Joel and Paul continued to drink beer and watch, the bright white reverse lights snapped on. The van ripped the air apart as it stormed right at them, the tires spitting debris and smoke. Paul threw his arm up as if the reverse lights were too bright. Joel continued to stare at the rear doors bouncing against the sides of the van. Joel dropped his beer and tackled Paul, who inadvertently dropped his beer. The van turned slightly toward where they landed on the ground.

As the reverse lights swept across them, Joel tried dragging Paul away. An ear-piercing squeal split the air as the van slammed on its brakes. Joel stood up just as the remaining bodies flew out of the back of the van like torpedoes. One body hit Joel, causing his legs to buckle backward. There were a couple snaps, possibly the fibula or patella. More bodies piled on top of them. Then the van took off, the back doors bouncing and swinging from side to side. One door slammed shut, but the other hung to the side as the van squealed down the road. Joel and Paul were buried in bodies, their own bodies stationary under the pile.

CHAPTER 5
UP THE RIVER

Along Highway 130 were seventeen squad cars with their flashers on, an ambulance, and a firetruck. The squad cars stretched along the highway, which made a sharp turn north just before Lone Rock. Some of them were on the bridge, their emergency lights illuminating the entire area. Floodlights shined down on the river from the bridge and along the cliff side of the road.

The bridge was made of steel; its girders were an aquamarine color. Steel girders on either side of the suspension bridge towered into the air about twenty feet over the roadway. Connected to the metal were more cross members that spanned the length of the bridge, all painted the same color. Other cross members crossed over the roadway and connected the other side of steel girders. All the girders appeared like large letter A's and V's spanning the length of the roadway over the Wisconsin River. Every V had another steel girder straight up and down through the center. The two letters overlapped each other along the length of the bridge.

Along the riverbank, a braided cable was looped around the axle of the undercarriage of the UPS truck from a winch mounted on a firetruck. They had tied the truck down as the Wisconsin River pushed violently against its side. Cops were on the embankment and in the water, swarming around the truck. Two cops were inside it.

Just then, Mark roared up in his car, parking next to Officer Darcy. He jumped out . "Where's Jeremy?"

Officer Darcy pointed down Highway 130 where a sandy beachfront curved up to the road. Near it were paramedics and an ambulance. "He's with the paramedics, sir."

Mark ran across the road to see the UPS truck upside down in the river. He looked upriver at the paramedics. Then he glanced down at the bridge where squad cars and a firetruck were setting up. He looked back at the belly of the UPS truck. Something wasn't sitting right with him. He couldn't quite put a finger on it. He was beaten down like a tomato for salsa. The memories of Stan's truck burning in front of his house were real. Suddenly, it hit him.

"Get out of the water!" he screamed.

Some policemen shined their lights at him. On the bridge, the firemen watched Mark jump and wave like a madman. The firemen ran around their truck as they realized they may be in danger. The four squad cars on the bridge didn't move, as the firetruck inched between them, working its way off the bridge. The UPS truck continued to bob in the water just below the bridge like a buoy.

Farther downriver, Bonzo and the tattooed man were crouched behind some shrubs on the opposite side of the river from where local authorities were swimming around the wreckage trying to remove their buddies from the area. Mark was farther down the embankment, screaming and hollering for people to move away from the truck. Cops were swimming through the water, some still alongside the UPS truck. One cop had just jumped from the truck's undercarriage into the water.

Bonzo held his radio to his ear. "Boss, you there?"

"Yeah, I'm here, you numbskull," Watches replied. The van he was driving sideswiped a stop sign and then bounced through a pothole and threw him around inside the cab.

"It's in place, boss!"

"Good. Blow it!"

"Roger that!" Bonzo tossed the radio at the other guy, who juggled it before he caught it. From his breast pocket, Bonzo extracted a square metal box with a switch in the middle. He smirked at the other man, who dropped the radio and placed his hands over his ears. Then Bonzo flipped the switch.

The firetruck nudged some squad cars with its bumper as it attempted to flee the bridge. A couple of squad cars were in a line behind the firetruck. Then the rear squad car shifted into reverse and flew backwards toward the opposite entrance. Mark was just entering the river, pulling a cop by his shirt, when the UPS truck exploded, pushing water in every direction.

Fire consumed the bridge. Mark and the cop flew up the embankment as fire soared over them, burning grass, twigs, and leaves. Most of the blast's force nailed the underside of the bridge. Pieces of the UPS truck shot through the doors of the squad cars on the bridge as they flipped over, and four significant cracks whipped the night. The squad car driving backwards nailed the buckled roadway as it blew upward. The car rocketed into the steel girders as the undercarriage scraped along them. It flipped upside down and landed in a blaze of fire.

The fire engine's rear tires dropped where the bridge separated from the hardtop. The firemen hollered for the driver to keep going. A fireman hanging off the side of the truck watched the bridge behind them detach from the roadway. The entire bridge was full of fire. One overturned squad car behind their truck exploded, and the force blew another squad car over the rail as it bounced between a V section in the steel girders, stripped the siren and lights off the rooftop, and splashed down into the river. The force bounced the fire engine upward, which allowed them to continue driving away from the collapsing bridge.

A wheel from the UPS truck flew at the fireman hanging on the side of the firetruck. He dove off the side as the wheel slammed into where he had been hanging. The wheel bounced off the truck and flipped off the road. The firetruck dragged the axle of the UPS truck upward as a section of the steel girders slammed overtop of the firetruck's rear end.

Mark looked up to see the wheel falling at them. He grabbed a cop and pushed him down the embankment into the water. They hit the water as the wheel nailed the embankment where they had just been. It took one final flip and then splashed into the water right in front of them. The cops who had been in the water near the UPS truck were nowhere in the sight.

The bridge was collapsing. Some metal girders slammed over a couple of cops. More girders darted toward squad cars on the road, plunging through their windshields and slamming across their hoods, rooftops, and trunks. Police dove to the ground, covering their heads.

Mark pulled the wheel overtop of them as steel girders slapped the water nearby. A streetlamp fell over top of the firetruck. The steel girders bore down on the rear end of the firetruck and bent the ladder as the roadway collapsed into the river.

Officer Darcy ran toward the ambulance on the sandy beachfront to avoid being crushed by girders. The paramedics moved Penske around the backside of the truck out of harm's way. Girders pierced the ground and squad cars near Darcy as he shrieked and ran through sparks from sirens being mangled on the rooftops. He dropped and rolled through the sand.

On the other side of the river, a van drove up with its headlights on. No cops were on that side of the river. Mark pushed the wheel aside, and the other policeman emerged from the water. The river remained restless, but no more girders were flying around. The bridge was still collapsing into the river, making splashing noises, but most the devastation was becoming quieter.

Upriver, Bonzo and the tattooed guy crawled away from the water and hobbled up to the van, jumping inside.

Mark spun around in the water, looking in every direction. Some floodlights were still shining near the firetruck, but the other floodlights were gone. Between the blurred vision of water in his eyes, the lights, and the fire, he noticed the van's headlights across the river. He raised his arm from the water. As water dripped from Mr. Steely (his personalized pistol), he shot at the van. Other cops realized what his target was, and suddenly they were all laying down fire.

Watches ducked in the driver's seat and backed up. He cranked the steering wheel, and the van dropped into the ditch. He paused briefly and stared at Mark. "Mickey!" he grumbled.

Grass and rocks shot backwards as the tires spun. The van turned, and they drove off down Highway 130.

Mark lowered his gun and helped the other cop, who was struggling to catch his breath behind him. He was clinging to the wheel like a little kid to a floatie. "I'm outta shape man!" the cop admitted.

Mark grabbed him by the shirt and stood him up. "You OK?"

The water they were in wasn't very deep. Once the cop was standing on his own two feet, he smiled. "Yeah, thanks!"

"Friggin' rookie!" Mark shook his head as he exited the water, only to see the van's taillights disappear from view toward Lone Rock.

Just then, the sun peeked over the horizon. Mark still hadn't slept, but at that point, he felt relentless. He wanted the one man he thought he knew. He wanted his WITSEC handler, Wayne Richards, a.k.a. Ralph P. Fallway.

He wanted answers. Supposedly, that guy was his protection. He had been inside the House on the Rock when all the havoc took place. He was there with Mark's sons when they helped take down the devil. Mark wanted him here now.

CHAPTER 6
THE INVESTIGATION BEGINS

After numerous hours down by the bridge, they were able to extract what was left of the UPS truck from the river. Bodies were piling up at the curve on Highway 130 near the river's sandy beachfront. The area was where people could back their boats into the river. Now two ambulances were on scene, as were several squad cars and a shitload of emergency personnel.

Mark brought a team back through the House on the Rock. They entered the carousel room to find the gruesome display of the three dead policemen. Mark walked over to the officer buried in the ivory keys of a grand piano and a pool of blood, kicking broken keys across the red carpet. A few other officers walked through the room while others searched the carousel.

"Mark, you might wanna see this!" an officer shouted.

Mark stood up and crossed the room toward the carousel. As he approached, he saw a streak of blood in the red carpet. It had been made by Tom's body, which continued to bounce around as the carousel dragged it in circles.

Mark walked over to a panel and killed the power to the carousel. Before long, other cops entered the room, and crime scene investigators began marking areas where bullets had struck. They quarantined the room to reduce foot traffic. It was a crime scene now.

Mark asked the coroner what he thought about the situation.

"I've never seen such evil before," the man replied.

"Where did this come from?" Mark asked, nudging the piano with his foot.

"Look." The coroner shined his flashlight at the ceiling. "If I were a betting man, this piano was mounted up there. Whether it decided to give way at the worst-possible time—at least for this guy, anyway—or some mystical force ripped it from the mounting bolts, I have no idea. If you look up there, you can see the bolts that held it up are still intact, though they're bent all to hell, and the framework on the piano clearly shows the bolt heads stripped through it."

Mark had a vision of Watches standing in the doorway of his old house. The door slammed shut without Watches moving an arm. Then he saw a kitchen knife willed into the devil's hand from his yard. He also saw an image of Watches' glass eye getting crushed by his wife's crutch. Then he saw him cackling hideously on the floor of a parking garage as the concrete structure collapsed around them. He continued to see images of Watches using telekinetic force, an unexplainable power.

The coroner stood up, and Mark followed him as he approached another dead policeman. "This guy over here has a throwing star embedded in his head," the coroner said. "It's so deep you can only see one point protruding from his nasal bridge. At the rate of speed that this star had to have been going to carve through that nasal bone and at that depth, would have been impossible for a human to achieve merely by throwing it. Unless after it was thrown into his head, someone pounded it in farther with a hammer. But as you can see, there are no bends in the metal points, no dings, and no scratches. It's just a sharp throwing star. It seems like it was launched by a cannon, not mere human force."

He stood up, and Mark turned to follow as the coroner continued his explanation. "The third policeman was lassoed, and his body was pulled through that railing over there." He pointed, and Mark walked over to inspect the blood on the railing. "The rope was previously tied off before someone lassoed the body and the carousel acted as a pulley," the coroner said. "He was still alive when his body was yanked through that railing. The torn torso suggests that the carousel was the driving force behind the abdominal tears between the ribcage and hips. Whoever did this is an evil you wouldn't even want to tell your kids about!"

Mark stood up slowly from the railing. "This evil you speak of is dead. He was blown to bits in the Infinity Room from a grenade launcher."

"We had a coroner van stolen from us last night, Mr. Emerson. Two of our guys were attacked. Both are in critical condition. I can't begin to explain, but the body count still seems to be piling up. If I were a betting man, I would bet on revenge. I would bet on the devil before any Christian could tell me otherwise. There's no safe place anymore. You got yourself a devil on the loose and a cannon willing to fire at your battleship, and there's nothing you can do about it but pray to God it misses."

Mark turned slowly and looked at him. Suddenly, he recalled being under that bridge as fire was burning on the water all around him. He remembered raising his hand toward the van across the river and shooting at it. Mark spaced briefly as he remembered a silhouette staring back at him through the window. When Watches whispered his name, Mark swore he could hear it in his imagination. He glanced over his shoulder to see other policemen on the main highway above him firing at the van as well. The van was catching some heat from all the firepower.

"Mark you still with me?" The coroner asked.

Mark snapped out of his short spell and turned toward him. "Do you have the information on that van?"

"Yeah, I can email it to you as soon as I get back to the office. You think you'll be able to find it?"

"I can put a bolo out on it," Mark whispered. "Keep up the good work, Randy!"

"Yeah, there's a mess here. We have witnessed the work of Satan. I swear to God, I have never seen anything like this. I can tell you that. No way!"

CHAPTER 7
RAIDS

On the east side of Madison, the Oscar Meyer plant, two miles from the Dane County regional airport, was very much alive that morning. Employees were parking their cars and heading for the doors. But just off toward Huxley Street, lights were flashing on squad cars and SWAT vehicles outside a house. It was under siege by local law enforcement as SWAT team members moved around on each side. Mark was leading officers toward the front door. Squad cars were lined up and down the entire street, which was barricaded at both ends.

A couple of SWAT team members held a ramming device to the front door and waited for the teams at the rear of the house to get into position. A few knocks at the door met with no response. They rammed the front door in, and the officers swarmed into the house.

Inside, a woman was sitting at her kitchen table painting her fingernails and listening to music through a pair of headphones. Smoke rose from a cigarette in an ashtray beside her as she glanced up to see the muzzles of several guns in her face. Her eyes rolled toward each man as she paused with the fingernail brush in hand, giving them a baffled look. One of the SWAT personnel pulled her headphones off her ears as he stood behind her.

"Where's your scum boyfriend?" Mark asked.

"I don't know," she snapped. "Why? What did he do now?"

"When was the last time you spoke with him?"

"A month or two ago; I don't know. I hardly ever see him. He comes and goes as he pleases."

Mark dropped a Polaroid on the table. He pressed his finger over it and slid it at her. It was a picture of a dead lady from the House on the Rock. "Tell us, or we'll give you some nice jewelry to wear on your wrists while you go down to the station."

"Yeah, whatever!"

Mark stepped into the table as she resumed painting her nails. Her brush slipped, and she painted down the back of her hand instead. She rolled her eyes at him. "Don't toy with me, lady," Mark said. "I'll have you thrown in jail so fast it'll make your head spin. It'll even give you a reason to roll your eyes at me twice."

She snapped her tongue.

"Give her the jewelry, boys!" Mark ordered the officers standing behind her. The two men swung their rifles onto their backs and stood her up to handcuff her. She resisted a little, so they slammed her face into her ashtray. She exhaled and puffed ashes across the table. Her short skirt exposed her bare buttocks, and a SWAT member in the kitchen shook his head at the sight. It was too late to take back even the slightest peek—no recovering from that. The scorn on his face reflected his agony as he observed the snatch of some poor shmuck's girlfriend. She remained bent over the old, beat-up wooden table breathing ashes across its dull finish.

* * *

Barbara Felter, Duffy's mother, flipped the sign in her floral shop to read "Closed." Inside, Mark had an entire task force ready to storm the office above. It was being rented by someone from his past who was supposedly a third-party constituent for WITSEC who had put Mark's entire family into witness protection. It was supposed to be someone they could trust. But now the tables had turned. After the House on the Rock incident, Fallway had vanished. Although Mark's sons came out of the incident alive he had no faith in Fallway, and he wasn't about to quit pursuing him either.

"Listen up," Mark said. "Everyone know what do?"

The entire squad of men nodded.

"Alright, move out!" Mark said.

Half the group stormed out the floral shop's front door. The other half went out the back. On the backside of the building, a fire escape led up to the second floor. Out front, to the left of the floral shop, a doorway led up to the same floor. The coffee shop around the corner was being evacuated into the park across the street, as was Barbara.

When the teams arrived at the top, they paid particular attention to their wristwatches. Suddenly, smoke canisters blew through the upper set of windows. Smoke twirled from the barrels of the launchers, held by the officers crouched down on the street. Both teams stormed the office, moving in from the back and the front. But the place was empty.

A lonely lamp caught anyone's eye to the right side of the only desk in the main office, which also contained filing cabinets and chairs. Teams swept through the back two offices, and then every officer reconvened in the center office.

As a few men opened file cabinets and desk drawers. Mark stood before a wall of photographs. They included pictures of his family and the families of his close friends: the Carsons, the Felters, and the Fifers.

One officer looked up from a drawer he had opened. "Uh, sir, ya might wanna have a look at this." Mark spun away from the wall of photos. Some of the men backed away from the desk and headed toward the doorway. Mark glanced into the desk drawer and realized it was packed with C-4—military-grade explosives.

"Hold on!" he shouted, holding his arms up. He crouched down and peeked inside to see a single wire leading up through the desktop to the phone, which was hooked to an answering machine. He slid the phone an inch to expose the wire. A couple SWAT guys glanced at each other, concerned about him moving the phone.

Suddenly, the phone rang. Some of the men aimed their guns at it.

"Evacuate!" Mark yelled. "Everyone move out now! Go, go, go!"

The teams ran back down the stairway. Mark picked up a pair of scissors and prayed briefly. The phone was going into its fourth ring when he snipped the wire leading up through the desktop. He closed his eyes for a moment. Sweat was spurting from every facial pore. He opened his eyes and then walked around the desk and headed for the door.

Suddenly, the answering machine tripped. "Wrong wire, Mikey," it said. "You lose, buddy!"

Mark bolted through the door. He missed a few steps on his way down and charged for the door at the bottom of the staircase. Before he got there, the explosion sent him through the glass door. He sailed over a parked car as fire roared over the rooftop, and the windows shattered across the entire face of the building.

Barbara dropped to her knees in the grass across the street and watched as her floral shop was engulfed in flames. Mark's body landed right next to her, and she fell over. He stiffened in pain as she shrieked. His face was badly cut, and he was bleeding slightly. She rolled over to him and placed a hand over his bleeding neck. "Mark, are you OK?" she asked.

He looked up at her, grimacing in pain. "Sorry about your floral shop, Barb." Then he passed out.

The next thing Mark recalled was opening his eyes to see Mary, Danny, and Billy standing around him in a hospital room. He looked at all their faces, which were overwhelmed with joy. Mary kissed him on the forehead. That was when he realized she was holding his hand, but he couldn't feel her squeezing his fingers. He couldn't feel her kiss either.

"Mary!" he said with a sigh.

The boys placed their hands on his shoulders. He closed his eyes. He could hear his family's excitement, but he didn't have the strength to open his eyes. As he lay there, he remembered helping Mary out of the café at the House on the Rock and Billy standing next to Wayne Richards instead of Mark. *How could his own sons look up to that man? What were his boys not telling him?*

Then his mind backtracked to 1974 where he was fighting the devil through the framework of his extension ladder in his front lawn. He had seen the look in Stan's eye when he tried dropping a yard ornament on his face. Then Stan was blasted by a current of water as a fireman came to Mark's aid. His mind jumped to the fireman strangling Stan with the firehose. Mark was lying near a firetruck grasping a rifle. He was looking back at Stan when he fired the shot that killed Stan's brother, ending his life in front of Stan.

His flashback skipped forward a couple of years when a UPS truck drove down the hillside right toward his house. He was trying to evade the destruction but instead watched as his wife ran out the door with baby Billy. In his flashback, he was stuck in his family room chair, wearing a robe and holding a TV remote. That was odd, because that wasn't how it happened. He had escaped with his wife. Instead, his mind had him in a front-row seat watching the fiasco unfold. He saw his LP tank roll through his kitchen. It took out the dining room table and rolled backward, crushing some chairs.

Then the UPS truck flew through the wall, and the floor in front of him collapsed into the basement. Now he was able to stand, and he climbed out of his chair to watch the LP tank fall in after the truck. It bounced off the side of the truck and bashed into the furnace. The furnace jumped backwards and separated from the gas line. In front of the truck, the wood burner tipped over, and ashes and flames spit out the open door.

Mark peered through the windshield of the UPS truck and saw Stan sprawled across the seat staring back at him, smiling with bloody cheeks. Mark raised his TV remote, only now it was a pistol, his pistol, Mr. Steely. He fired a round through the windshield, but flames flashed in his face as his house exploded around him.

The next place his mind took him was to Wayne Richards's office above the floral shop. Mark aimed his pistol right at Wayne as he sat behind his desk. Then Wayne pointed a pistol at him in his outstretched hand next to his typewriter. Mark lowered his gun and sat in a chair in front of Wayne's desk.

They had their talk about how Stan had threatened Wayne and how Wayne had to fake his own death to escape him. He remembered Wayne was in their house asking them if they were OK. He was there. He was their handler. Mark had confided in him, trusted him. Now he was torn between friend and foe. The same guy who had sworn to help protect his family had annihilated his own office, but the voice on the recorder wasn't Wayne's. It was Watches.

Then he remembered the last words he said to Wayne. "Yeah, after that, you and I are getting into this." He implied that after his family's trip to the House on the Rock, he wanted to interrogate him. But now it appeared as if Wayne wasn't to be trusted.

Mark closed his eyes and fell asleep.

CHAPTER 8
THE VIDEOGRAPHER

Unlike many larger cities, Verona had certain people who were always familiar, and a familiar face was always nice. If someone walked into the local sub shop, the folks behind the counter would start making their sub of choice before they ordered. And hopefully, the customer didn't have a different taste that day. That was what small town USA was all about.

Verona had some entrepreneurs who liked to see all of Wisconsin, even filming its true beauty. They ventured through prime tourist destinations and visited some of the glorious exhibitions that Wisconsin had to offer.

One day, after the House on the Rock incident, a scrawny man showed up at the police station holding a camcorder. Mark stood up from his desk and saw it was the high school art teacher. Since Danny was in his class (scoring straight A's), he felt it necessary to say hi. The art teacher was talking with the desk clerk when Mark approached. "How ya doing, Philip?"

"Oh, great, Mark." He smiled and shook his outstretched hand.

"What can we do ya for?" Mark asked.

"Say, listen, I'm not sure if it's anything huge, but I videotaped the destruction of the House on the Rock."

"Oh, great, as long as it isn't of you 'n' the missus, whatcha got?"

"No, it's not me and the missus," Philip replied.

"Never mind. Whatcha got?" Mark asked, throwing his arm around Philip's shoulders. "I believe we have a VCR in the squad room. It's a *very crummy radio* though. You can hardly get a tune out of the thing."

Philip looked at him with an absurd expression. "It's VHS!" he clarified.

"Oh, right, video!" Mark joked. His grasp on modern technology was irrelevant.

He grabbed the cassette from Philip and rolled a TV cart toward the tables. The room was like a school classroom. It had windows facing the hallway and along the exterior wall. The front of the room had a chalkboard. The back wall was bare. Heat vents were located below the windows on the exterior wall.

As Mark popped the cassette in, Philip brought him up to speed. "My wife and I were hiking the bluffs near the House on the Rock that day. We stopped to get a bite to eat—bologna sandwiches, as I recall. Suddenly, we heard what sounded like gunshots and explosions. She filmed it. But we saw the strangest things."

"Oh, really. Well, let's have a look."

The video was scrambled and fuzzy at first, a white screen with black specks flickering with a constant hiss. Then the image came on, revealing trees. Philip directed his wife to move the camera up. It made Mark dizzy at first. Then she zoomed in on the underside of the Infinity Room. It was still intact. A moment later, they saw brilliant flashes of light, and flames poured from the sides. One flash sent some red misty stuff out a wall, followed by a blob descending toward the valley. She followed the blob down and then moved the camera back up to the Infinity Room once the blob disappeared behind the trees.

The Infinity Room was dangling from the wall structure. It was true chaos. People were screaming due to simple electrical sparks or sirens from ambulances, firetrucks, and police cruisers. When the smoke cleared, the tourists were driving out the gates to head home. Everything seemed to be calming down. But that moment when Danny and Pete hammered the Infinity Room with an infinite amount of firepower, it was the Infinity Room that hung by a thread—or was it?

The moment when Watches buried a throwing star through Danny's collarbone and headed toward them was terrifying to say the least. His skin was flapping off one cheek, sending stomach bugs in motion. They watched as he had the strength to retaliate against them even after two explosive charges tossed him around like a rag doll. There he was again, cackling that hideous cackle as he strode with an unknown force even after his leg had been torn open by rounds from Danny spraying 5.56-mm lead through it.

When Watches fell out the viewing window from the last grenade Pete bestowed upon him, it was a moment to remember. The continual lashing that those boys dealt him would go down in the history of the House on the Rock. But the truth of the matter was they wanted to end the evil. They wanted to send him packing fifteen stories south and bury him where the sun didn't shine right there in Iowa County, Wisconsin. They wanted him to wear the Infinity Room forever. Swaying from a snapped steel girder, they were ready to end that horrific chapter of their childhood, or so they thought!

Pete's idea to tie the rope that thwarted Watches into believing that was their exit strategy was brilliant. It guaranteed Watches would be quarantined in the Infinity Room with nowhere else to go. If Pete could go back to that thought, however, he might explain it differently. He might be thinking, *Well, in the heat of the moment, I thought, fool him once, shame on me!* In actuality, the shame hadn't even begun. The swaying Infinity Room had taken a beating, but it wasn't the only thing hanging by a thread. The other half was Watches, who dangled from a string—several braided strings, to be precise.

The truth was, Pete's idea to thwart the enemy had allowed Watches to escape. When Watches flew through the viewing window, as seen on the videotape, he found himself falling into the rope, which continued to lash him as he fell. However, with enough slack for him to grasp, it was the rope that saved him. As the fire and debris rained down upon Watches during the Infinity Room's collapse, it carried him down to the face of the cliff on which the House on the Rock was built. Watches grabbed the rock wall and pulled his body tight to it as the Infinity Room swung into the rock face, forcing dust in all directions.

At one point, he had to kneel due to his torn legs. They had a few holes in each one. Danny had managed to hit his target even though he struggled through his own pain from the throwing star lodged in his collarbone. Had that throwing star not been in that shoulder, his aim may have been a bit higher and allowed him to close that final chapter they were seeking.

Watches let go of the rock wall and stretched back, leaning against the underside of the Infinity Room, grimacing in pain. Philip's wife zoomed in on Watches as he wrapped an arm around the side of the Infinity Room, revealing a significant glowing red bead, which was his only good eye.

His eye patch was bunched over his eyebrow, exposing a gaping hole in his head. His upper lip curled, his gangly teeth showed, and he cackled the same awful electronic-toned, monochromatic, hideous word: "Watches, Watches, Watches! Ha ha!" Again, he pronounced his "W" like a "V." He reached up for a better grasp of the rock wall and leaned to his side. His eye glowed red once again. Of course, none of this could be heard on the video recording, but that's what happened as she backed away from the lens as it appeared he looked right at her.

His shredded trench coat waved in a slight breeze. A couple of crows squawked above. The breeze felt good on his fresh cuts. A throwing star was still lodged in his upper leg from when Duffy chucked it at him. The crows were just waiting for their fresh meat. He glared up at them, his white hair flowing over his shoulders. Though upset over another failed mission, he was just getting warmed up; he was ready for part two.

The camera turned toward Philip. "Did you see that man out there on that ledge?" he asked

"Yes, honey," his wife replied. "Poor guy!"

Then the feed was cut off. No matter how pixelated the image was, there was no question that a man had dropped out of the viewing window and swung to safety against the rock wall as the Infinity Room crashed into it.

"He's still alive!" Mark whispered.

"We filmed him some more," Philip said. "He managed to climb the rock wall right back into the House on the Rock!"

Mark thought back to the House on the Rock. He recalled returning to the scene with his men to find three dead police officers in the carousel room. Their deaths may have happened after the initial attack. They may have died at the hand of Stanley Watches Markesan after he returned back in the house. The devil was at large. The devil knew where his family lived. The devil was coming for them.

CHAPTER 9
THE DUMP

One Saturday afternoon, Billy, Danny, Duffy, Pete, and Wesley decided to get together. Their meeting area was the community dump. The five boys strolled through the dump, turning stuff over with sticks to see what treasures people were throwing out. As the saying went, one man's junk was another man's treasure.

Suddenly, a car rolled around the piles of trash and stopped behind the boys. It was a Dodge Charger. A long-haired man wearing a trench coat stepped out and circled the car to approach the boys. He had little round sunglasses and an olive-drab cap. Billy walked over to him and shook his hand.

"I'm sorry we have to keep meeting like this fellas," the man said, "but there are people after me, and your dad is relentless."

"Yeah, we know, Mr. Fallway," Danny said. "If they aren't onto you, they're at least trying."

Fallway nodded. "Exactly."

"What are we learning today?" Wesley asked. "I have to be back by two."

"I was thinking more martial arts and some target practice. What do ya think, boys?"

"Yeah!" they responded in unison.

They followed Mr. Fallway to the Charger's trunk. He popped it open to reveal ropes, weapons, ammunition, knives, sandbags, and a few wooden crates. The boys' eyes widened. It was a treasure trove.

They set up targets on junk piles, and the boys fired at them from a prone position behind some sandbags. They spent the remainder of the morning doing target practice. Then Mr. Fallway handed them grenades, other explosive devices, and ropes. Although they never set off any real grenades or explosives, Mr. Fallway instructed them on the proper holding techniques and what to expect. They also set up Claymore mines, learned how to tie knots, and did some martial arts.

"Now, these aren't real hand grenades," Mr. Fallway said. "They're only smoke. However, the weight of this smoke grenade is equivalent to the real deal. When pulling the pin, you want to have your thumb here and your eyes out here, OK?" Mr. Fallway waved his hand as if they were to maintain 180-degree viewing at all times. "Not only should you be constantly scanning for the enemy, you should also be identifying the best possible placement of the grenade to cause the most casualties. In addition to finding the best spot to toss the grenade, you also need to detect the best possible cover. You want cover that will protect you from shrapnel. Each grenade . . ."

Mr. Fallway went on and on about grenades. The junkyard was far from any residential area. They were in their own little world. The boys would practice lobbing hand grenades. Different colored smoke patterns amongst the junk piles identified the dispersion of shrapnel. He used the colors to help explain where the destructive path fanned out.

From the wooden crates he pulled out Claymores. He had each boy set one up using detonation cord. They would run the cord far enough away from the Claymores and then trip them. They threw out colored patterns as well. The color helped to show the boys exactly where the packed ball bearings would go from the real mines.

The boys were having the time of their lives learning from him. He continued to explain different types of explosives and how they worked. Then the boys demonstrated how they operated. They briefed Mr. Fallway on the setup and destructive paths of each explosive device. They walked him through different scenarios and explained what he had taught them.

Mr. Fallway brought out ropes and showed how to make lassoes and how to tie different types of knots. They lassoed junk from the junk piles, and they demonstrated different knots over a wooden post at the edge of the dump.

Even though months had passed, nothing had changed. Mark was still hunting Mr. Fallway, but here he was in Mark's own backyard. None of their parents had any idea the boys met up with him once or twice a week. It was a top-secret club. As Mr. Fallway explained it, it was a club to provide them with the necessary tools they needed to survive and track and, if necessary, *to kill*. They were sworn to secrecy about their meetings with him.

They were being trained to defend and protect themselves. They were learning weapons systems and survival tactics, similar to what the military would teach new privates. But Mr. Fallway took it a few steps further. He took them beyond the limits, to the edge, and had them leap off. They even did some rappelling from a rock quarry near the junkyard.

Each boy had his own piece of the puzzle. Billy and Pete enjoyed weapons. Pete really admired knives. Duffy primarily enjoyed ropes and different techniques to tie up the enemy or use lassoes. Duffy enjoyed martial arts and the use of weapons as well. Danny enjoyed martial arts, but they all were sharpshooters, especially Billy. Wesley was "team strength." He was built like an ox. He usually put Mr. Fallway on the ground during hand-to-hand combat training. Billy was the same way. They lifted weights together at the workout center downtown.

Mr. Fallway gathered all the weapons, and the boys helped him carry the stuff back to his car. They stood in a semicircle around him as he gave some final instructions. "I want you boys to know something. No matter what curveballs life throws at you, you're ultimately the decision maker for which path you want to go down. I can train you until you're blue in the face. But the true nature of the beast is that you must want this. You have to want it in order to learn it, live it, and love it. My teachings are only good if you truly want to grasp the nature of it all. Now, I wish I could drive you fellas home, but I mustn't be seen in town. It's too dangerous for me there. I'm staying up north in Little Rapids. But I want you all to know that I took an oath to protect you kids from the enemy. There's speculation that Watches is still alive."

"Yeah, but how?" Pete asked. "We destroyed him. *I* destroyed him."

Mr. Fallway swallowed the lump in his throat. "Pete, you did a great job. But if you remember the night of the House on the Rock, several deaths happened after the destruction. They died after the cleanup crews had already gone through. And a car chase resulted in the destruction of the main bridge just a few miles from there. I've been investigating ever since. For that reason alone, we need to remain vigilant, and I must remain incognito."

"Huh?" Duffy asked.

"It means I have to keep in hiding," Mr. Fallway explained.

"That sucks," Billy said.

"Yeah, well, your dad really doesn't like me right now," Mr. Fallway said. "I have no one else to trust. I have no one to turn to except you kids. And I really do appreciate the amount of effort you guys are giving this club." He walked toward the driver's door and then stopped. "You know, you kids really should come up with a name for yourselves. A club isn't a club without a good team name." He smiled, tipped his hat, then got into his car and drove off.

"You see?" Duffy said. "I told you guys we need a team name. How about the Duff Busters?"

"No way!" Billy said, laughing.

"Fool Fighters!" Wesley shouted.

"I think there's a new band called that!" Pete said.

"No, that's Foo Fighters," Billy corrected.

"Kid Killas!" Duffy suggested as the boys started walking away from the dump.

"No!" the others shouted.

Duffy threw out more suggestions: "Boy Brats, Brat Boys, Billy Brats, Billy and his Brats!"

Billy stopped walking and swatted him on the back of his head. "Keep our names out of it, bro!"

They continued walking.

CHAPTER 10
THE ARMYBRATS

With much distress over what the future might hold, life was tense for those five boys. Over the years, the boys had discovered new passions in life. They were intrigued by families with military backgrounds and local law enforcement, much like Wesley Fifer's family, who often relocated due to military reassignments. Hence, their new club name came to be. But the knowledge they gained from these life positions and self-defense training was extraordinary. They created their own pact, an elite group that became well known as . . . the Armybrats.

Mr. Fallway had become a third-party-parent. He took the Armybrats under his wing. His approach to everything was professionalism. He corrected their inappropriate manners and taught them unimaginable things. Appearance and decency were a must, as was respect. Proper English was a key factor to remaining on his good side. If they cursed out of context, they were punished. He made them do pushups, squat thrusts, and combined the two into burpees or made them run a few miles for every infraction of his rules. Everything they did or said had to be proper and respectful.

Aside from manners, Mr. Fallway taught them a boatload of other shit. His main goal was to get them up to speed on hand-to-hand combat and self-defense. He taught them martial arts up the yin yang! Self-defense was all about attentiveness. How could anyone defend themselves without being alert? "Stay alert, stay alive," he always said. The way he taught them was so specific that it felt like they were back in the third grade. They picked up on his material like they had learned to tie their shoes at three years of age.

However, the ultimate test awaited them, his test of their skills, knowledge, and abilities.

Even though he spent all his time training the boys how to act more professional and defend with pride, he wasn't going to walk away and assume they knew it all. He prepared a testing ground to see how far they had progressed. It was located ninety-four miles north deep in the forest near Little Rapids, Wisconsin. He had scheduled an entire week of hardcore testing. It was planned for the first week after their school year ended in the summer of 1995.

The Armybrats' etiquette was a definite change. They walked tall and stood proud. They no longer disrespected their parents or their teachers (aside from seeing Mr. Fallway behind their parents' backs). They helped other students rather than bullying them. They were no longer divided from others. They were distinguished. They took on any high schooler who challenged any poor shmuck.

Schoolchildren separated themselves into smaller groups, otherwise known as cliques. The Armybrats tended to clash with the preppy, popular students. Then there were the middle-class kids who remained neutral. Before all their training, that was the faction with whom the Armybrats identified. At the lower end of the chain were the nerds, the students who weren't as noticeable because they kept to themselves or focused on their pocket calculators. They didn't care what anyone thought about them. They knew they were geeks, but they were the smart ones. The Armybrats often defended them. But it didn't matter which end of the food chain anyone fell on; the Armybrats would defend them all with honor.

The Armybrats were unique. Thanks to Mr. Fallway's long days and nights of showing them the ropes, they had matured a lot. It spruced up their attitudes toward life and their parents. People noticed, which was important. The popular kids wanted to butter them up and pull them into their cliques, but the boys knew better. The Armybrats were their own clique. Yet their parents remained skeptical, especially Mark. *Why the changes?* he wondered. *Where were the boys learning such things?*

All the boys wanted to do was promote a healthy, mature environment. They knew what it took to survive, and they wanted to see everyone else survive too. They didn't care what clique or nationality people belonged to.

Everyone was in this life together, and the Armybrats promoted unity. People all lived on the same planet and breathed the same air. They all wanted to survive, and the only way to do that was to work together. Many students didn't see that because that was how they were raised; and other people didn't matter.

It was a shame, but all the Armybrats tried to do was make people realize that egotism and selfishness were no longer their cup of tea. This was what Mr. Fallway taught them, and they were about to be tested on their strengths, their weaknesses, and their wits. They were about to be tested in all categories of life. They had no clue what awaited them in that deep dark forest up north.

Mr. Fallway had been keeping to himself lately. They weren't training as much anymore, but he kept in good contact with Billy, providing details on the test dates. All they could do was live one day at a time and wait. It was like a pop quiz without the pop. They knew when it was going to happen. They just didn't know what it would entail.

School was winding down. Nothing during classes or between classes was entertaining for them. The boys were constantly putting a kibosh on kids' antics. Take, for example, the lunchroom when little Nate Shelley was about to get an entire milk carton dumped in his hair just for looking at a football player wrong. Duffy was beneath the table with a rubber band contraption attached to a food tray with several piles of mashed potatoes and gravy on it.

He looked up from beneath the table to see Will Silverman opening the carton behind little Nate Shelley's back.

"Now!" Duffy hollered, and Nate slid to his left, where no one was seated. Duffy released the tray, and it flipped right into Will's crotch, sending a trail of mashed potatoes and gravy oozing down his shorts and legs. The milk carton splashed back at him as he let go of it. Duffy slid out from beneath the bench and kicked Will's shins. Will hit the tabletop with his face, smashing into another tray full of cake slices (which had been placed there previously for effect). Duffy picked up Will's legs and pulled him backward, slamming his face into the bench as Will slid off the tabletop carrying the pile of cake down with his chin.

Duffy stood up after retrieving the tray. "Apologize to Nate now," he demanded.

Half in a daze, Will glared at him and as he struggled to his feet. Duffy wound up and gave him an uppercut with the metal tray. Will's face wiggled toward the skylights in the ceiling, and he sank back onto the bench.

"Apologize or stay benched," Duffy said. "And you know what it's like to be benched, Will."

By then a crowd had gathered. Everyone was intrigued. Duffy was about to put an Armybrat beat-down on the jock. Will wasn't having fun anymore. His practical joke had turned on him, and rather quickly. Duffy sat on the bench and ate a French fry off another tray. As he enjoyed the fry, an elbow came toward his face. Duffy held up the tray with his arm and elbow secured to the backside, and Will's elbow slammed into it. Will dropped to his knees, holding his arm in pain.

Duffy continued chomping the fry as he glanced at Nate. "I'm sorry, Nate, but it looks you're not getting an apology today." Duffy whipped the tray at Will's buddy, who had advanced on him to protect Will. The tray caught him in the trachea. Then Duffy kneed Will in the back, and he fell forward onto his head as his friend fell on top of him, holding his throat. "Same place, same time tomorrow, fellas?" Duffy asked, glancing at his wristwatch. "Sorry, kids, I gotta run."

Duffy turned his tray in at the cafeteria window. A gentleman grabbed it from him. "Extra heat on this one," Duffy warned. "Lots of blood." The man dumped the tray through a hole, and slop splashed out of it.

Duffy grimaced. "Aw, man, looks like the sink just gave birth to a baby elephant. That's disgusting, man." He watched the man shut off the spray nozzle and roll a blue barrel out from under the sink. Duffy grimaced as stuff sloshed around inside. The man threw a lid over the barrel and clamped it shut. Duffy noticed another barrel just like it out the back door of the kitchen. "Gross." He sighed and walked away.

That night, Duffy's eyes snapped open while he was lying in bed. He glanced at his ceiling fan and heard the clock ticking in the hallway. He sat up slowly when he heard voices outside. He turned toward his bedroom window. It sounded as if some kids were playing in the park.

He threw off his blankets and approached his bedroom window. It was open slightly, the curtains waving in a slight breeze. Sure enough, some kids were playing in the park across the street. He watched a girl swinging and a couple of other kids on the teeter-totters. He backed away from the window and slid into the hallway. Just then the cuckoo clock in the hall struck midnight. It nearly dropped him onto the seat of his pants, but he continued walking.

He passed his parents' bedroom door and walked down the staircase. He slid his feet into his dad's slippers, which were huge, but he wanted to see who those kids were and why were they playing at midnight. Something about it seemed off.

He opened his front door and walked out into the street. He saw the swing swinging and the teeter-totter moving up and down, but as he drew closer, he noticed something strange.

No one was out there. Not a soul was in the park.

Suddenly, a swift breeze caught him by surprise, and a flash of light flickered at the top of the slide, reflecting off the slide's polished metal surface. The light was coming from the shelter above the slide.

Unable to see inside, he crossed the street and crept over to the stairs that led to the top of the slide. Another breeze blew his brown hair around as he glanced back toward his house. Then he started to climb.

Partway up the steps, he smelled a sweet tinge in the air. It was a familiar smell—the smell of a cigar. "Hey, who's up there?" he muttered.

Suddenly, the light vanished. Duffy leaned around the steps to see if anyone had slid down the slide. Nobody was at the bottom. He climbed a bit farther, finally making his way to the top. He raised his head over the lip to peek inside. The shelter was empty.

He gripped the railing and looked over his shoulder at the ground. Mulch blew in circles as a breeze swept through. He turned back to the shelter, only to find himself face to face with the ugliest, scar-faced bogeyman he had ever seen. Watches!

"Boo!" Watches said. Cigar smoke puffed into Duffy's face as he let go of the steps and flew straight back. He fell to the ground, landing flat on his back. His eyelids squeezed shut in agony as he rolled over to ease the pain.

Once he regained his composure and focused on the shelter, no one was there. He must have been dreaming. He grimaced in pain as he stood up, brushing himself off. He paced backwards, not wanting to take his eyes off the slide. Once he felt the asphalt under his dad's slippers, he spun around and hightailed it back to his house. He ran upstairs and jumped under his bedsheets.

After taking a moment to catch his breath, he realized the voices had returned. He pushed himself off his bed and approached his window again. Kids were playing in the park—swinging, teeter-tottering. Something was off. Then the slide lit up again. A man's tattered face appeared before a lighter. Duffy dropped to the floor beneath his window and cowered there for a moment. This wasn't happening. How could Watches be alive?

Then he heard the kids screaming. He built up enough courage to peek out the window. A man was tossing the kids into a box truck parked on the road. Suddenly, an orange blur inside the window caught his eye. Then Watches was standing on his roof lighting a cigar, his one eye glaring at Duffy. Duffy flew backwards and stared at the faint orange glare in the pane. The window cracked, Watches' cigar smoke fogged through the crack, and then . . .

Duffy woke up, sweating profusely.

A breeze pushed his curtains open, and he glanced at his window. There were no cracks. It had just been a dream, a nightmare. He lay there catching his breath. Then he rolled onto his side and noticed his dad's slippers below his bed and bark mulch scattered across his floor. Suddenly, children's laughter floated through the open window. Duffy glared at his window with discontent. Then he rolled over and threw his pillow over his head, ignoring the laughter.

CHAPTER 11
1,000 LICKINGS

The Armybrats' confrontations never lasted long, but the impressions they made lasted forever. The Armybrats had everyone wondering why kids still felt the urge to bully, especially when they knew they were about to get their asses handed to them. Every bully got a role reversal. They were dished the slop ten times worse than they planned to give. But the bullies weren't bullied; they were taught. Sometimes they needed a beat-down or what their parents used to call "lickings."

After-school football games were always a blast. Except one night, where two kids named Sam and Shawn tried performing some extracurricular activities after one of their winning games. They had two of their classmates—Vicki and Clarissa—in the bed of a pickup truck in the farthest corner of the parking lot, making out with them. Danny liked Clarissa, and Duffy had his eyes on Victoria. Unfortunately, the Armybrats weren't popular like the football players. They had their boy toys, and that was how it was. There was usually no intervening with other guys' girls. However, this horrific night rolled up rather quickly as the parking lot emptied out.

Speaking of rolling, that was how the Armybrats solved this problem. When the two boys were taking advantage of the two girls, they were struck by justice—Armybrats justice.

It was almost a double date rape that night as music blared from the truck radio, and the girls were screaming "Stop!" and "No!" from the truck bed. But these two nincompoops had only two goals in mind—wet penises and downing bottles of beer—and they didn't care what the girls were saying.

A cooler sat near the truck, and all four of them were intoxicated. The Armybrats weren't having that on their turf.

Each girl had been pinned down against her will. Vicki had a shoulder strap off her dress yanked down below her elbow with her left tit pointing at the midnight sky. Clarissa's panties were down to her ankles as Sam struggled to undo his pants. She screamed and pulled on his arms to stop him. Each boy was shirtless—and mindless. But what happened next was priceless.

The school cafeteria had a full kitchen. Some of the traps below the sinks held remnants from cleaning trays, silverware, and drink cups. In another area, food waste was chopped to bits and collected in barrels below a sink near the tray collection window. Duffy remembered seeing them the other day, and that's where he got the idea. The blue barrels were chilling in the corner out behind the cafeteria next to the dumpsters. They held some of the slimiest lard. Billy and Wesley rolled the smelly barrels down to the truck as fast as they could.

Two sets of ropes were flung over each boy. With their pants down and booze running through their bloodstreams, they didn't realize what was happening until the ropes stretched, and the cars they were tied to drove forward. The boys were kinked inside the ropes, which stretched up over the truck's cab. The other ends of the ropes were tied to the rear bumper of the truck. Sam actually had the worse deal because one of the ropes tightened over his erect penis and mashed it into his gut as both boys slammed against the cab's window. Their faces were pressed tight to the window, and Danny spun around in the front seat smiling and waving at them. Billy and Wesley undid the ropes from the car and tied them to the truck's front bumper.

Pete and Duffy ran up to the tailgate of the truck and helped the girls bail out before the guys realized what was going on, their dicks hanging out like two baby elephants' trunks swatting at flies. Shawn tried to lunge at them, but he was held back by the rope. Meanwhile, Sam was crying over the rope burn on his dick. The Armybrats had planned a quick attack followed by an equally fast escape.

Vile and grotesque as it was, the next occurrence happened as soon as the tailgate slammed closed. Two barrels had been positioned, one over the bed rail and the other over the tailgate. Billy tilted his barrel, and Pete and Wesley hoisted the other barrel over the tailgate. The fifty-five-gallon barrels of lard filled the truck bed with fat, food particles, and stench. Smelly waste byproduct rose clear up to the boys' mid calves. Sam and Shawn were shirtless, caught pants down buried in nasty slime. It oozed between their legs and buried their pants (at their ankles) deep in the shit.

When they tried to jump over the bedrails, their bodies were yanked back into each other from the tightened ropes, and they hit the bedrails, falling back into the pool of slop. Danny had started their truck. Billy and Wesley climbed in with him. Danny jammed it into reverse to jerk the would-be rapists around. Both boys flew into the sludge and slammed into the cab. Now it was fair game. Particles dripped off the boys' chins. Hairdos from the eighties couldn't compare to the gel packed deep into their scalps.

Danny drove the truck in circles around the parking lot, subjecting the boys to a nasty whiplash of lard as Duffy and Pete ran with the girls toward the school entrance. Sam and Shawn were in a bed of the slipperiest crap as Danny spun around the lot, basting the two turkeys with juices of lunches past.

Suddenly, Pete's car whipped out in front of the truck, and Danny followed him onto the main road toward a veterinarian's office, which was also a rescue shelter. Duffy and Pete had Heath, the veterinarian's son with them. The two girls sat in the backseat with Duffy, who was coddling them—of course!

Heath turned to Pete. "Man, I'm going to get my ass whooped for this."

"Trust me, you're doing these two beautiful women a solid!" Duffy shouted. "They're gonna thank you all senior year!" Heath turned his head and smiled bashfully.

They reached the rescue shelter, which wasn't too far into town, and Heath out of Pete's car. The funny part was, the two naked boys smothered in lard and other remnants of waste were clueless. They shouted profanities and tried to vacate the truck bed while they slipped in their own vomit. But Danny continued to drive them dizzy in the veterinarian clinic's parking lot.

Heath opened a garage door on the back side of the clinic, and Danny backed the truck inside. The two turkeys basted in the truck bed heard the barking of dogs, which grew louder when the garage door closed. It was dark inside. Only moonlight glistened over the lard on their naked bodies.

Danny flew out and opened the tailgate, then jumped away as lard poured out of the truck.

Inside the main hallway, Heath and Pete ran inside the garage and shut a couple of doors to the main hall. The barking grew even louder.

Sam and Shawn sat inside the truck bed, unable to see what was going on. They screamed and asked what was happening, but the Armybrats didn't reply. Duffy worked a winch off the truck and let loose cable drape across the concrete floor.

As the Armybrats fled the garage bay, which was for horses, the winch wound up. Sam and Shawn fought with the ropes. The dogs and other animals barked and scratched at the doors, which wiggled violently. Sam and Shawn couldn't see through the sludge. Then the winch yanked the door open.

Suddenly, Sam and Shawn were overwhelmed by mangy mutts. All the dogs were in heaven. The two naked boys with slicked hair, glistening chests, and chunks of fat and doused underwear and shoes grabbed their privates while the dogs went into attack mode—mostly licking. The Armybrats, Heath, and the two girls were driving away by the time the silent alarms were triggered, and squad cars came rolling into the lot. Sam and Shawn got what they deserved—not just one licking but several thousand "lickings."

The police officers entered the unlocked compound and scampered inside.

"Please help us!" Sam hollered at one of the officers with a significant whine from the back of his throat.

The cops aimed their flashlights at the animals and scanned the truck as slop dropped off the bumpers and slapped the floor. They backed away, blinking their eyes, and gasping for fresh air. Officer Penske looked at Officer Darcy. "What the hell is this?"

"You boys from the football game?" Darcy shined his light in their eyes as Penske killed the truck engine and the blaring music.

"Yes!" Shawn cried. "Get away, dog!" Another dog ripped his underwear clear off his ankles, and he slipped, bashed his head on the bedrail, and got mauled by slobbering tongues.

Darcy laughed. "Damn! Those are some hungry mutts!"

Penske flashed his light in Sam's face. "What kind of shenanigans are you two pulling?"

Darcy couldn't stop laughing. "I think . . . I think it's a hazing, probably some senior prank!"

Penske shined his light in his face as he gripped his Billy club and tried to stay upright but fell against a wall with a gut-wrenching laugh. "You're doing the paperwork on this one, Darcy! Do we need Hazmat for this?"

"Oh, shoot, let the dogs finish cleaning it up!"

"Call the veterinarian. We need to collect these dogs!"

"You boys been drinking?" Darcy asked.

Both officers laughed. They couldn't contain themselves from the gruesome display of shenanigans. Tails wiggled in the air as the dogs dug into the slop. Sam and Shawn remained roped inside the truck bed surrounded by fur balls and slobbering tongues.

CHAPTER 12
SCHOOL SHOOTER

This happened about midyear. School was actually postponed for a couple of days afterward. But it all ended in the gymnasium that day.

It started at the back entrance near the courtyard, where the kids played. The kid in question was no longer attending the school, but that day he was on a mission. Although he had a target in mind, he never made it that far. As a matter of fact, he never made it into the north wing at all.

It was about the third hour into the school day. The bells rang for the change over to the next class. Students ran through the halls to switch books at their lockers, use the bathroom, and get to their next class. When things were just settling down again, outside in the playground, the kid strolled through the swings, the basketball courts, toward the high school.

He wore a trench coat and had short hair and thick, black eyeglass frames. An earring shimmered in one of his ears. A silver ring looped through his eyebrow. Another oddity about the kid was his use of eyeliner. He had outlined his eyes in black. He stopped beside a "No Smoking" sign, lit a cigarette, then continued toward the school. At his waist was a pistol.

After passing through the first set of doors, he took a drag of his cigarette. A teacher noticed him smoking in the entryway. The boy kept the cigarette tucked between his lips as he used his shoulder to open the next door to enter the main hall. The teacher held up his hand to stop him as he approached the kid with a book from the library.

"Hey, there's no smoking in here. I'm going to have to ask you to extinguish that cigarette."

The boy entered the hall and watched the instructor set the book on a cart, then turn around to lecture him about the school's smoking policy.

Instead of listening, the boy raised the pistol and shot him. The instructor flew backwards over the book cart, flooding the library entrance with bloody books.

The librarian stood up from her desk and adjusted her bifocals to take in the devastation. The boy stood over the body in the doorway and glared at her. She held up her hand to stop kids from leaving the microfiches and ordered them to stay behind the shelving units. The kid glanced at the shelves to see the kids between the books. Then he looked at the librarian once more and walked away from the library. She slumped in her chair and reached for the phone, but her nerves made her drop the receiver. Then she picked up the phone again to call the main office upstairs, struggling to dial with her shaking hand.

A couple of students came down the staircase to the boy's left and caught him off guard, so he shot them. The students—a boy and a girl—were plastered to the lockers and fell to the floor, motionless. It seemed like this kid was on a mission. Any deviation from that was met with angst and attitude.

He threw open the door to the theater where students were acting on stage. An instructor was sitting in the first row with a clipboard and a pen. The room was dark, though the stage was well lit. The shooter walked between the last rows of chairs and sat down in the center.

A janitor entered the theater and shined his light toward the instructor. The instructor spun around. What the janitor didn't realize was the shooter was just to his right. As his pupils were adjusting to the darkness, a shot rang out, and the janitor toppled over a set of chairs.

The flashlight spun beneath the rows of seats, and the light flickered down the aisle. The students on stage screamed and then lay flat. The instructor fell to the floor as well. A girl continued to let out a wretched cry on stage. She was lying on the stage floor, shrieking. A bullet nailed her side, and her eyes bugged out. She rolled over, grasping the fresh wound. The shooter exited the theater.

Duffy, who was the lighting coordinator, witnessed the muzzle flashes from the booth. He flipped a bunch of switches and turned all the lights on inside the theater. He adjusted one light on the wounded girl on stage.

Then he jumped up, grabbed the emergency kit off the wall, and ran toward her. He had been so focused on the lighting that he hadn't realized what was happening until it was too late. He grabbed an actor and pulled him toward the wounded girl.

"Here, take this!" he shouted, then handed the kit to the kid. "Apply pressure here, OK?"

"OK!" the kid said, nodding as he followed Duffy's instructions.

Duffy bolted back toward the booth. He grabbed his backpack and pulled out a slingshot, then flew out an exit door that led down a flight of stairs to the main hall.

The Armybrats were scattered throughout the building. They were not in the same classes. Billy had already graduated, so he wasn't even in the building.

Duffy threw open the door and entered the hallway. He peeked around the corner to see the shooter stomping out his cigarette in the hallway and advancing toward the stairway at the end of the hall. Two students were lying in the hall near the theater, curled into balls. One was holding onto a fresh bullet wound while the other lay motionless. Kids were running and screaming down the halls. Upstairs, teachers were trying to keep kids inside the classrooms. Some kids roaming the halls were escorted single file along the wall into other classrooms.

That's when Duffy noticed Pete poking his head out from the library directly across the hall. He was straddling a body in the doorway, a pile of books surrounding his feet. Duffy pointed at the shooter, and Pete nodded. He already knew about the deviant but had no weapons available, unlike Duffy, who had his slingshot. But they were trapped behind the shooter with nowhere to go.

The school entrance was behind them, but they didn't want to leave; they wanted to deescalate the situation. There were two floors. The lower entrance, near the theater room, extended down to where the gymnasium was on the opposite end of the hall. The upper floor was where most of the seniors were. A few different wings branched off the study hall at the top of the stairs that divided each level.

Danny and Wesley watched an economics instructor step into the main hall and confront the shooter. "Hey, kid, let's talk about this."

Wesley looked at Danny. "This might not be good."

"OK, now or never," Danny replied.

Just then their art teacher, Philip, stepped into the hall and cut them off. "Where do you kids think you're going? Get back inside."

"The gym!" Danny said.

"No, get in the art room now," Philip insisted.

"You know what?" Wesley said, "that sounds like a splendid idea. While you're in there, pray for us."

They darted around him and down the staircase. Philip attempted to grab them on the way past, but they were too quick for him.

The economics teacher had his back turned to them as he reasoned with the gunman. "Something is ailing you," the teacher said, "and we must discuss it."

The kid was crying as he leaned inside the doorway to a restroom, aiming his gun at the teacher. "No, I'm here about one person and one person only. Whoever stands in my way is liable to get shot. Do you wanna get shot?"

"Well, no, but no one needs to get shot, son."

"If you don't move, you're gonna die."

Just then, the kid noticed the Armybrats running behind him toward the gymnasium. "Where do you little fuckers think you're going?" he yelled, pointing his gun at them.

The economics instructor turned one hand in the air. His other hand maintained a hold on his coffee mug. "Kids please, get out of here."

Duffy pulled a slingshot out as Pete picked up the book cart and lined it up with the gunman.

"Mr. Freeman!" Danny shouted. "Please go upstairs, and let us sort things out here." Danny pointed toward the staircase. "It's for your own safety, sir."

Mr. Freeman did not budge. "What?"

"Look, you're just a teacher. We're kids. Only kids get through to other kids. He's not gonna listen to you, especially if he's already messed up in the head, hopped up on cocaine, or whatever."

The gunman growled.

Mr. Freeman held onto his cup of coffee as he shook his head at Danny, trying to motion him out of the hallway. Then he spun around just in time for the kid to smash the pistol into the bridge of his nose, sending him to his knees. The shooter aimed at Mr. Freeman, who was waving him off, his coffee cup still in hand. They were standing at the foot of the staircase.

Duffy placed a metal ball inside his slingshot and cranked it back to his ear with a stiff arm forward. Danny and Wesley crouched in the doorway to the gym. Suddenly, a squeaky wheel on a book cart was heard. The shooter glanced up to see it flying across the hall toward him. He raised his gun to shoot at Pete. A bullet smashed into the wooden doorway to the library as Pete eased around the metal casing.

"Mr. Freeman, get out of here now!" Pete shouted.

Mr. Freeman seemed a bit puzzled as he looked at the boys surrounding the gunman. The gunman regained himself after the book cart smashed into his thigh. Danny pranced around Wesley and then ducked inside the gym, Wesley right behind him. Then the gunman noticed Duffy and turned to aim at him. Duffy released the round hunk of metal. It streamed right down the sight posts of the kid's handgun and through his front teeth. The kid dropped his handgun and bent over, holding his face, and slammed his head over the book cart. He flew over Mr. Freeman and cracked his head on the stairway railing. A tooth bounced across the floor.

Mr. Freeman reached for the gun, but the kid kicked him in the back of the head. His coffee cup flew across the hall and shattered, sending coffee streaming down the grout lines. The kid crawled over Mr. Freeman and grabbed his gun. He turned toward the gymnasium where all the Armybrats had gathered and shot at the door as it closed behind Pete and Duffy, who had run past the shooter when he was down. Pete had been flinging books at him the entire time the kid was losing teeth.

The Armybrats were inside the gym, and the kid was left toothless on the hallway floor. Lying on his side, he fired at the gymnasium doors. Mr. Freeman fled up the stairs behind him. The kid shot one round at Mr. Freeman's feet as he disappeared up the steps.

"Man, I busted him right in the schnauzer!" Duffy shouted as glass and wood blew over him.

"I think you pissed him off!" Pete said.

Duffy cocked his head toward Pete. "Oh, and you didn't? You beat him up with a book cart!"

Bullets flew through the door and took out the glass backboard on one of the basketball hoops.

"Every time I'm with you, we're getting shot at!" Danny shouted. "Why do you insist on drawing him toward us?"

"Because if we're his target, we have his undivided attention," Duffy explained.

"You're crazy!" Pete hollered.

Suddenly, the bullets stopped. "Get ready, guys!" Danny screamed.

When he peeked through the windows, he saw the kid charging the gymnasium, bleeding from his mouth and aiming at the doors.

Pete killed the lights, and they dispersed into the darkness.

The kid entered the dark gymnasium. "You little fuckers are dead!" His voice echoed into the empty space.

"Ooh, berry, berry scary!" Duffy screeched, his voice echoing across the gymnasium.

The kid shot a towel cart along the bleachers. His clip empty, he dropped it and dug out a second clip. Suddenly, a screeching sound rattled the gymnasium floor as a section of bleachers opened out toward him. He popped the second clip in and fired into the wooden bleachers. They usually left them folded against the wall during gymnastics class. If they held assemblies at the school, they would extract the bleachers and have hour-long ass pains listening to instructors or special guests talk.

While the kid fired at the wooden benches, a dodgeball winged out from the other end of the gym and bashed him in the back of the skull. His gun sailed across the gymnasium floor and slid beneath the bleachers, which continued to extend in his direction. As he stood up, Pete rammed the towel cart into him. The kid flipped backwards and bashed his head and shoulder into the gym floor.

Duffy laughed in the distance. "Oh man, I felt that way over here."

The kid stood up, clutching his shoulder. "I don't know who you kids think you're messing with, but—"

Wesley, who had snuck up behind him, crawled on all fours and twirled on his wrists, slamming his legs into the back of the kid's knees. He sailed backward and slammed into the ground. Wesley stood at his feet and smiled. "I don't think you know who *you're* messing with, brotha."

The kid stood up and scowled at him. "You're going to wish you never did that, boy." Wesley kicked the kid in the groin, and he fell to his knees. Then Wesley kneed him in the face and walked away. The kid rolled onto his back in agony. Wesley walked toward a cart of dodgeballs, whistling to himself.

"I'm gonna kill you brats!" the kid cried, then crawled toward the bleachers to retrieve his gun.

Duffy swung from a rope hanging from the rafters. Kids usually climbed it during gym class. He swung past the shooter as he crawled across the gymnasium floor and kicked him in the face. The shooter's body squeaked across the floor, and an echo rattled through the gym when his head bashed the bottom of the bleachers. Duffy swung backwards and dropped in front of him. "That's the Armybrats to you, you pathetic waste of oxygen."

The kid was bleeding from his missing tooth as he crawled through his own bloody saliva to reach for his weapon. Danny was lying beneath the bleachers holding onto his gun, which he had stripped of ammo. He locked the slide hammer back, which exposed the empty ejection port.

The kid reached between the benches. His outstretched fingers felt around on the floor trying to retrieve his weapon. Danny guided the ejection port into his middle finger and nudged the release lever, causing the slide hammer to slam over his finger. The kid bellowed in agony but couldn't retract his hand from the bleachers because the pistol had wedged him in. Danny shut him up with a quick tug on his arm and a swift kick to his face between the bleachers. Wesley and Pete joined Duffy, who was standing behind the shooter. He was almost subdued at that point.

Meanwhile, kids were pouring out of the school. Police surrounded the building and led students far from the main entrances. Ambulances were parked on the grass behind the theater. Policemen entered the school from both levels. A few students and teachers were hurried along behind the policemen.

Some teachers led policemen straight for the gymnasium. As they approached, they heard awful clanking and screeching sounds. The lights flickered on, and the police scattered inside, circling all the walls. In the middle of the bleachers, which were folded back against the wall, an overturned dodgeball cart leaned over the wood with a pair of legs sticking out of it. The shooter's pants were around his ankles. "I'm your shooter!" was written on a flag that protruded from his brown sphincter.

The police surrounded the kid, who was hanging upside down and tangled inside the bleachers, his wrists tied to a cross section beneath them. The shooter was literally in a jam. The Armybrats had closed the bleachers over his body, stopping as soon as they heard his bones crack.

The Armybrats were nowhere in sight. They had left out the gym's back door and cut through the forest out back. No one was the wiser except for the flag that Duffy had wedged into the kid's ass crack. The flag was one of the signatures that they liked to leave behind.

A policeman looked at the principal as he stretched out the flag. "Who the hell is this?"

The principal shrugged. "This is your shooter, I guess."

School was dismissed early following the shooting incident. All students had to undergo searches and seizures in a quarantine area at the far end of the school parking lot before they could be released to go home. Many parents were held at a church across the road. The entire perimeter was blocked. No vehicles were allowed in, and no one was allowed out. The entire school was wrapped in police tape. It was a crime scene.

Farther behind the group of frantic parents, on the south side of the church, a lonely van was parked along the curbside. Someone jogged over to the passenger door. It was Bonzo. He extinguished a cigarette before jumping into the van. "That kid you paid failed. He never got the art teacher, boss."

The man in the driver's seat snarled and tipped his flop hat upward, revealing his scarred face. It was Watches. "The art teacher is still alive?"

"Yes, boss, some kids managed to stop the shooter!"

"The Armybrats," Watches snarled.

"Want me to whack the art teacher, boss?"

Watches dropped the back seat with the push of a button, revealing a rifle. "See that bell tower on the church roof?"

"Consider it done, boss."

Police were escorting people through the lines for searches. Among the students were teachers and other emergency personnel. Some teachers were intermixed throughout the lines. Mark Emerson was walking past the line trying to read people's faces, trying to understand who might have seen what had happened. He was also questioning students in the line. He couldn't find Danny or any of his friends.

Bonzo crawled up the shingles of the church roof, the rifle slung over his back, the skyline widening before him as he neared the peak. He glanced over his shoulder to see the van still sitting by the curb. He climbed farther up to the bell tower, straddled the railing, then hopped inside.

Easing around the bell so as to not disturb it, he slid the rifle over the railing and propped himself inside the wooden structure. He nestled himself firmly against the framework and ran his sights across the line of people. He saw Mark and opened both eyes for a second. Then he leaned in.

Suddenly, a shot rang out. A few students shrieked, and kids in the line either scattered or dropped to the ground. Blood dribbled down a "No Parking" sign as a body hit the pavement with a thud.

Mark moved the kids into the parking lot between the parked cars, screaming for them to get down. He crawled toward the body lying against a curb.

As he neared it, he saw a fresh hole between the man's eyes. Suddenly, he recognized the face. He grabbed the body's shoulders. "Philip! Oh no, Philip!" It was his son's art teacher.

Moments later, the van drove away from the church.

* * *

Later that evening, squad cars roared into the driveway of a rancher home. The front door was wide open. Police swarmed inside. It had been tossed. Things were upside down and out of place. A den in the corner right off the living room had been scavenged. Cabinets were flipped over. Drawers were out of the desk, and video cassette tapes lay in a pile. However, one video cassette case was empty, lying open on top of the desk.

Mark realized this wasn't a robbery or an amateur hit. It had been done by a professional.

In the laundry room, they found Philip's wife, Mrs. Georgeson. Her body was slumped over the washing machine, her head buried inside. Apparently, she had been drowned. The washing machine was still full of water and was quietly batting her face around during the rinse cycle.

At that moment Mark remembered Philip coming to his precinct with the videotape and watching the video of Watches escaping the House on the

Rock. This was a hit, and Mark was pretty sure the devil himself was slowly emerging from the shadows.

Back in the living room, he tipped the videocassette tape to read the outside, which was labeled: "Our hike around the House on the Rock, June 1994."

The Armybrats had saved lives that day. They were like quiet heroes. This was just one of the many tales of the Armybrats' legacy in high school.

Despite their efforts, one student died. Her funeral was held the following weekend. Three other students were in critical condition, as were one instructor and the janitor. As for the Armybrats, they decided to design a strategy in the event such a thing ever happened again. Their strategy was to have a rally point, such as the gymnasium, to lure the shooter in. As a team, they had managed it quite well. Unfortunately, they were unable to meet sooner due to being in different classrooms at the time. Since weapons weren't allowed in school, they had to improvise, using only the props the school had to offer. Duffy's slingshot was nice to have, but it was not allowed in school. He just didn't care about rules.

School was out of session for a while. Funerals were held for the dead. Verona had become a little more shaken. People were on edge. Things were becoming more and more terrifying. If Stanley Watches Markesan was still alive, he wasn't going to kill Mark and his entire family; he was going to torture them. He was going to rile the herd, wake the farmers, and scare some chickens. He was going to make them suffer, and it wasn't over. It wasn't even beginning. The devil was just warming up.

CHAPTER 13
BEANER

School was back in session the following week. Diesel fumes drifted hazily through the air. Kids' nostrils succumbed to the scent of burning fuel as they marched up the steps and into their buses early on Wednesday afternoon. Being released early was an excellent feeling. But knowing they were being released for the last day was even better. It was the last day of eleventh grade for the Armybrats. For the last time, the buses were lined up in front of Verona High School. The following year, they'd be refueled and ready to take them to their final chapter of high school, senior class.

Pete strode up the steps onto his bus and sat in his usual seat. No sooner had he plopped his rear end down than an older kid named Greg stapled him against the window. His upper arm pressed over Pete's shoulder as Pete looked back at him. It was the same bully who had picked on him throughout high school. When Pete had a sleepover with his friends, he had bruises on his face, and Greg was the cause.

Lately, Pete had a lot on his mind. He was thinking about his mom a lot more. She was still lying in a hospital room in a coma. Now that school was out, he planned to visit her more often. He had been thinking about her until Greg interrupted his thoughts. He hadn't ridden the bus for most of the junior year just to avoid this kid. Instead, he rode his bike. Unfortunately, it had been raining that day. Since it was the last day of eleventh grade, he decided to ride the bus and close that chapter of his life. A conclusion with the bus bully would have been extraordinary, especially since he was never going to see him again.

"Can I help you?" Pete asked, his lips mashed against the window as the bus exited the semicircular drive between the high school and the middle school.

"No, but you can give me all your money though," Greg said. "Remember, I told you that I would come for you on the last day of school. And I told you that you'd better have my money. Where have ya been, Peter? You owe me big time now, dumbshit."

"I was under the impression that I didn't owe you jack." Pete said. "Oh, wait, I do owe you something: a bill! So is there anything else you need before I retrieve your billing statement and ask you to stand down, kind friend?"

Greg released him. He had a friend on the bus who usually supported him with his conniving ways. On one bus ride when Greg's friend held a knife to Pete's head, he had given away money and his favorite handheld gaming system. He had emptied his pockets and became a pawn in their evil games. Whatever money he had on him, he shelled it out to those boys. This time he did not concede. He knew exactly why he had paid them before: to avoid pain. But he wasn't about to retreat. He wasn't about to take heed of these boys anymore. Instead, he was ready to give some right back.

Pete brushed off his chest. "I've calculated the amount of money that you owe me. I have been suckered in to your bully antics, and I have paid you a total of four hundred and twenty dollars and sixty-three cents. So, there's one way I look at your presumption. It is backassward, my friend. You owe me money." Pete smiled and slapped a billing statement in Greg's lap. "Read 'em and weep, cowboy."

Greg slid away from him and unfolded the piece of paper. It read:

> Brackstin Eberly and Greg Wilkinson owe Pete Carson a total of **$420.63**. There are two options for how to respond to this good faith billing statement. Option A: pay it in one lump sum by the end of this bus ride. Option B: if you refuse to pay and instead resort to violence, I promise not to end your lives, but the hospital bill will cost you more than the lump sum shown above in bold. Please choose your option carefully. Thank you for your cooperation in this matter.

Greg wasn't used to any sort of retaliation from Pete or any of the other kids he had bullied over the years. He couldn't even tease him because he didn't know how to measure up to his potential. Unfortunately, he was about to make the scene more provocative. Too pushy to accept a devil's advocate plea, Greg's eyes became narrow slits in his fatty cheeks. His skin folded around his eyes, nose, and mouth.

Pete smiled. "What's it going to be? Are you going to continue asking me for money, or am I going to have to beat some dollars and *sense* outta ya? There's option A or option B." Pete indicated the first option with one finger, but on option B, he made a fist.

Greg looked forward. He didn't have anything to say. Pete focused on what he was looking at. The bus driver's curly gray hair waved in the breeze coming in through her side window. They could see her hair in the rearview mirror, and that was all they could see. At that point, Pete felt like slipping away from the kid, but he had already opened up the door for a settlement. So, he just sat there enjoying the scenery whip by.

That was when Pete noticed Greg's arm in the window's reflection. The bully was reaching forward to draw an elbow into his back. He was probably going to pick him up by the shirt collar like he used to. Then he would attempt to shove Pete through the window. It was a mild threat tactic that was about to fail miserably.

Pete intercepted his elbow by grabbing a hold of Greg's wrist and twisting his arm behind his back. He did it without even looking. Then he turned and placed a hand over the kid's shoulder and mashed him against the backside of the seat in front of them, digging his thumb into his jugular.

"So, you made a decision. You went with option B. Would you rather hold hands for the rest of the bus ride?"

Pete watched Greg as his other shoulder moved, and he caught his other arm as he tried to throw a fist into Pete's face. Pete grabbed that fist and wrapped it behind his head. However, that freed his thumb from Greg's jugular, and he could breathe again. Greg proceeded to move his head back. He was going to headbutt him, but Pete turned his shoulder outward, so Greg headbutted his shoulder bone. Greg pulled away from him and clutched his own forehead with a grimace. "Ow!"

"Option B then?" Pete asked.

Greg looked up at him with one squinty eye. He didn't say a word, but Pete watched his shoulders. Shoulders explained a lot about where punches would come from. Greg wound up for a good hit with his right fist, but Pete intercepted it and yanked, expanding Greg's momentum across his lap. With his other hand behind the bully's neck, he curled his arm downward and smashed Greg's face against the window. The smack was so hard that a crack webbed down the window pane. Pete raised his knee into Greg's sternum and dug his boney elbow into the small of his back, trapping him in the corner.

"OK, I'm going to let you go," Pete said, "but I expect that when I do, you will leave my seat. I won't bother you anymore for the money that you owe me. We'll call it Option C, a truce. How does that sound?"

Greg breathed heavily, and the window fogged up. Some blood seeped out of his nose. Pete let go. Greg backed away quickly. He straightened his shirt and looked confused. He remained seated, but Pete felt that the worst part wasn't over yet. Greg turned and twitched his head, cueing his buddy to advance.

"OK, here comes Beaner, your better half, a true negotiator and money manager." Pete smiled and shook his head. "I'm not tracking, but hopefully, once he gets here, we can sort all this out like adults."

Pete ogled Beaner as he eased from seat to seat up the aisle. Then he stared at the bus driver's head in the fat oval mirror angled just overhead as she adjusted herself for comfort. Pete didn't break a sweat though. He glanced out the window again to enjoy some more scenery and occasionally looked back at Beaner to verify his position. Greg turned his back to him as Beaner sat in the seat behind them.

"This kid thinks we owe him money," Greg whispered.

Beaner snorted as he laughed. "Is that what he thinks? What happened to your face?"

Greg placed a finger over his bleeding nose. Blood smudged across his upper lip and then looked at his finger to see the blood. "Yeah, he thinks we owe him money. Isn't that true, dipshit?" He turned around, but Pete was gone.

Beaner jumped over the seat. "Where'd he go?"

They both stood up and looked around. Greg started toward the back of the bus as Beaner searched the front. That was when a hand shot out from under one of the seats. Two girls looked up at Beaner as he fell. The hand that grasped onto his ankle suddenly stopped his forward momentum, and at the same time he noticed the girls looking up at him, he fell over and clocked his head on the floor. Pete sat up between the two girls. "Excuse me, ladies."

By the time Pete was sitting between the girls, Beaner was already on his feet looking down at him. He pulled out a knife and held it in the small of his back, hidden from view. However, Pete caught some sunlight that reflected from the blade through the window behind him. He withdrew his arms from the girls' shoulders and crossed them over his chest like Mr. Clean in the Power Scrub ads. He buried his hands beneath the flaps of his trench coat, much like the one Mr. Fallway always wore.

Beaner leaned against the back of the seat in front of him. "You're going to wish you never did that, kid." He held the knife behind his back and looked at the girl near the aisle. "Excuse me?" he said, motioning for her to vacate her seat.

Pete leaned into her shoulder, speaking on her behalf. "No. It's her seat. Not yours, Beaner the wiener." The girls were a bit startled by the situation.

"Listen here, you little friggin' twerp."

"I'm listening, ya big ugly fucker."

"Excuse me?"

"You heard me. I didn't stutter!"

Beaner whipped out his knife. Pete's arms unfolded from his chest. In his left hand, he swung out a bone-handled knife from a sheath—given to him by Mr. Fallway. It had been hard for Pete to accept the knife as a gift. He didn't know it was a gift; Mr. Fallway just gave it to him. Pete really wanted to keep it, but at the same time, he wanted to give it back. However, in the present moment, it came in handy. He grasped Beaner's arm with his free hand. Beaner's eyes bulged from their sockets. Then, with his hand gripping the bone handle of this eight-inch blade, Pete trapped Beaner's four-inch blade against the seat.

Pete headbutted Beaner's nose and slammed his face against both blades. He rotated his knife so that the blade bunched into his cheek and then slipped the knife downward. A fresh slit appeared across Beaner's face as he fell backwards across the aisle into the laps of two other students, screaming and clutching his bloody face.

Pete leaned forward and smiled. "Huh, mine's bigger than yours. Now we know how you don't measure up, Beaner."

The girls dropped their jaws as Beaner lunged at Pete across the aisle. Beaner wanted to thrust his knife into him so badly, Pete could sense it. Pete reached up and slid his hand along Beaner's handle, pressed a nerve in his arm, and ripped the knife out of his hand. He twirled the knives, so the blades tucked back beneath his wrists and folded his arms again; the knives were hidden.

Suddenly, Beaner was pulled back by Greg. Both of them stared into each other's bloody faces.

"What?" Beaner growled.

"We agreed, no knives, Brackstin." Brackstin was Beaner's real name. He had developed the name "Beaner" from constantly sucking on marijuana seeds. Kids referred to them as "beaners." He and Greg were heavy weed smokers.

"What are you talking about? I don't have a knife," he joked, since Pete had confiscated his. Just then, Pete dropped Beaner's knife. It bounced on the floor in front of Greg. Greg looked up at Beaner. "Oh yeah? Then what's that?"

"What are you going to do about it?" Beaner asked.

Hesitating for a moment, Greg considered knocking him out of the picture for the way he was acting. Beaner bent down to retrieve the knife. All Greg felt was the knife's blade scrape through his nostril. Suspended from his bony nose was a slab of skin that twirled on a bloody strand of cartilage that looked like a bloody rubber band. His nose bone was visible behind the fresh slice. He hollered in pain and held onto what was left of his nose.

Beaner brought back his elbow and nailed Pete across the cheek. His triceps mashed the face of the girl who was sitting closer to the aisle. Pete's head bounced back and cracked the window as he flew over the other girl, landing on her lap. Pete's lips smashed against his teeth as Beaner sat on top of him, crushing him. Then he saw Beaner's knife. Blood was smeared across the tip.

Life was short, and Beaner was about to spray Pete's insides across two pretty girls. Before Beaner could think about it, blood squirted from his other cheek. He screamed, held onto a fresh cut, and jumped out of the seat.

He glanced up at Pete's hand and the bone-handled knife, which held some skin bunched up over some blood across the blade. The slice to his cheek had freed Pete from Beaner's death grip. Pete had a solemn look across his face. He didn't want Beaner to make a move, so he kicked upward through his chin, then hopped backward off one of the girls and stood up.

"So, option B it is," Pete said, waving his knife at them.

Unfortunately, Pete was standing against the window as he lunged up and held Beaner by the neck. The only way of getting to the aisle was through him. Beaner glared at him, bleeding from both sides of his face. He raised his arm to throw his blade. Pete grunted as he struck Beaner right behind his elbow joint, causing Beaner to drop his knife. Pete slid casually down between the seats and crawled beneath them. Beaner's hand cracked through the window, cutting his arm on the glass. His knife landed in the girl's lap, and she screeched, more concerned about the blood spatter on her nice yellow dress than the blade.

Greg watched Pete crawling beneath the seats. His sensitivity for Pete brought forth a trust that had never been shown before. Pete knew Greg was much more sensitive than Beaner, and he expected that he would stick up for him one day.

Beaner looked back at Pete. He withdrew his bloody hand from the cracked window, grabbed his knife from between the girl's legs, and stepped into the aisle.

"What am I . . . what am I going to do about it?" Greg asked. "What am I, ha ha, well, ha, precisely this." His fist cranked forward, and his knuckles slammed into Beaner's nose with a bone-crunching snap. Beaner flew backwards into the girls' laps.

"Hey, sweetie." He smiled at one of them, blood pouring down his lips. Then he grabbed her right breast. She snapped her tongue with disgust and pushed him onto the floor. Bloody fingerprints outlined the curve of her breast on her dress.

He lunged upward, retrieved his knife, and shoved Greg backward into the seat across the aisle. They wrestled. They didn't have much room to move around and punch each other, but they were at each other's throats. A few kids gathered around the surrounding seats to watch. One kid screamed as part of Greg's nose detached and bounced off his white shirt, leaving bloody streaks.

The bus came to a screeching halt, and they rolled off the seat. Their bodies nailed the back of another seat and collapsed to the floor with a thud. Everyone shifted forward. The bus driver fought with her seatbelt and finally got it undone, then tried plowing through the flock of students to take control of the situation. Pete decided it was time to get off the bus, so he crawled over a few seats and headed for the folding doors at the front. He wasn't too far from home, so he planned to hoof it from there.

Greg was lying on the floor, and Beaner was on the seat. He held up his arm to punch Greg in the face with the knife clenched in his palm. Greg reached up and grabbed his wrist with his left hand. Beaner tried striking him with his other hand, but Greg grabbed that wrist as well. He clamped his neck with each arm and stood him up, inadvertently knocking the bus driver over. She landed on the two girls across the aisle. The weight of all three people came crashing down on them, causing the girls to grimace in pain. As the driver struggled to get up, Beaner forced Greg backward, shoving him down the aisle.

Pete stood near the curb behind the bus, staring at it. Then he shrugged and walked away. Suddenly, he heard glass shatter. He spun around just in time to see Beaner shove Greg through the window at the back of the bus. A few beads of blood were splattered across the glass.

Greg looked up and noticed Peter standing outside. "Run, dude," he whimpered. Greg couldn't move. The glass was in his neck, and blood was spurting from his wound. A boy in the back seat caught specks of blood across his cheek, and he winced while pulling away.

"You two stop it right this instant!" the bus driver demanded as if she had any control over the situation. She stepped back when she noticed Beaner had a knife and held out her hand. "OK, hand over the knife, Brackstin." He looked at her and then turned around.

Students were surrounding the scene. The quickest way out was the emergency door behind him. Greg was still hanging through the window. Beaner thrashed the blade through the bus driver's left palm. She fell to her knees, clutching her hand. "Shit!" she cried through clenched teeth. She squeezed her wrist as blood drooled off her fingers like saliva from the chin of a slobbering baby.

CHAPTER 14
THE OUTSIDER

Beaner forced the emergency door open and jumped out. Greg's body swung outward, hanging lifeless on the glass. Pete's eyes widened. "Oh no, not again." His arms swayed outward as he spun around and ran. Beaner noticed him right away, and the chase began.

"Peter!" he shouted. "You're dead!"

Pete rounded a group of pine trees along the road. His house was about one hundred yards ahead. He stopped about a third of the way and glanced back at the group of trees. They swayed from a slight breeze. The road remained dead silent. He whipped his head in every direction, but no one was around. Birds chirped overhead, and he glanced up as a couple of smaller birds picked on a large crow.

Suddenly, an arm wrapped around his throat. The chokehold forced him to his knees. He was stuck. The guy held him tightly and wouldn't let go. He tried looking back, but he couldn't see him. He knew it was a guy because his arm hairs tickled his nose, and it wasn't Beaner.

"Hey, Peter, remember me? Watches, Watches, Watches? Ha ha! I want you to stay right here, Peter. This is your death call. Time to die!"

Out of nowhere, Beaner darted down the road. Pete screamed and struggled, but Watches just tightened his chokehold. In no time at all, Beaner was hovering over him. He couldn't see Watches; he could only see Pete flailing his arms while kneeling on the road by himself. Suddenly, Watches let go and kicked Pete forward. He landed on the road, coughing and trying to catch his breath.

Just when Pete was ready to put up a fight, the oddest thing happened. Watches was nowhere to be seen, but suddenly a man wearing a black suit and a black ski mask forced Beaner backward. Pete stood up.

"Go now, Peter!" the man said.

Pete hesitated. *Who is this guy? How come he knows my name?* However, that was his cue to leave. He ran, obeying this black-suited stranger. He didn't want to see what was about to happen. He didn't feel like sticking around. Things were getting too weird for him—too hairy. This was the type of nose tickler that would create endless sneezes. He didn't know who the newcomer was, and he didn't plan on sticking around to find out. Had Watches really been holding him against his will, or was it all in his head? When he hit the ground running, thoughts flourished in his mind. He ran past his mailbox toward his house.

Beaner caught air for a split second and then hit the rough road with a thunderous crack. Somehow he missed his footing as the black-suited man took all the stability away from him. He flipped him around like a pancake on a griddle.

Beaner jumped to his feet and spun around holding out his knife. "What the F?" His voice died when he saw no one was around. Blood ran down his neck. Each cheek had a bloody gash from Pete slicing them earlier.

The mysterious man was right beside him, but Beaner didn't even know it. He turned in every direction, but he didn't see a soul. He swung his knife around, cutting thin air. "W-who the h—"

The man elbowed Beaner in the jaw, cutting his question short. Beaner continued to swing his knife. The man's gesture was so professional that it almost appeared too easy as he blocked the kid's swiping maneuvers. The black-suited man punched him in the face. Beaner wobbled backward, took another blow from the man's elbow, then flew onto the seat of his pants as the stranger stood over him.

Beaner pulled out a lose tooth. "Ow! My tooth!"

The man kneed him in the face, and Beaner rolled backward. He walked on his hands and then stood up, waving his knife around like he was swatting flies. The man grabbed his wrist, and his other vinyl glove enclosed the handle of Beaner's knife. Using both hands, the man threw him forward, and

Beaner dove onto the road's surface. The crack of his collarbone sounded like a party popper. As Beaner sat up, he saw the stranger was holding his knife.

"Uh! M' damn shoulder!" he cried, then gasped when he saw his knife floating in midair.

Beaner watched the blade as it slid upward through his chin. He fell over once again, rolling around in agony. He grasped his chin and nailed the road, lying on his side. The mysterious man took off through someone's yard and ran away from the chilling display.

Beaner lay motionless, soundless, and functionless as a puddle of red flowed from beneath his head onto the pebbles embedded in the road. His mouth was knifed shut. He was like a real beaner now, the seed that never grew.

Pete flew through the front door and ran up to his dad in the kitchen. "Dad!" he said, grabbing him. "Watches is alive."

Jake, who was sitting at the kitchen island, burped in his face. "It's good to keep time, Peter. Never lose time. Always carry watches."

"What?" Pete asked, then backed away from his dad, waving his hand in front of his face. "What? No, Dad, you're not listening to me. And you're drunk!"

"Pete, your mom's in a coma," Jake said.

"I know," Pete replied.

"You should go see her, son."

"Dad, we were there last night."

Jake looked away from him and stared at the bubbles in his beer. His head fell onto the counter, and he wept. Pete, who was trying to catch his breath, walked up behind him and placed his hand over his shoulder. "Dad, everything will be alright. She's a strong woman!"

Jake lifted his head and sobbed. "You really think so?"

"No I know so, Dad. Are you going to be alright while I'm gone?"

"Where ya going, Pete?"

"Oh come on, Dad, we talked about this, remember? The Armybrats and I are going up north on a camping trip. We're going to have a sleepover at Duffy's house tonight, and then we'll be on the road in the morning. But I don't have to go if you're not gonna to be OK."

"No, son, you deserve time away. I'll be all right," Jake said. "I'll be all right!"

Pete hugged his father and then ran into the basement. He sat on one of the five stools in front of the wet bar downstairs and dialed the Emersons' house. Mary answered.

"Hi, Mrs. Emerson, is Danny home?"

"Well, yes, Pete. As a matter of fact, he just walked in the door."

A brief silence was followed by a scuffle. "Hey, Pete."

"Danny, listen, the strangest thing just happened to me."

"Oh yeah . . . puberty? It only happens once in a lifetime, ya know."

"No, Danny, I'm serious!"

"Me too."

"No, I think Watches is still alive! And there was some other guy, but I'm not sure who he was. He was dressed in black."

"Come on, Pete, don't start crap. You're only trying to get me riled up before we go camping. It's like the ghost story before the camping trip, right?"

"No, I'm dead serious, dude! He held me down in the road. Of course, that was right before I almost died from Beaner. He just held me there." Pete tried keeping himself busy by flicking pens through the air and catching them. He accidentally stuck one into the ceiling tile over his head. Then he looked at a cup full of pencils on the bar and raised his eyebrows in glory.

"What? Pete, you're making no sense. Look, if Watches were anywhere near you, he would have a bone to pick with you. Probably over a hundred bones! Remember, you blew him up with a grenade."

"Wait, what? You were there too. You and I both dished him a whoopin'!"

"Oh, I know, but you pretty much made him swallow a grenade, man. If he's coming after anyone now, it's definitely you. But don't worry—I'll try to save ya!"

"Shut up, Danny. I thought we were the Armybrats, man. All for one . . ."

"We're not the Musketeers."

"I still think we need a slogan."

"Hey, we gotta get off the phone. Duffy could be calling any minute."

"Yeah, you're right," Pete replied and chucked a pencil in the air. "OK, see ya soon. Bye."

The moment Danny hung up, the phone rang. Danny picked it up. "Pete," he said, "I'll talk to you when—"

"What?" Duffy replied. "Did you just refer to me as a geek?"

"Oh, crap, I thought . . . oh, never mind. Pete's got it in his head that Watches is still alive. I just got off the phone with him."

"Yeah, Pete's got a lot of screws loose, but we still love him. Hey, what's the big idea? I said I would call you at 1715 hours, and it's now 1720 hours."

"You're late. You should have called me five minutes ago."

"I did, but your line was busy!"

"Sure," Danny said, smirking.

"Are we on or not?"

Danny looked at his mom, who had just closed the refrigerator door and walked farther into the kitchen. "What about your parents?" he whispered.

"Dad's out of town on business, and Mom's oblivious. Actually, she went with him—although I did tell her we were all going camping together. What did you tell your parents?"

"Are you kidding? Mom thinks I'm going to your place for a few nights and then Pete's for a few more."

"Something tells me your story will hurt us. Well, hurry up and get over here."

"Alright. Just let me grab my bag, and I'll be right over!"

CHAPTER 15
CLEAN-UP CREW

Outside the Carsons' house, an ambulance hauled Beaner's motionless body away. Mark was there, as were a couple of other police officers. Although Beaner still had a pulse, he remained unconscious. Yellow tape blocked off the scene. Just ahead, the school bus was parked alongside the curb. Students were pointing at Pete's house as a paramedic tended to the bus driver's hand. They had Greg sitting along a curb. His nose was bandaged, as was his neck.

"Officer, is Brackstin going to make it?" Greg asked Mark.

He nodded. "Yes. But you need to rest. That ambulance is going to take you to the hospital along with a police escort. You have some explaining to do here, young man."

Greg sighed. "I never wanted any of this to happen."

"Yeah, neither did I," Mark replied. "I'm supposed to be on my way to the airport. I have a meeting in Washington, DC, and thanks to this, I might miss my flight. Now get along like I asked, young buck."

Greg held his head low and followed Officer Penske toward the ambulance. Mark walked over to Officer Darcy. "I have to run, but I expect a full report on my desk when I get back," Mark said. "Until then, if you have any questions, and I mean *any* questions, don't hesitate to call me while I'm in DC."

"Sure thing, boss!" Darcy replied.

"Later," Mark said and then climbed into his car.

After emptying his mailbox, he entered his garage. He noticed his hedge trimmers hanging out of place on the wall. He walked straight over to the tool bench to straighten them out. Then he glanced over at a dogfood bag and saw dogfood spilled onto the floor. He had a flashback of the night he fought with a pile of white gloves holding onto knives. He remembered how that dream ended: with him stabbing the devil through the back of the head.

Once inside, he opened an envelope, unfolded the piece of paper inside, and picked up the phone. He had decided to give his old boss a call in Granite View.

"Hey, Mike," Tony said. "Are you heading to Washington tonight?"

"Yup. I'm going to speak to whoever is in charge up there and find some damn answers."

"You haven't located the suspect yet, I presume."

"No. It's like he vanished."

"What's Billy been up to these days?"

"He's got it in his head that he's going to become a cop. I told him that dream died a long time ago for me, but he doesn't buy it. He still wants the cop life."

Tony laughed. "Oh, that's awful, Mike, but he'll make a great cop. Say, listen, when are you going to come out of hiding?"

"When I can get some answers from Washington. Do you remember the name of the guy who called you that day and told you Wayne Richards was found murdered?"

"No, but the transcript I just sent you shows exactly where the call originated, and you have the address, right? That should also be on the documentation."

"Thanks for all the information, Tony. I wanted to call you and thank you for all the help before I headed out."

"No problem, Mike. I hope you find everything you're looking for."

"Thanks, Tony."

He entered the kitchen and kissed his wife, who was chopping celery for homemade chicken noodle soup. He opened the fridge and grabbed a beer. "Honey, where are the boys?" he said. "I want to say goodbye to them."

"They aren't here, sweetheart. Remember? Danny has the sleepover, and Billy had his interview for the new job!"

"I still don't want him to become a cop!"

"Why not? I know a darn good cop he can learn from."

"I'm serious. A cop's life is neither glamor nor glimmer."

"Hon, I don't want him to be a cop either. But there's a time where you and I must step back and let our sons become who they want to be."

"You're such a realist, and that's why I love you."

"Aww, well that was the sweetest thing you told me all week." Mary smiled.

Mike sipped his beer, his face going grim. "What if I don't find any answers in Washington?"

"What if they don't even know about us?" Mary asked.

Mike looked at her in surprise. "What are you saying?"

"Well, what if everything was a hoax from the start, and we were displaced?"

"No, I won't even consider that. I won't even . . . I don't know what I'm going to discover out east, but we can't just wait here and expect something to get done."

"Honey, calm down! You've done a great job of protecting this family. You've done so much in your career. You know what's best for us, and for that I trust this trip is necessary. We need answers. We can't keep wondering 'what if'? I trust you'll find what you're seeking in Washington. We both need this. We need resolution, Mike!"

Mark glanced at her. He knew that whenever she used his real name, she meant business. If the answers were in Washington, he had to go for the sake of his family. He could tell she was scared. As she hugged him, he noticed his suitcase near the stairs.

"Are those my bags?"

"Yes, dear."

"You packed them for me?"

"Well, you started, I just finished for you. You have enough clothes for a few days. The smaller bag on top has all your toiletries."

"Aww, that's the nicest thing you've done for me all week." He snickered, and she slapped him playfully. "Just kidding, sweetheart."

"Are you ready to get going?" she asked.

He smirked. "Are you trying to get rid of me?"

"Come on, silly, I'll drive you to the airport." She replaced the lid over the crockpot after dumping the celery slices inside and turned the dial to low.

Mark opened the lid, took a whiff, and followed his wife toward the garage. "Oh sure chicken noodle, and I don't get any!"

As they backed out of the driveway, Billy arrived home. "Hey, Dad!" he shouted from the front door.

Mary hit the brakes. "Hi, Billy. I'm sending your dad away for a few days."

Mark laughed and leaned across her. "What's the verdict, son?"

Billy dropped his head toward the sidewalk and trudged toward them. His mom grimaced, and Mark's smile faded. "Well, son, don't give up hope just yet," Mark said. "You can always—"

"I got in!" Billy hollered.

"Oh, that's great, sweetie!" Mary said.

"Yes, we're proud of you, son," Mark said. "We knew you could do it. Well, I have to get going, or I'll be late for my flight—if I'm not already."

Billy pointed at him. "Have a safe trip, Dad. Love ya."

"Love you too, Billy."

On the way to the airport, Mark turned to Mary. "Are you sure you'll be OK without me?"

"Would you stop worrying?"

Mark smiled. "No."

"Do you have the paperwork from Tony?"

"It just came today in the mail. Talk about timing. It's right here in the car. But it's probably another dead end. Where'd you say Danny is staying the night?"

"Pete's. Oh, have you heard from Jake?"

"Not lately. Why?"

"I heard through Danny that he's not doing so well with Julie laid up in the hospital."

Mark nodded. "Yeah. I'm going to call him as soon as I get back. I need to be there for him. I can't imagine what he's going through."

"He was always there for us when we relocated here."

"Yeah I know. He was always a real help."

As soon as they pulled into the airport, a plane took off in the background. Mary pulled up to the curb right outside the Delta terminal, then threw her arms around him. "You be careful. You hear me?"

"Don't worry about me. *You* be careful. Do I need to send Darcy or Penske by the house every night to check on you?"

"Oh stop it." She giggled and slapped him on the shoulder, practically pushing him toward the door.

Mark opened his door and stood outside on the curb. "One more thing . . ."

"Yes?" she asked, smiling.

"I love you."

"I love you too!"

He stepped back and then put his hands on the window. "One more thing . . ."

"Yes?"

"Where's my kiss?"

She undid her seatbelt and threw herself across the seat to the passenger window. They kissed. People passed by on the sidewalk. Cars passed by the driver's side. A security guard directed traffic around a forklift parked farther up the curb near another terminal. A man watched them kiss as he smoked on a concrete bench. He tilted his head down to glare over his sunglasses.

Mark stepped back. "Oh, one more thing . . ."

She laughed. "Would you get going, silly? You're gonna miss your flight!"

"No, seriously, I need you to pop the trunk."

"Oh, ha ha." She clicked a button. A metallic click sounded, and the trunk hinged upward. Mark jogged back and grabbed his suitcase.

He slammed the trunk, and she waved as she pulled away from the curb. He rolled the suitcase up the lip of the curb and headed toward the terminal.

The man on the bench opened a flip phone and held it to his ear. "He just arrived!" he said. Then he shut his phone, flicked the cigarette into the street, and stood up. He slid his sunglasses farther up the bridge of his nose, straightened up, and tugged the lapels on his gray suit coat. Then he followed Mark into the terminal.

CHAPTER 16
JAKE'S DISORDERLY CONDUCT

Pete had no idea that the Beaner incident was going to come back to haunt him. His dad was upstairs swallowing back several bottles of whatever he had fermenting in a "secret" cabinet in his den. He drank more often now that his wife was in a coma.

The entire Carson family had been traumatized by Julie being drowned by the demon. An incident such as Beaner's trauma making Pete a suspect and placing him in a juvenile hall would most likely drive his dad into complete insanity—although he may have held his own since he was a psychologist. Julie Carson's vital signs were still present, but when on earth would she regain consciousness?

The phone rang, and Pete answered it. Upstairs, his dad opened the door, thinking it was the doorbell. He was startled to find two policemen on his doorstep, one of them just about to press the doorbell.

The phone rang again, and he slammed the door in their face to go answer the phone. The two cops stared at each other. Mr. Carson stopped after the phone had stopped ringing. The doorbell rang, and Mr. Carson slowly turned back toward the door. He walked back to the door and opened it.

When they asked for his son, Jake questioned them right back. He wasn't even aware that Pete had made it home yet, even though he had just spoken to him a few minutes earlier. He was worn out. He had scruff on his chin from not shaving for a while. He was taking a leave of absence to spend time watching over Julie. He hadn't slept for the past few days, and his breath reeked of alcohol.

"What?" he snarled.

"Verona Police. Hi sir—"

"No shit. I thought you were from Chicago. But there isn't any Chicago-style pizza here, coppers. Sorry, ate it all this afternoon." He swung the door open a little farther, and it nailed a table in the foyer. A greasy cardboard box slid forward and hung over the edge of the table. Several pieces of pizza crust and sausages rolled across the floor. The cat ran up to it and sniffed a sausage before batting it with her paw. It rolled beneath a rocking chair, and the cat reached underneath, batting its leg back and forth.

"Ya stupid cat," Jake said. "Leave my sausage alone, damn it."

"Excuse us, sir, but we're looking for Pete Carson, your son. Do you know where he is?"

"Do you know where your kids are? Do you ever friggin' know where your kids are?" Jake screamed. "Hold on."

The cops looked at each other in confusion.

Pete hung up from talking with Duffy. Earlier that morning, Jake had agreed to let him have a sleepover all weekend at Duffy's house. Pete had been waiting by the phone to get the final word on whether or not the sleepover would happen. As soon as Duffy told him it was on, he booked it out the exposed basement patio door and ran through the backyard, cutting through the woods out back. He decided to run all the way to Duffy's. It was only two miles. He could manage it.

"Pete! Get yer stinkin' ass up here!" Jake yelled, glancing at the cops. "What the hell did ya do now?"

Jake wandered off to look for him in the basement. That was usually where Pete hung out. The officers followed him downstairs. The phone on the bar was dangling from a barstool, left off the hook. Pete had been so anxious to leave that he didn't even hang up the phone properly. The cops stood over Jake as he struggled to untangle the cord from the barstool. Instead he ended up strangling himself with it, and the cops had to step in to help him.

"I forgot, I told him he could have a sleepover at his friend's house."

One cop backed away and waved his hands in front of his face from the alcohol fumes. He opened his notebook. "Sir, how many drinks have you had today?"

"I don't know," Jake snapped. "Why on earth would I count them?"

"OK, if I could have a name, please?"

Jake stumbled and bumped into the other officer. The officer helped sit him in a barstool. Jake glanced at a picture of his wife on the wall behind the bar. "How about Julie?" he asked and then smiled.

The cop wrote "Julie" in his notebook.

"Do you know my wife, sir?" Jake asked.

"No, I do not."

"Well, she's in a coma right now, and we hope she makes it. I hope my wife comes out of it OK."

"Julie is your wife?"

"Yes, sir," he answered, drunk off his rocker.

"That's not what I asked, Mr. Carson." The cop scratched Julie from his notebook.

"Well, you said you wanted a name. So, I gave you a name. And that's who I have on my mind at the moment."

The cop was growing aggravated with Jake's drunken remarks. "No, sir, I want to know where Peter Carson is—your son! If you have a friend's name, that would be great!"

Jake held up his finger and shook it at him. He nodded and then got up and headed toward the bathroom. The other cop followed, thinking Jake was getting something for them. He stepped back out of the bathroom as Jake hung over the toilet and released a foul outburst of liquids and half-digested Chicago-style pizza. Then he passed out and fell onto the floor.

Jake was too intoxicated to give them a straight answer. As they stood there with puzzled glances, a pencil bounced off one cop's head. Still holding the notebook in one hand, he looked up at the ceiling. Another pencil bounced off his forehead. They backed away, looking up at the ceiling. Hundreds of pens and pencils were protruding from the ceiling tiles above the bar. They looked at each other and shrugged. Pete had way too much fun. While he talked with Danny and Duffy on the phone, he whipped writing utensils at the ceiling, so they would stick in the tiles.

One of the cops walked back into the bathroom to check on Jake. He exited a moment later and shook his head. "He's out cold!"

Duffy's house was located a couple of blocks down the road from Danny's house in Cross Country. Danny lived on the corner of Mid View Road and Crossing Pass. The park in front of their house—across Mid View Road—was visible from Duffy's house, two blocks south. The slide in the center of the park was a double-decker swirl slide. The steps faced Danny's bedroom window. The slide ended toward Duffy's front door. A while ago, Duffy had heard children playing in the park at midnight. He had seen Watches puffing away on a cigar at the top of the slide. He doubted there were any children at all. It may have all been an illusion. After Danny mentioned that Pete thought he saw Watches, Duffy slumped back and hung his head. He didn't say a word.

Along the park was a dead-end road that led to a cul-de-sac. The road was called Slamming Drive. Local residents assumed it got its name from the basketball courts in the park. Kids always overthrew the balls into the cul-de-sac. Slamming Drive was the road where Drifts Construction had built the newer homes where the Armybrats had water balloon fights years earlier—until one night that involved Watches and an explosion. They never had another water balloon war after that.

Now every board was up, and every nail was in. The houses were as complete as the families who lived inside them. Drifts Construction had replaced the home that Watches destroyed. The Armybrats were grounded as a result of that episode.

Mr. Fallway had inspected the damaged home and found all sorts of broken gas lines but no indication of who had caused them or how. He made up a story to Mr. Felter about an electrical cord sending sparks down a concrete section of the house. The gas line valves were faulty. He claimed the loose cord caused the fire. Mr. Fallway knew the truth. After talking with the Armybrats, he knew it was Watches' handiwork. He was the only one who believed them.

The insufficient information about the explosion led to more investigations. Nothing was confirmed as a possible reason for the explosion. Now all that was behind them. The Armybrats were looking forward to their next level of training, preparing to meet Mr. Fallway up north. Once morning rolled around, they planned to be on the road. They were all meeting at Duffy's late that afternoon. The stories were jumbled with every parent. Everyone was sleeping at everyone else's house.

A half a block south of Slamming Drive, a forest wrapped off to the right. It was the school forest. The school owned the acreage of trees with public path in front of Duffy's house that provided a peaceful half-mile walking trail to the school from the neighborhood. It ended at a grassy field behind the middle school where a quarter-mile track wrapped around a football field. The path had been torn up from teenagers illegally driving down it and parking on other trails to have parties. Most of those parties were sexual in nature and involved alcohol.

Duffy's house was the frosting in the cookie. It had white shutters, a white garage door, and a white front door. It seemed like too much white. A dark-brown house with a black brick foundation sat on the left. What threw off the entire frosted cookie concept was the house on the right, which was brown with dark-brown shutters and a dark-blue front door.

The evening was well planned. The entire clan got together at Duffy's for two reasons: his parents were out of town on vacation, and they were planning to go up north for the ultimate test. Mr. Fallway had left his car at the high school for Billy to pick everyone up in the morning. They would meet ninety-four miles north of town. The gas was all on Mr. Fallway. He left them a full tank and snack money under the visor.

They all sat in Duffy's garage as Billy smoked a cigarette. The garage was empty with exception of Mr. Fallway's beautiful 1968 Dodge Charger. Billy showed up early. They hadn't expected him until the following morning. The garage door was at half-mast, so smoke couldn't fumigate the house. Duffy didn't want his parents to smell it upon their return.

Billy sucked in a drag of smoke and then quickly exhaled. "About tomorrow, we all know what's going on, right?"

The other boys nodded.

"OK, little bitches, listen," Billy said. "I'm going to bed soon. No one is to bug me because if you do, after the long drive, I will squash you."

"Ooh, ninety-four miles, look out," Danny teased.

Billy whacked him on the back of the head. "Ninety-four miles of driving at zero dark thirty in the morning is not my thing, thank you very much.

I'm going to bed, and I don't want anyone bugging me. I'll sum it up in two words: Peace and fucking no noise whatsoever. Got it?"

"Do you know math?" Pete asked. "Like beginners, like pre-math? These are numbers, add them up, and you get more numbers!"

"What the hell are you talking about?"

"I'm talking about summing it up in two words. Use your fingers and count. Jesus. That was, like, six words."

"Hey, don't use the Lord's name in vain!" Billy said.

"Are you in beginner's English too?"

"No, tell me why, Pete."

"I don't know. The last time I checked, peace and no noise mean the same thing, stupid."

"Oh no you didn't! I know that Pete Carson didn't just call me stupid."

"Wow, deaf and stupid. So, what are you going to do about it?"

"Throw down." Billy tossed his cigarette onto the garage floor and mashed it with his foot. A streak of tar stained the concrete. Duffy winced.

Pete stood up. "With pleasure."

Billy stood up. The rest of the guys smiled. They knew what was about to happen. Billy was just testing his wits. Pete had the same knowledge that Billy had. The fight may not have seemed fair since Billy was older than Pete, but when Billy threw the blows, and Pete blocked every single one, their hand-to-hand skills were, by comparison, pretty damn similar. Mr. Fallway had taught them all the same skills. They were just learning how and when to utilize them. Billy and Pete were kickboxing right there in Duffy's garage, but neither of them harmed a hair on each other's heads. They ended the fight by becoming a pretzel as they clung to each other's arms holding each other against the floor under a tool shelf. Wesley just sat there and laughed.

Finally, Billy got up and brushed himself off. "This week is gonna rock!"

Pete smiled. "Heck yes!"

Duffy threw Billy's cigarette butt into a trashcan.

"Goodnight, boys!" Billy said. "Don't forget to get some sleep before tomorrow!"

Duffy laughed. "Are you nuts? It's only quarter after nine. Dude, my parents don't even make me go to bed this early on school nights. It's time to crack open some of my dad's brewskies and party hearty, dog!"

They all followed Duffy to his old man's liquor cabinet beneath the china hutch in the dining room. Billy went downstairs and stood in the basement, turning his head back and forth. Then he whipped out a sleeping bag, sending dust balls fluttering through the air as he snapped it open. He waved his hand in front of his face and coughed.

Discipline went out the window that night. The Armybrats upstairs drank some hardcore mixtures, and for some of them, it was the first time even smelling alcohol.

CHAPTER 17
PRACTICAL JOKES

Later that evening, around 2230 hours, they ran from the lighter-brown house's front yard, Duffy's neighbor. Objects hiding in the night lunged out at them as the neighbor hollered and bolted after them. However, he tripped on some hedges along his driveway.

"Darn you kids! Toilet paper all over my front lawn. Go to bed!"

"OK!" Wesley hollered.

The man rolled onto his butt and stood up, staring across the road. They kept the laughter to a minimum as his eyes searched the brush for them. He waved them off and unraveled the toilet paper from his ankles and his shrubs. It was a practical joke but a cruel one. It was Duffy's neighbor, but he didn't recognize Duffy or any of his friends. He was a grumpy old man who beat his dog a lot. He yelled at Duffy all the time for being reckless. So, Duffy had wanted to toilet paper his hedges.

Their heads bobbed over the ditch on the other side. The guy finally finished tearing down most of the toilet paper and retreated inside his humble home, hugging a huge wad of shit paper. Strands of it flailed under his arms and around his waist, waving behind his bare feet as he walked inside. Feeling no remorse, they were about to climb out of the ditch when they dropped back down and held each other back, concealed in the tall grass.

A rust-colored car eased past them and shut off its headlights. It turned down the trail leading toward the school. It bounced as it dropped off the road, and the kids inside hit the ceiling. Duffy glanced up at the sign that stated in small print, "Motorized Vehicles Prohibited." Some kids were illiterate, or perhaps they just didn't care.

However, the Armybrats knew exactly where they were headed. They were going deep into the forest to party hard. A long time ago, the Armybrats had built their fort in the valley. That was where students loved to gather and toke it up. Weed was becoming more popular in town.

"Let's follow 'em!" Wesley urged.

Duffy grabbed his shoulder as Wesley proceeded into the dark, damp forest. "Hold on, high-speed. Did you see those pretty gang colors?"

"You mean the black flag with the white skull on it hanging from the antenna?" Wesley asked.

"Exactly, cheese head. Skulls, crossbones, and black flags. Do you know what they'll do to you if they see you?"

"What?"

"Wait, I have a better idea," Duffy said, smiling. "Follow me, guys."

"Here we go," Pete sighed.

Duffy's parents bought him anything his heart desired. He was spoiled. At least once a month, they'd go shopping and bring back Christmas. They'd buy him the store if he wanted it. All he had to do was say he needed something, and they would get it for him.

Pete was spoiled too, but only because he pulled good grades. Lately, with his mom in a coma, he hadn't gotten a thing; his dad doesn't go shopping. As long as his mom was in a coma, that's how it would continue. When she was well, his mom would come home with a shirt or a pair of pants or shoes and a brand-new model car for him to put together. He had even gone to the hassle of cleaning his room and making it spotless before his mom had to tell him to do it. In other words, he was a complete brownnoser. But at least he showed good reasons for being spoiled. Duffy, on the other hand, just got stuff. He didn't have to bury his nose in anyone's crack just to receive a treat.

All five bikes in the garage were his. Two dirt bikes were in nice shape. One brand-new mountain bike was a gift from his grandparents. Then there were the old hand-me-downs. One was a racing bike his dad owned. The other was a mountain bike that Duffy's dad had bought for his mom. She didn't use it though. It was a guy's bike, and Duffy ended up with it. It was a nice bike. His mom expected that he would take care of it, so she gave it to him. It must have been nice being an only child. At the Emersons' household, Billy would have gotten the bike before Danny.

Wesley stood in front of the hand-me-down racing bike. "It's a good bike," Duffy said, repeating what his father had told him word for word. "It's gone through hell and back, but it's still a good bike."

"Ya think?" Wesley asked, noticing a spoke hanging sideways from the rear rim. "Hope you don't plan on biking anywhere really fast."

"Don't be such a wussy," Duffy said. "That's a racing bike. It'll go faster than my mountain bike or my dirt bikes."

"Then I'll ride that one if you like this bike so much. You can have this one."

Duffy laughed. "What, are you kiddin'? Not on my life." He pushed his favorite bike out of the garage as the other boys picked other bikes.

Before long, they were positioned behind a foothill. Somewhere in the midst of the gully, alcohol fumes and other illegal toxins filled the air. A small fire was burning in the center of this gaggle. Trees around the fire flickered orange. The Armybrats stood in a row, each boy loaded with fresh store-bought eggs. Egg cartons sat between them. They had split the eggs six a piece.

Wesley chuckled. "Ready?" he whispered.

"Now," Danny said.

They kept their voices low, but the snickering was a tough egg to crack. Danny threw first. Duffy and Wesley followed suit. Pete lobbed his eggs over easy—pun possibly intended. Their laughter grew louder, but they kept their distance as the egg cartons became emptier. The music stopped along with the hooting and hollering. A few girls chirped in disgust as the yokes showered down on them. A car engine started. Danny was the first to notice.

He quit throwing eggs. Actually, he was fresh out. Duffy held up the last egg. Danny grabbed his arm and intercepted the forward motion and attempted to simmer his snickering. An owl gave a short hoot in the distance, followed by a faint rumble. When their shadows swung past a few trees behind them, they realized they were deep in the scorn of the teenagers' headlights. Their hearts pounded with anticipation. The teenagers' hearts pounded with animosity as they chewed up the trail toward them. Their headlights bounced the boys' shadows like they anticipated bouncing their little heads.

From an open window, the Armybrats heard a kid hollering. His voice was only a mumble since it was competing against an American motor. But at one point, the profanity was indeed coherent.

"You punks! Ya little assholes!"

A flame flashed above the mirror on the passenger side. A loud snap followed the flame, and their ears tingled. A small bell clinker on Wesley's handlebar rang as it blasted into a million pieces. All that was left was the small clasp around the steel handgrip on which the bell had been mounted. Another crack sounded, and a small limb was blown off a tree. Danny was covered with branches; they webbed over him as he hurdled his bike seat. Everyone else hit the deck due to the shots. Wood chips stuck to their foreheads, and twigs twined through their hair.

"Aw, geez!" Wesley hollered. "They're shootin' at us!"

"You don't say!" Duffy joked.

Pete turned toward Duffy. "Always . . . every time I'm with you . . . I'm being shot at."

They scurried around in circles to get on their bikes. More shots rang out. Several prickles shot down their spines like sharp needle pokes. Uncertainty throbbed within the cells of their minds. What if their stomachs burst open, and their insides sprawled over the handlebars? Where was the gun aimed at that moment? Such questions sent their blood cells sailing through their veins, shivers rattling through them.

"Pedal harder, and swerve all over the place!" Danny said. Just then, his seat snapped off the mount, and his leg started bleeding. "Good Lord, I've been shot!"

Duffy glanced over and laughed. "That's just a scratch. You're not shot. Keep going."

Dirt puffed up from the ground in small explosions around him as they bounced up the winding trail on their bikes. According to Duffy, they were well-oiled machines. Danny glanced over his shoulder to see the license plate. However, the jagged yellow glare of the car's headlights bit at the spokes of his wheels like Watches' teeth dug into his mind.

Wesley scratched his nose. Suddenly, the handle that his sweaty palm had clung to cracked open. The foam grip was annihilated. The bullet's force turned the handlebars and forced his bike to the side. Three more spokes popped out of his wheel. His wheel wobbled, and he looked as if he were riding a unicycle, shifting quickly from side to side. He stood up and gripped the racing handles. Suddenly, he leaped off the side of the bike and lobbed it over his head.

He didn't look back after that, but the bike cut through their windshield and sent cracks deep and wide. The bike sat in the windshield as they drove.

Duffy hit a pothole and flew over the handlebars. He sat up and reached for the bike, but the headlights cut the underbrush in his direction. Instead, he took off running with Wesley. Danny and Pete biked out of the woods. Despite the horrendous sound of the car driving over Duffy's bike followed by a loud bang that echoed through the trees, no one looked back.

Soon, they reached the road. They glided across the center line, hopped the curb, and hit Duffy's lawn. Then they jumped off the bikes, panted for air, and lay there behind some shrubs. All they had accomplished was upsetting a group of teens who now had an even greater incentive to rebel. Their blood pressure shot through the roof as they stared at the vacant trail. It remained dark for what seemed like a half an hour. The car's headlights never chewed their way out, and the Armybrats wondered whether or not they had turned around, went a different way, or just plain stopped. Or maybe they were staring back at them. Maybe they were waiting for them to make a move.

Finally, Duffy stood up. He truncated their death thoughts and the many "What ifs?" What if the teenagers caught them? What if the gun was aimed at Duffy right now as he stood before them? What if they shot him?

"It's time for bed," Duffy said.

Duffy, Wesley, and Pete walked toward the front door of the house, but Danny remained flat in the grass. The moonlight was bright, making their flesh, the houses, and the road shine. Danny wasn't finished with the sudden rush of death. It had been an incredibly exuberant escape. He couldn't let it go. About thirty-five minutes earlier, a brown Trans-Am had wanted to eat them up with its grill and squash them dead like toads in the street. The conclusion was not OK with him since there didn't seem to be one.

Before entering the house, the other boys turned around and saw him lying in the grass.

"Wow, did you see that?" Danny whispered in amazement.

Duffy walked toward him. "No, I missed the whole damn thing."

"Come on, you guys," Wesley said. "I've had to take a dump this whole time. I was pedaling with no seat, steering with one handlebar, and praying for dear life. That lasted for about three quarters of a mile, but I ran the last quarter, so if you want to stay out here, good for you, but I'm gonna go take out my anxiety on Duffy's washing machine." He pointed at Duffy. "Good bike my ass."

Danny sighed. "We were chased."

"I must have missed that too." Duffy smiled and turned around, heading toward his house. "No defecating in the washing machine."

"We got away, we waited, and nothing happened," Danny said. "I say we go back into the woods and—"

"Are you nucking futs?" Duffy screamed, turning around to face him.

"Don't be stupid, Dan," Pete said. "Listen, they saw us biking, and they probably see us standing here right now. I think it's over. We did what we wanted to do, and now it's over. We would be stupid to go back."

"Yeah, I suppose you're right. We need some sleep anyways," Danny said.

Duffy sighed. "Good answer. You pass."

When they entered the basement, the television flickered to a commercial. Billy had fallen asleep with the remote in one hand. Duffy threw blankets and down-stuffed pillows onto the floor for everyone. Talk about comfort; Duffy was spoiled with luxuries. All the blankets and pillows were extras—stored in a pantry.

CHAPTER 18
PETER COTTONTAIL

Pete's eyes snapped open. The first thing he looked at was the kitty clock hanging on the wall. Its tail and its eyes whipped back and forth every second. The clock said it was 0118 hours. He lay there in a trance from watching the tail and its eyes. Then he watched the rest of the Armybrats toss and turn and talk in their sleep. He closed his eyes, then opened them to see a flashlight on a table near the television.

He sat up. His sleeping bag rolled down off his fully dressed body. He stood up and walked over to the table. He picked up the flashlight and pushed the button. Billy's face lit up. When Billy flinched, Pete dropped to the floor. He held the light against the carpet until he figured out how to shut it off.

Billy stood up and walked toward a lit-up room down the hall. Pete stood up and headed upstairs toward the front door. Grabbing the doorknob, he turned it and walked outside into the cool, dark night.

Billy walked out of the hall and mumbled as he tiptoed into one of the support poles. "Ouch." He stumbled for his sleeping area and tripped over Duffy.

Duffy looked at him from his bundle of blankets. "What were you doing in the laundry room?"

"What kind of question is that?" Billy asked. "I mean, what do people normally do in the . . . in the laundry room?"

"You pissed in the laundry room?" Duffy hollered, sitting up.

"Shut up," Danny groaned, rolling over. "Go to sleep."

"Well I . . ." Billy began.

Danny sat up and yawned. "Wait a minute, what did you do with who in who's laundry room?"

"No," Duffy said, his voice growing militant. "Billy just pissed in the laundry room!"

"Man, that's gonna reek," Danny said, still half asleep. "I mean, you at least peed down the drain hole or something, right?"

Billy fell back and slammed into an end table. Bottles fell onto the concrete slab in front of the fireplace. They were empty beer bottles. Billy had been drinking. Wesley rolled over.

"Whoa, you drank all that?" Duffy exclaimed.

"I don't remember." Billy yawned and lay back down.

"Hell no, you're gonna have to clean that up. Remember the food fight at Pete's house? We aren't reliving that here."

"Where did you pee, bro?" Danny asked, somewhat confused.

"Ah, I guess I made a huge mistake then."

"Whyyyyy?" Duffy hissed.

"Well it may have been the dryer . . ."

"Say it ain't so!"

Billy laughed hysterically. "Duff-buster, ya know how every bathroom has a toilet? I assumed that the dryer . . ."

"Oh no, you didn't."

"Well, I may have been half out of the bag, and the dryer looked like . . ."

Danny laughed. "Like a toilet? In whose world?"

"Oh, that's just great!" Duffy said. "You mean to tell me that you—"

Billy shrugged. "I could be wrong."

"You peed in the dryer?"

Wesley sat up. Danny's jaw fell open.

Billy sighed. "Oops."

"There's a fresh load of clothes in there, and you—" Duffy's cheeks bloated, and he could hardly finish his statement. "You pissed in the dryer?"

"I think that's all I did."

"Oh no, you didn't . . ."

"No, no, no, no! No number two; don't worry. I don't think so anyway," Billy said uncertainly and turned toward the laundry room.

Just then, the washing machine began its rinse cycle. They all stared down the hallway leading into the laundry room.

"Oh, maybe it was the washing machine. Oh, maybe I did take a dump."

Duffy looked over at him. Then he lunged at Billy and pushed him over. They rolled into the couch as Duffy choked him. More beer bottles fell off the end table.

Billy's story may have been a bit farfetched, but he was having fun playing around with his little fib. And the truth was too dull. Billy had a few changes of clothes, and he had spilled beer on the shirt he had been wearing, so he decided to wash it with some dirty clothes that he had brought along. That was what he had gotten up to do. He had been checking on his clothes. He laughed and hit the pillow.

Duffy jumped over his legs and grabbed his collar. "I don't see how any of this is funny, bitch."

Wesley smiled. "Well, at least he flushed."

"Turning on a washing machine isn't flushing," Danny said.

Billy chuckled. "I, uh, I couldn't sleep, so I got up to shut off the laundry room light. That's all."

Duffy groaned. "OK, yeah, but you flushed the washing machine. All I know is that right now it's throwing your crap back and forth inside there. There are going to be some awful shit stains on my clothes."

"No," Billy said, laughing. "Well, I did have jalapeño pizza for dinner, and I had some pretty nasty runs the night before."

"OK, that's not funny." Duffy pounded Billy's chest. They rolled around, messing up the blankets. Duffy was furious. They rolled over Wesley and kicked Danny, but Billy couldn't stop laughing.

"Get off me, silly!" Billy hollered. "I just did my laundry—that's all!"

Danny laughed. "Holy cow! I think you guys just mashed Pete!"

They were lying on top of Pete's blankets. They quickly scattered from his sleeping area, asking for a response from him. Duffy threw the covers away from his pillow. Pete wasn't there. Then he cast his eyes around the entire basement scanning for any signs of him. Billy and Danny searched the bathroom. Danny came out of the den shaking his head. Duffy walked back downstairs from checking the kitchen.

"I have a good guess where he might be," Duffy said.

Across the street, in the woods, the brown car was leaning against a tree. It appeared like a missing section of the woods, like a cutout of the underbrush. A light shined across the doors, and Pete stood before it, holding the flashlight. He crept toward the rear door on the driver's side. He shined the light through the window.

No one was inside. He shined the light across the crinkled hood and up the large tree that had stopped the car. An owl flew at him from a limb higher up, hooting as it flapped past his head. Suddenly, Pete's feet rocketed out from under him, and he fell onto his back. The owl perched on a branch on a much smaller tree behind the car.

"Friggin owl . . . stupid bird . . ."

He stood up and placed his left hand on the car's door handle. He yanked upward. It was locked. Then he tried the back door. With a loud squeak, the door budged a little. He looked back at the owl. It cocked its head and watched him. He yanked even harder, and it cranked open and swung into a tree. A bang echoed through the woods like a cannon. At the same time, a fluttering gush of wind threw him backwards once again. Strangely, another owl flew over him. Apparently, it had been trapped inside the car, and Pete had just freed it. But he had no idea where it really came from.

"Friggin owl . . . stupid—" He was about to repeat what he had said earlier when he froze. "Déjà vu . . ."

His flashlight lay against a tree. That was where it had landed after he was knocked over. The light shined up toward the branch where the first owl had landed earlier. The second owl flew up to that same branch, but the other owl was gone. It could have been the same owl, but Pete wasn't aware of the first owl ever moving.

The smell of weed billowed from the open door. The windshield was cracked, the bicycle still sticking out of it. Smoke radiated from the hood where it had struck the tree. More smoke slithered through the cracked windshield. Pete jumped onto the floor of the car when he noticed another car driving up the trail. The car had its headlights off as it crept down the trail, which was why it had taken him by surprise.

"Oh Lord," he whispered.

The car was Mr. Fallway's Dodge Charger. Billy hopped out of the driver's door. "Pete?"

Danny jumped out the passenger door. "Pete?"

"Peter?" Wesley also called for him.

Pete crouched as low to the floor as he could. "Mommy," he cried, then crawled toward the other window to see who was outside. Suddenly, a hand wrapped around his mouth. He squinted as he struggled to look up the arm to see who it belonged to. The boy's face was unrecognizable. Pete didn't have his flashlight, and he couldn't scream for help. He had no idea what was going on. The kid made him hush.

Billy walked slowly toward the Trans-Am. He saw it shaking and rocking. The hub bounced over the wheel. He hesitated for a moment. The car continued to bounce, and then it stopped. He eased toward the back door once again. The kid holding Pete was lying across the seat with Pete on top of him. Pete's eyes widened when he realized the kid was aiming a handgun at the door as Billy approached.

Pete couldn't do anything as Billy grabbed the door handle. Suddenly, Pete kicked his foot through the open window and nailed Billy in the forehead. Billy jumped back and fell, clutching his head. A bullet flew through door. Billy rolled over as more bullets flew toward him. The kid holding Pete had a red face and steam oozing from his brow, since Pete had given away his position. He reached out the window and tried to shoot Billy as he crawled around the front of the car. The other boys scurried away.

Pete seized the opportunity to strike the boy in the back of the head and pin him against the door. He rolled the window up and cinched him inside. Cracks formed around the bullet hole in the glass. The kid flailed and screamed. Pete opened up the door, and the kid's body swung outward. Billy ran up and punched him in the face. The kid swore at him, but Billy continued to punch him until the kid hung silent. The door swung back and mashed the kid's body against the frame. The gun fell from his hand and bounced beneath the car. Pete climbed out and stood before Billy.

Suddenly, a car door slammed. Duffy and Wesley had jumped back into the Charger. Danny was nowhere in sight. Duffy and Wesley peeked over the back seat. Twigs snapped beneath the feet of a group of teenagers as they approached the Trans-Am. It was the same gang who had danced and screamed to the loud music in the woods, the same gang that the Armybrats had egged, and the same group who had chased them earlier. They hadn't made it out of the woods because of the car wreck against the oak tree.

Three girls stood behind five guys. They were older than most of the Armybrats, though Billy was the oldest member of the group. These kids had just graduated high school and in their celebratory moment, the boys had interfered. Billy and Pete backed away slowly. Billy was still searching for Danny but figured he had crawled inside the Charger as well, though he saw only Duffy and Wesley cowering behind the seats. He glanced back at the group of teens advancing toward them. His eyes fluttered back and forth as he searched the trees, wondering where his brother was.

That's when one of the guys in the group held out another gun. Billy glanced at the ground near the Trans-Am in search of the gun that the other kid had dropped. The kid stood in front of everyone else. One girl slid her hands over his shoulder and stood sideways against him. She wore a denim jacket, and it was evident that she was wearing nothing underneath. Each time she stood on her tiptoes to lean across the guy's shoulder and rub his cheek with sexual glances, her jacket flapped open. Her zipper reflected moonlight as it brushed across her nipples. Whichever way her body moved, her breasts were revealed. It was almost sexy, but the situation was too overwhelming to care about beautiful boobies.

The kid holding the gun walked forward and stood near the side-view mirror on the driver's side of their Trans-Am. He lifted the boy's head that was hanging through the window. Then he dropped his limp head and aimed the gun at Billy. His eyes were fixed over the sights, and Billy stared right down the cylindrical hole of the barrel. It was a 22-caliber pistol. Toying with death was not on Billy's mind that evening.

The guy glanced at the body hanging from the window. "What should I do to them, hey, Tim?" Obviously, Tim was unconscious from Billy's blows, and the guy who had spoken to him had asked a question that his unconscious buddy couldn't answer. "Oh gee, Clint, I don't know, perhaps kill them for destroying your car," he said, answering on behalf of his friend. He glanced at Billy. "Poor little Timmy speaks." He held the gun up high to shoot Billy. "Maybe I'll just finish this. Yeah, I think I'm going to kill all of them now, Timmy."

Suddenly, his ankle burst open, and blood sprayed across his shoes. He screamed and aimed his gun into the air, pulling the trigger. A round burst into the night sky as he fell against Tim, bouncing across the ground.

Another guy stepped forward, and a fluttering owl smashed into his face as it fell from a tree. Pete looked down at the dead bird.

"Hey, the owl," he said, smiling. "Aww, he shot 'im."

Danny rolled out from under the Trans-Am and picked up the other gun that the guy had just dropped. As he stood up, he pointed both guns at the three girls and the other two guys. They shrieked. Danny glanced down at the owl. Its wings were fanned out over the guy's head. It must have rendered him unconscious, since he wasn't moving. Danny was confused about the whole owl bit. His nose wrinkled, and his lip curled as he looked back at Billy and Pete. He kept the guns aimed at the others.

The girl wearing nothing beneath her jacket smiled at him. She winked and licked her upper teeth. Danny peeked over the barrel of one of the guns and withdrew his aim as he noticed her perky nipples.

"Hey, you, open your jacket."

She dropped her smile and pointed at herself.

Danny aimed the guns at her again. "Yeah, you. I think you're hiding some weapons under there."

She slid the jacket halfway down her arms and turned her entire upper body. Her hard nipples pointed out from her beautiful breasts. Danny lowered the guns to his sides.

"Holy shit!" Pete whispered.

"Holy shit!" Duffy and Wesley echoed from inside the car.

Billy didn't trust her. "Danny . . ."

Danny raised the guns again. "Thank you."

A car door slammed, and everyone looked over to see Duffy walking toward Danny. He reached for one of the guns, stripping it from Danny's hand.

"Give me that." He aimed at one of the other girls in the crowd. "All right, now you suck on her tits."

The girls looked at each other.

Billy was aggravated. "Duffy . . ."

"What?" Duffy said over his shoulder.

"We're not here for that. Let's go."

Duffy lowered the gun to his side and sighed. "So gay."

"We need to get out of here," Billy said.

"Aww man, where's the love, huh?" Duffy asked.

They backed up toward the Charger. The dark-haired girl wrapped an arm around the other girl's waist and drew her closer. Gently, she rubbed her left nipple with her index finger. The nipple rolled over her finger like a raspberry. Duffy stopped walking backwards and lowered the weapon when she bent over and licked it, the other girl's nipple rolling over her wet tongue. Duffy saw the saliva shimmer in the moonlight. His jaw dropped. So did Wesley's.

"Ohh . . ." Pete whispered.

Wesley passed out in the back seat.

"Ohh . . ." Duffy sighed.

Billy slapped his hand over his shoulder. His reflex pulled the trigger, and twigs and dirt exploded over his shoes as he shot the ground in front of him. Everyone dropped. Billy grabbed the other gun from Danny.

"Get in the car, you two," Billy demanded as he looked at the two girls embracing each other on the ground. "Goodnight, ladies." He turned to follow the other Armybrats to the car.

Billy tucked each gun into the back of his pants. He sat in the driver's seat and looked at everyone. They were all in a trance as they gaze out the windshield at the two full-figured broads on the path, sucked out of reality into an erotic world of exotica. Their minds were lost.

Wesley sat up and grabbed his crotch. "And we have liftoff!"

Billy looked at him. "TMI, Wes, TMI."

Duffy sighed. "Sick."

"TMI?" Wesley inquired.

"Too much information," Billy explained.

"Hey, I can't help it. Them are some hot chicks out there, man. And we egged them. Why did we egg those hot chicks? We had the guns and the time. We could've had them both naked and . . ."

Billy shifted into reverse. He kicked the gas pedal and screamed out of the woods. The tires dug up dirt and pushed them forward into their seats. As the Charger ripped out of the woods, he swerved to the right and backed right into Duffy's driveway. They entered the garage, and the door closed. Billy grabbed the garage door remote and unclipped it from the visor. He climbed out of the car and put it back on the bench near the toolboxes.

"Are you guys alright?" he asked.

"We're fine," Duffy said with a sigh.

"Let me get this straight. You egged a bunch of teenagers who were partying in the woods?"

Danny shook his head in an odd circle while biting his bottom lip, unsure how to answer him. "Yup."

"You guys are asking for trouble." Billy said. "I don't want to know what happened earlier tonight. But I want you guys to sit here and think about what you did. Mr. Fallway has taught us many important and valuable things. But you guys were about to fuck it all up tonight, weren't you? What were you thinking?"

He walked inside the house. The other boys remained seated inside the Charger. They didn't even look at one another.

"Thanks, guys," Pete said.

Danny looked at him. "What were you thinking?"

"I don't know. I guess I had to see for myself."

Danny sat there thinking about those kids. Everything was their fault. They had egged them, broken their windshield, and caused them to crash. Except for the fact that the teens had guns and shot at them, it was pretty much the Armybrats' fault for instigating the whole thing.

Pete was thinking the same thing. He was asking himself why he even went back out there.

Duffy wasn't thinking about anything except the mental image of the girl's nipples. They were the size of nickels. And the dark-haired girl was lying on top of her sucking both of them, left then right. Wesley was in outer space as well. They were two peas in a pod.

CHAPTER 19
DEAD FROM DUBIETY

The sad part about that night was that the Armybrats were drunk out of their gourds. They finished a couple of bottles of Duffy's dad's liquor. They were hungover by the next morning, and their thought process was lagging. After all the stupid stuff they had done the previous night, they had no idea what they started. They had emptied Duffy's parents' egg count, booze count, toilet paper stash and ruined a couple bicycles. They had also ruined a perfectly good Trans-Am and angered some teens. What more could the boys get into?

Pete ran from the laundry room to the Charger in the garage. He stuffed clothes inside bags then tossed the bags into the trunk and ran back inside the house to gather everyone's belongings. As he continued to toss bags into the trunk, Billy was snoring in the driver's seat.

Pete slapped Duffy across the face. "Get up." It was 0500 hours, and everyone was sleeping, except him. He walked over to Wesley and stood at his feet. He bent forward and wrapped his arms around his ankles and pulled him out from beneath an ottoman. Wesley didn't budge. Sometime during the night, he had rolled beneath it. Pete pulled his feet once again, but this time he backed away and waved his hand in front of his nose, signifying wretched foot odor. "Have mercy."

All four of them began sleepwalking toward the garage. They climbed inside the car. Billy was still snoring in the driver's seat. Pete was striving to keep them awake, all of them fighting a hangover. Wesley's hair was sticking out in viscous points. Duffy was functioning, but his eyes were shut. Danny was the same way. Pete helped Billy crank the key to start the engine. Billy was the only guy Pete didn't have to struggle with since he crashed in the driver's seat. Pete looked at the garage door opener near the tool bench. He opened his door, climbed back out of the car, and pressed the button on the garage door opener.

The door opened slowly. Sunlight poured into the garage, blinding them. Billy rolled over, and his knee popped the shifter into neutral. The car rolled slowly out of the garage. Pete walked toward the car and exited the garage. He clicked the button once again to shut the garage door. As it closed behind him, he realized the car was still rolling away from him.

"Whoa, wait!" Pete shouted, running after the car.

Down the road, a police officer was sitting in a squad car along the curb. He glanced up from his coffee and spilled a little on himself when he saw the Charger rolling toward him in his rearview mirror. He rotated the radar in their direction and clocked Billy's speed. Red digital lights blinked from thirteen to fourteen then back to twelve to eleven and back to twelve miles per hour. He glanced into the rearview mirror and saw the Charger's grill. It was headed right for his rear end. He leaned forward and squinted when he saw Pete running behind the Charger. "What the . . .?"

Pete threw the door open, hopped on one foot with his other foot inside the door, and struggled to jump inside. He landed on the passenger seat and slammed the door. He noticed Billy's face hanging over the side of the seat and glanced out the windshield in fear. He looked at the label across the trunk of the car in front of them, which read "Verona Police." Then he glanced at the emergency lights on top of the car. He noticed the police officer's eyes as the cop stared back at him in the mirror. He slapped Billy's face and tried to wake him up, but Billy just slid to his left, and his cheek mashed against the driver's window. He snored and fogged up the window with his early morning dragon breath.

"Billy," Pete whispered, tugging on his shoulder as he looked up at the police car. He turned back to Billy. "Billy, wake up!"

The police officer's eyes widened. He glanced down at the side-view mirror and then spun around to see the Charger's hood ornament right next to his trunk. He was trying to understand if it was really happening.

Pete stretched across Billy's knee with his leg and mashed his foot on the brake.

The police officer flinched and dropped the entire cup of scalding-hot coffee into his lap. The steam fogged up his glasses near the bridge of his nose. The front of his pants were soaked. He smacked the dash with his fist as the Charger's bumper tapped his rear end.

The policeman clenched his teeth from the burning sensation. Then he lifted his head to glare at the sleeping boys. Billy's window was dense with fog as he continued to saw logs. Pete shrugged when the police officer's eyes fixated on him. Then the cop spun around, dropped the shifter into drive, and did a U-turn to park behind the Charger. He threw open his door and approached the driver's door, walking if he had been sitting on a toilet for hours. He walked slowly as if he had a bad case of hemorrhoids, waddling like a duck from the coffee burn.

He peered through the window, then made a fist and pretended to roll down an imaginary window, so Pete would follow suit since he was the only one awake in the car. He noticed Pete was straddling the transmission hump on the floor with his foot mashed over the brake. Pete cranked the window down, and Billy's cheek stretched with the moving glass.

"What the hell is this?" the cop asked.

"Morning, officer." Pete smiled as Billy continued to snore.

"Does he have a license?"

"Of course." Pete fumbled through Billy's pocket and yanked his wallet out. He flipped through it. He had a little trouble since there were many nude pictures of his ex-girlfriends. He gawked at the pictures for a bit, taking his time.

"Give it here, son," the cop demanded, snatching it from Pete's hands. He flipped through it in one direction, taking his sweet time as well. Then he went back the other way. He completely ignored Billy's license as he slipped something from the billfold. "And what the hell's this? His license is expired!"

"Seriously, officer." Pete clenched his teeth and shut his eyes in disbelief.

"You kids wait here." He tossed Billy's wallet onto Pete's lap.

Pete smiled. "We're uh . . . we're not going anywhere, officer."

The cop walked back to his car and dabbed his seat with a handkerchief after throwing his paper cup onto the ground. He littered, which Pete thought was odd. He leaned over and hollered in Billy's ear. "Waaaake Uuuup!"

Billy's head bumped the ceiling when his rear end shot off the seat. He honked the horn, and his foot hammered the gas pedal. The engine roared. Billy braked, shifted to drive and drove. The tires ripped over the pavement, hopped a curb, and the bumper knocked a fire hydrant over. Then he slammed on the brake and rubbed his eyes. Water pitter-pattered across the car's hood and windshield as pressurized water thundered beneath the car's front end. It sounded like a bowling ball rolling down an alley, racing toward the pins. Billy had no clue where he was, what he was doing, or how he had gotten there. He quickly rolled up the window as mist pelted his face.

"Huh, it's raining." Finally, he was awake. "What? Where am I?"

Pete groaned. "You don't remember?"

Billy's eyes drowned in tears as slants bundled beneath his eyelids when he yawned. "I don't remember waking up, Peter."

"There's a cop back there, and he already has your license."

"There's a . . . a what?" Billy adjusted the mirror and slapped his back pocket for his wallet. His fingers crawled over the smooth handle of the guns from the previous night. He grew extremely nervous. He knew that if the cop got him step out of the car, he would be charged with illegal possession of firearms. But he couldn't see anything out the rear window with all the water gushing down it. "Uh-oh!"

"What?" Pete asked.

Billy didn't want to tell him about the weapons. "Where's my wallet? I don't have my wallet."

Pete grabbed his shoulders. "Billy, I have it."

Billy wrenched Pete's hands from shoulders. "You have my wallet?"

"Yeah."

"Give it to me!"

"You want your wallet?"

"Yes, now give me my wallet."

"If you stop shaking me . . ."

"Yeah?"

"I'll give you your wallet."

"OK." Billy stopped shaking him and sighed. "Sorry!"

Pete reached behind his back and grabbed his wallet off the seat. "Here's your friggin' wallet."

"Thank you," Billy replied. He rolled down his window while picking at a sleeper in his eye. "I thought it wasn't supposed to rain today." He quickly rolled the window back up.

"It's not."

Billy sighed and shook his hands at the water spraying on the window. He was drenched. "Look at me. How could it not be raining, Pete? And where's this cop?" He looked out the back window. He still couldn't make anything out. He squinted and looked in each direction, trying to figure things out.

"You sort of, well, you ran over a fire hydrant."

Billy glared at him. Danny sat up in the back seat, having just awoken. "Are we there yet? Why's it rainin'?"

"Is there anything else you'd like to tell me before the cop—" Billy looked out the back window again and then turned back to Pete. "Wait a minute, what cop?"

Pete squinted and jerked his head back. Between the bent illusions of water over the glass, the curb remained empty behind them. "He's gone."

Billy looked in the side-view mirror. "He's gone, huh? Well then, that means we're gone. Good thing too, Pete. You would have been paying my fine. Plus, you would've been bailing me out of jail for having these guns." He pulled one out and pointed it at him.

"Whoa, Billy, I had no idea," Pete said, raising his hands.

"Remind me later to shoot you." Billy shook his head and then put the gun away. "I'm outta here."

"But he has yer license. I watched him take it."

Billy opened his wallet. His cheeks turned cherry red when he noticed Bridget Mcmahon partially nude inside a plastic protector. She was sitting on a bed wearing nothing but a black pillow with red stripes across her tummy. Her upper extremities were beautifully hung over top of the pillow. Her nipples were harder than pencil erasers. She was shaven and very young. His license was there. However, when he checked the pouch, the $180 from Mr. Fallway was missing.

"Pete, was there some sort of friggin' fee for this, or did that prick steal all Mr. Fallway's money?" He looked over the seat and watched out the window as he shifted into reverse and hit the gas. He backed the car down off the curb. The fire hydrant rocked backward, and they drove away from the geyser.

Once he reached the road, he turned to Pete. "Why didn't you wake me up?"

"I beg to differ."

"You did not."

"I did so."

"Where are we? Why is it raining?" Danny asked a second time.

Billy and Pete turned around and glared at him. "Shut up!"

Danny slumped back into his seat. Billy looked at Pete, and Pete glared back. "Why couldn't you just wake up?" Pete asked.

Billy smiled. "I downed a whole bottle of rum last night after we got back to the house. After what you guys put me through out there in the woods."

Pete sighed. "Now I get it."

Somewhere down a residential road, a happy, crooked policeman drove around town $180 richer. He was excited. A crooked cop, he used his authority and power to benefit himself, stealing from young kids. However, this sin was about to become his last. The evil in the world was faced with more evil. The cop had committed a crime, and he was about to be punished for it.

Out of nowhere, an arm flew around his neck and put him in a chokehold. He gagged and attempted to yank down on the stranger's black sleeve. With one hand on the steering wheel, he continued to drive, but he had no intention of stopping to fix the problem. He slid his hand down to his holster, but nothing was there, and the snap remained loose. That's when a cold gun barrel jammed into his right temple.

"Don't have yer little gun, do ya?" the stranger said.

The cop's eyes widened as he tried to see the man in the rearview mirror.

"Cuz I got it," the stranger said, "an' I got you good. Keep drivin', copper, while I read you your rights." The black-suited man pressed the barrel into the soft skin near the cop's right ear. Two big white eyes behind a black ski mask stared back at the cop in the mirror. He sideswiped a parked car and continued driving. "Whoa, where'd you learn to drive?" The police officer had his eyes closed from the tension over his throat. A tear dove down his cheek and dripped into his lap.

"You have a right to think long, deep thoughts," the stranger said. "You have something that doesn't belong to you, copper. You stole those boys' lunch money. Instead of writing a citation, you pocketed their cash. How could you possibly think about stealing money from my friends and think you could get away with it? Think again."

Then he switched to an Irish accent. "Hey, man, stop yer bloody cryin'. You're a grown lad, a policeman with hope and good fortune. Yeah, a big heart and strong bones." He laughed, and the tone of his voice grew deeper, almost like Watches' voice. "Cry, bitch, cry! Ha ha. You have the right to hang on tight, and there's no reason to put up a fight. Now take yer foot off the gas, and close yer eyes cuz you're in for a big mutha fuckin' surprise. Place yer fingers in yer ears, and forget about the tears cuz this is gonna be loud."

The police car's side window cracked outward, bubbles of blood swirling around the glass. As soon as the bubbles splashed against the rough surface of the road with the glass sprinkling around it, the car stopped. Then the horn gave a constant ear-mangling honk when what was left of the cop's forehead fell against it. Blood joined the tears in his lap as the black-suited man stepped out of the police car, a wad of cash in his vinyl gloves. Then he placed the revolver in the policeman's hand and dropped the money on the seat along with a bag of marijuana. Such stories were unusual for the *Verona Press*, the town's daily newspaper. The headline would probably read, "Crooked Cop Commits Suicide While on Duty!"

CHAPTER 20
NEWCOMER

It was 0720 hours when everyone awoke. Beams of sunlight streamed in and out of the trees of Little Rapids, Wisconsin. The trees darkened the path that led them to their destination, their limbs wrestling with one another in the short gusts of wind. Verona was about sixty miles behind them. Mourning doves fluttered across the road like gnats. One was resting silently on the road and staring at the Charger as the grill scooped it up and sent it flying.

About twenty miles of farmland and open fields seemed to stretch endlessly before they entered Little Rapids. They drove up a narrow road with an incline into the heavens, pushing up dust clouds as the Charger ripped up dirt from recent mudslides. Danny glanced back through the rear window. When the dust clouds cleared, he saw a car.

"Uh, guys?" he said. Frantically, he tapped his brother's shoulder and screamed as a beaten-up, brown, rust bucket slammed against the Charger's rear end, giving them all early morning whiplash. Another tug on Billy's shoulder from his brother detached his grip from the steering wheel. Considering the fact that he had woken up not too long ago, he still didn't have a firm grasp on consciousness.

Their pursuer bashed into their bumper a second time, sending them spinning into the ditch. Their back end slammed against an uprooted tree. That tree saved their lives, keeping the front corner of the car on the road. To their left was a hillside that declined gradually for thirty yards before a drop-off that would have sent them to the base of a cliff in a ravine far below. Now they were in a rut, and they had Danny to thank for it.

Billy rubbed his neck and sighed. "Thanks a lot, bro. You crashed Mr. Fallway's car."

"Me?" Danny said. "You're the one who let go of the steering wheel."

Billy glanced over his shoulder. "You guys OK?"

After the others verified they were, Billy's door flew open, and some kid yanked him out of the car. The rest of the Armybrats had knives to their throats. The gang of kids who had overtaken them demanded they get out of the car.

It was the same gang from the night before. They were seeking revenge for their prior engagements with eggs, their damaged car, and the fact their friend had been shot in the ankle. The Armybrats had been caught completely off guard.

The rusty brown Trans-Am sat on the road near the Charger's tail end. Their hood had a huge dent in it from trying to climb a tree in the woods. The car was still operational, though it had cracks in the windshield. It appeared to have gone through hell and back.

The tall, skinny guy who had been driving the Trans-Am the previous night hobbled behind Billy to the front of the Charger and shoved him against the hood. His ankle was torn apart from the round that had mangled it when Danny shot him from beneath his car. A white cloth was wrapped around it, soaked in blood.

"You're the brats who screwed up the front end of m' car, threw eggs at us, and shot me in the leg." He threw a fist deep into Billy, a real gut bruiser. Billy rolled off the hood, clutching his stomach. "Stand up," the guy said. "I'm not through with you, ya little cocksucker." He grabbed Billy's shirt and threw him against the grill.

A long-haired dude wearing biker gloves was holding Pete against the driver's door. The smell under his gloves reminded Pete of sweat built up beneath a wristwatch. Wesley was trapped on the ground near the passenger door. The guy pinning him wore an eyebrow ring, a nose ring, and what looked like a miniature barbell in his left earlobe. He was shorter than the other gang members, but his veins were large, bulging from his muscular arms. In his right hand was a knife. His left foot pinned Wesley to the ground.

Duffy was also chewing dust particles as he lay face down on the dirt road near the trunk along the driver's side. Black army boots wrinkled his shirt as the tread pressed a new design in the fabric and gouged into his lower back. Meanwhile, Danny was wedged over the trunk.

Pete peeked at the knife that was scraping his neck. "Hey, that's like the knife in Rambo!"

"Shut up," the guy said in a low, crackly voice. "Face the ground, punk!"

"OK, but would you move this hand?" Pete nudged his shoulder to signify which hand he was speaking of. "Your glove smells like carc-ASS."

Smelly raised the knife to Pete's cheek. "If you don't shut yer piehole, boy..."

Pete closed his mouth and tucked his tongue beneath his upper lip, cringing.

After Billy stood up, the tall boy pounded him again, responding to a sudden urge. He punched him twice in the gut and then shoved him to the ground.

Two girls climbed into the Charger's back seat. One girl jumped onto the hood and sat down. Billy glanced up, holding his stomach. Beneath her short skirt he could see the great divide toward the solemn place of baby making.

"Get that coochy slut to remove her fat ass from the hood before her crotch crickets scratch the paint from all that hepatitis jumping out," he said.

The boy towered over him, "Excuse me, what was that?" And he punched him across the jaw. Billy's face slammed into the hood.

"Get yer slingshot whore off the car," Billy said, spitting blood from his lips.

The tall boy kicked at him, but Billy grabbed his foot and twisted it until the guy's face drove into the ground. The kid stood up slowly after the sneak attack and kicked Billy in the face. Billy's head flew in the opposite direction, spewing a wad of blood and saliva into the Charger's grill. The girl backed away and screamed as blood landed on the hood before her open skirt.

"Go ahead, say that again . . ."

Billy spat, and dust particles fluffed outward from his saliva bubbles and blood as it landed in a small patch. "Slingshot whore," he growled.

Once again, the rock-hard sole of the guy's right shoe swung into Billy's gut. Billy rolled over and slapped the ground with his right hand. Then the guy knelt down and picked up a branch. He cracked it over Billy's back as if he were splitting wood for a fire.

"Noooooo!" Danny screamed. "Asshole!" He had no idea how badly beaten his brother was. Danny was lying across the trunk, and Billy was on the ground in front of the car, so Danny couldn't see him. A squeak rang out as his chin smeared across the trunk. Danny was growing restless, and the guy was throwing his entire weight against him to keep him pinned. Danny saw the other guy holding the branch through the vehicle's windows. The two girls were still sitting in the back seat of the car as Danny watched over their shoulders. Slowly, they turned around and looked at him as he rocked against the car. He stopped wiggling and winked at them.

The tall boy walked slowly around the side of the Charger. "Whoo-hoo...we got a feisty fucker back here, don't we?"

Danny's forehead wrinkled with anger. When he looked up through the windows, he noticed the tall guy advancing around the Charger. All he could see was his chest to his waistline. He figured it was his turn for some bruises, skin abrasions, and other marks of interrogation.

"What have we got here?" the guy asked, his face expressionless.

Duffy looked up from the road. "You know, from this angle you look like the leaning Tower of Pisa—a 'pisa' shit, that is." Duffy tried to squirm away from the guy's foot, but the guy mashed it even deeper into his shoulder.

The tall guy looked away from Duffy as he continued walking toward Danny. Then he heard a snap. He spun around to see a black-suited man's hand close over the Trans-Am's antenna and break it off. The man used it to whip the face of the boy who had his foot on Duffy's back.

The tall boy pulled out his knife and spun around. "Get him!" he ordered the guy with smelly gloves who was holding Pete.

The guy who had been holding Duffy on the ground had a reddish welt across his face from the diagonal slash of the antenna. He swung his knife at the newcomer, but the blade scraped against the antenna as the man blocked his swing. The stranger spun around, grabbed the boy's arm, and flipped him head over heels, so his army boots nailed smelly boy's face. They both hit the ground, but the guy with the welt jumped up to attack again. He charged at the man, knife in hand, but the man stepped back and whipped the boy's wrist with the antenna.

The boy dropped to his knees, clutching his wrist. "Ahhh!"

The mysterious man jabbed the broken edge of the antenna straight through the boy's neck and slipped the knife out of his hand. He gave him a nudge as he walked away, and that knocked him over. Then he ran toward the other boy as he stood up. Lowering his shoulder, the man swung upward with the knife, and it carved vertically through the kid's face. However, the dark-suited guy gave him no time to feel the sting of fresh air pushing against his new slice as he tripped him. With an outstretched arm, he held the knife upward, so the guy fell face first right into the blade. The blade shot out the back of his head, sending blood trickling through his hair.

Danny and Pete cringed and turned away to avoid the gruesome display. Most of the Armybrats were finally released. They grouped together and stood on the road to watch. Danny was still trapped against the trunk, and Wesley was still trapped against the ground. From the corner of his eye, Wesley watched. The man was their "knight in black armor," and he was seeking justice for them.

The man slipped the knife out of the lifeless body. The boy's head dropped, and his chin bounced off his chest. The man approached the tall boy who had beaten up Billy. The boy swung the branch at the newcomer, but he stepped aside and hacked at the branch with the knife, chopping it in half. The kid lunged at him to spear his chest. The man swung downward and hacked another good-sized length off the branch. The boy swung the branch to bash him on the head, but the man held up the knife, and the blade lodged into the wood. He pulled on the handle, yanked the branch from the boy's hands, and then dropped it to the ground, the blade still lodged in it.

The tall boy stepped forward and threw a punch. The man swiped downward with his right palm and grabbed the tall boy's fist. With his other hand, he grabbed the boy's other wrist. He shook him until he had complete control of his body. With the boy's arms crossed over his chest, the stranger pressed against them with each hand against the boy's shoulders, running forward as he forced the boy backward. The boy limped from the pain his shot ankle. Then he stopped and swiped his foot into the boy's heels. He released the boy's arms and raised his entire body off the ground, then sent him sailing through the air. The tall boy felt nothing but a sharp pain in his head as his body launched through the Trans-Am's back window. Then the stranger lifted the boy's legs and rammed him farther into the car.

"I would have picked on someone my own size," the stranger said, smiling as he held his right hand over his chest and then pointed at him. "If you had only picked on someone your own size."

He knelt down and stepped on one end of the branch, then wiggled the knife free. Then he walked toward the Charger. The boy who still had Danny pinned against the trunk placed his knife snugly over Danny's throat. The mystery man stared at him. The boy stared back with beady eyes and a forehead drowning in sweat.

"Whoa, man! I can't believe you just killed them. OK, drop the knife, or I'll make this boy breathe through his throat."

"After what you've just seen me do, do you really want to threaten me, son?"

"Drop the knife, or get ready to catch this boy's head," the boy warned.

"If that's what you really want," the stranger replied.

He didn't hesitate; he held onto the tip of the blade and lowered it toward the ground. Then he flung through the air. It passed over the trunk just above the hinged gas cap, burrowing itself in the boy's neck. He flew backwards onto the ground, and Danny jumped aside with a shout.

That's when the short, little muscular boy stepped off Wesley's back, jumped up onto the Dodge Charger, ran across the top, and flew off. He landed on the stranger and knocked him over. They rolled around on the dirt road until the stranger managed to get back onto his knees as the little dwarf put a chokehold on him. The dwarf stood over his back. At that moment, the stranger was as tall as he was because he was on his knees. The dwarf clamped his hands over the stranger's wrist to ensure his grip on him, so he could not escape from his chokehold.

However, the black-suited man wrapped his hand around his head, threw his weight forward, and smashed the dwarf's face against the rear bumper. The powerful blow made him jump away. The dwarf webbed his hands over his face to comfort his nose. The stranger spun around and grabbed the boy's shirt, wadding a handful of fabric in his fist. Then he punched him in the face.

Releasing the boy's shirt, the outsider jump-kicked him in his gut, and the dwarf flew backwards and bounced off the side of the Charger. The man jump-kicked him in the stomach a second time, sending the boy ricocheting off the Trans-Am.

"Oh, and that's another thing," the man growled, "You will never touch these kids." He kicked him. "Ever . . ."

He grabbed the boy by the shirt and spun him around, walked closer to the brown car, and released his shirt. Then he gave him another vomit teaser as he kneed him in the gut and finished his statement, "again!" The boy flew backwards, and his left arm smashed through the driver's window. He wobbled forward, and the stranger walked over to him. He wrapped his hand around the dwarf's chin and spun his head around until his neck cracked. The man concluded his victory by ripping the barbell ring out of the kid's ear. He smeared the dwarf across both doors and then slammed him to the ground.

The man picked him up and tossed him into the brown car. Then he walked over to the Charger and stood beside it. The two girls were still sitting inside, cowering and whimpering. The third girl still sat on the hood. She covered her mouth as tears trickled down her cheeks.

"You, off the hood," the man demanded. She nodded and then slid off and stood in the middle of the road, crying her eyes out. He opened the back door. "You've both got five seconds to get outta the car." They climbed out, both of them crying. "Now, all three of you, walk that way, and keep walking. As long as you keep walking, no harm will come to you. Now go!"

The stranger helped the boys push the Charger back onto the road. Then he piled the bodies inside the Trans-Am. He put it in neutral and walked the car toward the edge of the road. When he bailed away from the side of the car, the door swung shut. The Trans-Am rolled down the hill and angled over the edge of the cliff. It dove off and plunged several feet, smashing into a rock face. The transmission hung down as it curled over and dove into the ravine, flipping over the trees far below.

What the stranger had done was unbelievable. He had saved the Armybrats, but how he had handled the gang was a bit much. After the Armybrats watched the car go up in smoke, they realized they were alone. The mysterious guy had vanished. They could no longer see the girls down the road either.

Then, out of the blue, someone else joined them on the road. It was Mr. Fallway. "Now boys, what's going on?" he asked. He grinned with excitement as he sat on a mountain bike, startling the living daylights out of them as they huddled in the middle of the road. Wesley's eyes were larger than baseballs as he looked at him. Then he fainted.

"Whoa, Wesley, what happened?" Mr. Fallway asked as he caught Wesley's limp body. "Did I miss something?"

Uncertain, Billy shot his head toward his brother. His brother's eyes narrowed as he glared at Mr. Fallway. The same went for the other two. They weren't sure what to think. Mr. Fallway had appeared right after the mystery man disappeared. Who was the man in the black suit? Were he and Mr. Fallway one and the same?

Mr. Fallway listened to their entire story as he tossed his bike into the trunk. They tried to point out the Trans-Am at the bottom of the cliff. However, no one could see it through all the trees, though smoke billowed from far below. All Mr. Fallway wanted to do was get going. He seemed to be in a hurry to get out of there, so he cut their story short. He wanted to get to the campsite. They didn't the discuss the story after that. Once again, another fairy tale was left unexplained.

CHAPTER 21
TABLES TURNED

They headed down a narrow dirt path. Even though it was midday, the forest was so dense that they drove with the headlights on. Branches rubbed against the car, and Duffy ripped leaves from them for fun. Mr. Fallway had secured the trunk with a bungee cord, but every pothole caused the trunk lid to bounce and clank against the bike.

Duffy was ripping off a palm full of leaves as Pete smirked at him. One leaf landed in Wesley's lap. When he looked down at it, he saw hundreds of slimy caterpillars sticking to the leaf and crawling around his legs. He screamed and swatted them away. Duffy jumped back against the window. The caterpillars looked like little humans with arms and legs and tiny heads. When they crawled off the leaf, they crawled up Wesley's shirt. Mr. Fallway looked in the rearview mirror trying to figure out what was going on as he squirmed and shouted.

He slammed on the brakes as the caterpillar-humans piled over Wesley's chest and turned into a pile of goo. The slime soaked into his shirt and disappeared. Duffy sat forward and looked at Wesley. They stared at each other in confusion. Mr. Fallway hung over the seat trying to get answers for why Wesley was screaming. The caterpillar-humans were gone. Mr. Fallway noticed a caterpillar crawling along the headrest, and he flicked it out the window. Danny noticed it and thought for a moment. He remembered the catwalk at the House on the Rock when that leaf fell past him and the little caterpillar-like thing crawling on it.

After that little ordeal, the trip continued. As they headed farther down the dirt trail, the boys began to wonder if the trail would ever end. They were about to get an answer to that question.

Finally, after traveling about three miles through the trees, the Charger came to a dusty halt. Mr. Fallway climbed out, and the Armybrats followed. Everyone was carrying a backpack. Mr. Fallway had a backpack as well, an army-issue rucksack. They had a change of clothes and some snacks, but that was about it.

They helped him snap branches off trees and shrubs to conceal the car. Then Mr. Fallway asked them to follow him. He walked along the edge of a cliff and led them to a rock stairway that descended down one side of the cliff. Their hearts raced out of control.

This was it, the day of their ultimate test. The test that Mr. Fallway had been planning to give them for quite a while. Once and for all, they were going to be tested in all categories. As a reflection of Mr. Fallway's teaching ability, the test was to show him how much information each boy had retained. The knowledge that he had passed down to them was grand, and no other boy their age could measure up to their potential.

Danny could not recall a day in his childhood when the sky was as blue as that day. He remembered a girl from school who had worn a blue silk shirt to English class, and he couldn't help but compare the memory of that shirt with the silky sky that morning. The clouds reminded him of the white buttons. A couple of birds flapped past, and he thought of the girl's long, soft, brown hair as it waved around her shoulders whenever she turned her head and how her hair bounced off her breasts, rhythmically colliding strand by strand. With school being out, he was sore that he had to go the entire summer without being able to look into her gorgeous brown eyes as they sparkled like a varnished tabletop. A sparrow chirped, and Danny heard her name within the three-syllable sound: "Clar-iss-a!"

Once they reached the bottom, a bridge extended to the other side of a river. With the bridge being about fifty feet above the river, the Armybrats backed off. Four thick braided ropes hung from one side all the way to the other. Boards connected the lower two ropes. Crossing it would require a significant amount of trust. The bridge was suspended between two rock ledges that were several feet lower than the ridge where the paths led them through the trees on either side. From far away, it looked like a hammock. To the naked eye, it seemed trustworthy, but was it?

"Aw, cool, a bridge!" Duffy hollered and ran for it. Wesley followed.

Mr. Fallway ran and tackled them right before they reached it. "I'd advise you not to go on that bridge."

They backed away, sharing awkward glances. "Why?" Duffy asked.

"Cuz I'm afraid of heights," Mr. Fallway said, "and I know another way around. Follow me." He walked away.

A second glance at the bridge made them back away. The bridge swayed, twisted, and creaked in the wind. The boards seemed rotten. Some were missing, and others were broken. The ropes were black from age. A few ropes wound through the boards to connect the handrail, which was nothing but a rope with mold growing on it. If they squinted, they could see that not all the boards were consistent with each other. Some were slanted, crooked, and lopsided.

"You're, uh, afraid of heights, big guy?" Duffy asked sarcastically, though he had a serious look on his face.

"Yeah, but don't get me wrong," Mr. Fallway said, "we'll be rappelling later this week."

Duffy smiled. "Awesome!"

"So, in one week, we'll all be hardcore fighters," Billy said, "but you'll still be afraid of heights, and we'll still get to go home?"

Mr. Fallway gave his odd inaugural speech about what was supposed to take place that week. "Since your parents have enrolled all of you into our new program, you're going to begin the second stage of training. Basically, after Pete's mom was put in a coma, your parents got together. They contacted me and were concerned about your safety. I assured them that this program was amongst the safest legions, and many are involved in the community. It will allow you kids to become more alert during your daily activities and become more aggressive. I plan for us to spend a week to ten days up here to cover some tactics that I may have missed during your previous stages of training. You will have some hand-to-hand combat training, including some martial arts, and you've already learned weapons and cover and concealment. Up here we'll also find time to have fun, but we're going to learn how our minds work under stress. We want to learn how to deal with things while under pressure. That is what the world offers: pressure. As adults, we must deal with the pressures in life." Like a single air molecule in a balloon, that was the pressure holding its shape, but without hope, their minds would deflate. Mr. Fallway was there to make sure that wouldn't happen.

"All along you've mentioned that our parents enrolled us into this program," Billy said. "This program is fantastic, but if it's so great, how come they haven't even told us about it?"

"Billy, this isn't the real thing," Mr. Fallway replied, "it's just the beginning of the next worst thing, which can be *very* real."

With that, he walked away, and they followed him. Billy's forehead wrinkled like a shirt full of static. His mind worked double time and ventured off on a little voyage of soul searching. His parents had never mentioned anything about joining some program. He still couldn't get over the fact that they were a little over two hour's drive from home in the middle of nowhere to learn how to defend themselves. If most of the community was involved in the program, how come they seemed to be the only idiots playing games in the forest way up north? All he wanted was to see Watches' body dangling from a noose. Soon, he snapped back to reality and realized he was alone. He ran to catch up with the others.

Once he caught up to the them, he jumped in front of Mr. Fallway and forced him to stop. "Wait a minute," Billy said. "Our parents never signed us up for this. If they did, they would have told us, don't ya think? Tell me if I'm wrong."

Mr. Fallway smiled. "You're wrong."

Billy crossed his arms stubbornly. "I'm not spending an entire week or so in the forest with a complete stranger like you."

Mr. Fallway sighed. "Aww, William, I thought we were past this. I'm not a stranger anymore. I thought we were friends now."

"I order you to take us home immmmeediaatt—" Billy stopped and thought for a moment. "Wait a minute," he whispered. "Wait one cotton-pickin' minute. That's why you lent me your car. You didn't want us to leave, did you?" He seemed as if he were thinking up each accusation right before he said it. "You hid your car. You don't want anyone to find us. And now you're on a winding route, so we have no clue where the fuck we are. You kidnapped us! And you allowed me to make it happen!" He stepped backwards.

Everyone else stopped dead in their tracks and thought how this all seemed too real.

Mr. Fallway turned and smiled at him. "William, get a hold of yourself, You're falling apart already. That's what this is all about. I want to see how your minds work, and it seems like your mind is already doing cartwheels."

"The truth, Mr. Fallway. The truth will set you free."

"Free? You must calm down. I didn't kidnap you. You came out of your own cognizance. I promise you'll be home in a week or so."

He placed his hand on Billy's shoulder, but Billy shook it away. Mr. Fallway stood there, dumbfounded, as he glanced from boy to boy.

He stepped forward with an outstretched hand and stated his name. Billy stepped back and whipped out the gun he had taken from the kids the previous night. Mr. Fallway stepped back, as did the Armybrats. Mr. Fallway raised his hands slowly. His puppy dog eyes were mysterious, but he seemed as confused as the rest of them. The sun was bright, the brightest day they could remember. Mr. Fallway's lazy eye was fixed on Billy as his other eye scavenged for hope.

"I've been waiting for this moment, Mr. Fallway."

"Billy, don't be stupid."

"No, I've seen this moment in my dreams. You haunt me just like Watches does. And sometimes I feel as if you are him!" Billy shouted, shaking the gun at him. "But I know that even if you aren't, you at least have something to do with him." Billy put his other hand behind his back and squeezed the other pistol tucked into his pants. "I watch the news, Mr. Fallway; I'm not stupid. You're wanted in Illinois, Iowa, Minnesota, and Wisconsin. Children are getting murdered throughout each one of those states, and you're using them as bait to lure him in. You're almost running out of options to get your man, aren't you, Mr. Fallway? So, what are you going to do next?"

The new information fell into each boy's mind like a rock on a bare foot. Mr. Fallway had operated his investigations in all the states surrounding Wisconsin, but no one knew that except Billy. They had no idea that the story had escalated beyond the boundaries of their assumptions. They thought all the murders, all the drug smuggling, and all the illegal activities were miniscule, but Watches' posse was more upscale than they had expected.

Mr. Fallway smirked. "Billy?"

"You're going to make this club sound like cotton candy. You want to use us to solve your case. Then you're going to feed us to this insane freak, so you can hunt him down. That's your ultimate goal, isn't it? And who's the man in the black suit?"

Wesley's eyes bugged out. Danny and Duffy looked at each other, then Danny stepped forward. "Yo, bro, cool it, man."

"Danny, you guys walk the other way," Billy said. "This is between Mr. Fallway and me."

Duffy sighed. "Does this mean we won't be rappelling? Because that sounds awesome right now."

"Duffy, shut up," Billy said. "Get out of here now, guys."

Wesley stood there watching as Danny, Duffy, and Pete walked backwards. No one could believe what was happening. Was the entire test a mind game? Had it started already, and were they already failing due to Billy's abrupt actions? He continued to push Mr. Fallway backward, keeping the gun aimed on him as he drilled Mr. Fallway with accusations and waited for answers.

A leaf swirled down from a limb above Billy's head. It floated back and forth like a feather, swinging like a pendulum between Billy and Mr. Fallway. Wesley watched the leaf, and Billy noticed it through the handgun's sight. A little caterpillar-human grew from the surface with raised arms and webbed fingers. Inside the slimy, little human figure's head were small black holes for eyes. Its mouth opened, and slimy strands connected its lower lip to its upper lip as it screeched at Billy. Wesley stepped forward, stating Billy's name. Billy pulled the trigger at the bug. The bullet burned right through the figure, and it exploded like a melted marshmallow, the leaf scattering through the air.

The bullet kept going as the leaf particles floated to the forest floor. The human figure on the leaf was of no importance, and gobs of its remnants splashed Wesley's cheek and a smaller tree behind him. Yes, Billy shot and destroyed the leaf, but who cared? The bullet kept going—straight through Mr. Fallway's upper chest, near his shoulder.

Duffy's jaw dropped as Mr. Fallway's body flew backward and bounced away from a tree. His rucksack jumped over his shoulders, and he fell off the trail. He rolled down a foothill and landed out of sight, surrounded by branches and shrubs. Billy lowered the gun and looked at Wesley, who was crying and shaking as he looked up at him. Billy didn't even break a sweat.

He kept his cool. That was what kept Danny from freaking out. However, Duffy and Pete had the same expression as Wesley.

Pete broke the silence as he raced toward Mr. Fallway to help him. Before he could leap off the trail, Billy grabbed his arm and shook his head at him. Pete looked away from him and noticed Mr. Fallway's body behind a log. Danny and Duffy walked slowly to the edge of the trail to see it for themselves. All they could see was one leg propped up over a log. The other leg was cinched behind it, the tip of his shoe just visible.

"Forget him, and let's go," Billy said.

He turned and walked away. The rest of the Armybrats huddled in a group and stared at him as he passed. Billy tucked the gun into the back of his pants. His job was done, and now he was leaving. All along, he had wanted to confront Mr. Fallway. He had held these thoughts about Mr. Fallway throughout his life and never shared his true feelings with the others. He had never trusted him. Mr. Fallway had him so bothered that he had resorted to shooting him. None of the other Armybrats had suspected that.

Wesley walked over and rejoined the group. They were all as still as the trees with no wind. Danny stared at his brother as Billy made his way back up the trail. Billy never looked at them as he walked by, and he never looked back at the others after he passed them.

"Billy," Danny said. "Billy . . . Bill! What the heck just happened?"

Billy spun around, walking backwards. "What are you, blind? Come on."

"Listen, bro, you just shot him."

"OK, and now we have to go."

Danny looked at Duffy. Duffy panted as his eyes rolled over to Danny. "We can't just leave him here," Danny said.

"Is . . . is he dead?" Pete asked.

"Hey, I don't feel like standing around right now," Billy said. "I got a million things on my mind and a sting in my ear because I can't hear a friggin' thing you're sayin'. Damn, that was loud." He sighed and wiggled his right earlobe. "All I want to do right now is walk. So, let's regroup somewhere else to talk about this, OK? At least until I regain my hearing."

They followed him without conversation. The day was still bright, but they felt gloomy. A stranger who had once came up to them with millions of odd questions was now lying on the ground with a hole in him. Maybe that was why Danny felt it was the brightest day he could remember. And he remembered something Mr. Fallway always said, "Never go anywhere alone. Always go together!" Now that they were together, he felt very much alone. He had trusted Mr. Fallway a little more than his brother had, obviously. Now they had no clue where they were headed.

Wesley was thinking about his grandfather. Visions of his childhood raced through his mind. Then he saw his brother walking down a staircase. That was the night he got hammered after prom. His girlfriend had dumped him for another guy that night. It all happened at the high school gymnasium. All along, his girlfriend had been seeing the other guy. She had decided to let Wesley's brother in on their secret during prom. He went out to some bars after that, and somehow his underage friends got hold of some alcohol. They got really drunk. That reminded him of what Billy had called the girl sitting on the Charger's hood, a "slingshot whore." He smirked, and his head twitched. His brother had referred to his cheating girlfriend in the same profound manner.

Wesley's parents were on vacation, so they weren't even home to witness his behavior. His older brother was supposed to be at home babysitting. Instead, his brother had gone out, and when he came home, he took his anger out on Wesley. Ever since that night, Wesley had had a twitch in his neck; though, he recovered just fine from the hospital. His brother had been sent off to boot camp. Wesley couldn't find it in his heart to forgive him, and he would never forget how much that night scared him. This was another scary moment in his life.

Pete had one thing on his mind: his mom. And all he could hope for was that she would recover. He was wondering if Mr. Fallway was the reason why she was in a coma. Maybe he had thrown her onto the pool cover that almost drowned her, or was Watches to blame? Now that Billy had shot Mr. Fallway, Pete was wondering who the real monster was. All he could think about was his mom's bright smile when she entered the kitchen in the mornings, her flip-flops slapping the floor. He missed that, and he missed her. He missed her so much that he even missed the picky things about her like how clean she kept everything. With his mom gone, Pete and his dad were creating a disaster at home, and his dad would take his aggression out on Pete more often. Things felt like they were falling apart.

Duffy wasn't thinking about anything. He merely followed Danny. Pete was behind him, and behind them was Wesley. Duffy was in a trance. He didn't know what to think. The Armybrats were lost. They had no idea that Billy even felt that way about Mr. Fallway. Billy said he couldn't wait for *the moment*. Well, now it had happened, and a big question mark loomed. A million question marks swirled around Duffy's head like a halo. He wasn't able to think straight at all.

Danny, on the other hand, was very confused. When he first sat down and discussed Watches with his brother, he felt that Billy trusted his instinct. And his instinct was to follow Mr. Fallway's lead. Mr. Fallway could help them get through this entire thing. Without Mr. Fallway, a huge piece of the puzzle was missing.

Family was on Billy's mind. He didn't want to accept this stranger. He had lied to Danny to protect him from the truth—that the office above Barbara Felter's floral shop haunted him. That was the turning point in his aggression toward Mr. Fallway. The pictures of their families on the wall were deceiving.

Billy knew what he wanted to do. He wanted to go straight to his father and let him know about Mr. Fallway. That was the correct thing to do. But now that he had shot Mr. Fallway, he had a lot more explaining to do. However, he felt as though he had it all figured out. When Mr. Fallway taught martial arts and how to kill people, Billy accepted all that information. But he didn't accept Mr. Fallway's ways. He felt as if they were a part of a secret cult, and they were on a manhunt to murder Watches. Billy had ridden it all out to see what Mr. Fallway was intending to do. But as they walked through the deserted forest hearing nothing but nature sounds, it was almost too real.

Unfortunately, the Armybrats were now lethal weapons. They knew how to kill. They knew weapons. They knew self-defense. They knew what Mr. Fallway knew. This wasn't a training site; it was where Mr. Fallway was going to build his cult for the kill. He had kidnapped them. They could not trust him; Billy knew that. Billy also knew he loved his family. He loved his brother, and he wasn't about to involve them any further with this stranger. It was time to let his dad know what was going on. The night Danny was attacked at the bridge was the night they should have told their dad. The whole thing may have already gone too far . . .

CHAPTER 22
FREE FALLING

Suddenly, they stopped on the path. Below was a drop-off where a rope bridge stretched to the other side of the river. They had returned to the same bridge as before.

"OK, we need to get to the car," Danny said.

Billy looked back at his brother. "What good is that going to do us?"

"We need to get out of here," Danny said. "Leave his body, and let's go."

"Yes, I think that would be a wise course of action, Billy," Duffy agreed.

"Yeah, brilliant," Billy said. "By the way, do either of you have the keys?"

Duffy looked at Billy for an answer. Danny shook his head, as did Wesley. Pete sighed. "Mr. Fallway has 'em."

Billy smiled. "Bingo."

"Does that mean we're going back to the body?" Duffy asked.

Billy looked at Wesley. Danny read his mind like an open book. He closed his eyes and shook his head again. Then they trudged back down the trail. Many bad things were happening to them, and now they were going to dig through a dead guy's pockets to get the car keys that could free them from all of it. They could drive away and leave his body in the forest to rot. It sounded like a nightmare.

They rounded a corner of the trail. Just over the ridge at the end, a foothill divided their line of sight from whatever was on the other side. And on the other side, they already knew what lay ahead . . . Mr. Fallway's body. It was lying there with one leg draped over a log and blood all over him.

From that moment on, the slope seemed longer than before. The trail seemed like it never would end. They felt exactly how they did when they first entered the trail and continued riding in the Dodge Charger. Back then, Mr. Fallway was leading them. Now they were headed toward Mr. Fallway as he lay dead in the brush.

When they neared the end of the trail, sunlight was streaming overhead. Billy whipped out the pistol and looked at his brother. Danny heard the gun brush Billy's pants as his waistband snapped, and his shirt ruffled upward. Billy sighed, and then they continued onward until Billy motioned for them to stop. He pointed at Wesley. "You're gonna go down there."

"What?"

"You're gonna go down there."

"But—"

"Don't worry, I got ya covered," Billy assured him and then walked off the trail to position himself behind a tree.

Wesley did not want to go down there. He was already scared enough. His knees were locked together. Reality had him jammed in a tight spot. He stood in the middle of the trail, and his neck twitched as if he were having an epileptic fit.

Danny walked over to him and stared into his eyes. Wesley's head continued to twitch. Danny walked away from him, and Wesley panted while holding onto his knees. Billy watched his brother walk calmly down the trail. He leaned on the tree and squeezed the pistol grip. He fixed his sight on the foothill. Danny made it to the end and then stopped.

"Tell me what's up, Danny," Billy said.

Danny turned around slowly and then looked in every direction. Then he looked at everyone on the trail, his eyes stopping on Billy's face beside the tree. "He's gone."

Billy frowned. "What do you mean?"

Danny pointed at the ground behind him and shook his finger. "What I mean is there's nobody here. No *body*."

Billy stepped out from behind the tree and speed-walked toward his brother. At the end of the trail, some dead branches were lying on the ground. Leaves continued the rustle from swaying trees, but as soon as he caught up to Danny, he stopped. The two brothers exchanged a worried glance.

Billy opened the pistol's chamber. One round gleamed in the sun. He opened the other pistol's chamber. Only one round remained in that one as well. He sighed. "Oh, shit. Let the games begin."

They both spun around, and Billy waved the gun to signal the others to come over. The boys jogged toward them. The trees were still rustling as Billy rested his head on the barrels of the pistols. He closed his eyes and thought for a moment.

They huddled together. No one said a word; they just looked at each other. Just then, an owl flew through the group, and they all fell over, screaming. Billy spun around as a couple of squirrels ran past too. He pointed the guns in different directions as he lay on his back. Everyone else was cowering behind trees and undergrowth.

Finally, Pete worked up enough energy to break the silence.

"Billy, tell me what's going on!" Pete demanded.

"Hey, calm down Pete."

"Look at us, Billy," Duffy said. "You're telling him to calm down while we're all hiding from birds and squirrels."

"OK," Billy said, standing up. "This is it. If we get split up after this, our rally point will be on the other side of that bridge back up there at the top of the hill. Do you guys remember how to get up there?"

"Yes," Danny replied as the others nodded.

"Do you guys remember what Mr. Fallway taught us about shooting a back azimuth and about resection 'n' all that crap with our maps?"

"Yes!"

"You all have your compasses?"

They nodded.

"Good, now, we have to find the main road to get us home. We're gonna get out of here now," Billy slammed a map against the ground and pointed out the main road. "The road runs close to this field, and this field isn't too far off. Let's go." He tucked the map back into his bag.

He knew that Mr. Fallway could be anywhere with his sights fixed on them, but he didn't care. He stood up to show them courage and leadership. He looked up the trail and saw emptiness. The entire forest seemed empty. Nothing was happening. Leaves were rustling, animals were doing their daily deeds, but other than that, they were stuck in the middle of a screwed-up situation. As quiet as it seemed, they had no idea they were walking billboards in a forest of green and brown, but they did know they were over ninety miles from home.

They all climbed out of the ditch. If they could at least get to the main road, that would lead them back toward civilization—not necessarily back home, but anywhere seemed better than the deep, dank forest.

They walked up the path toward the bridge. Just then, Billy grabbed everyone and stopped. "We need to find the Charger."

"Do you have the keys?" Danny asked sarcastically.

"Shut up!" Billy hissed. "If Mr. Fallway is going anywhere, he's going to go back to his car."

"I say we slash his tires," Duffy said. "Guarantee he can't leave."

Billy's eyes rolled back toward Duffy as he nodded. "Not a bad idea."

They headed back up the trail. As two of them searched the right side, the other two searched the left, and Wesley walked up the center of the trail. When they drove down the trail, they had parked on the right side, which meant it should have been hidden on the left side. They backtracked up to the bridge, but they couldn't find the car. Billy hopped in and out of the shrubs, busting branches and clearing out areas in search of the car but found nothing.

Billy walked farther into the forest. He strayed from the trail, pushing shrubs aside. He stepped out about twenty feet and looked beyond the trees. Up ahead, an empty field collected sunlight, though gray clouds were moving in. The trail ran north and south. The sun was behind him, setting in the west, and the great wide-open field darkened slowly. He smiled at the beautiful tall green grass.

Billy spun around. "Hey, there are no trees straight ahead. It's a field."

Pete stood on the edge of the trail and made a whooping sound, sarcastically acknowledging the remark about its beauty.

"Hey, Pete, this will be our rally point, OK?"

"Whatever!"

Pete and Wesley were up on the trail watching Danny and Billy circling the trees and bushes along the trail. They stared out at the empty field. Duffy was now the only person along the right side of the trail. He stopped searching and turned to look at the brothers kicking shrubs aside and searching for the car. He glanced up the trail and then walked over to the other side, continuing to watch the brothers.

"Hey, you guys, we're saved!" Wesley yelled, pointing over Danny and Billy's heads.

Danny walked over to the edge of the forest and looked out at the field. Billy stood next to him, and they saw what Wesley had noticed. "Uh, guys," Billy said, "let's head back the other way . . . now!"

Wesley stood in the center of the trail staring at something in the field. Pete walked forward a bit and then hid from the view of some people heading along the fence line that divided the field from the forest.

"Ohhhhh shiiiiiiiit," Duffy said. "He's alive!"

A group of individuals were walking toward them just around the bend. Their faces were unfamiliar. The lead guy had his head down, and he was wearing a trench coat. Billy and Danny stepped onto the trail, and the Armybrats walked back the other direction away from the group of people. They glanced over their shoulders and picked up the pace.

Billy tried to hush them up, but it was too late. "He's still alive!" he snarled.

The lead person lifted his head. His one red eye glowed. His eye patch appeared like a black hole in his head. The group of people stopped behind him. It was Watches. He held his arms out to the side to halt the group and cocked his head to the side like an owl. It must have been his lucky day.

The boys turned and ran in the other direction, which led them deeper into the never-ending wilderness of dirt, trees, and undergrowth. They ran for their lives. Without direction and nowhere to go, it seemed hopeless. But they didn't look back. Trees were far below them to their left as they approached the end of the trail. The only way to go was down.

Watches and his men stared at each other. Then Watches growled and grabbed one of his men by the collar. He shook him for gratification. "Get them!" His eye lit up, and he pointed at the boys running the other way. Watches threw the man away from him and spun around. "Go now!" he screamed at the others. They took off running, pulling out fully automatic weapons.

Watches followed slowly behind them, climbing casually onto the trail. His men stopped for a few seconds and shot at the boys. However, the trail curved left, then right, and the Armybrats disappeared from sight. Wesley fell, but Pete picked him up and encouraged him to keep going.

By the time Watches' men caught up to them, Billy was already halfway across the rope bridge. Unfortunately, he was suspended through a hole in the boards, and Pete's body was dangling from the railing, which was a thick fibrous rope. Danny was crawling out to help them. He finally got Pete back onto the bridge, but Danny was still clinging on for dear life. Below him, the Wisconsin River raged.

"Hurry!" Billy hollered.

Pete knelt on the bridge and hugged the rope railing for support, panting. Danny kept crawling toward his brother. "Hang on, bro, I'm coming."

"Crawl faster! I can't hang on much longer."

"Pull yourself up, wuss."

"Oh, I'll show you, wuss!"

"Yo, I can't go any faster," Danny said. "I feel like this bridge is gonna collapse." Just as he finished that statement, his body broke through a few boards, and he swung underneath the bridge. He was hanging onto one board as he slammed into Billy's gut, accidentally nailing him in the crotch with his shin.

"Aggh!" Billy shrieked. "You kicked me in the nuts!"

Danny grabbed a loose rope hanging from the railing. Billy kicked him in the side, and the rope snapped away from a few boards. Danny swung around Billy's body, and the rope wound around Billy's neck. Billy choked and gagged, his face turning red. "Got Gammit!"

Duffy's head poked through the hole from the other side. He made it past the damaged section where Billy had fallen through. He was already on the opposite side from the other boys. Duffy held his arm out for Billy to grab.

Danny climbed up the rope, and Pete poked his head through the hole for the rescue. He reached down and hollered Danny's name. Danny looked up at him. As soon as Pete grabbed him, he stepped off Billy's shoulder, and they flew up onto the bridge. The rope released from Billy's neck, and he could breathe again. Danny and Pete looked up from where they had fallen. Billy's fingers were clinging to the end board before the hole in the bridge. The rope was swaying beneath him. He glanced back at Duffy and reached for his outstretched arm.

Suddenly, the board snapped. Billy screamed and fell. Danny and Pete struggled to turn around and crawl over to the gap, screaming his name. As they peaked over the edge, they saw Billy below. The rope had wound beneath his armpit, and he was swinging from it. He cursed as he looked up at them.

Billy lifted one arm off the rope and pointed at Pete. "When I get up there, I'm kicking your ass!" Then he pointed at Danny. "And I'm throwing you off the bridge!"

"Then I guess helping you is out of the question!" Danny smiled and turned around.

"Yeah," Pete agreed and stood up to turn around as well. He glanced at Duffy, who was standing on the other side of the gap with his arms reaching for the sky. Wesley was sitting on the bridge following suit.

They grouped together and stared at a crowd of Watches' men aiming their weapons at them. Immediately, they followed Wesley's lead and threw their arms into the air. Billy remained quiet after an upward swing of the rope gave him a glimpse of Watches walking down the trail. The swing of the rope had finally calmed down, and he just hung at the center. The strain on his fingers continued to place pressure where the fibers pricked him, but he kept quiet. Watches' men separated as Watches stepped onto the first few boards of the bridge.

A main rope snapped, and the bridge bounced. Billy grabbed the rope with both hands and spun a little as the movement rotated him. He looked up at the two boys. He could see part of their faces through the hole on the bridge. They were on their knees with their hands in the air. They were looking in each direction trying to figure out how to escape. Nothing looked promising.

Billy glanced up. The three of them were suspended in the center of the bridge. Watches was standing before the bridge pointing his weapon at Danny and Pete, but he hadn't noticed Billy hanging below.

"Where are your friends, fellas?" Watches asked. "Oh, OK, there's Peter, Wesley and Duffy. Say 'Hi,' Duffster."

"Hi," Duffy mumbled.

"Soooo, where's Billy, fellas?"

Billy's back was swinging toward Watches. He tried to spin around to see him more clearly. *Oh shit,* he thought as Danny peeked down at him.

Billy's head whipped back and forth from Watches to the river far below. The bridge was a setup. It was something Mr. Fallway didn't want the boys to be on right away because it was supposed to be part of the training course. The goal was to cross it as a way of overcoming stress while under pressure and allow everyone to reach the other side safely. But halfway was the farthest they had gotten. Now a big, ugly goon held them back with nowhere else to go.

"Come on, where's Billy? Let me know, or I'll have to off one of ya." Watches aimed his weapon at Danny. "Well, kids, you think you can handle me? You think the world would be a much better place without me? Instead it's full of little shits like you who think everyone can just get along. I have some unfinished business to attend to, and it's in Verona, right under my nose, and it has to do with you little shits. Can you believe that? You 'n' your brother live a *fake* life, Danny. *Emerson.* What kind of name is that anyway?"

"Oh, hell no!" Danny hollered. "What kind of name is Watches?"

"Ooo, ballsy, son. Must I remind you that I'm the one with a gun to your face?"

Duffy wound his finger around his ear. "Cuckoo . . ."

Danny rolled his eyes in Duffy's direction.

Watches shot Duffy. Danny jumped back, and Watches aimed at Danny again. "Forget about him, son. Focus, Danny. Where's your brother?"

Wesley looked down at Duffy who wailed as he clutched his shoulder. Wesley wanted to aid him, but he was afraid to move.

It started sprinkling. Watches raised an Uzi at them and growled. Anger swelled in everyone's minds. Watches blinked his one eye as the water droplets tickled his eyelashes. Beads built up on his eyepatch. "Well, if no one will talk, I guess this is the end of the road for all of ya." As he prepared to hose them down with automatic rounds, his shoulder burst open.

Watches held onto his shoulder and looked down at Billy. Smoke poured from the barrel of Billy's gun. Billy blew the smoke away and glared at him. "Fuck you, Watches." Watches dropped the Uzi, and it fell down the side of the cliff, bouncing into the crook of Billy's arm. Billy tossed his pistol and sprayed rounds up the hill with the Uzi instead.

Watches screamed and ran across the bridge. Billy shot the wood above his head. Splinters flung over Watches as he charged at Danny. Some rounds split the support ropes. The bridge dropped a foot, and Watches moved to his right, trying to hold onto the railing. He was only a few steps away from getting those boys. The clip emptied, and Billy dropped the Uzi, grabbing the rope to regain his balance. The gun nailed the sandy shoreline below, sending up a puff of sand.

Watches flew backwards and landed on his back. When his body hit the bridge, the last two support ropes snapped, and the entire bridge broke in half.

Billy clenched the rope even tighter. It was over. He was tired, and he decided to end the pain. As he swung downward, he let go. All the pressure relieved from his biceps, and he held his arms as he fell toward the river. Danny let go of the side and dove in after his brother. Both of them splashed into the Wisconsin River.

Watches jumped backwards and grabbed onto a few ropes as he swung against the cliff face. The other side of the bridge swung toward the other rock face across the river, Watches' men clinging to it for dear life.

Wesley helped to support Duffy, who was holding on to the bridge with one arm, his other arm mangled from the bullet wound. Pete supported his legs.

Boards from above fell onto Pete as the boys climbed above him. The boards pelted Watches as he hung upside down with his legs between a couple of boards. Everyone else managed to hold on as the other half of the bridge smashed into the cliff and blew apart below them. Pete crawled up toward the top of the cliff. Duffy and Wesley were above him. Wesley helped Duffy over the top. Then they turned back and rooted Pete on.

"Die, Peter!" Watches pulled out a pistol and shot at him.

Pete held onto a rope at his side as bullets cracked a few boards in half above him. He wrapped the rope around his hands and ran along the rock wall. The bridge swayed as he ran with the free-hanging handrail. It appeared as if Watches was sitting on the side of the cliff shooting up at him for fun. While Pete became a moving target, he forced the entire bridge to sway, including Watches.

Pete stopped running and swung back in the other direction. The rope rubbed across the rock ledge where the boys were cheering him on. Sparks shot upward from the jagged rocks as more bullets snapped boards farther up the bridge.

Duffy and Wesley turned their faces away from the ledge as Watches grabbed another board, which prevented him from falling. A few boards separated beneath his legs, and he was dangling in midair.

Duffy and Wesley jumped at Pete's rope. Only a few threads remained intact. Wesley grabbed the rope with both hands, and the only fibers that held Pete up curled as the tension was relieved and then snapped. Duffy grabbed Wesley's pant leg with one arm and kept Wesley from sliding over the ledge. Wesley was the only one holding Pete up while Duffy's weight kept Wesley from sliding over. Pete looked into his eyes and reached a rock at his side that stopped him from swaying, then climbed toward him. Duffy and Wesley hurried him along. Duffy tugged on his leg as Wesley reeled him in.

Pete looked up at Wesley. "Wait."

"What do you mean?" Wesley shouted.

"Yeah," Duffy said through clenched teeth. "Sure we'll wait."

Pete pulled out his bone-handled knife and glanced down at Watches struggling on the ladder below. "Yo, Watches!" Pete yelled, "ever heard of the song 'Free Falling' by Tom Petty? They say it's a real heartbreaker." He sliced one rope, and Watches dropped a few feet.

"Don't even think about it Peter Cottontail!" Watches said.

"Too late," Pete replied. "Already thought about it—half acted on it even." He sliced the last rope. The remaining portion of the bridge and Watches toppled toward the river.

Once Pete reached the top, he threw his rucksack off his back and lay down for a moment. Then he regained energy and opened it. He withdrew a dirty map and dropped it next to the bag. As Duffy opened the map, Wesley tied a long sock across a wadded-up rag over Duffy's wound. Duffy brushed off the map and followed the river around the basin with his finger. It wrapped around and then headed back toward the main road. Where it curved, heavy contour lines extended farther away from the river. That meant there were no longer rock cliffs on either side. That was, more than likely, where Billy and Danny would exit the river.

It was getting dark. Duffy stood up and looked at Watches' men on the other side of the gorge. Then he spun around and put his arms around Pete and Wesley. "Let's go."

CHAPTER 23
SINKHOLE

Mr. Fallway had built training sites throughout the forest. The boys were experiencing misery by not knowing what was to come. The bridge looked real, but it was a confidence course. What was next was a mudslide that led to a sinkhole—another one of his creations. They didn't know it, but a few hundred feet below another ravine was a plastic tarp runway to the pit of gloom where Mr. Fallway had constructed a hellhole mud trap. Before they knew it, they were stuck on a cliff with no way down except a rope suspended at the center. It was another training site. If there were more training sites, they were bound to find them.

The rope was suspended in the middle of a fifteen-foot gap between another gorge. It hung quietly from a huge tree limb that was wide enough to shelter them from the rain. The rope eased back and forth in a timid circle.

The boys stared at the rope as it hung suspended between the ledges. Out of the blue, as blue as the sky, a burst of energy swelled inside Pete. He ran between them and hurdled himself through the thick air. His backpack lifted briefly from his shoulders as his outstretched arms cut through the air and grabbed the rope. His backpack fell against his back again, and his momentum carried him to the opposite side of the gap. As soon as his feet touched a rock surface on the other side, he reached out and caught a small tree with one hand and hoisted himself up.

Wesley opened a zipper, and Duffy watched him pull a banana out of his pack. He peeled it and bit off a huge chunk, mashing it between his teeth. All he could do was stare with hunger. Suddenly, he noticed Duffy looking at him. "What?" he mumbled.

Duffy stood there in awe for a moment. It seemed almost unreal that he had taken time to eat a banana. Since they had slept for most of the trip, they had missed the option of making a pit stop at a McDonald's or a 7-11. The crooked cop had stolen their money, but Wesley had grub in his bag. Duffy couldn't remember if he had brought some of his favorite crackers. They were dying to take a break and munch, but no one else had brought any food. Soon, their guts were talking to one another. Either that or a pack of tigers had joined them on the trail.

Pete stepped back and whistled. "Hey, Duffy, think fast."

He tossed the rope over to him. Duffy stepped closer to the end and concentrated on the swing of the fibrous rope. He caught it, but before he stepped off to swing, he glanced back and noticed Wesley's gut. Automatically, a number popped in his head from an estimation of the limb, rope, and Wesley's weight. He wasn't in physics, but his fragile, little mind hurt at the thought of Wesley swinging. He considered his weight and the torque on the stress point where the rope was tied to the limb and decided he was swinging next, but he had no idea how accurate his thoughts were.

Duffy hung his body off the edge and looked down the cliff. He pulled himself back and noticed movement through the trees. Someone had advanced on their location. He snapped back and looked toward Pete on the other side. Danger may have been bestowed upon them all over again as a person jumped down a foothill and jogged toward him. Pete made a hand signal, whistling while Wesley hurried to zip up his bag and tossed his half eaten banana over the ledge. Pete pranced about, instructing them both to swing across at the same time. Duffy understood him, but his head whipped back to Wesley's gut and then to Pete. He shook his head in fear of the added weight. He had the same feeling as before, but now he was stuck with the actuality of it. Wesley jumped up after noticing the guy running through the forest and reached for the rope. Duffy yanked it back as they both clung onto it.

"Get away from me, banana boy," Duffy whispered.

"Come on, we have to go together."

"No, we don't," Duffy insisted. "No . . ."

Wesley struggled to take the rope from him.

"No!" They both leaned over the edge. Wesley pushed and pushed. Duffy leaned farther and winced from the pain of torn flesh on his arm. "Nooooooo . . ."

Unexpectedly, they both toppled over the ledge.

The man running through the trees looked up when he heard the screams. There was a crackle before the crumble. He didn't notice Duffy and Wesley plummeting through the gorge, but he heard the commotion. Pete looked up and realized who it was: the black-suited man. He ran up to the ledge and held out an arm with concern for the two boys as they plunged into the deep, dark abyss. Then he noticed Pete. "What are you doing here Peter?" the man asked, squinting.

Pete stepped back and grabbed a small tree in shock. "Who are you?" His mouth dropped, and he dragged his chin across his chest. He was in a state of lockjaw.

The man held a finger to his lips. "No! Shh . . . keep it down, kid. Listen to me very carefully, OK?"

Pete shook his head as he took a few more steps back. "What's going on? Where's Mr. Fallway?"

"Listen to me," the man said. "I don't care right now. Forget about Mr. Fallway for a moment and listen to me . . ."

More screams echoed from below until the boys found themselves wrapped up in a net at the bottom of the ravine. The limb that had broken from the tree fell straight for them. They crawled separate ways as the limb bounced between them. The net curled inward and tossed them back into the air. They collided with each other as the limb bounced back up, split them apart, and tossed them like a couple of ragdolls. Branches slapped their faces and broke over their bodies.

Several corners of the net had been strung up midway to separate trees. A few sides snapped, and the net curled. The branch rolled to one side and stopped. Duffy and Wesley were tangled in portions of the net. Tree limbs stapled them against it, but they clung on tightly. Part of the net squeezed over Duffy's cheek as he stared at Wesley out of the corner of his eye. The net squished his lips together like a duckbill. His eyes bugged out. "Tubby little bitch-ho!" he shrieked. He pulled his lips out. "Just great," he whined. They both crawled for the limb and grabbed a couple of different branches.

Pete squinted at the man and sighed. "Huh?"

"My name is Ron," the stranger said.

"Where's Mr. Fallway?" Pete asked. "No, listen to me. You were kidnapped, kid. This Watches guy is a villain, and you guys are in a bad place."

"Well, no shit."

"Look, he's after you kids right now."

"Well, aren't you a bright, shiny star."

Pete looked down at his friends, who were clinging to the tree limb. He took a couple more steps back and shook his head. A tear rolled down one cheek. He saw an image of Mr. Fallway lying over a stump, bleeding from his shoulder and his cheeks, but now he was missing. Was he hiding from Watches? Pete turned back to the dark stranger. "You killed those teenagers."

The man nodded. "Yes, I did." His eyes rolled up at Pete, glaring at him. "And they would have killed you!"

"Me?" Pete shook his head, causing his cheeks to wiggle.

"I was out of my mind before, but now I see what's going on. Think about what you're doing here. You kids are in trouble. Serious trouble! You were kidnapped. I'm here to help you."

"Kidnapped?" Pete asked.

"Yes. Watches brought you here. I need to get you kids out of here. I have a car up on the main road."

"What are you talking about? Watches didn't bring us here."

"Then who did?"

"What are you talking about? You're making no sense. Mr. Fallway brought us here."

"Pete, you were kidnapped. So were your friends."

Pete pointed at him. "I don't know who you are, but all this is making absolutely no sense."

"Listen to me, and please don't point at me. It's wrong to point at people, ya know."

Pete was reminded of his statement to Mr. Fallway a few years back when Mr. Fallway pulled him out of his class. During his speech, he introduced the boys to each other and in doing so pointed at Pete as he told his life story. Those were his exact words. "You're Mr. Fallway!" Pete said.

The man in the black suit stepped back. "Excuse me?" The guy, whoever he was, closed his eyes in response to Pete's distrust. But he gave Pete no reason to trust him. He had hidden his identity, so how could Pete trust him? He kept taking cautious steps backwards. Ron opened his eyes and stared at him. He took a step back. One hand slid beneath his tight black shirt. Pete spun around and flipped out the bone-handled knife that Mr. Fallway had given him.

The truth was untold. The mystery was this man who seemed to be moving in and out of their lives. In the beginning, they ran from Mr. Fallway. Then an interest in him led to a new friendship with him. Now this guy claimed he was their guardian angel, but who was the true assailant?

Pete whipped his knife as the man drew a pistol from beneath his coat. The knife slipped through the trigger guard and sliced Ron's index finger. The pistol flew out of his hand, and the knife pinned it to a tree. Ron screamed and grabbed his finger as blood crawled out of a black-threaded opening in his bodysuit and down his joints. It trickled along the black spandex over his palm. He glanced back at his pistol hanging upside down from the knife blade that was stuck in the tree. He looked at Pete, who stood there glaring at him from across the ravine. Then he spun around and ran through the trees like a drunken cheetah.

Ron grasped the knife handle and wiggled the blade. He held onto the pistol with his other hand and screamed over his shoulder. His biceps bulged as he yanked the knife out. He turned and aimed the gun at Pete and screamed. Pete ran around a tree and raced down a hill, disappearing from sight. Dust puffed around the tree, and the guy held the weapons in front of him. He lifted a few of his fingers to read the inscription on the side of the knife: "Ralph P. Fallway."

When he rotated his hand, the knife spun around. He caught it with the blade facing upward. His eyes rolled toward the sky, and he looked beyond the blade in Pete's direction.

Pete rolled onto his side and hid behind a fat tree. He peeked around the side at Ron, who saw him and put his gun away. Still holding out the knife, he scowled. "Kid, I won't hurt you. Just tell me who Mr. Fallway is. I want to help you." He shook the knife in the air and then pulled his trench coat aside and slid the knife under his belt.

Pete turned around slowly and headed back up the trail, crying. He dropped his head against the tree and wrapped his arms over his chest. He felt cold inside. The shivers pushed his blood cells into clots of pulsating questions. He rolled his head back and forth, feeling the bark press against his skull. The soothing massage eased his mind a little, and he fell to the ground in a ball.

Down below, the net finally snapped at both ends and gave way. The limb speared the ground as the boys hung onto it. It tipped backwards, and they flew off and landed in a mudslide. Little did they know it was the runway to the mudslide to hell. The flowing mud took them farther downhill to another course that Mr. Fallway had designed to test their wits.

Pete heard new voices as he ran. He searched the woods but saw no one. Once again, a voice echoed through the trees. It belonged to someone else on his spook chain hierarchy of fear. He heard faint laughter that belonged to the demon himself.

Watches hollered from the riverbank far below. Pete couldn't see him, but he was standing in the dense undergrowth near the base of a cliff. Watches pulled out a grenade and yanked the pin out. "I'll get you, you little shits!"

Pete watched a tiny object fly over the river at Billy and Danny as they swam away. As it whistled through the air, Pete slowed down and grasped a small tree. He noticed the rope bridge swaying beneath Watches' men as they stood up on the cliff. Watches was nowhere in sight.

Billy and Danny were nearing a bend in the river as the grenade looped through the air. It landed in the river farther upstream. A moment later, it exploded.

Pete dropped to his knees and watched as the two brothers were engulfed in a wave of water. Waves hurled into the air and splashed the cliffs far below him.

Billy glanced back and grabbed Danny. He pulled him behind a log jutting up from the river bottom. Water blasted around their bodies. Watches' men watched the weeds for movement on the other side of the splashes to see if the brothers had survived the blast.

Down below, Wesley was lying on his back as the mud flushed him backwards. He saw the blue sky and the explosion of dirt, fire, rocks, and water above. When the grenade exploded, it spit objects off the cliff where they were. He turned to Duffy, who was lying on his stomach in the mudslide.

"Did you see that?"

Duffy lifted his head. The side of it was caked with mud. Mud splashed over his head as his arms flailed at his sides. "I c-c-can't see-a-a d-d-amn th-thing, W-e-s! Th-this issss alllll y-y-yourrr fault!"

They continued down the winding hillside in a river of muddy water. A fish flopped around in front of Duffy, and he waved his hands to push it away. He slapped it, and it flipped into Wesley's nose. "Hey!" Wesley shouted. Another fish hit Duffy's shoulder, and he whipped that one aside as well. It also clobbered Wesley in the head. "Stop throwing fish at me!" Wesley shouted.

Finally, they toppled over a mud fall and splashed into a huge pool of mud. They both fluttered around and tried to reposition themselves. Wesley was behind Duffy, who was facing an uprooted tree that was angled into the pool in front of him. Beyond that was a whole section of the forest. The sunset sprayed ongoing arrays of nothingness through the trees.

"Take the backpack off my shoulders!" Duffy screamed, feeling overwhelmed by its weight.

Wesley reached up, but he could barely lift his arms, never mind reach the bag. "I can't."

"What do you mean? Take my backpack off."

"I can't move!"

"OK, after I get out of this, I'm gonna to kick your ass!"

"Fine, go for it, ya loser."

"Loser, oh yeah?" Duffy tried to turn around to fight him, but he couldn't.

Wesley looked at his arms as they lay flat on top of the mud. They were sinking below the surface. He was stuck. They both were.

"Get off me!" Duffy shouted.

"Oh, you would know if I was on you."

"Yeah, yeah, you're probably right."

"Umm, we're sinking," Wesley said.

"You're sinking?" Duffy asked. He laughed. "Lard ass."

"No, we're really sinking!"

"Cuz you eat a lot."

"No, we're both sinking!"

"I'm not." Duffy spat mud off his lip. His chin was going under. "Oh, damn!"

"Yeah, see?"

Both of them freaked out and swished their bodies back and forth to get out of the mud, but the more they moved, the faster they sank. Duffy was going down a lot faster though. Wesley remained calm. He was farther up out of the mud than Duffy, but he was still sinking slowly.

A branch slapped in front of Duffy's face. His eyes rolled up the branch to see Ron holding it out for him. He was wearing a ski mask, so neither of them could see his face. It was the same man who had attacked Greg, the bully in front of Pete's house, and who had rescued them from the teenagers in the brown Trans-Am. The same guy who had come face to face with Pete just moments ago, bringing his gun to a knife fight. He was here for another rescue.

"Who are you?" Duffy asked as his eyes widened, spitting mud.

"I'm here to save your dumb asses!" the man said.

"Oh yeah? Well, OK!"

"Yeah!" the man whispered.

"Well, I don't trust you."

"Shut up, Duff," Wesley said.

Ron withdrew the branch and held it at his side. His other hand went to his hip, and he stood there with his feet shoulder width apart. "Well, is that a fact?"

Duffy's face was all that was above the surface. "Hey, give that back!"

"No, I think we should take a couple of minutes and talk about this whole *trust* thing a little more in depth."

"I'm going in a little more depth too," Duffy said. "And I'm going under if you don't help me!"

"Yes, I see that," Ron said. "And I said I was here to save your dumb asses. What part of that didn't you understand?"

"All right, I suppose we don't need this confrontation right now," Duffy's lips were about the last thing left at the surface as his head tipped back and mud engulfed his ears. Wesley was still better off; his shoulders were above the surface.

Ron stuck the branch into the mud until it bumped into Duffy's cheek. Duffy's hand emerged slowly and gripped the branch. Ron tugged hand over hand, and Duffy emerged from the mud, panting for air.

Wesley grew restless, suddenly realizing how bad off he was. When Duffy was completely out, they realized the branch wasn't long enough to reach Wesley.

"OK," Ron said, "you guys trust me now, right?"

"Yes," Duffy said, wiping mud off his face.

"Yes, yes!" Wesley screamed; his head was the only thing above the surface.

Ron looked at Duffy. "OK, I trust you. Do you know that? That's why I trust you guys will save me, OK?"

"What?" Duffy asked.

Ron pointed at Wesley. "OK, kid, I want you to climb across me. You got that?"

"Across you?"

"Just climb across me, OK?"

"OK, whatever!"

Duffy watched as Ron took off his ski mask and whipped it behind him. Then he stepped forward.

"Sir," Duffy said. He wasn't sure what Ron meant until he realized what his plan was. Ron belly flopped into the mud with the branch outstretched. Then he hollered for Wesley to grab the branch and pull himself out. He watched the level of the mud as his face slowly went under. Wesley stared into the man's eyes. They were brown, except one eye, which seemed hazy.

"Look, you're drownin' the poor man!" Duffy yelled. "Move your fat ass, Wes!"

"I can't!" Wesley cried.

"Pull yourself up!"

"I really can't! I'm too fat."

"No kiddin'!" Duffy laughed and then crawled over Ron's back and grabbed Wesley's collar. He dragged him with all his might. At that point, Ron took a deep breath, and his entire face went under. Duffy scrambled back to the edge of the mud pool. Wesley followed him as they crawled up Ron's legs. Mud drooled off Wesley's large belly and slopped over Ron's black suit.

Once they both got to safety, they grabbed Ron's legs. At that point, at least two minutes had gone by. Duffy and Wesley dragged him backwards, but Ron's face was still under the mud. He had held his breath for a good three minutes or so by the time they got his body onto the solid ground. Duffy cleared mud from Ron's mouth. He gasped and spit up mud. With his muddy hands, he wiped more mud from his face as the boys helped clear his nostrils of quicksand.

"Thank you, boys," Ron said, gasping. "I knew I could trust you."

"Who are you, mister?" Duffy asked.

He brushed more mud off his neck. "I'm Ronald."

Duffy turned and looked at Wesley. Then he sacked him and pushed him over. "I wouldn't have sunk if it weren't for you."

"OK, you guys, I'm only going to tell you once, shush," Ron said. "We have a problem here, and if this man hears us, we're all dead. Now, where are your friends?"

"Oh no," Duffy said. "We have to go meet them back at our rally point."

"Rally point," Ron said, "are you kids rangers or something?"

"No, we were trained by this really smart man and—"

"Where is he?"

Wesley smiled. "We shot him."

Ron's eyes widened in surprise. "You shot your buddy?"

"No, Billy shot him." Duffy looked at Wesley.

"OK, how many buddies do you have out here?"

"Pete, Danny, and Billy. Danny and Billy are brothers."

Ron nodded. "I know who they are."

"How do you know them?" Duffy asked.

"Never mind that right now. We have bigger fish to fry."

Wesley gave Duffy the evil eye.

"How are we going to find your friends?"

Wesley removed his bag and pulled chunks of mud off the zipper. He unzipped it, and brown bananas fell out. "Aww, man, my bananas."

Duffy laughed. "Oh boy. My friend seems to have lost his bananas."

Wesley glared at Duffy's remark and then pulled out some muddy drawers and whined again. He whipped them onto the ground, and it made a loud squishing sound. The underwear piled onto the ground as mustard-colored mud drained onto the forest floor. Duffy cringed. "Oh, man, don't you ever wash your underwear? That's disgusting."

Wesley found a map and laid it across the ground. He wiped a few pieces of mud off the bottom and unfolded it. He reviewed it for a second and then glanced up at Ron, who looked up at the two boys. "You guys made a rally point?"

"We sure did," Duffy said.

"Where?"

"The other side of that bridge in a field . . ."

"*Where?*" Ron snapped, seemingly startled.

"On the other side of that rotten bridge up the trail. There's a field back there near the main road!"

"Oh no you didn't!"

"Yeah, we did. Why?"

"I think that's another one of your other friend's training courses that he designed."

"You mean Mr. Fallway?" Duffy cried.

Ron smiled. "Oh, it's only a field of simulated land mines! Nothing too extravagant! This bozo friend of yours planted steel canisters the size of Campbell's soup cans throughout that entire field. There's got to be at least a hundred of them out there."

Duffy and Wesley turned and looked at each other.

"Your rally point is a mine field," Ron proclaimed.

CHAPTER 24
UPHAM WOODS

It was dusk. Pete walked slowly through an open field, pushing the tall grass away from his body as he whispered everyone's names. The sun was going down quicker than the boys had sank in the quicksand, and the moonlight shined over the tips of the grassy field. The green grass looked white in the moonlight.

Billy and Danny were approaching the backside of the field. They stopped and noticed Pete in the center. He turned around and saw the two of them standing at the edge. He couldn't quite make them out, but he could tell they were sopping wet from head to toe as they walked slowly toward him.

Suddenly, Pete's body rocketed sideways as flames shot up his arm. His body broke through some branches and grass, which had camouflaged a hole in the ground. Pete fell six feet and hit the bottom of a deep, dark hole, which Mr. Fallway had dug as a trap. Pete rubbed his arm as he lay inside, shocked. Blood ran down his arm. He heard Billy and Danny screaming for him as they ran toward the hole. He grunted and crawled up to peek over the top. The two brothers were headed straight for him.

Pete screamed at them to stop. They were running side by side until one of them set off another simulated land mine. The boys' bodies were blasted apart from each other. They twisted through the air and then disappeared in the tall grass. A rock slammed down next to Pete's hands where he held onto some wet grass. Roots tore from the soil, and the grass gave way, sending Pete back into the pit with a thud.

Fire burned, and portions of the field were sizzled. The boys were dazed and confused over the mini explosions. They needed to get out of there. It felt like they were at war with the earth. Plus, they were drawing too much attention to themselves.

Duffy, Wesley, and Ron ran up the trail together. They had heard the pop of the gunpowder that lit up the field, but they couldn't see the small fires that continued to burn as they drew close to the tree line.

The sound of the land mines carried quite a distance. Back up on the main dirt road, a young couple was walking quietly, staring into the field. They saw mushroom clouds of debris in the distance. The girl was wearing a gray tank top that hugged her washboard stomach and her breasts like cellophane. There were sweat spots between her breasts. She leaned over and threw both of her arms around the young gentleman.

His tank top was gray as well, and his shorts were the same color as hers, both of them tight spandex. They were counselors for a nearby camp out for an early evening jog. They watched the smoke from the fires curl into the night sky. Grass shot up along with dirt clumps as the boys set off land mines left and right.

The counselors remained as silhouettes over the road. Her body showed more shapes and curves as he pulled her near him. The sound of the blasts startled her, and she yelped. The man was just as frightened. She punched his upper arm and warned him that they should seek help. He nodded in agreement. Their clothes ruffled against their bodies as they continued to run with a much swifter pace than before.

"Oh, man, I did not like that one bit," he said over his shoulder.

"Poachers ya think?" she replied in her soft voice.

"I have no clue what that was," he said, "but I doubt they were poachers."

They turned onto another dirt road, which was deeply rutted. Two wooden beams adjoined another wooden beam at the top that crossed the width of the road, and an oblong wooden sign hung from it. The edges of the sign had been cut by a bandsaw. It appeared to be made of old barn wood—rustic.

A gust of wind blew in from the main road, and the sign swayed back and forth. Lights were strapped to the poles, angling up at the sign. It swayed in and out of the light. When it tilted backwards, it grew dark. When it swung forward, it lit up again. The chains creaked as the sign pulled the links against each other through metal D-rings at the ends of the steel rods. It crept forward into the light, revealing the words "Upham Woods."

Trees on either side of the road rustled from another mild gust. It wasn't sprinkling anymore. The trail became brighter and more open as empty fields surrounded the runners on either side. Four-foot-tall light posts stood about twenty-five yards apart from each other on the left. The runners' bodies faded in and out as they ran past them.

They ran through a parking lot and past some picnic tables. To their left a field of hay bales was lined up uniformly for archery practice. Two trails wound around a few buildings, rejoined, and led down to a beach. Recreational activities were set up, such as volleyball, horseshoe posts, canoes, and more. A few parking lots sat deserted beyond some basketball courts off to the left just after the archery field. Cliffs towered over the parking lots. Cabins were located along the ridge at the top. On the right were baseball diamonds, a storage shack, and another stretch of land.

The joggers ran around a flowerbed that surrounded a flagpole that stood tall and proud as lights shined at it from the flowerbeds. The lights made the colors shine as the American flag snapped in the silent sky. Similar snaps came from a Wisconsin flag below it. A third flag wiggled below that. It was an Upham Woods flag. It was white and pictured a couple of pine trees, a campfire, and a tent.

A circular drive surrounded the flowerbed. Off to their right was a log cabin. It was the camp clinic, where nurses treated injured or sick campers. Up ahead was the main office, where Wesley's grandfather worked. They jogged up the steps, leaped across the wooden deck, and the door squeaked as the guy threw it open. They both ran inside.

A light hung in the foyer; a beautiful chandelier with crystal lights. Their pupils adjusted, and they tried to catch their breath as they leaned on their knees for support. On their tank tops was a sketch of a family trying to hold onto their tent as the wind attempted to sweep it away from them. The treacherous winds were blowing the fire sideways in the fireplace. Smoke rose from the pit of charred logs, creating the words "A CAMPING RESORT FOR ANYONE!" "UPHAM" was written above the sketch, and "WOODS" was written beneath it. On a pocket in the upper-left corner, it stated: "CAMP COUNSELOR."

An elderly man walked down the stairway in the hall and glanced up from a book in which his nose had been buried: *WAV File*. He noticed them standing in the foyer. Both of them were worn out from running. The guy was sweating around his collar and down the middle of his back. The lady had sweat rings outlining her perky breasts as each of them bounced from her breathing.

"Greg, Samantha, what's the matter?" the old man asked. "Looks like you've seen a ghost."

"We heard gunshots and saw explosions again, sir," Greg said.

"Did you just come from the recreational hall?" the old man asked as he headed to his office. The two counselors followed.

"Well, sir, we cleaned the rec hall and got caught up with all the staff duties, so we took a light jog together."

"Where?" he asked sarcastically. "To Madison and back?"

Samantha smiled. Greg looked at her and shook his head.

The old man sighed and sat in a chair behind a desk. On the edge of his desk was a wooden block that read: "Gerry Fifer." "See, I thought you guys were doing a little hanky-panky again down at the boathouse. I don't know about you two. This is almost becoming a habit. I don't pay you to play hanky-panky."

"We took a break, sir. Marsha and Scott took over for us," Samantha replied.

"So that's sex sweat. Is that what you're dripping on my office floor? Sex sweat? Look at that, puddles of sex on my floor."

"No sex this time, sir," Greg said. "But we need to contact the authorities."

"Probably hunters or poachers," Mr. Fifer grunted. "Leave 'em alone."

"I know the difference between pellet guns and shotguns," Greg said. "But do you know the difference between a rifle and maybe a fully automatic or a nine-millimeter pistol?"

"Yes, sir," Samantha said. "It was a continuous burst of gunfire."

The room was dimly lit. Mr. Fifer's desk sat in a corner. Floor-to-ceiling windows surrounded it on each wall. It had a corner window, an expensive bay window made for joining corner walls. The view was gorgeous during the day. A long stretch of grass led down to the beach. The yard was packed with grills and picnic tables. Greg walked farther inside the office. Sam stood in the doorway.

Near the doorway, a lamp rested on a table off to the right. A leather couch sat against the wall straight ahead from the doorway. That lamp was on its highest setting, but it still wasn't very bright. Samantha knew the couch was brown, but it looked black in the lighting. A florescent desk lamp was on Mr. Fifer's desk. He hit a little orange button on its base, and his desk lit up. The florescent tube reflected in the glass corner window behind him. Watches' face seemed to loom outside the pane.

"This issue has nothing to do with me," he said as he sat back in his chair. The cushioning squeaked. "A few people are camping out there just outside of my property, and they choose to do a little target practice late at night. So what? I'm tellin' ya, leave 'em alone! If they aren't bothering you, why bother them? They certainly aren't bothering me."

"We have a few families up at our cabins on the north ridge," Greg said. "Those sites are close to the main road. There are innocent lives at stake here, and you're sittin' on yer ass without concern reading some smut novel, nonetheless. I'm telling ya, as a camp counselor, it's my job to make sure the camp is secure and safe for those who wish to be here. People are shooting out there." He made a gun with his fingers. "Bang, bang, bang!"

"Greg, I think you need some sleep. Too much sex and little sleep can really get to a man," Mr. Fifer said. "You need a vacation, son. You're pretending to shoot me now!"

"No, I'm not pretending!" Greg smiled and threw up one arm. A pistol slid into his hand. "I'm just practicing!" He lowered his arm, so he was aiming right at the old man.

Mr. Fifer put down his book and sighed. "Greg?" Then he looked at Samantha. "Samantha?"

"I'm sorry, Gerry," Greg said.

"Greg!" Samantha shrieked and joined Greg standing at the center of the office. "I thought we were doing this until midnight."

"You can't pay either of us more than what we were offered."

Mr. Fifer hit a red button on the underside of his desk and pulled a shotgun up to his shoulder as he stood up. "You little bastard! I knew I couldn't trust you two." Greg yanked on the trigger. Sparks flew past Mr. Fifer's cheeks as the round hit the shotgun's barrel. He flew backwards out the corner window.

Greg did not see him push the little red button, however. That button was a direct link to the local sheriff's office, a panic alarm. The shotgun mounted to the underside of the desk was something Mr. Fifer had added within the last year for self-defense. It saved his life when the bullet grazed the barrel. Greg didn't see Mr. Fifer land on a lower deck and crawl away.

Samantha sighed. "Phew, that wasn't so bad."

Greg nodded. "No, of course not. I told ya I'd end it quickly."

She walked across the office and sat down on the leather couch. Greg placed his weapon on the desk and then sat in Mr. Fifer's chair and opened a cigar box on the desk. "Oh, cool," he said, smiling. "I could get used to this."

"What?"

He tilted the box toward her. "Want one?"

She snapped her tongue. "No, thank you." She picked up a magazine from the end table and flipped through it. Greg lit up a stogy and spun the chair around in circles. She looked over at him. "Now what?"

He spun back to face her. "Now we wait."

"I don't want to wait around here. This place gives me the creeps. Did you know his wife died in some restaurant up north? And that old man sees her spirit?."

"Look, we did what we had to do, but it's not over. We have to wait for our boss."

"Why is there always a boss?" She shook her head. "I don't get it."

"It's life, Sam, and unless you have a few years of schooling under your belt and some knowledge, you will always be working for the man."

"Shut up."

"Wow, I could take over this camp." He spun around in the chair and kicked his feet up on the wall. The chair reclined, and he placed his hands behind his head.

"No you won't," a voice said, drifting in from the doorway.

Greg spun around and slammed his hand over his weapon when he saw Mr. Fifer standing in the doorway. Samantha threw down the magazine and screamed. She glanced at Greg for guidance. He was lifting the weapon off the desk, but Mr. Fifer yanked the trigger on the shotgun. Greg's guts blew inward, and the chair rolled backwards. Greg aimed the gun at him but dropped it. It bounced across the desk and bumped into a plastic file rack. The rack fell off the desk along with the gun, which flipped toward the couch. Papers fluttered across the floor. Greg's head fell against the cushioning on the back of the chair. His arms fell to his sides, and the chair rolled into the wall along the desk.

Gerry moved toward the desk maintaining his aim at Greg. "You screwed up trying to kill me." Mr. Fifer said, then looked at Samantha. She stopped screaming and began whimpering. His eyes lit up as he snarled. "I'm a Native American. How do ya like them apples, sweetheart?"

She screamed again.

"Pipe down, Chiquita." He smiled. "I couldn't shoot a woman." He briefly lowered the shotgun.

She calmed down to a pant. Her breasts rose with her gasps. Feeling relieved at his words, she slid Greg's pistol toward the couch with her foot.

"But you ain't a woman . . ."

She smirked until she understood what he had said. As he raised the shotgun to his shoulder, she reached for the pistol. The trigger went back like she went back. She landed on the couch after bouncing off the wall. She broke the picture frame of an overblown aerial shot of the campground. A Billy Bass mounted to the wall must have caught some shrapnel because it began to sing "Take Me to the River."

He lowered the shotgun and hollered at her even though she lay dead on the sofa. "That's what you wanted to do, right? Take over my camp? Bust my beautiful picture, upset my Billy Bass." He turned to face his desk and the broken window. "OK, I need some tequila, man!"

CHAPTER 25
RONALD

Back in the simulated minefield, the boys were crawling through the grass, whispering to each other. They were laying down some guidelines on how they planned to backtrack through the field, so they could get safely back to the forest. But they needed to wait for the others. They couldn't leave them behind, and they didn't want them to encounter more land mines.

A hard, white chunk nailed Billy's arm. Billy groaned. "Ouch."

Danny felt another chunk strike his leg. He glanced up at his brother, and they both looked back at Pete. "Run!" he hollered and then bolted.

Suddenly, hundreds of ice chunks fell from the sky. It was hailing. The hail was thick, and the boys dropped to the ground and covered their heads. The hail nailed the earth with such force it actually tripped the land mines all around them. Billy lifted his head and noticed Pete trying to catch up to them. Hail was pelting his arms, back, head, legs, and neck as he pulled himself with his elbows, keeping his head covered with his hands interlocked over it.

Billy and Danny yelled for him to crawl faster. Pete looked up and could barely open his eyes to see them. Hail smashed over the bridge of his nose, and he dropped his head. Blood ran down his cheeks due to the hail slicing him. A mine discharged between him and the other boys. Flames whirled over his back. He lit up, and then Billy couldn't see him anymore. Hail bounced off his forehead as more mines went off in the distance.

The hail ripped small limbs off trees, sending leaves fluttering through the air. Billy crawled out toward Pete. All he could do was use dead reckoning to find him. Billy gripped the dirt and pulled his body through the hailstorm.

When he reached out for another grasp of the ground, a slimy pile of dirt crawled up his arm. As he pulled himself up onto his knees, he looked down and realized his arm was sinking through a pile of worms.

However, the worms were not normal worms. They were crawling up his clothes. They had small hands and little fingers. They were more of those human-caterpillars. He brushed them off, but they continued to bunch up in large quantities, and they overwhelmed him—almost suffocated him. When he looked over, he noticed two prongs sticking up from the ground. It was another simulated mine. He couldn't breathe. They were crawling around his throat and his face.

He rolled over and slammed his arm over the prongs. The mine popped up and discharged flames across his stomach. The human-caterpillars sizzled and fried as the flames burned them. Billy rolled back onto his other side and screamed from the pain of the explosion and the burning remains across his body. His arms were now free, but the hail was tackling him as he tried to stand up. He stomped on a few piles of caterpillars and brushed off the dead ones that he had toasted. The ice balls continued to rain down on them.

Danny sat in a rut covering his head with his backpack, watching his brother through the ice storm. Before he knew it, Billy was next to Pete, and he toppled over him. Danny screamed as he watched Billy fall over but then ducked from the hail.

Billy sat up and noticed his limp body piled in the green grass. Ice slit his cheeks as the hail whipped into him. Billy crawled over Pete's back and covered him to protect him. He glanced up, and those caterpillars were dashing through the mud and crawling up Pete's legs. Billy dragged him back toward the edge of the field where Danny was waiting for them.

Suddenly, Pete came to and jolted as he noticed the human figures crawling up his legs and biting him. The bites were like pinches, and he screamed. Billy fell over, and Pete lay there screaming. Some hail pushed these caterpillar things off him, yet more kept coming. Billy hollered his name as Pete slapped at his legs and arms.

More mines went off in the distance, and Billy turned and saw another set of prongs sticking up from the ground. He stepped forward and kicked a long sharp rock with his foot.

He dropped to his hands and knees and grabbed the rock. Pete screamed louder. With the rock, he dug around the prongs, scraping the dirt away from the canister. The mines were designed to shape their charge. The prongs were set in temperate plates. As soon as the prongs contacted the transmitter beneath the plate, the explosive would force the plate off with fire and heat. The canisters were strong enough to withstand the force. Stepping on the prongs wasn't the issue; stepping off of them was. All they had to worry about was the plate flying off or a little burn from the flames. The residue burned away as quickly as the contact moved from the transmitter inside. *How many of these things are out there?* Billy wondered.

He yanked the canister from the ground and held it over Pete's head. Pete looked up at him, and his eyes bugged out while caterpillars jumped up his stomach and arms. "Turn your head!" Billy hollered. Pete shifted his head in the opposite direction, and Billy slapped the prongs with the rock and grabbed the canister with both hands. Flames fanned out over Pete for a few seconds. Billy swished the canister back and forth until the flames died down. He tossed the can into the field and dragged Pete once again. The caterpillars were charred; some fell off him as he was being dragged. Pete flicked off the live ones.

As Danny crawled out of the hole, the hailstorm settled. No more flames shot into the night sky, and everything seemed to calm down.

A man ran up to the edge of the forest with Duffy and Wesley. It was Ron. Billy and Danny looked up at Pete. They both turned around as they lay on the ground. Billy stood up, lifted his shirt, and pulled out a pistol. He aimed it at Ron, who took a step back, his eyes wide.

Billy fired. Ron lunged through the air. Branches slashed his arms and his face. He broke through thick undergrowth and cowered next to a tree. He stood up slowly behind the tree. "Damn it, Billy, will ya just hear me out?"

Pete crawled back into the rut and peeked over the edge. Billy paced toward the man. "Who are you, mister?" Billy fired his last bullet. Instead of hitting his target, he hit a tree limb behind Ron. It swayed down, broken.

Ron stepped out from behind the tree. "My name is Ron."

"And you're who?"

"Billy, face it, you and your friends are in a predicament here. I'm here now, so you must listen to me very carefully."

"Yeah," Billy held his arms up sarcastically. "A predicament! The last time someone told us to listen to him very carefully, he kidnapped us."

Pete jumped out of the hole. "Don't believe him, Billy. He's a fake. He told me that Watches kidnapped us."

Ron jerked his head to the side and looked beyond Billy toward Pete. "That's right, Pete."

"You tried to kill me!" Pete shrieked. Billy glanced at Pete as the new evidence came to light.

"Pete, you scared me. You pulled a knife on me. What was I supposed to think? I didn't know who you were. And how the hell did you do that thing with the knife so that my gun was hanging from the tree like that? That was awesome."

Billy lowered his gun, realizing he had no more bullets. He squinted and wondered what they were discussing.

"Never mind," Ron said to Pete. "There are some things you kids must know, and that Mr. Fallway character may be one of those things you need to know about."

"Just tell us!" Pete said.

"Hey, we can't hang around here much longer. Listen to me: I have a tent set up in the woods. Let's go back and eat, huh? I know you're hungry. I guarantee you're all hungry right now. I have fresh northern pike that I caught this morning. Let's batter those babies up, cook 'em, and eat 'em. What do ya say? Huh? Come on, fellas."

It started sprinkling again. Pete looked up and blinked as some drops hit his eyelids. He shook his head. All along, he had believed in Mr. Fallway. Earlier when Billy shot him, he didn't understand the power of Billy's madness. But now he understood Billy's lack of trust from all the lies. Maybe this was someone they could finally trust: Ron, the black-suited man. What did he have to hide? Billy tucked the gun in his pants and nodded at him.

"OK, Billy." Ron smiled and pulled out what appeared to be binoculars from a satchel strapped to his back beneath his backpack. "Walk straight at me right through the center of the field." They were night-vision goggles, and he used them to find land mines in their path.

They trudged toward him with their heads down searching for prongs hidden beneath the grass. He encouraged them by letting them know where to walk each step of the way. "Go straight, straight . . . OK! Billy stop, go right a little. That's good, now straight in."

Finally, they cleared the minefield. Then they followed Ron through the forest. It was a long walk, and no one talked. They feared for their lives. They thought if they were quiet, it would help keep them safe.

Ron had a red lens over his flashlight. The flashlight was attached to his belt and facing the ground. The Armybrats followed the red light as it bounced around.

Billy was right behind Ron. He wanted to be closer to the mystery man rather than putting any of the other Armybrats' lives in danger. A couple of them felt the muscles tightening in their heels as they pressed on through the dreary night. But at least they were making some good distance. However, the whereabouts of Watches or any of his men was unknown. The camp wasn't too far up the main road from the minefield that Mr. Fallway had built. Perhaps Watches' men were already there.

Ron looked back. "OK, careful, stay right behind me. I have trip flares up ahead and concertina wires around the campsite, so don't go running off in the middle of the night, or you could get chopped in two."

He rested his flashlight on a picnic table and lit a grill. The Armybrats checked out the army tent that was resting between a few trees on flatter ground. A stove inside was burning. Billy and Danny wandered inside to dry off. They were cold from the river, rain, and hail, and they were muddy from crawling through the field. Grass hung from the tongues of Billy's shoes, and he sat on a cot to pick it out.

One cot had a sleeping bag and a pillow. The sound of sleep was music to their ears, and the smell of food was even better. Two poles at the center held up the tent. A flap at the rear of the tent whipped in a slight breeze. In one corner, a cardboard box was full of munchies. In another was the stove. Danny and Billy grabbed a bag of potato chips. The rest of the Armybrats attacked the box for more munchies. There were more cots in a plastic trunk and more sleeping bags in another. Billy rummaged through them with a curious mind.

Duffy lay on the picnic table with a stick between his teeth. Ron approached as Wesley pinned Duffy to the table. Ron held a glowing knife blade from the firepit. He glanced into Duffy's eyes, which widened when he saw the glowing blade in his pupils. Ron opened Duffy's shirt around the bullet wound.

"I ain't gonna lie," Ron whispered. "This will hurt."

Duffy bit down on the stick. Ron dug the blade into the wound. Duffy closed his eyes and bit harder. He snapped the twig just as Ron flipped a bullet from his arm into a pan. Ron twirled the pan around to get a good look at the piece of lead lying in swirls of Duffy's blood and flesh.

Wesley noticed Duffy was unconscious. "Is he gonna be alright?"

"He'll be fine," Ron assured him. "Wrap him up with that fresh linen there."

Wesley grabbed the white cloth from the picnic table and wrapped Duffy's arm with it. The other boys came out and helped carry Duffy into the tent and set him on a cot.

Ron opened a cooler and pulled out a few fish filets. The rest of the Armybrats sat on the table as he cooked the fish. They gobbled the food down when it was ready. Wesley was so hungry he even bit his lip. For the remainder of the night, he sucked on a napkin to stop the bleeding. Eventually, Duffy joined them. Danny walked into the tent, and Billy threw his napkin down and followed his brother.

"I just caught these fish this morning before you guys showed up," Ron said. "Billy, Danny, can you hear me from inside there?"

Billy and Danny were holding their hands over the stove and looked out the partially open tent flap. "Yes," they replied as steam billowed from their wet fingers.

"I want you to trust me. I'm sorry about everything thus far. I wasn't sure how to gain your trust. You guys believe me, right? Pete, you believe me, don't you?"

Pete shook his head. He glanced at Wesley who readjusted the napkin over his bottom lip. "I still don't know you." He looked down and whispered. "Ronald McDonald."

"Pete, do you know what?"

He looked up at him. "What?"

"My mom is in the hospital in Madison. She's in a coma there."

Pete's eyes lit up. "So is my mom!"

Ron sighed and nodded. "Yes. My mom's name is Dukes."

"OK, who are you again?" Pete asked.

Billy overheard his question and stood up from the cot. Both brothers exited the tent to join the others at the picnic table.

"I have a little problem, fellas," Ron explained.

"How do you know our names?" Billy asked.

Ron scratched his head. "I'll tell ya what, I only knew your name and Danny's name and Pete's name." He pointed at Duffy and Wesley. "I did not know your names until tonight!"

"OK, there's something you're still not telling us," Billy said, "and we'd like to know what it is, sir."

Ron finished chewing on a granola bar and swallowed. "Billy, are any of us who we say we are? We live to get somewhere in life, but the question is . . . *are we getting anywhere?* I want to get somewhere. And yes, I want to help you understand. But I'm going to ask you a question first before I answer that."

Billy nodded. "OK."

Ron drank some soda and leaned forward, causing the board on the seat of the picnic table to creak. "Do you know who I am?" he asked.

Billy shook his head. "No. Well, you look familiar, but I don't recognize you, so I guess not."

"Look at my suit," he said.

Billy glanced down at his uniform. It was tight spandex and black. Ron held a ski mask over the table. Billy jumped back and stared at the mask. Then he glanced at him. "I know you."

"I knew you would."

"You saved us from those kids out on the road. You pushed the Trans-Am into the ravine."

Ron smiled and nodded. He turned toward Pete. "And you know me too?"

Pete's eyes widened as he swallowed some fish. "I do?"

"Yeah, ya do. I saved your life."

"You did?"

"Yes, you were attacked by a kid on the school bus. Do you remember that?"

"Yes. Beaner."

"Yes. You handled him very well on that school bus, by the way. But then you got off, and he came after you. You were sitting in the road, helpless, almost like you couldn't move."

Pete's eyes widened even more. Then he sighed. "Yeah, I couldn't move because Watches had me. He was holding me there." Pete looked like he was in a daze.

Billy wrapped his arm around him. "Pete, you OK?"

He wiped a tear from his cheek and nodded. "Yeah, I'm fine."

Ron stood up and threw his can of soda into the firepit. A couple of charred logs turned over, and sparks blasted through the air. They wound through the branches and leaves on the trees above.

"Damn it!" Billy stood up from the table. The other boys perked up as Billy looked at the firepit. Soda poured out of the can and sizzled against the hot coals. He held the pistol up and aimed it at Ron.

Ron didn't even turn to look at him. "There's no need for that, Billy. You can holster that weapon because I'm not a threat to you kids." Billy didn't put it away. He was concerned about how Ron knew he was aiming it at him since he was standing by the fire and hadn't turned around. "He has you boys right where he wants you," Ron said. "Scared and helpless. He's put so much fear into you kids." He turned around. There were tears on his face. The firelight shined on his wet skin. "You have every right to be scared, and damn him for doing that to you."

Ron stirred the campfire with a stick. He called them over to sit around it. Then he broke out a bag of marshmallows. Their pants were warmed up as the fire roared. Marshmallows roasted within the flames as they held them out on the ends of whatever branches they could find. After a good roast, it was a swap festival for whoever wanted the least crispy or the crispiest puffball. Everyone had a favorite. Wesley was a nut for extra crispy. Duffy was right up there for the blackened ones as well, as was Danny. Ron didn't have a single marshmallow. But he brought out the box of graham crackers and chocolate bars.

He stood up and walked in circles around the firepit. "What I'm about to tell you might scare you a little, but I don't want you to be scared. I want you to trust me; that's all. That's why I'm here."

The boys agreed. Wesley seemed to be a bit sleepy, as was Pete.

"I lost my dad a few years back around the same time I lost my mom to a coma. I'm searching for this villain who goes by the name of Watches. I believe he's after your father, Billy and Danny. That's why I know you. I've been following this guy most of my life. I know where he's been and what he's been up to. And I promised myself that I would find this man. He's a drunken bastard and deserves nothing out of life. And I'm going to kill him."

"Well, maybe he needs some psychological help," Pete said. "My father's a psychologist."

Ron turned toward Pete. "I know that. But this man deserves no help from anyone. And the last thing he said to Billy and Danny's father was that someday he would come back, and he better hope and pray he wasn't around on his delivery day. And if he ever had kids, he better hope and pray he knew where they are at all times."

Billy and Danny looked at each other. They had deceived their father. He was in Washington and believed they were at Duffy's house for a sleepover. Even though love was strong in the family, trust was an issue. However, Mark was so involved with his work that his work had started to follow him around. Stanley Markesan was out to get him. And Mr. Fallway, the investigator from the destruction of the Emersons' old home in Granite View, had taken their father's place by becoming a parent to them. They had spent more time with him than they had with their own father. When Mr. Fallway disappeared, they lost that trust. Now a new tempter was taunting them, and identity of the black-suited man had been revealed.

Billy loved his dad. He couldn't believe he had let this drag out this long. Though he was strong, he had not been thinking rationally. None of this would have been happening if he had told his father the truth. But he bought into the subliminal messages Mr. Fallway had preached about not telling their parents a thing.

Unfortunately, their parents had no idea their boys were in the middle of a forest over ninety miles away from home with a complete stranger trying to solve a mystery on their own. Billy couldn't trust Mr. Fallway. He had held on for so long, keeping the secret and not intervening with what the other Armybrats were doing. The other boys may have been buying Ron's story, but Billy merely sat there and soaked up all his information. He would listen to whatever anyone had to say, but unless it came straight from someone he could trust, he wouldn't accept it. And if the story involved Watches, he knew he couldn't trust the guy.

Billy looked back toward the tent as Ron told the same story Mr. Fallway had told about the woman getting smashed by the refrigerator. Her son was left home alone, and when his parents came home early from a bar that morning, his father, Watches, smashed his mother with the fridge. Mr. Fallway had told the same story word for word, but Ron's story was in first person, whereas Mr. Fallway's story was in third person. He hadn't been there, but maybe he had been an investigator at the scene.

Billy looked inside the tent at the two trunks that he had dug through earlier. He couldn't help but think how there were enough sleeping bags for an entire army. He looked back at Ron. Things seemed blurry. Actually, his vision was going in and out. Two other boys were already sleeping.

Billy's mind had led him to believe that Ron was Mr. Fallway, even though Ron had dark hair and Mr. Fallway had light-brown hair. Ron had arrived shortly after Mr. Fallway. If Ron removed his black suit, would his shoulder have a bullet in it? Billy decided not to say anything about it.

"What's going to happen, Ron?" he asked.

Ron, who was fascinated by his own story and seemed startled by the interruption, turned to face Billy. "What do you mean?"

"We came up here with a man named Ralph P. Fallway."

"I don't know him."

"I know that. But he seems to be missing, and thankfully, you came along to feed us and, I'm hoping, shelter us tonight. I find it very interesting that you have enough sleeping bags here for all of us. So, what are we going to do while we sit in the middle of what appears to be a death trap? We can't stay here."

"Billy, you're right. Who is Mr. Fallway?"

"He's an investigator who's after the same man you are, sir."

"Oh really?" Ron's eyes lit up. "Does he want to kill him?" The way he dipped his head and the sparkle in one of his eyes sent chills down Billy's spine.

"No, sir," Billy said. "He wants to put him in a mental ward."

"That's a joke." Ron shook his head and tossed a marshmallow into the hot coals. It burned and oozed down a black log. "We can't let that happen. Watches is the devil. He doesn't deserve help. He deserves to die! No offense to your father's line of work, Pete, but he's a nutcase, and no one in the world could help him." He turned to Billy and Danny. "Your dad saved me once. I was only a little boy then."

Billy's eyebrows shot up in surprise. "My dad saved you?"

"Yes!"

Billy looked over at Pete, who snored and choked, then turned back to Ron. "My father could handle Watches."

"No, no he could not."

"Yes he could."

The boys sat quietly around the fire. It had turned out to be a long day. Their minds had consumed a lot of information, and now Ron was filling them with more. He cut down Mr. Fallway's integrity and Pete's father's loyalty to his career just like Mr. Fallway had cut down Danny's father for being a cop. Mr. Fallway said he was the only man who could stop Watches, and no cop in the world was capable of doing so. He talked their ears off all night about Watches. To the Armybrats, it was a comfort to finally rest. They fulfilled the daily tasks with minimal bruises and scars, but the training seemed to be a hoax thus far. Mr. Fallway had hoped to train the Armybrats, but it ended before it began.

* * *

Later that night, Billy sat near the rear of the tent with both pistols in his hands. He was on guard. Ron had more .22 LR rounds and 9 mm rounds for the weapons, and he reloaded them. They were going to take turns throughout the night pulling shifts for guard duty, so everyone could sleep peacefully. But if Watches truly was the devil, how could any trip flare, any weapon, or any person help them? How could the boys defend themselves?

Billy was thinking about the wound on Mr. Fallway's shoulder. He glanced over at Ron through the tent window. He looked away and stared off into the trees. Then he thought about Ron's story about pulling Duffy and Wesley out of quicksand. If he wanted them dead, he could have easily killed them by now. If he didn't want them to survive, why had he fed them? Mr. Fallway had taught them combat skills and gave them hope, so why couldn't they trust this man?

Billy couldn't trust him because of the danger he had placed them in. He understood what Mr. Fallway was trying to do. He wanted to use them like a worm on a hook, dangle them before the enemy . . . *Watches*. So, Billy had shot him. But had the test really begun?

CHAPTER 26
NIGHTMARES AND TRAINING

Either fog had rolled in or Billy wasn't feeling well. Perhaps no one was feeling well. Billy's eyelids snapped open, and the firelight from the stove lit up his cheeks. The orange glow was dim, but his eyes were bright white. The light flickered in his eyes. His sleeping bag curled away from him. He was fully clothed. He even had shoes on. He slipped between the cots and peeked out the tent window. Duffy and Wesley were standing along the picnic table with pistols in their hands. They were on guard watch for the next hour after relieving Ron. Throughout the night, they each took a turn at guard duty.

Duffy hit Wesley. "Man, why did you make me fall today? You fat bastard."

"Why did you throw fish at me?"

"Because you made us fall."

Ron was the closest to the tent's front entrance. Billy brushed by the stove and kept low as he paced toward his bunk. He stopped at the foot of Danny's bunk and looked at his shadow, crouching to make himself inconspicuous. He went around his bunk and waddled up next to Ron's bunk. Then he stood up and leaned over him.

Ron was as still as a rock. The only thing that moved was a down feather protruding from the end of the sleeping bag as he exhaled. Billy pulled the sleeping bag away from Ron's shoulder. His eyes remained shut, and his mouth was closed. He wasn't snoring. Billy was looking for a wound on Ron's shoulder, underneath the blanket. He appeared to be shirtless.

Suddenly, Ron's hand shot up and clamped over Billy's wrist. His other hand held a claw-hook knife to Billy's neck. The curve of the blade dug into his neck. Ron rolled onto his stomach, then released Billy's wrist and wrapped his arm around his gut. As he lifted him up, Billy didn't make a sound.

"Billy," Ron said, cackling wickedly.

He stepped out of his sleeping bag and dragged Billy out of the tent. He had a black long-sleeved shirt on. It was unbuttoned and flapping at his sides. He was also wearing blue jeans. He held Billy up with the knife to his neck.

Duffy and Wesley were missing, no longer sitting on the picnic table. They were walking down a trail in the dark woods. A blue fifty-five-gallon barrel rested against a tree. They heard a mumble for help, but they weren't sure where it came from until they stumbled upon the blue barrel. The barrel bounced back and forth and slammed against a tree. Finally, it fell over, and the lid popped off. Wesley jumped against Duffy, and they hid behind a fat tree.

Duffy held onto both pistols as Wesley pointed the red-lens flashlight at the barrel. A body lunged out of the top. Wesley dropped the flashlight and fell over Duffy with a scream. Duffy attempted to push him off, but Wesley had to roll off. Duffy kicked him as he stood up against the tree holding the pistols around it. Wesley grabbed the flashlight while lying on the ground and held it up. The light shined over the barrel—and the body.

The man was alive but tied up and gagged. He was wearing a ski mask which was partly up his face hung up on the bridge of his nose. His hands were tied to his ankles. He was mumbling and whining. Duffy looked at Wesley. Wesley was shaking, causing the red light to bounce all over the place. Duffy kicked him in the side and told him to hold still and shine the light at the guy's face.

They moved in on him. His head was lying on the dirt. The guy noticed the red light through his mask, but he remained calm. He was wearing an all-black suit. They were curious since Ron had worn the same sort of suit earlier.

Back in the tent, Ron lowered the knife from Billy's neck. Billy looked up at his shoulder. The campfire flickered, the flames curving over a log as a gust of wind blew through. The flames illuminated Ron's hairy chest. No bullet hole. His shoulder was perfectly fine. Billy looked at Ron's face in confusion.

"What's wrong, Billy?"

"Oh nothin'. I thought maybe you had a shoulder wound. Where's Duffy and Wesley? They're supposed to be watching the camp."

"I don't know." Ron smiled and rotated his shoulder as if it were sore. He had no idea what Billy was talking about. Billy stared at his shoulder.

Duffy and Wesley approached the black-suited man. Wesley knelt down and grabbed the elastic material along his neck to remove the mask. He slipped it up over his forehead. As soon as he removed it, the guy hopped forward and growled at them. They both flew backwards. Wesley dropped the flashlight and shrieked. Duffy fell onto his butt, his hands still aimed toward the body.

In the tent, Ron grabbed Billy. "What was that?"

"I'm not sure."

Ron glared at him. He leaned forward, and his left shoulder lit up. Billy smiled and shook his head. Ron turned his head a little and smiled. He didn't even know which shoulder Billy had shot him in. Ron's shoulder had a bullet hole in it. His shoulder was torn, but no more blood seeped from his wound. He stood up straight and grabbed Billy's neck. Billy's eyes were wide. And he couldn't help but wonder what was going on. He gagged. "Mr. Fallway?"

Duffy and Wesley looked down at the flashlight. It lay next to the stranger's head, the red light shining into his face. He squinted and blinked. He was gagged, a rag wadded up in his mouth. Duffy and Wesley's jaws dropped. It was Ron. Duffy slid a Leatherman tool out of a holster around his waist and cut the ropes away from Ron's wrists and ankles as Wesley pulled the gag out of his mouth.

"The others are in trouble!" Ron yelled as soon as his mouth was free. "We have to hurry."

"What happened?" Duffy asked. "We thought you were sleeping."

Ron stood up and ran down the trail. Wesley looked in the barrel and wondered how Ron had fit inside. He sighed. "No way. Man, if I was in there, I'd puke all over myself."

"You'd start eating yourself, right?" Duffy joked.

Wesley nodded, still staring at the barrel. "Probably . . ."

Duffy looked down the trail as Ron booked it toward the campsite. Ron looked back at the boys. "Hurry!" he shouted. They raced after him.

When they reached the camp, they were confused. Mr. Fallway was strangling Billy near the picnic table.

Billy stood up from the picnic table, and a lantern tipped over and broke open. The heat mantles burned dimly and then ignited the fuel, sending flames whirling over the picnic table. Mr. Fallway turned toward Duffy and Wesley. A soda can rolled off the picnic table. Coke dribbled out of the top and seeped into the dirt. Billy stood still as if he had pooped his pants. Mr. Fallway knew what Billy had seen. He knew what he was up against. Ron stood there in confusion. Instead of one stranger, now there were two.

"You know what hurts worse?" Ron asked the imposter Mr. Fallway.

The fiend turned slowly to face Ron. Ron ran at him and pushed him backwards. Their bodies smashed over the picnic table. It broke apart, and boards bounced across the ground. All that was left was the frame. The Armybrats were confused as they kept track of the wrestling in the dark.

Ron and Mr. Fallway stood up while strangling each other. A slight push separated them briefly. Ron charged at him once again. Mr. Fallway backed away. He took Ron on by surprise as he flew over top of him. Their bodies fluttered over top of the tent.

Suddenly, Billy and the rest of the Armybrats were lying in the cots being smothered by the tent. Billy watched the tent collapse over top of him. He sat up and screamed. Everyone else woke up.

He had dreamed the whole story about Ron being Mr. Fallway. The tent was still intact, and the campfire was still burning in the firepit.

* * *

Mr. Fifer's office door creaked open. A shadow grew across the floor. The chandelier lights pushed the shadow farther away as a medium-sized beast entered the room. A patch covered one eye, and his other eye was bright red. The man stood in the doorway. It was Watches. His men entered the office and checked the two bodies inside, Samantha was dead, but Greg, who hung across Mr. Fifer's desk, slowly lifted his head.

Watches growled. He turned toward a man standing next to him. "I want that old man. These two are useless to me. They failed."

"Hey, boss," Greg mumbled, "I screwed up. I shot him, and then the old bag of bones shot me."

"You did screw up, Greg. I promised you money if you did the job correctly. That's all I asked you to do, to do it right. This is not what I asked you to do."

"That was part of the bargain. I got you into the campground without any complications, and Mr. Fifer was a complication."

Watches grabbed Greg's hair and yanked his head back. "I don't suppose you know where the combination to this man's secret place is, do you?"

"No!" Greg whined.

"That secret place includes roughly forty-six billion dollars." Watches rubbed the whiskers on his chin. "But this man is so tight, his shoes squeak when he walks." Watches dropped Greg's head onto the desk and walked over to the broken window behind him and stared down at glass scattered across the lower deck. "Do you know where this particular secret place could be?"

"No!"

Watches bobbed his head sarcastically. "Oh, you don't?"

"No, but I got you into the office. I got you what you wanted."

"No, you didn't. You screwed up. And you upset my only lead! And now he's running around loose—a very angry Indian. So now you don't get paid." He slammed Greg's head onto the desk once again. Then he walked away from him and sat next to Samantha's body on the leather couch. He wrapped his arm over the back of the couch.

Greg looked up at him from the corner of the desk. "That wasn't the bargain, mister. Maybe you don't see things too clearly with one eye, huh?"

Watches looked up at him. His upper lip curled. Watches' men smiled as they stood over the chair behind him. Greg blinked. Watches glared at him. Then he cackled. "You idiot," Watches put his hands together like he was praying. "Thanks for closing the deal. Goodbye, Greg."

Watches opened his praying hands, a beam of light shot through Greg's forehead and tossed him out the broken office window. Blood dribbled off the jagged chards of the busted window pane along with brain matter. A few papers (from the desk) followed his body through the broken glass. His body wiggled as he flew backwards through the patio railing with his legs out and his arms spread. His head swung against his right shoulder over a woodpile far below with a significant crunch echoing through the dark.

The men caught the chair as it bounced away from the window frame and shoved it toward the desk. Watches circled the desk and pushed the cushion down in the chair. "Ooh, I could get use to this." A box of cigars sat on the beautiful desk. He pulled one out and lit it. He blew smoke out and snarled.

A guy with long hair and a suit walked away from the broken window. "Boss, I'm not so sure this is going as planned."

Watches spun around and stood up. He stood by the man's side and looked out the window, then pulled the cigar away from his lips. He blew smoke over his shoulder and looked over at the other guy. "Bonzo . . ."

"Yeah, boss?"

"Where's Mr. Fifer?"

"Well, he shot the counselors, and my guess is the authorities are on their way. He's probably with them now."

"Yeah, I concur, Bonzo." Watches grunted and pointed out the window.

A bunch of glass was lying across the deck below, but there was no sign of the old man. He had disappeared. Blood stained some boards as well. Specks of blood around the broken glass dripped between the boards and beneath the deck.

Watches smiled. "But the old man is still alive." He sighed. "And now I don't know where he is." He punched the wall near the broken window. Glass fell and shattered across the lower frame.

They both looked back at Samantha lying on the couch. Then Watches looked at Bonzo and blew smoke in his face. "Well, oops. Guess we have to find the old man ourselves, huh?"

"What are we going to do about those meddling kids in the woods?" Bonzo asked.

"I know exactly what I'm going to do to them. But that will come tomorrow morning."

"What?"

"A surprise . . ."

"Oh boy, I like surprises," Bonzo smiled, which wasn't much of a smile.

* * *

Billy sat on his cot in a cold sweat. Then he jumped up and worked his way over to Ron as the tent came crashing down around them. He pushed

Ron over. Ron fell off his cot and rolled against the hot stove and screamed as it sizzled against his bare back. He flew forward onto the ground as the tent wrapped around him. Billy started to unwrap it from his shoulders. Ron flinched in pain, wondering what Billy was doing. Billy crawled out of a bundle of canvas, but no one came out after him. He had expected Ron to follow.

* * *

Suddenly, Billy was back inside the tent as he awoke from yet another dream. He sat up against Danny's cot and cried. Ron scooted up next to him. His back was burned, and his shoulder was bleeding again. He was in pain. Billy looked over at him. But it wasn't Ron anymore; it was Mr. Fallway. A hole at his shoulder spit blood across his chest, and his back was rippled with skin folds and more blood.

"I'm sorry I didn't trust you, Mr. Fallway!" Billy cried. "I didn't mean to shoot you, but that leaf had a worm thingy on it. It was a little worm from hell, man. It had arms and tiny fingers, and when I saw it, I lost it, and I pulled the trigger. I didn't mean to! I just wanted that little weird worm to die." He held his hands to the sides of his head and shrugged. "What the heck is going on with me? Where's Ron?"

"Ron? Billy, calm down. You'll understand everything once the training is over."

"Training?" Billy stopped crying and stood up. "What do you mean?"

"What? I figured this would be the true test for your young, warped minds."

"What?" Billy asked.

Mr. Fallway's eyes rolled up at him. "You still don't trust me? The training will continue as planned tomorrow. You guys had a long day. Now get some rest."

"How can we train when we're being tracked by the devil? Wait a minute, what day are we on?"

Mr. Fallway sighed. "Day three. Get some rest, Billy. I need you to have energy for tomorrow."

"Day what?" Billy asked, but Mr. Fallway had already slipped back inside his sleeping bag and zipped it shut. Billy blanked as his vision slipped away.

* * *

Suddenly, it was morning. The entire tent was lit up. Smoke withered outside from the firepit. Billy stepped out of the tent and noticed Danny was sleeping with his head resting on the picnic table, a gun in his hand. He was the last person to pull night watch. Bill spoke his brother's name. No response. Billy approached the picnic table. He turned around and noticed everyone else still sleeping inside. Then he stood over Danny. Across the picnic table's maroon boards was a gush of thick syrup streaming toward one end and dripping off.

But wait, he was hungry and thinking about pancakes. That wasn't syrup. His brother had been shot in the head. He was dead. Billy grabbed him and screamed. Everyone fell off their cots inside the tent. A rumble outside grew louder. Billy spun around and saw Mr. Fallway smiling at him from a distance. He held onto a rifle with a scope.

At that point, headlights streamed into the tent. Billy looked up as a Trans-Am drove right for them. He looked down at Mr. Fallway's cot, and his bag tipped over. A black suit fell out with a ski mask, which rolled to the foot of Billy's bunk. Mr. Fallway stood up, only now it was Watches. Billy's head whipped back toward where Mr. Fallway was standing.

"You're the man in black."

Watches smiled and stood in the doorway of the tent. Everyone was still inside as the brown car tore through it. Billy fell over the picnic table, hugging his brother's limber body and sliding through the syrup. The teenagers bounced around inside the car as it flattened the Armybrats under the canvas. Watches was beneath the canvas as well and disappeared in the headlights. The car kept driving through the trees.

As the brown car took out the tent. Billy rolled across the dirt holding onto Danny's limp body. The brothers were the only ones left in the forest. He rocked Danny and squeezed him with all his might, crying. Smoke poured over the Trans-Am's hood as it slammed into a tree in the distance.

Suddenly, it was like a replay of the night of their practical jokes. A bike was sticking out of the windshield. The passenger in the front seat flew against the dashboard. A couple of girls fell out the back doors. The tent was folding down over squished bodies everywhere. Red blood soaked through the canvas.

An owl landed on top of the Trans-Am. Suddenly, the tent was gone. Duffy stood up, and the picnic table was nowhere to be seen. Pete held onto a flashlight. It wasn't covered by a red lens this time. It projected a bright white light. It was Duffy's flashlight from his basement. He shined it at the Trans-Am. The teenagers were inside the car, only now their limp bodies were strung all over inside as if they had suffered a horrendous crash. The driver was hanging over the steering wheel.

Suddenly, they found themselves back in the woods with the juvenile delinquents. The car looked like it had driven off a cliff. Then Billy remembered that it had. Ron had pushed it off the cliff. But it was up against a tree, and the roof was caved in. All the teenagers inside were dead.

* * *

Danny sat up and screamed. He was still in Duffy's basement. Billy wasn't the one having the nightmares this time. Danny was dreaming about his brother having a nightmare. Danny had created the entire dual between Ron and Mr. Fallway. They were all sitting on the couch. He stood up and walked in circles. No one was watching TV anymore; they were watching him. He was sweating profusely.

"Oh, it was a dream," Danny said, panting.

"Was your dream about the training?" Billy asked.

Danny stopped pacing and looked at his brother. "Yes, and it was too real. We were being shot at. You even shot Mr. Fallway and—"

"Did Mr. Fallway call himself Ron, and was Watches in your dream?"

Danny tilted his head. When Billy said that, he wanted to wake up again. He wanted to be somewhere else. He was having nightmares. And they wouldn't end. He looked at his brother. Billy didn't seem concerned. He was smiling as if he already knew the whole story. If Danny was still dreaming, he wanted to be awake for real this time.

"Yes!" Danny sighed.

"So did I, and the rest of the guys had the same dream."

Danny looked over at Duffy, who was rocking in a rocking chair in the corner. He was too quiet for it to be real. He was always cracking a wise joke, but he didn't. Pete was sitting next to Billy on the couch, sucking his thumb like a baby. Wesley was sitting on the floor near the television eating pizza. Nothing but snowy static was on the screen.

"We were all discussing it, and we think we shouldn't go up to see Mr. Fallway tomorrow. Instead, we should tell Dad about it. As a matter of fact, we should tell him everything."

"Yes!" Danny agreed. "But I'm still dreaming, aren't I?"

Billy leaned forward on the couch. "Danny, wake up."

Danny tilted his head at him once again. He was confused why Billy would ask him to wake up when he was standing right in front of him looking at him and talking to him. He wasn't sleeping; he was wide awake, and he was certain he wasn't sleepwalking.

"Danny, wake up," Billy said. "Danny, wake up!"

CHAPTER 27
BARREL ROLLING

Danny opened his eyes. He was surrounded by darkness. The moon was bright, but he couldn't see anything. It was early in the evening; he could tell by the crickets chirping outside—that and the stickiness he felt in his eyes. He was surrounded by hard blue plastic, but it looked black in the darkness. He screamed and pounded his fist against it. Even though he was screaming, he felt as if his vocals weren't working. He felt dizzy, nauseous even. Billy was trying to calm him down. Suddenly, someone kicked the plastic from the outside and told him to zip it. The dream was over.

Far below, a long grassy hill led down to a ridge. Below the ridge, a steep drop-off led to the Wisconsin River, which rushed violently through the woods at the bottom. At the top of the grassy hill, six fifty-five-gallon barrels were lined up. The steel lids were strapped shut by steel rings. Watches had kicked one of the barrels as Danny simmered down. Danny heard his voice and realized he wasn't in a good situation. He was trapped.

All the Armybrats were locked inside the barrels. Their fearless leader was standing outside, arguing. They could hear him talking to Watches. There were holes at the bottom of the barrels, and Danny crouching down to peek out. He couldn't see anything. Then he heard Wesley whimper. He didn't know the exact whereabouts of the others, but he could tell from their voices that they were in the same predicament.

"Billy, I think we should tell Dad," Danny said.

Watches laughed. "Ha, too late, Danny boy! Your daddy will just have to discover your body when they fish you out of the Wisconsin River."

"No, I will not watch you drown them," someone said. The boys couldn't decipher who the voice belonged to.

"This was your idea."

"Not exactly . . ."

Watches laughed wickedly.

Billy's head rested against the side of the barrel. "A little late for that, bro," he replied to Danny. His barrel tapped into Danny's as he threw his body against the plastic inside.

Watches laughed wickedly. The Armybrats felt tired, but they were wide awake. Fear made sure of that. Danny must have been a heavier sleeper to sleep through the entire thing. He couldn't remember being shoved inside a barrel and brought to the top of a hill far from the campsite. Billy had been trying to wake him up for fifteen minutes. Danny had been having nightmares for months prior to this. It was nothing new. He just had no idea how badly the dreams paralyzed him or how badly he ignored reality from being in such a deep sleep.

The blue barrels were another one of Mr. Fallway's courses. He was going to roll them down the hill one at a time and test their agility. He wanted to distinguish their motor skills by having someone at the foot of the hill try to stop all the barrels before they went over the ridge at the bottom. However, he hadn't planned on rolling the boys down the hillside inside the barrels. The course seemed dangerous, but now it was a role reversal as Watches planned to roll all of them over the hill with them inside the barrels. And he wanted the man at the bottom of the hill to stop the barrels before they plummeted to the river far below. However, Ron, who was at the bottom of the hill, was bound with his hands tied behind his back.

"This is a great course, son!" Watches screamed.

Danny squinted as his eyes adjusted through a peephole. He thought he saw a pair of legs. He knew what was going on. He didn't have to see it to believe it. But he was preparing himself for a real gut teaser. The courses Mr. Fallway had built were for testing, but Watches was using them for his own personal game. He was playing chess with them. The world was one big board of squares, and they were his game pieces, his pawns.

"You're driving me nuts!" Ron said. "I'm sick and tired of this. I really am. I hate this. I hate myself. My whole life I've been after you, you sick, twisted fuck."

"Oh quit your bellyaching," Watches replied. "I'm disappointed with you, son."

"I have no idea what you're talking about, Dad."

Danny was no longer dreaming. This was real. However, he had no clue what was really happening anymore. *How far back did my nightmares start? What happened to Ron? What did happen and what didn't happen?* He had just had a few nightmares in a row, but now he found reality just as hard to believe.

He pounded the plastic barrel with his fist. The others continued to whimper from the other barrels. Pete whimpered like he had on the night of their balloon wars when they were younger, and Watches had beat his body against the two-by-four studs.

"What do you mean?"

"You're just as stubborn as I am," Watches muttered.

All the boys could do was listen to Watches and Ron argue.

"How is that?" Ron shouted.

"You won't quit."

"You're right, I won't."

Watches laughed. "Why are you trying to save these boys?"

"Why are you trying to kidnap them?"

"Me?"

"How dare you?"

"How dare I?" Watches said. "No, how dare you?"

"Did you know Mom's still alive?"

"Don't bullshit me, son."

Now each boy sat in wonderment. Ron was Watches' son. Ron was after his dad, and Watches was after Billy and Danny's dad. Unfortunately, their friends were caught up in all this, and now the training site had been turned into a death trap.

"Oh, I'm not, Dad. Can't bullshit a bullshitter."

"I have some unfinished business here," Watches whispered, "and you keep interrupting me, so I don't believe you. You're just trying to change me."

"Believe what you want."

"What were you teaching these boys anyway?" Watches asked as he tipped each barrel onto its side. He was growing more upset with his son, who was kneeling at the bottom of the hill with his hands tied behind his back. Watches' men were standing at the top of the hill aiming their guns at him.

"No, don't."

"*Endurance . . .*" Watches nudged Danny's barrel with his foot. Billy screamed for his brother as Danny screamed and rolled downhill.

"They'll drown!" Ron said.

"*Speed . . .*" Watches said, ignoring Ron's cry as he pushed Billy's barrel over. Billy wailed as he began rolling downhill.

"Stop it, Dad!"

"*Motivation . . .*" Watches kicked Duffy's barrel. Duffy cursed left and right as his barrel beat him to death on the way down the hill.

"You'll drown them!"

"Then maybe it's all about courage," Watches said as he kicked Pete's barrel. "Or is it about duty?" He pushed the second-to-last barrel, and Wesley cried out. Watches turned to face Ron. "What are you waiting for, son? You have a duty to protect these boys."

Pete felt the hillside pound his barrel. His body hit the sides as he flopped in circles. Dizziness kicked in as the hard plastic beat against him. Ron ran in one direction to throw his body in front of Danny's barrel. With his hands tied, he managed to knock the barrel vertical and then run over toward Billy's barrel. He dropped in front of it and stopped the barrel from rolling any farther. He snapped the lid off, and Billy rolled out.

"See those barrels?" he yelled, pointing up the hill. "Stop 'em!"

Billy sat there for a second while the world spun around him and tried to focus on Ron, but he was running sideways away from Billy and then upside down.

"Where's my brother?" Billy shouted. Ron pointed at the barrel standing upright at the bottom of the hill just before the drop-off. Billy jumped up and tried to run toward it, but he fell onto his side. It seemed as if the hill had knocked him over as it spun around him. He tried regaining his footing as the hill spun over his head. He glanced up at Ron, who was running toward Wesley's barrel. Billy also saw Pete's barrel heading right for him. Just beyond that, he thought he caught a glimpse of Watches standing at the top of the hill, puffing a cigar, but as the world spun he noticed an odd tree in place of the false image of Watches. However, he heard his muffled cackle. Men stood at the top of the hill clutching their weapons. Billy fell down again as he tried to regain his strength, his vision, and mobility.

Danny sat in his barrel and closed his eyes. He was dizzy and trying not to puke on himself. He had suffered through nightmares all night. *How did yesterday end and today begin?* All this was happening so fast. Just when they thought they were leaving this place, they were stuck in the next nightmare. He tried to regulate his breathing and then suddenly remembered that Pete had a mild case of asthma, so he grew extremely worried for him. If Pete was stuck in one of these godawful blue barrels as well, he was probably worse off than the rest of them.

Farther uphill, Ron ran after Wesley's barrel. It nailed a rock and took a turn. It rolled through some trees into a wooded section of the hillside. Ron leaped into the air, brought his bound hands under his feet and in front of his body, then looped his arms over the end of the barrel. The barrel rolled toward the edge of the cliff, pulling Ron with it. Rocks rolled over the edge. The ground collapsed beneath him. As he struggled to stop it, Ron looked over at Danny's barrel. It still rested upright a good two feet from the drop-off.

Inside his barrel, Wesley did one last belly-flop, pulling Ron a bit farther, and then it stopped, crushing Ron's arm. Ron wailed in agony, but Wesley managed to pop the lid and crawl out of the barrel.

Ron grabbed Wesley with his bound hands as Wesley teetered along the cliff and pulled him back uphill.

Wesley shivered. "Where's Watches?"

"Forget about him," Ron said. "Untie me. Then we need to save Duffy."

Billy lay flat across the hillside and let Pete's barrel slam into him. He managed to spin the barrel, so it was parallel with the slope, which kept the barrel from rolling any farther, though it rolled a bit as Pete's body took one last fall inside. Billy popped the lid open, and Pete crawled out. Vomit flew downhill. Pete looked up the hill, and moonlight shined over five paths of flattened grass that appeared white instead of dark green. They were the paths the barrels made. He looked back down the hill and saw nothing but darkness and a ravine below the cliff. He rolled out of the barrel and tried to stand but slipped on his own vomit. He heard a gushing sound drawing closer.

"Whoa," Billy said. "Give it a few, Pete. Lie down for a second if you need to."

As Pete lay on his back, the gushing sound became even louder. He rolled over and realized what was making the sound. Duffy's barrel was drawing near.

Pete pushed himself up with what little strength he had left, then all three of them made their way toward Duffy's barrel. They turned around and saw that Ron had finally freed Wesley as he ran toward them and then stopped. He turned around to see Ron standing in the middle of the hill.

Suddenly, an explosion rocked the hillside, shooting dirt and grass skyward. He dropped behind a large rock embedded in the grassy hill as a brilliant explosion burst over Duffy's barrel. They looked up at Ron, who shot at Watches' men as they chucked grenades at him.

"Run, Billy!" Ron screamed. "Save yourselves!"

Billy peeked over the rock and looked up the hill. Ron was shooting into the trees. "Where's Watches?"

"Don't worry! I got him under control. Just go."

Meanwhile, Duffy was cussing up a storm as his barrel rocketed back up the hill. He was crying about going through all that again. Duffy could feel the heat and the impact of dirt, grass, and flames. He didn't want to roll anymore. "Billy, get me the hell out of this thing!" he cried.

Another explosion took out Ron's side of the hill. He rolled toward Wesley. Moonlight shined over his back. His entire right side was bloody. His shirt was torn, and his pants were soaked with blood. Ron pulled out a grenade and hollered for Billy to run.

Duffy's barrel took another bounce backward and sat at nearly a forty-five-degree angle on the hill. Duffy leaned back against the uphill side. His neck lunged forward as he trapped vomit inside his mouth. A bullet whizzed past his neck and out the front of the barrel, allowing a new stream of light to glow in his face. Suddenly, he couldn't hold it in, and puke flew across the barrel, shifting the weight forward. Everyone outside his barrel heard the grotesque splash inside. Some squeeze out the new bullet hole.

"No, no!" Duffy panted as the barrel tipped forward.

Danny's eyes were still closed. He heard gunfire and explosions from inside his barrel. He heard his friends running around as well. That gave him some comfort, until more moonlight shined through two fresh holes just above his head. Two stray bullets had found his barrel. The bullets actually pushed the lid up slightly and wrecked the seal. Danny reached up and pushed on the fresh crack in the plastic. He could almost get each hand out the top. However, if he knew how close he was to the edge of the cliff, he wouldn't have been bouncing around like he was.

Wesley turned around and approached Ron. He grabbed his arm and stopped him from tossing the grenade. "Man, look up that hill," Wesley said, smiling. "There's no damn way you could lob this grenade even a third of the way up there. Pin that sucker. Let's focus on saving Duffy."

Billy took off running toward Duffy's barrel. Ron rolled onto his back holding his gun up as another explosion farther up the hill tossed up dirt. A couple of small trees fell over and rolled down the hill.

"I hate you, Watches!" Ron yelled. "I'm going to rip your heart out, you stupid cocksucker!"

As Ron raced up the hill, a group of Watches' men approached. Billy stopped. They waved at him. Confused, he looked back at Ron, who dropped and shot at them. When Billy glanced back up at the men, they dropped and crawled back into the tree line. One of Watches' men knocked over the sixth blue barrel and tossed it downhill at him. The barrel rolled toward Ron but bumped into a rock, spun onto one end, and tipped over with the open end facing downhill. The lid popped off and slid a few feet. The ring rolled over the rock and got hung up on a clump of roots.

Watches' men aimed their weapons at Ron and the boys. Ron raised his arms. Dirt and grass whipped upward like a mushroom cloud as they shot rounds all around him. Suddenly, Ron accidentally dropped his grenade, and it rolled past Wesley's feet. Wesley scooted it off the cliff with the toe of his right foot and dropped against the hill, covering the backside of his head as Watches' men continued to sweep the hill, spraying rounds.

Ron stood up and advanced up the hill. The force of the explosion at his back sent him flying uphill. He slid, and dirt bunched up against his chest until another rock embedded in the soil stopped him. He did a cartwheel uphill and slammed into the rock with a thud, crying out in pain. Then he pulled out a handgun and fired uphill once again.

Billy looked back at the gunplay as he ran to escape the clearing. Farther down the hill, Ron took a prone position behind the rock and shot at Watches' men. Their leader was nowhere to be found. His men jumped out with fully automatic weapons and sprayed bullets at him. Ron rolled back and hid behind the rock as dirt, grass, and weeds sprayed over his back.

"You're gonna pay for this one!" he screamed. "You hear me, you stupid-ass no good sons of bitches?" He took potshots around the side of the rock without caring about his aim.

Duffy's barrel was still rolling down the hill. Wesley charged toward it, as did Pete and Billy. Pete managed to grab the barrel. He had the worst time controlling it (still a bit woozy), but he finally stopped it. They lowered it to the ground, popped the lid off, then pulled Duffy out. Another explosion farther up the hill forced Duffy to puke on himself again. They were about to be blasted off the edge of the cliff.

Pete backed away from the barrel as soon as he saw yellowish vomit pour out of it. It reeked. Duffy had already lost all kinds of stomach fluids. Pete encouraged Duffy to run, but Billy held up his hand to stop them. "Just wait," he whispered. "Give Duffy time to regain his strength." Duffy fell and rolled downhill, but Pete stopped him. Duffy struggled to get up. "Duff man, sit down," Billy ordered. He glanced up, keeping an eye on Ron, who was still firing uphill. Then he looked back down at his brother's barrel resting at the bottom of the hillside.

Several minutes had gone by when the exchange of gunfire stopped suddenly. Wesley had left the group, and Billy turned to see him crawling toward the sixth barrel, a body lying just outside of it. He was going to investigate it. Billy grew extremely frustrated with him. A long drawn-out silence enhanced the sounds of nature and the small fires burning undergrowth uphill. Other than the sizzling flames, it was pretty quiet.

"Wesley," Billy whispered.

Wesley was drawing closer to the barrel. Billy glanced back down the hill toward Ron, but he didn't see him. Then he noticed movement farther down the hill. It was a buck. It stood before Danny's barrel, which was hung up on a small tree. The buck dipped its head and nudged the barrel. Then it slammed into it. Billy heard Danny shout as the barrel rolled around the tree. The buck backed up slowly, staring at the blue barrel as if it had invaded his territory.

Wesley wrapped his arm around the barrel and spun it, but it slipped out of his grip and stormed down the hill. Bullets streamed down the hill again. Then the buck ran forward and headbutted Danny's barrel.

"Oh, hell no!" Billy hollered as he ran toward the buck, shooing it away.

"Nooooooo!" Duffy and Pete screamed as they ran toward the barrel, which wobbled around with Danny inside it.

Wesley popped the lid off the drum and Mr. Fallway rolled out. He was gagged and tied. Wesley jumped away from him. Mr. Fallway rolled his head up from the ground. The whites of his eyes rolled in his direction. Wesley tried helping him untie the knots and get the gag out of his mouth.

Gunshots echoed through the trees, and rounds penetrated the hillside. Danny's blue barrel grew smaller as it fell over the ledge. The Armybrats watched it from the edge of the cliff. The barrel dropped for what seemed like an entire minute, turned a bit, and then splashed into the river far below. They stared at it as the water splashed around it. The ripples fanned away from the sides for quite a ways as the barrel headed down river. Then it started to sink. In a few minutes, the Wisconsin River would swallow Danny forever.

The entire hill was on fire behind them. Wesley slowly crawled away from Mr. Fallway. In the distance more explosions blanketed the hillside as they stared at each other. Mr. Fallway wiggled toward him and Wesley scooted backwards. They both ducked, an explosion flushed debris across the barrel Mr. Fallway fell out of. After tucking his head against the ground from dirt, grass and twigs, he glanced up and Wesley was gone. On the ground was a red, folded, pocket knife. Mr. Fallway closed his eyes and smirked with the rag in his mouth. He wiggled toward the knife Wesley left him.

CHAPTER 28
SAVE DANNY

"Noooooo!" Billy screamed and scrambled down the rock face as the rest of the Armybrats ran along the cliff trying to find an alternate way down. All Billy could think about was saving his brother, and the rock face was the quickest route to the river. He was worried the barrel would sink before he reached the bottom and he would lose sight of him.

Billy reached a point where he couldn't climb any farther. He was stuck about halfway down the cliff. He stood there for several seconds, his eyes searching the river. He grew extremely nervous because he couldn't find the barrel.

Then he watched two crows swarming over a spot of the river. He looked below them, and, sure enough, the barrel was still bobbing at the surface. It wasn't very high above the surface, but he could still see it. Running out of time, he decided to swan dive right into the raging river.

His hands split the waves as he disappeared underwater. He shot back up to the surface and looked straight ahead. The barrel was gone. He swam toward where he had last seen it.

Wesley bolted down the hill after the rest of the group. The Armybrats made it down to the shoreline and ran alongside the river. They watched Billy swimming in circles. They ran with him and pointed ahead of him. Suddenly, he stopped swimming and treaded water for a few seconds, whipping his head around and cussing. Pete screamed at him from the sandy shore. Billy was too concerned about his brother's whereabouts to understand him. Little did he know Pete was trying to guide him. The other two boys jumped in, shouting Billy's name.

They stood about 50 meters away staring and pointing about 5 to 10 meters to his left. Billy finally realized they were trying to clue him in to where the barrel had sunk. He swam forward a little more and then stopped. They continued screaming, so he swam some more. Then the screaming stopped. They gave him a thumbs-up and nodded. Billy was in the right spot.

Beneath the water, Danny had a few seconds of air left as water quickly filled his barrel. He took short breaths as the water level climbed. When the water crawled up his clothing, he slammed his elbow against the lid, trying to bend it outward.

Billy popped back up to the surface and yelled for more advice. Suddenly, water splashed over him as two bodies brushed past him. An old man rose to the surface. It was Wesley's grandfather, Mr. Fifer. He grabbed a canoe next to Billy's head. Billy glared at him. He had no idea who he was.

"I got him, don't worry." Mr. Fifer smiled and lifted Danny out of the water. Billy treaded water and helped the old man hoist his brother into the canoe.

Billy heard a whistling noise and glanced at the hillside. It was too dark to see anything, but he could hear Watches cackling. The whistling noise grew louder, and he looked up. A black smoke trail arched up from the cliff, blocking out the moon and some stars in its path. Crows flew away, and a ball headed right toward them. Billy jumped against the canoe as Mr. Fifer pulled him over the side.

The ball struck the water, spraying one side of the canoe, which rocked, violently. A fireball burst under water and bubbled upward, slammed into the underside of the canoe. Mr. Fifer lay over Billy to shield him. Then they paddled to get away from the disturbed water. Billy threw his paddle down and held onto Danny. Mr. Fifer paddled the canoe by himself as Billy checked his brother's pulse. Billy looked up and noticed Mr. Fifer's black lips smiling back at him.

"Don't worry, Billy," Mr. Fifer said. "He's alive."

As Watches brought a grenade launcher back up to his shoulder, Mr. Fifer paddled as hard as he could. Billy grabbed the other paddle to help. The Armybrats ran down the shoreline.

The canoe curved around a bend, finally allowing them to escape the devil's path. Bulky trees were uprooted on the river's edge. They hung out over the water, the roots tearing away from the soil like outstretched fingers swatting river flies.

They paddled hard. Their lungs batted against their ribcages, and their hearts pounded as another grenade splashed the water behind them, sending their asses into their guts. But it actually helped move them along as it exploded and tossed a wave toward them. Water spouted into the sky and rolled under the backside of the canoe.

Mr. Fifer pointed around the small group of trees and directed the Armybrats along the shore. "On the other side, boys!" he said, and they ran deeper into the forest to meet them on the other side.

A grenade bounced off a tree and deflected into the water. An explosion ripped the roots from the soil, and three trees dropped into the water and pushed earth upward into the sky. Billy and Mr. Fifer ducked inside the canoe and then sat up slowly. They searched for the other boys, who were running behind the group of trees that had been annihilated.

Mr. Fifer turned the canoe toward the shoreline, and the other two boys hopped in.

"Where's Wesley?" Billy asked.

"He was right behind us," Duffy replied.

Just then, Wesley charged out of the brush. His skin tone seemed to hold blackened blemishes, smoke swirling over his arms.

Duffy smiled, "You're smoking!"

Wesley panted and climbed into the canoe. "I was in that group of trees over there."

Everyone looked at the burning embankment—trees slowly collapsed in a bed of sparks, spitting embers across the glimmering water.

Billy noticed Mr. Fifer waiting in anticipation. "We're good, go," Billy said.

Mr. Fifer looked at his grandson and shook his head. Then he continued to paddle.

After the water splashed down and some fish landed inside the canoe, Watches caught a glimpse of them heading for the bend. He aimed the grenade launcher ahead of the canoe in an attempt to cut them off, but Billy helped Mr. Fifer paddle as they turned beneath a tree leaning over the water and disappeared.

Watches lowered the grenade launcher. "Drat!"

One of his men stood next to him at the bottom of the hillside. "Boss, you OK?"

"Of course! Why wouldn't I be OK?" Watches grumbled.

"We got 'em right where we want 'em, don't we boss?" the man said.

Watches turned toward him and smiled.

Mr. Fifer was a Native American, so he could track well. He had hunting skills, and he was gifted with many outdoor techniques. He knew every inch of the soil around the forest and his campground. He could close his eyes, listen to the sound of the river, and know where the waves were hitting the shoreline. Not only that, he could pinpoint their exact location on a map without even reviewing it.

"What are you boys doing up here?" Mr. Fifer asked.

"We aren't exactly sure, sir," Billy replied.

"Billy, you of all people should know better. Does your dad know about this?"

Billy looked at him in surprise. "How did you know my name? Do you know my father?"

"My grandfather knows all the people of the land in and around his reservation," Wesley said.

"Yeah, OK. I'm talking Madison, population two hundred and five thousand people, hello."

"Oh yeah, Tommy Thompson stayed at my camp, why?" Mr. Fifer asked.

"Really?"

"Your family is in danger, William. You're dragging your family into the eye of the snake, and you don't even know it."

"Huh?" Billy said. "English please."

"You ignorant little white boy. Just sit back and let the old man drive the train, K?"

"Uh, excuse me, but you're lucky you're Wesley's grandpa, OK, old man?" Billy smiled sarcastically. "Cuz I would have driven this paddle right up your brown-faced racist ass," Billy slouched back and held onto his brother, who was still blue in the face but calm.

"And I would bury you under a force of water only the heavens could bear," Mr. Fifer said. "Without a life preserver."

"What?"

"This is a good guy right here, man," Duffy said. "He's our savior."

"What?" Billy asked.

"Watches always speaks in stupid-ass riddles, and this guy speaks about spirits 'n' stuff. He's the answer to all our problems. Listen to our brown savior, Billy."

Billy laughed. "Shut up, Duffster."

"Watches, the forbidden one, disgraced this land."

Billy sat forward with interest. "You know him?"

Mr. Fifer nodded. The canoe rocked as he glanced at Billy from the corner of his eye. "God, of course, he surrounds you 'n' me. He's all over."

"No, Watches. You know Watches?"

"Billy, the question is, have I heard of Watches? I'll answer that with another question: have you heard of the demon spirit?"

"What does he want?" Billy asked.

"He wants some numbers out of my head."

"Numbers?" Billy asked.

"He wants my fortune, which I buried in my campground."

"Can you fight this guy?"

Mr. Fifer stopped paddling. The canoe continued on its forward course. He turned around to look at Billy. He didn't say a word, merely shook his head.

Wesley's eyes grew wide as he looked up at his grandfather. "Yes you can, Grandpa," he said.

"No, Wes. The demon spirit is a wicked presence. You can't fight a spirit without strong love of your creator. Without him on your side, you might as well hold your breath and keep counting. You must get over your brother and prevail."

"Grandpa, you can fight him," Wesley encouraged. "You're strong!"

"Wes, choose me or the river."

"With you, Grandpa . . ."

Mr. Fifer whacked Wesley with the paddle, and he fell overboard. "Wrong choice, boy. You get the river."

"What the hell ol' man?" Billy shrieked.

"Yeah, that was your grandson!" Duffy said. "Holy crickets, man, what's wrong with this family?"

Billy and Danny helped Wesley back into the canoe.

"You know, I wish your dad named you that Indian name he had picked out for you," Mr. Fifer said. "But your mother wanted an American name."

"What was that, Grandpa?" Wesley asked, smiling despite what his grandfather had just done to him.

"Indians always name their children after the first thing they see."

"Oh yeah, what did dad see?" Wesley asked.

"I don't know. Your mother hit him so damn hard, he saw nothing but stars, and it was pitch black, so they agreed on Wesley instead of Brown Star."

"Yeah, I'm sure." Wesley nodded sarcastically. "Thanks, Grandpa."

"Come on, boys," Mr. Fifer said. "There it is."

Up ahead, a pier jutted into the water.

CHAPTER 29
BILLY'S BACK

"He's coming to!" Pete shouted.

Billy's eyes opened slightly. Mr. Fallway was standing over him. Billy closed his eyes again. Pitch black. But he could hear something beeping—a machine. Then he felt a slight sting on his arm, and he opened his eyes again. A nurse hung a fresh IV bag on a hook to his left. He heard his brother's voice.

"Billy you're awake?"

Billy opened his eyes again. Danny was standing next to Pete. Duffy was standing next to Mr. Fallway. He seemed to be lying in a hospital bed at some sort of clinic.

"Man, you had us worried, bro," Danny said.

"Yeah, I've never seen anyone leap like you did off a cliff before," Duffy said, laughing. "Well, except in the movies, of course!"

Billy blinked his eyes and noticed ice chips on a tray to his left. He glanced up at the nurse in desperation. He wanted that ice, but he didn't know how to ask. His lips felt numb. He felt incapacitated. He struggled to reach for it. Mr. Fallway grabbed the cup and looked at the nurse for reassurance. "It's OK, right?"

She nodded.

Mr. Fallway helped Billy take a sip of ice water. Billy's eyes narrowed as he drew closer. Billy felt the coolness ooze down his insides. It was a refreshing feeling, a reboot into reality. The nurse smiled. "I'll check back in a bit," she said and then exited the room.

Billy looked at Mr. Fallway. "Did I shoot you?"

The other Armybrats redirected their attention toward Mr. Fallway. He had a puzzled look on his face. "No, Billy. But you gave me quite the scare, that's for sure!"

"Scare?" Billy asked.

"Yeah, during the rappelling course, you slipped."

"I slipped?" He frowned in confusion. "How long have we been training?"

"Five days. We're going home tomorrow."

Suddenly, Billy closed his eyes once again. He could hear people talking. "And there he goes again!" someone said. "It's a good thing that Upham Woods had a clinic." After all the strength it took to drink a glass of water and ask a few questions, Billy slipped away from reality.

CHAPTER 30
AND THE NIGHTMARE CONTINUES

Billy opened his eyes. His body was rocking. He saw stars in the sky and a faint light on the horizon. Dawn was approaching. He sat up trying to understand which dream was real or if any of them were dreams at all. Was it an ongoing nightmare? Then he noticed he was soaked and holding onto Danny. He looked around and saw he was in the canoe again. Mr. Fifer was paddling hard. Mr. Fallway was nowhere in sight. They were making their way to somewhere, but he didn't know where.

An old rickety pier jutted into the water. Two fishing boats were tied to it. They swayed in the current and rocked up against one another. Mr. Fifer crashed the canoe right into the fishing boats. One boat pushed farther underneath the pier. He held onto his arm as if arthritis pains were acting up and led them out onto the rotten pier. Duffy and Danny started for the shore as Billy and Wesley helped Mr. Fifer out of the canoe. The moon was directly above them. They had canoed through most of the night.

They were on the backside of the campground. The sandy shores weren't as bright orange as earlier. Portions of the river were shallow, and sandbars stuck up from the center of the river in certain areas. A large wooden sign hung near the corner of the tree line before it opened into a private drive that led to the parking lot in the main section of the camp. Underground electricity serviced four lights below them. The sign was cut into the same shape and had the same design as the main entrance sign for Upham Woods Campground.

Farther up the beachfront, where the water neared the tree line, a two-story white-and-green boathouse sat along a private drive. Three bays beneath held three boats. The bays were built with rock and mortar. Two bays had fancy boats in them. The first was named *Wake Menace*. The second was named *Menace Part II*. The third bay held *Menace Part III*. All three boats and the boathouse were maintained well. Several canoes lay under a white-and-green storage shed next to the boathouse. Everything was clamped together, kept secure, and accounted for. The shingles were green, and the walls were painted white just like the house. The shutters and door were green.

Wesley's other grandparents lived inside the boathouse. They ran canoe rentals and daily sales in the convenience shop below the house, where they sold groceries, health and welfare-type products, antiques and artifacts, and Indian apparel and assorted arrowheads, books, and jewelry. The shop was clean and interesting to walk through.

Togetherness was the primary focus of the camp. Its purpose was to provide a cheap, pleasant camping atmosphere for families. In the past, local schools had reserved log cabins for students. Over the years, they enjoyed it as Mr. Fifer designed strategies for them to accomplish. The strategies included groupthink and problem solving. It was always fun. Verona High School reserved a three-day, two-night stay for their students during their senior year.

Billy had avoided that experience. He decided to go hunting with his father instead. His dad gave him permission to be excused from the school field trip, so they could spend quality time together. In a year, it would be the Armybrats turn to attend the camp (without Billy). Outside of groupthink, a lot of history lessons, among other activities, were available to the campers, including baseball, basketball, football, tennis, soccer, and volleyball. Beyond the baseball diamonds were archery and rifle practice ranges. Mr. Fifer hired camp counselors to supervise the ranges. The camp also offered boating, fishing, jet skiing, swimming, wakeboarding, and just about everything imaginable. On Sundays they held a church service at the chapel not only for campers but also for the general public. The camp had a dining facility and a medical facility. Mr. Fifer paid a small crew to operate the facilities at certain times of the year.

Even though it may have seemed like Mr. Fifer was shelling out a lot of dough for his staff—he had camp counselors, nurses, a personal doctor, cooks, and security personnel—he raked in quite a bit.

The landscape was beautiful, with the riverside and woodland area. It was more prestigious than one could imagine. The location was like any oil reserve to a farmer in Kuwait or Texas—a gold mine. The customers, mostly Christians, were always kind, with the exception of one customer that night whose religion lay somewhere down below where the two horned man engulfed in flames would call him the buddy . . . the deliveryman that Michael Anglekee had angered one dreary night in Granite View when he killed his brother right in front of him.

CHAPTER 31
SIMULTANEOUS EXECUTIONS

Mark Emerson slammed his fist on the desk. "You people relocated my family for this WITSEC program due to this maniac postman hiding a weapons cache. And the guy you assigned as my handler, Wayne Richards, has gone rogue. One of your agents already told me they've never heard of him, so who was my handler supposed to be? You have the documents right there in front of you. You have the list of contacts. What more can I provide to you?"

"Listen, Mike, this is the first time we've heard of this case, and we—"

"Wait, what?" Mark shouted. "What do you mean 'first time?' I jumped through hoops for you guys. Wayne Richards needed documentation to relocate us, and I listed everything on paper for you guys, and you're telling me my case doesn't exist?"

"You mentioned that you discovered an arsenal of military-grade weapons that your postman was hiding in the back room of his house somewhere in Wausau, Wisconsin."

"Yes, that information must be in that white box on your desk. Did you check, or is that just a light bright shining in your face?"

"Sir, I'm in the database, and there's no Mike or Mary Emerson listed as being relocated as part of WITSEC, and there is no federal discovery of weapons in Wisconsin."

"But we left everything behind," Mark said, "all our assets. We moved away from family. We became disconnected from our lives, and you're telling me all that was for nothing?"

"Look, Mike, if your family is in some kind of danger, we can protect you. We can open a new case, and I'll enter everything now. We can guarantee you and your family safe passage to a new location. We'll find you a new position in life, and you can get a fresh start."

Mark stood up. "I came here looking for answers. And your solution is to relocate my family all over again? I'm not putting them through that. I'm not going to relocate them and then have some other handler go off the reservation on us. No way."

Mr. Johnson stood up from behind his desk as Mark walked toward the office door. Johnson wore a black suit coat and a red tie. The daylight shined off his black forehead. "Wait, Mike, don't go doing anything irrational. What are you going to do?"

Mark scowled. "I'm going to do what I do best." He placed a hand on the doorknob.

Just then, Johnson's computer beeped. "Wait a second, my new search came back."

Mark turned to him.

"Do you know a guy named Ronald?"

"Well, yes," Mark said. "He was the boy, the one who called 911 for his mother. He was the deliveryman's kid."

"We had an agent working out of Wisconsin by that name."

"Well that doesn't make sense. My handler was Wayne Richards, but he was going by the alias Ralph P. Fallway."

"Well, nothing makes sense with criminals, Mike."

"Wait," Mark said, a thought striking him. "What you mean by *you had* an agent named Ronald?"

"It says here that he's DEA."

"Dead on arrival . . . what?"

"Oh no, he transferred to DEA. He's an agent with the Drug Enforcement Agency."

Mark's eyes narrowed in thought.

"Hold on, Mike." Johnson grabbed his phone and dialed. "Hey, Doug," he shouted a moment later. "It's Darrel Johnson with the Justice Department. Do you have a Ronald Markesan working for you?"

In anticipation, Mark leaned forward. Darrel hit the speaker button, and Doug's voice came from the speaker. ". . . ham Woods. That's where he's running a drug outfit at the moment. He's been working it for quite some time now, almost three years. We're waiting on the suppliers for the outfit he has organized up there. But he isn't running it alone. He has a few informants with him. The operations continue in northern Wisconsin."

Mark lunged at the desk, but Darrel muted the phone. "Don't talk, Mike. This is a secure line, and he has no clue I have you listening in."

"Ask him where they're running that outfit," Mark said.

Johnson grimaced.

"Ask him!"

Johnson unmuted the phone. "Say, Doug, where are they smuggling the drugs out of?"

"Some abandoned mill off the Wisconsin River."

"Right. What was the name of that campground again?"

"Oh, that, Upham Woods."

Mark's eyes lit up. He knew exactly where that camp was.

"Say, Darrel," Doug continued, "this is classified, and I know you already said you're on a secure line. But I'm no longer going to discuss this case with you. I have to remain vigilant with such things. Do you have a relocated family mixed up in all this? Are they part of the cartel?"

Johnson hesitated. "No, nothing like that, Doug. I was merely inquiring about our former employee. I had no idea he transferred agencies. Thanks for the intel, and good luck."

"Thanks, sir. Take care!"

"You too!"

After hanging up, Johnson glanced up, but Mark was gone. Johnson jumped up, cornered his desk, and dashed to his door. He glanced up and down the hallway, but Mark had disappeared.

Mark walked through the halls of the Justice Department trying to comprehend the new data he had gathered. People passed him, but he was oblivious to them.

A man standing near a water fountain wearing a gray suit coat and matching gray pants checked his watch and glanced at the office that Mark had just exited. It was the same man who sat outside the Dane Country

Regional Airport in Madison, Wisconsin when Mark's wife dropped him off. He crossed the hall behind him as Mark pulled a boxy cell phone out of his pocket.

The man in the gray suit knocked on the office door.

"Come in, Mark!" a voice hollered.

"Not Mark," the man said as he leaned in and waved at Johnson.

"Hey, Joe, I just had the weirdest confrontation," Johnson said while sitting back down in his chair and tucking his red tie down off the desk.

"What about?"

"Some old Wisconsin cop trying to plead his story about a federal case we didn't open back in 1976. He said we relocated him through the WITSEC program, but there's nothing on file."

Joe walked behind him to see his computer monitor. "Really? That's odd."

Darrel brought up the screen. "He told me Wayne Richards was their handler in Wausau, Wisconsin."

Joe leaned over Johnson's shoulder and stared at the monitor, which showed a picture of Ron. "Wausau . . . there was never a case in Wausau. I don't even know where Wausau is."

"I know, right?" Johnson said. "He said the local task force unveiled an arsenal of military weapons, but there's no search results for—"

A snap was followed by a muffled thump as Johnson gasped his last breath. His eyes rolled up at Joe, who released a hot muzzled silencer from his upper back. Johnson's eyes and his mouth remained wide open as Joe leaned in with his arm around Johnson's shoulders. He slid his chair aside and keyed in a few commands on the keyboard. The "delete" or "cancel" options flashed on the monitor. Joe clicked "delete" and then wheeled Johnson back to his keyboard. He sat with his head slumped forward and his chin mashed deep into his upper chest. A stream of blood rolled down his black suit jacket.

Joe reached across the desk and took a sip of Johnson's coffee. "Oh, shit, that's cold. Would you like a fresh cup, Darrel? What's that?" he cocked his ear toward him. "You're not thirsty? OK, well I must get going. I got a cop to kill, things to do. You know—bad guy stuff."

With that, he vacated the office.

Outside, Mark hailed a taxi. "Hilton Washington, please," he said when he got in.

"No problem," the driver replied.

During the thirty-minute drive to the hotel, Mark called his old boss in Wausau.

"Hey, Mike, how's your trip going?"

"We need to talk," Mike replied. "Offline!"

Tony leaned back in his chair. "Yup, I figured this call was coming."

"This just continues down the rabbit hole, Anthony. I'm going to need your help on this one."

"Anything for you, old friend. Anything."

"Oh, and we're gonna need a lot of resources on this."

"Yup, I figured that too."

"Good. It's good you know me."

"Why wouldn't I, Mikey?"

"I'm not hiding anymore. This has got to stop. I want to tell you everything, but I can't right now."

"Understood! See ya when ya get back. Safe travels, buddy."

"Thanks, Tony!"

Mark noticed the cabbie continue to glance from mirror to mirror. "Everything OK?" he asked.

"Everything fine, sir," the cabbie replied. "High traffic volume." His Indian accent was prominent.

"Is that normal?"

"Ah, yes sir."

Up ahead, a bus slammed on its brakes, and a motorcyclist flew up alongside the cab. Mark dropped to the floor as bullets blasted through the glass next to him. He heard a gasp as the driver fell into the passenger seat. He had been shot. Mark peeked over the seat as the motorcyclist flew around the bus. The driver's foot was still on the gas, and they were on a collision course with the bus. Mark wrapped his shoulder through a seatbelt just before the cab hit the bus.

Mark leaped out of the cab on the passenger side and dropped to the road. He could still hear the motorcyclist as he crawled toward the back of the cab. The motorcyclist had driven around the bus onto the sidewalk and shot through the passenger doors. Mark leaned over the bumper and peered around the taillight. Then he jump-kicked the motorcyclist in the visor. The motorcyclist wobbled off the sidewalk and slammed into a tree. His body flew over the bent forks and wrapped around the tree trunk.

Mark circled the cab in the center lane as vehicles drove around him, honking. Some slowed down or switched lanes. Others didn't. He threw open the driver's door and glanced at the cabbie. The bullet hole in his head told the story. He was dead.

Mark shoved the driver to the side and then jumped in and threw the cab into reverse. He backed away from the bus, the cab's hood crumpled and arched halfway toward the windshield.

Suddenly, two more motorcyclists approached on Constitution Avenue. Mark cut off another driver and swerved around the bus. One motorcyclist drove around the bus to the right. The other approached in the far-left lane. As soon as Mark got to 17th Street SW, he veered left. The motorcyclist took a few shots at the driver's door. Undaunted, Mark headed away from the hotel with the two motorcyclists hot on his tail.

He approached a mild traffic jam before the Kutz Bridge where a parking area jutted off to the right. He drove across the sidewalk and cut through the parking area. The motorcyclists followed suit. They shot out the cab's rear window as Mark swerved left and hopped a couple curbs.

Suddenly, a police car turned on its lights and flew up on Mark as he turned onto Kutz Bridge. The motorcyclists surrounded the police car and shot out its tires. The squad car drove up the guardrail and flipped, sliding toward pedestrians walking along the bridge. A few people screamed and jumped out of the way as the car bore down on them.

Mark opened his door and slammed on the brakes. The motorcyclist driving alongside him folded in half over the door and took the door with him as he slid farther up the road. The other motorcyclist slammed into the cab's trunk and flew through the broken window, bending the barrier between the front and back seats. His head and shoulders hung next to Mark. Mark glanced at him and smiled. "No free rides, buddy." Then he punched him in the face a few times.

Mark reversed the cab and drove over the motorcycle, then swerved toward the guardrail along the bridge. He skidded to halt and jumped out to check on the officer who was stuck upside down between the guardrail and the concrete pillars along the side of the bridge. He knelt down beside him. "Are you OK, officer?"

"No, not really. My whole world is kinda upside down right now," he joked.

"I'm Mark Emerson. I'm a cop from Verona, Wisconsin, and I'm here to help you."

"We must be stretched thin if you had to come all the way from Wisconsin to help me."

"Actually, I was the one you were chasing."

The officer laughed. "Of course you were."

Suddenly, bullets struck the side of police car. Mark jumped over the guardrail as a motorcyclist drove by shooting at them. Sparks flew off the rail as Mark slid between the car and the railing. He could hardly move. The motorcyclist cut off a few other vehicles and spun around when he realized he had missed Mark.

"I have no clue who these guys are," Mark said, "but they're relentless."

A pistol flipped out of the upside-down cop car, and Mark stretched his arm across the ground between the car and the guardrail for it. The motorcyclist came back into view, driving through oncoming traffic on Kutz Bridge.

"Oh shit!" Mark shouted. He grabbed the pistol as more sparks flew off the rail. He wrapped his arm beneath the guardrail and shot up at the motorcyclist. He hit him three times: twice in the chest and once in the face as he drove into a bus and impaled himself on a bike rack mounted to the front. The bus driver slammed on his brakes as the motorcycle bounced off the corner of the bus's bumper. Cracks spread through the window panes in the side door.

Mark twisted toward the officer, who remained upside down in his squad car. "Thanks," he said, indicating the gun.

Just then, police cars swarmed the bridge. "Can I have my gun back, officer?" the cop grumbled.

"Yes of course," Mark replied.

The police had to use the jaws of life to cut the officer out of his upside-down squad car. The man on the bus's bike rack was the same guy in the gray suit who had killed Johnson. Mark couldn't believe Johnson was dead. He had just spoken to the guy. After questioning him for most of the night, the police escorted Mark to the airport, probably to make sure he left Washington, DC.

* * *

A few police cars pulled into a driveway. Mark jumped out of one of the cars as police stormed past him and around the yard of the house. It was 1976. A wooden deck jutted from his house. His boss, Tony, was running to his left, and Mark followed him up the wooden steps. At the top of the wooden steps, it opened up to the deck and a door with an address on it. It was dark, but there were deck lights and a porchlight above the door.

The deck wrapped around the front of the house where a huge picture window was smashed. Jagged chunks of glass webbed inward. A huge hole spread across the center. Broken glass covered a sofa and a shattered coffee table. Police rammed the door and swarmed inside.

Mark and Tony led the way down a hallway immediately to the right. More officers poured into the living room and the kitchen. Tony and Mark worked their way to the end of the hall, clearing rooms. In a back bedroom, they heard a scuffling sound.

"Not clear!" Mark shouted.

Tony pulled the shower curtain aside, cleared the bathroom, then joined Mark in the bedroom. They both aimed at a closet door. Tony grabbed the doorknob, and Mark nodded while aiming Mr. Steely at it. Tony yanked the door open, revealing a boy with his head deep between his knees crouched over a pile of clothes. Mark holstered his weapon as Tony knelt beside the boy. "Son, you're OK now," he said.

The boy lifted his head and sniffled. Tears flowed down his cheeks.

"We're the police, and we're here to help you," Tony continued. "You're safe now."

Inside the kitchen, a police officer called for Tony. Tony helped the boy to his feet, and Mark took him from there.

Tony entered the kitchen as Mark and the boy exited the hallway. Mark could see between Tony and another cop where a refrigerator had been overturned. Mark turned toward another cop. "Take the boy outside to the ambo," he said. Then he knelt next to the boy. "This police officer is a good man. He'll take you to get looked at and make sure you're OK. There are doctors outside who will help you. My name is Mike. If you need anything, just ask for Officer Michael Anglekee."

"Yes, sir," the boy said. The other officer held out his hand to the boy, who reached up slowly and grabbed it.

Mark walked up behind his boss and noticed an arm sticking out from beneath the fridge. Five officers flipped the fridge sideways, revealing a woman, who let out a gasp. Tony checked her pulse. "She's alive," he said. "Pulse is weak, but she's alive."

Another young boy lay in her arms. The boy and his mother had been struck by the fridge. Mark checked the boy's pulse. He looked at Tony and shook his head. Dead.

Mark glanced up at the wall where the fridge had been. A piece of plaster had a hole in it, and wallpaper hung loosely. He reached up and pulled on the wallpaper, and a larger portion fell to the floor. Tony glanced up at him as EMTs tended to the woman on the floor. Mark dug, and more plaster fell off the wall. He revealed a two-foot-by-three-foot hole in the wall. He reached for his flashlight and shined it into the hole, revealing crates and racks of weapons. They appeared to be military issue. "Boss, this doesn't look good," Mark said.

Tony grabbed his light and checked it out. Then he spun around to face the other officers. "Everyone out! Get out!" He turned to Mark. "We need to get you gone. But first things first. I need you to contact the bomb squad. We don't know what's in that room, and I'm not about to presume it's safe here." Mark spun around and pulled out a phone while exiting the house. "Vacate the premises, now!" Tony shouted. "Move, move!"

Mark ran off the deck and turned around to see paramedics jogging with the stretcher and Rosalyn Markesan's body bouncing on it. Another officer carried the dead boy out the front door. Mark glanced over at the other young boy being cared for on the back of the ambulance. Then a flash of light shined over his face as the house behind the emergency personnel ignited. Bodies tumbled across the yard.

* * *

"Ladies and gentlemen, welcome to Madison, Wisconsin," a voice said. "The current temperature is seventy-three degrees, and the sky is partially cloudy. Please fasten your seatbelts. Flight attendants, please help clear the aisles, button up trays, straighten up seatbacks, and prepare for landing. Thank you for flying with Delta."

A flight attendant helped Mark straighten his seat back. A skinny kid seated beside him kept giving him awkward glances. "Dude, you were having a nightmare," he said.

Officers Darcy and Penske were waiting for Mark outside the Dane Country Regional Airport in Madison. Mark rolled his suitcase behind the car, and Darcy popped the trunk. Mark shoved his suitcase inside, then slammed the trunk and climbed into the back seat. He sighed. "Boy, am I glad to see you guys." Darcy handed Mr. Steely to Mark, who tucked it into his pants. "Thanks!"

"Fun trip, boss?" Penske asked.

"Let's not talk about it. What happened while I was away?"

As Darcy pulled away from the curb, Penske sighed. "Not much."

Suddenly, Mark's cellphone rang.

"Mark is that you?"

"Jake!" Mark replied. "I've been trying to call ya at the house, but I haven't been able to reach ya. I was actually startin' to get worried."

"Mark, thank God."

"Where ya been?"

Mark sat back and cast a scornful look toward Officer Penske. He tried interfering to justify what had happened, but Mark waved for him to shut up. Jake was shouting into the phone as he told Mark he had been admitted for detoxification.

Mark held his hand over the receiver. "What kind of bullshit is this?"

"Mark?"

"Yeah, Jake, let me put you on speaker. Hold on." Mark held his phone between the seats. His face was whiter than a cloud in the middle of a long week with rainstorms. But soon it turned redder than the upside-down cop in the squad car back on Kutz Bridge. Mark was a steaming teapot ready to hiss. "You guys need to explain something to me."

"Are you mad, boss?" Darcy asked, glancing into the rearview mirror.

"I haven't determined that yet. Do you guys have any idea what this is all about?"

"Yes." Penske said.

"No," Darcy replied.

"Oh, really. If the case was undetermined, what did you plan on doing about it?" Mark asked.

"I was going to question the lead witness in the incident," Penske stated.

"And did you?"

"Yes, and we couldn't get a hold of the boy," Darcy said.

"What about the boy's father? What's his name?"

Penske sighed. "Jake Carson."

Mark pointed at the phone. "I'm glad you know!"

"Oh, shit," Penske said.

"What?" Mark asked. "I don't want to hear 'oh shit.' I want to hear solutions. So, what did he tell you?"

Darcy leaned forward in his seat and turned out of the airport gate. "That was a few days ago, sir. He was going through withdrawal so badly that we couldn't talk to him."

Jake, who had been listening to the entire conversation, jumped in. "Bullshit. They sort of forgot about me here."

"Oh, shit," Penske said. Darcy merely laughed.

"Would someone please tell me what's so funny, Officer Darcy, ya bonehead?" Jake yelled. "I get one phone call a day, and I've been trying to get a hold of my son the entire time while you boneheads hung me out to dry. Thanks a lot. Now my son's missing, no thanks to you two clowns. Do you know where I am right now?"

Mark put the cellphone back to his ear and raised his eyebrows. "You still there, big guy?"

"Yeah, I'm still in friggin' detox section B, room eleven. I'm sitting in a friggin' white gown on an aluminum chair with a fat nurse guarding me, and she's pissin' me off. And this friggin' chair is freezin' my ass. Did you know they do anal probes here?"

"Excuse me," the fat nurse said.

"No, and I don't want to know," Mark said. "I'm sorry about that, Jake. I promise I'll have you out in less than one hour. I'm sure you're having a tough times with Julie in a coma 'n' all. Now Pete's missing, that means, my sons are probably missing too. And if anything has happened to any of them, these two officers will reap our wrath; I promise."

Penske and Darcy slouched deeper in the front seat.

Suddenly, shots rang out. A van struck their front bumper as it cut them off and then turned up a side street heading west toward Northport Drive. Mark and the other two officers watched someone in the van shoot at the police officers who were chasing it. Three squad cars were following the van. It was the missing coroner's van from the Iowa County mortuary. They turned up the volume on the CB radio. The tags matched the description the coroner had given Mark.

"Follow them!" Mark shouted. "Turn on the lights!" They joined in the chase as the van ran red lights and continued westbound. As they drove, they tried to follow the chatter over the CB radio.

"We're tracking two other chases," the lady from Dispatch said. "They're both UPS trucks. One is heading westbound on Highway 14 toward Spring Green, and another is heading up Highway 60 from Lodi." A brief silence was followed by static. Then the woman's voice returned. "Now we're tracking a third UPS truck going northbound on Highway 23 several miles south of Spring Green."

"What the hell is going on?" Mark asked.

Darcy smiled in the mirror. "Welcome back to Madison, sir."

"Two UPS drivers are 10-65. The third driver wasn't with his vehicle at the time it was stolen."

Another voice came on the radio. "We have a 187 at the corner of First and Prairie Street in Lodi. Subject is wearing UPS uniform with a single gunshot to the chest, over."

"Attention all units, attention all units," Dispatch said. "Please be advised UPS driver heading westbound on Highway 60 may be armed and dangerous."

Another voice jumped on. "We have a 187 at 601 East Leffler Street found in the Dodgeville Wal-Mart parking lot. Gunshot victim also wearing UPS uniform, over."

"Attention all units, attention all units, please be advised UPS driver heading northbound on Highway 23 may be armed and dangerous," Dispatch said.

"Well, this just keeps getting better and better, doesn't it?" Mark hollered.

The pursuit carried on for roughly twenty-three miles. They were heading north on Highway 12 crossing a hill and quickly approaching Sauk City. The highway that crossed the Wisconsin River was a highly traveled road. As the coroner's van climbed the bridge, another fleet of squad cars had the other side of the bridge barricaded. The van stopped on top of the bridge. The police had barricaded all side roads and main roads. No one was walking the street; no pedestrians were around. Flashing lights were everywhere. The bridge had squad cars on either end. The van was stuck.

"It appears all trucks have halted," Dispatch said. "Please advise."

Mark looked out the windshield as Darcy slammed on the brakes before the bridge. The few cars that remained on the bridge were slowly exiting the southbound lane, driving between the squad cars. A cop on a megaphone was telling the vehicles in front of them to turn around and vacate the bridge.

Mark grabbed the CB mic. "That's affirmative, Dispatch. Sauk City Highway 12 Bridge on the Wisconsin River, over." Mark opened the door and stood up slowly, peering over the squad car. Other officers were calling in their locations over the radio where the UPS trucks had stopped.

From across the river, a policeman shouted over a megaphone. "Driver, shut off the vehicle and dismount, or we will fire upon you."

Inside the van, the driver lit a cigarette. Mark stepped out of the squad car and walked slowly toward the bridge. Dispatch called for him once again, but he ignored it. He glanced upriver and then back in the other direction. Just upriver, another bridge crossed the Wisconsin River. It was Highway 60.

As the last civilian vehicle exited the bridge, Mark had a flashback to the bridge on Highway 130 near Lone Rock, Wisconsin. He remembered the UPS truck that blew up the bridge. Mark ran over to the cop with the megaphone and snatched it from him. "Fire!" he shouted.

All forces from each side of the bridge fired upon the van. Mark knew what was about to happen. The van exploded, causing the entire bridge to buckle and crack. Everyone stopped firing and took cover as debris pelted the vehicles. Mark flew twenty feet and landed on the hood of his squad car. Glass blew out the driver's window as cracks webbed through the windshield. Fire ripped through the night sky, and they felt the heat against their skin.

Suddenly in the distance, another explosion went off. The Highway 60 Bridge was annihilated as well.

Down in Spring Green, police were shooting at the UPS truck, and shots were being returned. Then an explosion lit up the night. A few squad cars were too close and were sucked down the embankment where the bridge used to be. The police managed to run away from the explosion and hunker down to safety, but the bridge was gone.

The same story repeated itself over and over. Reports came in later that night. Three other bridges had been blown up along the Wisconsin River at Highway 23, Highway 14, and a bridge on Interstate 39 going northbound. Most of the cops had been led to Highway 12. Now all the main supply commuter routes had been destroyed, including Highway 130 in Lone Rock from a couple months earlier (still under construction).

This wasn't just a coincidence; it was planned. It was something big before something even bigger, but what?

Mark's cell phone rang. It was Mary. "Danny and Billy aren't at Pete's," she said.

"I know, honey," Mark replied, groaning as he slid off the squad car. "I know where the boys are."

"Mark, be careful!"

"I will. I love you!'

Mark hung up and dialed another number. He stared into the river and watched the current carry away the remains of the coroner's van. "Tony, now's the time," he said when the call connected. "They boxed us in. They cut off all the main routes going north. I need support now."

"Didn't you just get back in Wisconsin today?" Tony asked.

"Yeah, and they destroyed every bridge along the Wisconsin River. Now I really need your help. We're going to get across though. I know exactly where to go. Oh, and Tony . . ."

"Yeah?"

"They got my boys."

"Where?"

"At the Upham Woods Campground. He has their friends too."

"Oh, that's terrible, Michael."

"This is where it has to end."

Mark hung up. Every police car followed him as they stormed northeast on Highway 188 toward the ferry crossing in Merrimac. Dispatches went out across the radio. Every unit was rerouted to Upham Woods. All Wisconsin police forces were fully engaged now. They were combining forces and racing toward a single location, but their path was about to be impeded . . .

CHAPTER 32
CELLAR

Wesley's grandfather had been running the camp since about 1962. Every building was built out of logs except for the boathouse. It had been built more recently out of two-by-four studs and drywall with metal siding. With an asphalt roof and a block chimney, it was more modern than anything else at the camp.

Wesley's other grandparents stayed in the boathouse, which was their place of peace, their retirement dream home. However, they were in the middle of ground zero that night—a holy war between drug kingpins and evil deliverymen.

The main entrance was a long, narrow straight road. The poles holding up the Upham Woods sign out front were like power poles. There used to be an old sawmill upriver. It was still standing but was now abandoned. In the 1960s it was the real buzz in that town. The sawmill came in handy for shipping lumber down to the camp. The river provided easy transport of the wood in those days. Much of the lumber supplied the cities along the river as well. Many employees had been laid off. Those employees were always talking about Gerry Fifer, who ran the Upham Woods Campground. They talked about his fortune there as well.

Nighttime was slipping away. Mr. Fifer wanted to see if the authorities had made it to the campsite yet. He had hit the panic button earlier, so it should have alerted someone. His next move was to contact Wesley's other grandparents in the boathouse to let them know what was going on.

The camp was calm, clean, and professional looking. A dog barked every once in a while. Families were allowed to bring dogs, but the dogs weren't allowed to sleep in the cabins unless people brought kennels. Other than that, it was peaceful, a night to cherish—if only the devil weren't included in their evening plans. If the starry sky were the only light streaks seen from spinning eyes, it was far better than a rain of bullets. But the forecast was calling for fire and heat.

The camp had storage shacks for all the sporting equipment. All the storage facilities, trashcans, and picnic tables were part of the scenery. Over the years, various people had moved the trash cans around, tipped them over, moved picnic tables, and forgot to return sporting equipment. Sometimes the equipment was recovered from cabins. Other times, people took it home with them. This hurt business, so now things were more secure. Tables were locked to trees, and trashcans were locked to light poles.

Back in the day, Mr. Fifer didn't give a squat about such things. Unfortunately, the world had changed, as had security. Nowadays, things may have been better as far as accountability of personal property, but the price was more regulations. All those things belonged to the camp. There should have been accountability and no reason for anything to be misplaced. He couldn't help it since every crowd had an ass ruining it for everyone else.

Inside the boathouse, a man in a UPS uniform tipped his flop hat forward and groaned. "I'm sorry this delivery was so late." As he raised his chin, the old couple gasped while sitting on the couch.

Watches had beaten Mr. Fifer back to the camp. Granted, the river was a straight shot, but who could beat the devil? He was anywhere and everywhere. It was a game of cat and mouse at that point, but who was playing mice and men?

"Such a sweet old couple," Watches said as his men carried a huge cardboard box through the store. "It's a shame you have to sacrifice for the cause. Any minute now, your son-in-law will be entering through that door to warn you about, well, ha ha, me. All I want you to do is invite him in for a cup of coffee or something. There are five boys with him. I only want two of those boys. Then the rest of you can all just go away." He waved his hand in a mystical circle as if he intended to make human souls vanish from existence, which he did. "So, I brought the package to do just that." His men tossed the box through the glass counter, knocking the cash register onto the floor. The drawer popped open as it rang, and money flew across the floor.

230

Outside, the boys followed Mr. Fifer across the sand toward the boathouse. Mr. Fifer stopped, and the boys circled around him. The house remained dark. It threw him off since Wesley's other grandpa usually got up to go walking around 0530. Even the bays beneath were dark. When he noticed a bit of moonlight streaming through the large picture window on the front of the house, he saw Watches' white hair glistening inside. The screen door on the shop was also propped open.

Mr. Fifer turned and faced the Armybrats. "Wesley?"

"Yeah?"

"Paddle back. Hard."

Wesley jabbed the paddle backward, and a man with a gun caught the end of the paddle in his gut. Pete lunged forward and whipped a knife over his shoulder. The blade buried itself in the man's neck, and he fell backwards into a pile of canoes. The canoes clanked like a bag of empty paint cans tossed into a dumpster, followed by the sound of metal on metal as they slid across the side of the metal shed. This abrupt noise redirected their attention to their surroundings. They scanned the beach and searched for more of Watches' men. Mr. Fifer guided them up toward the shed. "Come on boys, hurry!"

Pete took his knife back from the dead assailant and followed the other boys as they jogged with him toward the main office farther up the grassy hillside.

Three men were walking down the road from the main entrance toward them. Suddenly, a man lunged from the shrubbery on the other side of the shed and put Mr. Fifer in a chokehold. Danny, who had just come up behind Mr. Fifer, kicked at the man's legs, right behind his knees. The man arched upward through the air as Danny stripped his weapon from him and shot him through the underside of his chin as he fell over a block wall onto the beachfront.

"Whoops! Watch your step, buddy," Danny said. "Chew on your brain for a while."

Two men jumped over the man's body and raised their weapons to their shoulders. Danny took a knee and shot each man two times. Mr. Fifer practically pulled the kids up the hill, but Watches' men were closing in from every direction. Duffy raised a slingshot and shot a man lying on the roof of the shed. He gasped and rolled down from the sheet-metal peak, his rifle clicking the metal ridges with each roll. His body wrapped around the eaves, which tore away from the roofing as he landed in a canoe, which flew off the pedestal on which it rested. The canoe slid down the beach and stopped when it hit the head of the guy who Pete had knifed.

Pete turned around and then raised his hands as two more men encroached upon the walkway where the boys were standing. The men held weapons in one hand and then clutched their throats with the other. Pete's fists were at each man's throat. He released the handles of the knives protruding from their throats as they dropped to their knees. Pete stripped them of their weapons and nudged them so they fell over onto the sidewalk. Then he recovered both knives.

Danny was on the other end of the walkway wrapping two more men in their own weapon slings. He spun them around to face each other and then tied their arms to their necks. He twirled their rifles, so the straps tightened them together, their muzzles buried under each other's chins. Danny ducked backward as he tugged on the sling that wrapped them up like a pretzel. Their fingers mashed down their triggers. As Danny bowed down, the moon shined across his back. In the moonlight, two streams of pink mist arched in each direction behind him as both men dropped to the ground. He had forced them to shoot themselves without much effort.

"We need cover now," Danny said.

"Follow me," Mr. Fifer replied.

They ran around the office just below the deck. Mr. Fifer approached a cellar. Danny spun around and shot two men running across the deck. They blew through the railings and fell into the woodpiles. Wesley ran up to one man who was trying to stand up with his weapon at his side. Wesley grabbed a log off the pile, spun around, and released it. It cracked over the man's face, and he flew backwards, landed on his back, and didn't move.

Bullets buried into the woodpile as a man shot at Wesley. Wesley grabbed two more logs and chucked one. The log winged the tree where the man was crouched and knocked his weapon free just before a round sliced through Wesley's side and splashed fresh blood across the pile of logs. The man stood up against the tree and looked for Wesley but couldn't see him. When he turned around to retrieve his rifle, Wesley lunged at him from behind and jabbed a log into his mouth and nose. The man dropped to his knees, and

Wesley dropped the log over his skull, leaving him unconscious next to the tree. Wesley retrieved his rifle.

"I have some supplies down here in the cellar, boys," Mr. Fife said. "Follow me."

"Yeah," Duffy said.

Mr. Fifer grabbed the barrel of a man's rifle as he exited his office onto the deck. He tugged on the rifle and clotheslined the man through the doorway. The man landed on his back with his head on the door track. Duffy slammed the patio door into his head. Blood filled the track and spurted upward. They stepped over the body and entered the office.

Mr. Fifer led them into a corner room. The furniture was beautiful and antique. Right away they noticed Samantha lying dead on the leather sofa inside the main office. Danny walked over to the doorway and stared at her. Mr. Fifer pulled out a desk drawer, and it fell to the floor. He tossed a couple of books onto the floor behind him and dug around the bottom of the drawer. He felt around inside the drawer until he withdrew his hand, a set of keys dangling from his fingers.

Suddenly, Danny tossed a man through a china hutch. Duffy and Pete attacked another man who exited a hallway. The men threw punches at the boys, who blocked them. Danny moved a chair, so the barrel of the man's rifle was between the woodwork. As he shot the floor, Danny kicked the chair, which forced the weapon from his grip. Danny pulled a statue of a bear catching a trout over a downed log in a river. It was a beautiful four-foot ceramic statue, and it took quite a tug to tip over. The man looked up as the statue hit his face. Blood fanned out across the tile.

Danny turned to see Pete and Duffy struggling with another man near a hallway. He glanced at the centerpiece on the dining table. It was full of fruit. He dumped the fruit on the floor, and tossed at the man's neck like a Frisbee. Pete and Duffy were pulled backwards as they hung onto the man, whose body had just gone limp.

The Armybrats ran out a back door behind Mr. Fifer and crawled out to the cellar as small-arms fire came from near the boathouse. The patio door's glass separated from the frame as rounds penetrated it.

Wesley struggled off the deck clutching a weapon in one hand and clenching his side with the other. His grandfather tried to unlock the cellar door, his hands shaky from the blood pumping through his veins. It may have been a combination of that and arthritis or possibly too much coffee. Finally, he managed to unlock it and swung the door open. All of them crawled inside.

Just then, a helicopter flew overhead. Leaves whipped through the air. Their hair blew upward and fanned outward. A spotlight zipped across the ground as everyone ran inside the cellar. Wesley stopped when gunfire echoed through the trees. He looked back to see more men running up the hillside.

Mr. Fifer patted his shoulder. "Show them the tools in the far cabinet, OK, boy?"

"Yes, Grandpa."

All of them moved against the farthest wall of the cellar and stood still. A few of them were shaking. Wesley's neck was twitching, and his head kept turning to the side. The cellar was musty and dark. It contained shelving units that held boxes, canned food, crates, and other knickknacks. The boxes were full of junk. Gasoline cans sat beneath the shelves, as did different types of synthetic oils, car cleaning compounds, and milk crates full of rags made from old, cut-up blue jeans and shirts. Another shelf had a dual cassette player, record player, and a few other electronic components.

Another shelf had a red Craftsman toolbox with a black lid on it. It had five drawers. Billy opened the drawers and looked inside. The top drawer had fractional wrenches, a screwdriver, and Allen wrenches. He opened the second drawer and found fractional sockets. In the third drawer were extensions for the sockets and adjustable wrenches, vice grips, and a hammer. The fourth drawer had pencils, markers, tape measures, rulers, and small levels. A striker sat behind the ruler. The fifth drawer contained paper.

"Stand easy, boys!" Mr. Fifer shouted as he slammed the cellar door.

Wesley sprinted across the cellar, screamed and hopped the steps, only to discover that his grandpa had locked them inside. The cellar door barely budged as his body slammed against it.

"No, Grandpa!"

Mr. Fifer clasped the padlock shut and spun around to look at the boathouse. "There's a stove down there and some canned goods," he said, "but I need all of you to stay in there, OK? I love you, boy. You kids stay quiet. Grandpa's got this."

"But Grandpa—"

"No buts. Just do it."

He walked backwards a couple of paces. A key bounced off his boot and fell to the grass. It was the cellar key along with others. Mr. Fifer snuck toward the tree line around the propane tank to avoid the men firing at his office building.

Billy pulled out the striker and flexed his fist, throwing sparks from the metal cup inside. Wesley grabbed him and pointed at the fuel cans on one of the shelves. Billy's heart raced.

Watches looked out a window and snarled in anticipation. Just then, Mr. Fifer knocked on the front door. Watches turned to look at it. He smiled wickedly. As he walked toward the front door, he pulled out a handgun and cocked it. He didn't want the Native American; he wanted the two Emerson boys. He looked over at the old couple sitting on the couch. Their hands were tied and their mouths gagged. He aimed the pistol at the door and shot through it.

Watches' men stood at his side. The old couple shrieked and held onto each other. There were three fresh holes in the door to the shop. Watches opened the door and looked at the ground for Mr. Fifer's body. Just then, a leg whipped around the corner and ripped into his gut. Watches flew backward as Mr. Fifer slit through two of Watches' men's wrists. They dropped their weapons and fell to the floor holding their wrists, which were spurting blood. Mr. Fifer jumped into the doorway with two bone-handled knives— one in each hand.

"This isn't a gunfight, my one-patch wonder."

Watches glanced up at him with his one eye. The black patch covered his other eye.

Suddenly, several more shots were fired.

Down in the cellar, Wesley stopped and turned around. "Grandpa!" he screamed.

Billy slammed into his chest and held him back as Wesley slammed into the cellar door harder and harder. Finally, he knelt down, pouting. "Nooooo!" Shots were still fired as they continued to struggle.

"Pull yourself together!" Billy hollered.

Wesley lifted his tear-filled face. "Grandpa Fifer!"

A tear formed in Billy's eye, and he sighed. "I'm sure he's fine, Wes!"

They heard more gunshots. Billy looked over his shoulder in fear of being shot through the wooden cellar door. He helped move Wesley away from it. The gunshots were from down by the riverbank. He was confused why shots were being fired, but that didn't mean they weren't in danger.

Wesley got up and staggered toward a shelving unit. Danny walked over to his brother and pulled on his shirt. He was drenched in blood. Danny was concerned for him. "Bro, you're bleeding."

Before Billy could reply, a crash echoed through the cellar. It sounded like the entire house above them had exploded Everyone jumped to their feet. Wesley fell into the shelving unit. Boxes, cans, crates, and junk piled over him as his body crashed to the ground. The entire shelving unit twisted against the wall, turned, and metal shelves bent downward as a few more boxes dropped. The entire shelf leaned forward over him.

The other boys dragged it away from Wesley as he lay on the ground, motionless.

"Duffy," Billy said, "grab a rag out of that box over there!"

Pete cut Wesley's shirt away from his gut, revealing a gash where blood was gushing out. It ran down his stomach and dripped across the concrete. When Wesley was near the woodpile, one round had skimmed his belly.

"Holy crap!" Pete shouted. "He's lost a lot of blood!"

"Quick," Billy snapped as Duffy handed him a rag. He put pressure over the wound. "It's too damn wide to maintain. I can't stop the bleeding."

Danny grabbed one of the rifles from along a wall and dropped the clip from the chamber. He popped a few rounds out and jogged over to the toolbox. He found wire snippers and cut the lead from the casings. Then he grabbed the striker his brother had been playing with earlier and brought the items over to Wesley. Danny looked at Duffy. "Back away," he said, then he dumped the gunpowder from a few rounds over the gash and struck the striker. It flamed up and glowed bright orange until all the powder burned up over the wound. Pete wiped some remaining blood from below the gash, and Wesley's insides finally stopped spilling out.

Billy felt for a pulse. The boys hovered over him. He sighed. "Little bastard's got heart."

Watches lit a cigar as he stood on the sandy beach. His wide eye reflected a ball of fire blossoming toward the starry sky as the boathouse went up in flames. Fire swirled into the sky. White aluminum siding flew across the river as pieces of the house separated from the foundation. The chimney split up to the top and separated from the house. The question was, were Wesley's grandparents inside when it had gone up in flames?

Now the boys had a wounded buddy locked in a cellar and no way to contact anyone for help. To save themselves from this nightmare, they needed a miracle. Then the possessive spirit of the night grazed the uneasy little terminals computing all the chaos in their tiny heads.

Outside, they heard a whistle echo across the river and bounce off the hillsides. The whistling grew louder, followed by humming. Deep down, the boys knew what they were listening to. They were listening to the moments just before they met their fate. It was coming for them. It was on the prowl.

When the whistling and humming stopped, they couldn't even hear the river splashing on the rocks. All they could hear was the whisper of their fate. The whisper seemed almost as dreary as the first time they met Watches under a bridge.

"Oh, Armybrats," Watches whispered, "Oh, Armybrats. Come out, come out wherever you are. You can run. You can hide. But as fast as you think you might be, when you turn around, you'll see me. Watches, Watches, Watches, ha ha!"

A moment of silence followed Watches' cackle. The boys stood in the farthest corner of the cellar, waiting, listening, and watching the cellar door, hoping and praying the worst wouldn't happen. The coolness brushed their skin like a smooth breeze. The silence pierced their minds like a curse.

Danny crawled over to the rifles and popped the magazine back in. Duffy followed suit with the rifle Wesley had brought in. Billy raised a pistol and aimed it at the door. Danny knelt along the wall to left of the door, and Duffy knelt near the wall to the right.

The whistling returned, louder this time, as if Watches were on the other side of the door. The boys just stared at the door. It was a little brighter out. Daylight was creeping through the cracks in the boards. Then a shadow blocked the light. Beads of sweat tickled their brows.

Suddenly, the door wiggled. Danny leaned into his sites and aimed. They heard what sounded like two more helicopters. The cellar door wiggled even harder, jumping against the screws. Wood split around the lock. The boys were ready to defend their position.

Suddenly, the wiggling stopped. They heard gunfire and people hollering in the distance. Louder gunfire echoed through the cellar, and they saw muzzle flashes through the cracks in the door. The flashes disappeared, and new bullet holes appeared through the door. The boys covered their faces from flying debris. Billy lay over top of Wesley to protect him from stray bullets. The boys had no clue what was transpiring outside the cellar. All they could do was wait . . . and hope.

CHAPTER 33
CHOKE POINT

Civilian vehicles were told to exit the ferry, which was being loaded with squad cars. It was the last resort for any police force south of the Wisconsin River trying to go northbound to get to the Upham Woods Campground. A megaphone beeped, and a cop directing vehicles off the ferry asked people to stay back as cop cars boarded. The civilians drove around them.

Mark turned toward Officer Penske. "We're lucky we got this ferry, or we would have had to drive clear out to Portage."

"You don't suppose he would expect this do you?" Penske asked.

"What do you mean?"

"Every cop crossing the river on a ferry. Seems like we would have nowhere else to go. We're kind of stuck on this thing if you think about it."

Mark watched the gate drop and the rails move up as the last squad car entered the ferry. He got out of his vehicle and glanced from car to car. He scanned the river and then looked across it, scanning for anything suspicious. He glanced back toward the other side of the river where the ferry was pulled by a cable as it made its way across.

Officers Penske and Darcy watched him frantically checking the horizon. Other cops were either playing on their phones or listening to music in their vehicles, oblivious to any danger. But Mark knew better. After Penske suggested the most obvious thing to him, he knew it was true.

The ferry captain was standing at the helm when the door barged open, and Mark walked in. The captain turned to face him. "Hey, what's up, officer?"

"Sir, have you noticed anything suspicious on this ferry today?"

"You mean other than it's full of cops?"

"Yeah!"

"Nope, can't say I have."

"Any strange deliveries? Anything out of the ordinary?"

The man hesitated for a moment as he looked out at the deck, scratching his head. "No!"

Mark looked out the windows at all the police cars. Then he noticed one vehicle in the dead center that was not a cop car. "Whose car is that?" he asked.

The captain stepped up to the window. "Oh yeah, that Ford Pinto boarded this morning but the owner abandoned it. I was going to have it impounded at the end of my shift. Why?" He glanced over at Mark, but Mark was already gone.

Darcy and Penske stared up at Mark as he bolted down the steps. He startled an officer as he threw open a door and grabbed a megaphone. "Evacuate!" he cried. "Evacuate!"

Penske and Darcy ran to each squad car and tapped the windows, alerting everyone to get off the ferry as Mark continued to shout through the megaphone. "Jump overboard! Evacuate this ferry immediately! Get off the ferry!"

He spun around and charged back up the steps, grabbing the captain. "You aren't going down with your ship today, captain." He dragged him down the steps and tossed him overboard. Then he spun around and drew his gun. He ran toward the yellow car in the center. He had a flashback of the explosion at the diner in Granite View. He remembered chasing a little red car to the diner parking lot and the explosion when the car flew off the pavement. He had flashbacks as he approached the little yellow Pinto.

Officers ran past him and jumped off the ferry. Others were already splashing in the water. Officer Penske ran up alongside Mark and drew his gun, pointing it at the coupe. It was clear. No one was inside the vehicle. Mark peered through the window and checked for trip wires. Then he slowly opened the door. "Hold that trunk," he called over his shoulder to Darcy. "Don't let it pop open."

Darcy held onto it as Mark pushed the trunk release. Then he jogged back to Darcy. "I think you guys should get off the ferry."

Penske shook his head. "Not without you, boss."

"Suit yourself." Mark slipped a finger through the crack of the trunk and ran it along the inside. As he opened the trunk wider, he closed one eye in anticipation of a fireball (as if cocking his head would save him) and felt along the entire inside of the trunk. Then he threw it open to reveal a huge bundle of C-4 with wires connected to a timer. It was counting down. They had one minute and ten seconds left.

"Go. Now!" Mark shouted.

Penske pulled out his knife and ejected the wire snipper. "No, we're going to get your sons."

Marks eyes widened. "You can figure out which wire to cut in fifty-three seconds?"

Penske smiled. "No."

Mark rolled his eyes as Penske cut a blue wire. It was a moment to remember. The digital display did not stop. However, the fifty-three seconds quickly turned to thirty-three, then twenty-three. While Penske stewed over the fact that he didn't get it right, Mark was already carrying him to the side of the ferry.

It was dusk. The horizon was capturing the setting sun. Mark pushed Darcy's shoulder. "Run!" he shouted. Then the officers leaped over the side.

A moment later, Merrimac lit up like the Fourth of July. *Colsac III* (the name of the ferry, a portmanteau combining "Columbia" and "Sauk") spread across the river in pieces. The officers' bodies went sailing through the air. Officers in the water dove to avoid shrapnel and fire.

The ferry separated from the cable, which whipped upward and killed one cop in its path before burying itself in the wreckage. As Mark and some other officers resurfaced, a Wisconsin Army National Guard unit drove up to the north edge of the river. A Blackhawk helicopter landed on the embankment, and Mark swam ashore. A few other officers were right behind him.

* * *

A helicopter flew around the main camp a few times and shined a spotlight down at the buildings, illuminating the cabins as it swept across them. "This is the Madison Police Department!" a voice shouted over a megaphone. "The camp is surrounded. Come out with your hands up. I repeat: surrender your weapons and kneel in place with your hands up. If you do not comply, expect to be shot in place."

By that time, tons of campers were standing outside their cabins. Everyone was looking down at the main camp from the ridge. The helicopter belonged to the Wisconsin Army National Guard. Inside was a SWAT team along with Mark, Darcy, and Penske. As they continued to circle the campground, people wandered around screaming, and parents held children back to keep them from running into danger. Police cars poured into the camp.

"Little toy police cars," Darcy said, looking out the window.

"That's the Little Rapids Police Department!" Mark shouted. "They're the ones who informed me about this camp. Their silent alarm was tripped."

Suddenly, another helicopter flew by. "Holy shit!" Penske said. "The FBI is here!"

Mark nodded. "Yup. Tony called in the favor I asked for. He's my old boss. Good man."

They flew down by the river and shined the light at the remnants of the tattered boathouse. Another helicopter flew over the water and hovered near the shore. SWAT team members poured down on ropes, then charged the shoreline. Their helicopter circled and then flew back up to the main section of the camp.

"Who are those guys in the baseball field?" Darcy asked.

Mark replied, "DEA."

Still in the cellar, the Armybrats didn't know what was going on. They heard the voice on the megaphone but not what was said. The office above them suddenly echoed with the pitter-patter of many feet as teams ran through it.

The helicopter descended into the grassy field. Soccer posts tipped over from the wind beneath the blades. More SWAT team members lunged out and made a circle. From the main entrance, more SWAT team people moved in. They had all the directions covered as they closed in on the main section of the camp.

Suddenly, the boys heard people were running around outside of the cellar. People were wandering through the office above them yelling and screaming. They heard a few snaps of gunfire, thuds against the floor, and then silence. A few guys were talking outside, no longer running but walking. Billy looked at a steel washbasin under the shelves along one wall. The shelves had plastic pails and steel buckets on them. He squinted at the cans, then at the striker. He glanced back at the cellar door as thoughts flourished in his dirty mind.

Billy tipped the washbasin over and sat on it. Duffy and Pete grabbed a couple of buckets and sat on them. Pete looked at his watch. It was 0630 hours.

Down by the river, a few SWAT personnel pulled charred boards out of a fire and tossed them. The boathouse was destroyed. Nothing was left besides a couple of walls. Suddenly, a board fell over and rolled down a pile of debris. Sparks joined the smoke as they floated up into the night sky.

The guys dropped to the sand and rolled onto their sides. They aimed at the pile of boards. Five members of the SWAT team were there. Three men were lying near the pile of burning wood, and two more guys were farther down the shoreline.

Someone stepped out of the fire. The two guys in the rear cocked their weapons. The three guys in front lowered their sights—and their jaws. The man stopped between two of the men lying in a prone position and looked down at them. His UPS clothes were charred and dirty, and his shirt was torn and buttoned only halfway. His sleeve was on fire, and he jerked his head away from the bright flame that crawled up his cheek. He grasped the flaps of his shirt and ripped it downward. The dark-brown buttons popped off and fell onto the sand. He slid the shirt off and swung it over his head, then tossed it. He flexed, and his six-pack stuck out, shiny with sweat. Water beaded off his wet hair as it started to rain. He continued walking.

As he passed by the first three guys, they stood up and turned to aim at him. Watches kept walking. The third guy came between the two guys standing in front of the pile of burning wood. Watches passed the last two guys. They stood up and turned to aim at him as well. The men faced him in a "V" formation. The odd man out stood in the middle in the rear toward the boathouse.

"What the fuck was that?" one of the SWAT team members hollered.

"I don't know," another officer replied.

Watches looked over his shoulder. "I'm the devil. That's what the fuck I am."

Two officers gasped as Watches spun around and pulled out two pistols. He fired both guns from his sides and then took a knee. All four guys dropped as the bullets passed through them, one bullet per two guys. The last guy, the point man, held his breath and adjusted his gun to his shoulder. Watches twirled a gun in one hand and crossed his arms. The gun twirled upward and rested over his left arm. The revolver rotated as he slid the weapon up his arm. He fired a round through the guy's shoulder, which caused him to drop his weapon. Watches twirled his other pistol backwards, and it swung over his right arm for support. He fired another round right through the man's chest, and he flew backwards into the flaming pile of lumber. Wood rolled and clanked against a few other boards as the man burned up.

Watches twirled the gun in his left hand and spun the gun in his right until the barrels collided. He lowered his right elbow and drew back his left hand. With both barrels together, he blew the smoke away from the ends. He stood up and turned around, then walked toward the pier.

Police cars tore down the shoreline as Watches dragged a canoe toward the river. The canoe clobbered one dead man's head aside (the man Pete had knifed) as he dragged it through the sand. He jumped in and paddled downriver. Moonlight shimmered over the rippling water.

When the cops reached the edge of the river, they aimed at him as he sat in the canoe. "Return to shore immediately!" one officer hollered through a megaphone.

Watches stopped paddling. He held his arms into the air, a paddle in one hand. His back faced them, and they couldn't see his face, only his silhouette. Smoke rolled across the river from the burning boathouse.

A splash was heard as a blue barrel sat along the shoreline. The waves pushed it against a downed tree. It was hung up on the trunk. It was just like the fifty-five-gallon barrels in which the boys had rolled downhill. The waves pushed it against the tree limb in the water, creating a knocking noise. Everyone turned to look at it. Two cops closed in on the barrel. It bounced a couple more times, and they paused while aiming their weapons at it.

The barrel's ring was hung up on the top of the log, the lid lying cockeyed over it. The limb had fallen from a tree along the river. The log lay on the sand.

Water rippled around the base of the canoe. Watches spun the canoe around without even paddling. He kept his arms in the air as everyone watched him, including the two cops who had been approaching the barrel. Watches sat in the canoe, grinning. A big fat stogie hung from his lips. "Is it alright if I light my cigar, Sheriff?" he asked.

"No!" a sheriff hollered.

"Oh, come on now," Watches said. "All I want to do is smoke one last time before you take me to prison."

"Return to shore at once!"

He lit his cigar anyway and puffed it. "And what happens if I don't?"

"Ready, aim . . ." cops along the sandy shore took knees. Agencies of all types focused on aiming at the canoe.

Watches laughed.

"You will be shot then."

"Can't we work out a deal?"

Two National Guard soldiers ran down to the shore with an M60 machine gun and positioned it near the pier.

"We sure can!" the sheriff said. "Do you see that machine gun?"

Watches laughed. "You have a good sense of humor, Sheriff!"

"It's not a very funny deal, Stanley."

Watches held his arm over the edge of the canoe. "Then you're not going to like my counteroffer."

The sheriff watched the two cops approach the blue barrel once again as Watches glanced at them. Then the sheriff noticed the orange glow on the tip of Watches' cigar. He turned to his men near the shore. "Fall back!" he screamed.

Watches dropped the cigar in the water. Flames puffed up along his canoe and ran along the river beneath the pier. The flames wound toward the shore in the opposite direction. The cops near the blue barrel noticed the flames as they headed toward them. The guy on the machine gun lit up the canoe as they shot at Watches. The flames whipped up over the blue barrel. As the cops ran up the shore, the barrel exploded, and the waterfront moved back several feet. Sand rained down over everyone. The machine gunner fell over the weapon and covered his head.

Flames rolled up the shore and lit up some trees where the boathouse used to be. The machine gunner positioned himself behind the weapon once again waiting for the smoke to clear, but the river remained empty. All the cops were lying down on the sand. The machine gunner glanced over at the canoes tied to the pier as water pushed them into each other. Water washed over his legs from the forces of evil. More clanks were heard.

A few cops stood up. The canoes kept tapping each other from the explosion forcing waves upriver. The machine gunner looked over at the empty canoes next to him. Suddenly, Watches sat up from one of them and shot the machine gunner and his assistant. The sheriff fired at Watches as he jumped onto the pier, took a knee, and somehow retrieved the machine gun with a mystical force beyond explanation. The sheriff ordered his men to retreat as Watches fired at them. Cops' bodies were severed from the rounds that Watches fired. Sand trenches were carved out of the beach. The sheriff ran back down to the shoreline and jumped over a burning log in the river. The same one the barrel of explosives ignited over.

Watches turned and fired at him. Pieces of the log shot into the air. Water splashed at the base where ripples billowed outward from the bullets splashing into the river. Watches screamed and fired off the entire belt of rounds at the sheriff. He laughed and stood up. Then he pulled out his pistol and shot a couple more cops who were firing back at him from the canoe shed. Smoke rose from the M60's muzzle and waved in front of Watches' face. The barrel was red hot. One of the soldiers had his arm extended over the other troop pulling him back toward the pier for cover. Watches dropped the weapon on his buddy, and the hot barrel lay over the back of his neck. He screamed and rolled away from the burning metal.

Suddenly, the helicopter flew over them. It was flying downriver shining the spotlight at the shore. Watches glanced up at it and then shot at it. His pistol empty, he ran up the beachfront.

Moments later, a few paramedics arrived, along with more Little Rapids police officers, a total of four more cars. They tore through the sand and braked near the SWAT team. They positioned the cars in a "W" formation, and police officers stepped out.

Watches ran into the third bay beneath what used to be the boathouse. Ironically, the third bay remained empty. It was dark. The other two boats rocked a bit from the water ripples. Low-lying fog from the humidity and storms from the night before made for low visibility. SWAT personnel headed toward the open bay, but no one fired because visibility was awful.

Suddenly, the water lit up with another explosion. Water, mud, sand, and debris blasted out all three bays. The SWAT dropped and rolled to avoid it. Some cops dover for cover. Other cops flew out of their vehicles and dropped to the ground. Finally, the flames died down.

Sheriff Dunfri of Little Rapids, Wisconsin, stepped out from behind a log that actually was a lot smaller now, large pieces of it floating in the water and up the shoreline as a result of Watches unleashing holy hell on him with the M60 machine gun. It was amazing that the sheriff didn't step out with a few holes in him as well.

Mark Emerson walked up the shoreline toward him. They ran over to a couple of wounded cops on the sand. The sheriff pointed downriver at a canoe and conversed with them. Pilots buzzed them over the radios and explained that the canoe was empty. Two SWAT team guys slid down a rope and climbed aboard the canoe. They gave the all clear.

"Who was that man?" Mark asked Sheriff Dunfri.

"He's been haunting this camp over the past few months," Dunfri replied. "No one knows who he is. But I have to clear sand out of my throat because what I just went through sucked balls."

"We need to secure this camp immediately!" Mark hollered.

"I've got officers positioned on either end of the main road past the camp, so there's no way out for this man," Sheriff Dunfri stated. "Even if he goes downriver, we have guys stretched along the shoreline. We even have a chopper from the National Guard; I guess the FBI has their own chopper too! But I have no clue why the DEA is here."

A group of police officers gathered around them. Some SWAT members walked along the tree line behind the boathouse where Watches was last seen. They entered the forest and swept through it. They also searched the bays but found nothing but debris.

"The SWAT guys have the inside secured, but we need to search everywhere," Mark said. "The main office, the clinic, the dining hall, the recreational center, each individual cabin up there on the ridge, the bathrooms, the storage areas, and any underground wells or cellars. Even search through trashcans. I want this guy!"

CHAPTER 34
BLACKHAWK DOWN

The sun crawled over the horizon, lighting things up. The Madison police provided K-9 units to sniff out the entire camp. Police evacuated the facilities and sent campers to a quarantined section of the main parking lot. The campers were angry, and many were confused. A line of citizens was being patted down prior to entering the holding area. The cops were searching cabins and anywhere for clues. They entered bathrooms, tore down shower curtains, broke into lockers, and dug through trashcans. Storage shacks were emptied, as were cabins.

Mark looked over at Officers Penske and Darcy. He looked down at his watch. They were standing near a bell tower at the base of a staircase that led up to the camp's upper level. Penske was smoking a cigarette. Mark approached him slowly. "Look at the clock. You're on my time now. How does it feel to work for free? You could be enjoying the day off today, but I still haven't found my sons! And God help you if any one of them is harmed. Mr. Carson will be released from detox, and someone will drive him here. Got that? If he's not here in the next half hour, Lord help you."

"Yes, boss."

The K-9 units led police through the trees sniffing for clues. At one point the dogs stopped and licked a tree. Several dogs brought them to the same location. The dogs were sniffing at blood dribbling down trunks of several smaller trees. The police looked up and discovered a horrific scene. Wesley's grandparents had been nailed to a ring of trees. Their arms were spread out like Jesus Christ on the cross. Even their ankles were nailed together. Mark had ladders brought out. A few SWAT guys used crowbars and hammers to pry the nails from the bodies. Then they lowered the bodies carefully using cranes.

With the loss of blood and dehydration, they were lucky to be alive. The dogs sniffed two other trees, which were empty. However, there were nails in the trees, and all the heads to the nails had been filed off.

One dog pulled an officer down a hill. A hand shot out of a mud puddle. Mr. Fifer was lying in the water. He was covered with mud and blended in with the ground. The rain from the night before may have kept him alive as it flushed his wounds and kept him refreshed.

A stretcher was brought down to him, but he waved it off as he walked toward his office. A few officers tried to stop him, but he brushed them off.

Mark sighed. "Gerry? Gerry Fifer? It's good to see you again, just not under these circumstances." Mark waved the other cops off and walked alongside the old man, trying to keep up with his pace.

"Hi, Michael," Mr. Fifer said and then stopped walking. He lifted his arms, and globs of mud dropped down, some splashing on Mark's nicely polished boots. Only his white teeth and eyes showed as he smiled. "How's about a hug, big guy?"

Mark shook his head and thought about his name change. He looked up at the two officers who worked for him. They were unaware of who Fifer was referring to when he called him by his real name. He could tell they were confused, so now the heat was on. Mark turned to them and shrugged, pretending the old man may have forgotten his name when he really hadn't. Mr. Fifer was good with faces; he could remember the slightest change in anyone. Mark used to take Mary down to Ma and Pa's Diner every weekend. Mr. Fifer and his wife, Nadine, used to run the diner. They were old friends, but Mr. Fifer only knew him by his real name.

"Did you find them?" Mr. Fifer grumbled.

"Find who?"

"Your boys and their friends."

"You know where they are?"

"Of course! Follow me."

He led them out of the forest, whipping his arms downward to throw the wet mud off them. "My wife passed away a few years ago," Mr. Fifer said as they walked toward the office building. "The diner is no longer in business. After she passed, there was no way I could keep up with it. If you go visit it now, they put in one of those *Mac*Donald's. They make alright coffee, just not as good as Nadine's ever was." He pronounced "McDonalds" with a hard "Mac."

Mark looked at the two officers and smirked as Fifer continued to refer to him by his real name. He sighed and shook his head. "Oh no, that's a shame. I always enjoyed your wife's cooking. I would take my wife there all the time."

"Yes, every weekend. I remember you guys. Well, life goes on. And you remember Stan, right?"

"Well, I'd like to forget him."

"Yeah, he's the reason for all this mayhem."

Down near the river, a couple of officers were sifting through some rubble. Paramedics were tending to a few people near the pier. One officer approached a few canoes propped up against the boat shed. They were chained together by a padlock and stacked three deep with about six rows across. A cop behind him was working through some more rubble, moving wreckage away from other piles. He slipped, and his foot sank into the mud. He grunted and yanked his foot right out of his shoe. He landed on his ass and crawled back over to get his shoe.

Suddenly, a muddy arm shot out from beneath some aluminum siding and grabbed his ankle. One muddy eye peered up at him from the dark. "Help!" The cop cried, jerking away with sudden shock. The other cop jogged up and tossed the aluminum siding off the body.

The man in a trench coat was drenched in mud and blood. His upper torso was partly visible. The rest of his body appeared like a chocolate raspberry sundae dripping down the shoreline. The second cop glanced at the man. "OK, buddy, you're going to be alright. Just hold on." He glanced toward the pier. "Paramedic!"

Both paramedics (investigating the two dead soldiers) ran toward them. The cop grabbed the man's hand. "Buddy, do you know your name?"

The man lifted his head up from what appeared to be a tire, and his one eye rolled toward the cop. "Ralph," he said, then gagged and spit some blood across another stretch of white aluminum siding. "Fallway. I'm Ralph Fallway!"

"OK, OK, Mr. Fallway, just relax. Can you breathe?"

He nodded, and more mud dripped from his chin and nose, along with a string of blood. His hips appeared to be mangled, and his entire face was covered in mud. His one eye remained shut. He coughed, then dug his elbows into the ground and crawled over the tire.

"Whoa, buddy, relax," the cop said. "The paramedics are almost here. Is your eye OK?"

Mr. Fallway bobbed his eye and shook his head from side to side. "I don't know."

A paramedic crouched down and examined him, then turned to the other paramedic. "Grab the gauze rolls from the truck!"

The other paramedic left him some supplies and then ran toward the EMT vehicle parked near the road farther up the shoreline.

The first paramedic grabbed a towel and carefully blotted Fallway's face to check for gouges in his cheeks and neck. He shined a light in his one eye. "OK, buddy, how many fingers am I holding up?"

Mr. Fallway tilted his head back and scowled. "Two," he said, drooling as he said it. Mud was caked over his other eye.

The paramedic moved one of Fallway's legs back slowly. "Can you feel that?"

Mr. Fallway nodded.

"That's good, although you have lacerations along each leg. I feel a hip fracture too, and your shoulder is out of alignment. You have lacerations on your face and neck. I'll need to bandage you up, OK?"

Mr. Fallway nodded.

Mr. Fifer and Mark walked across the baseball diamonds. Mark let him know that Wesley's mother's parents were going to be alright. He was relieved, but the first thing he mentioned was that he would have to build them a new house.

He headed straight for the cellar. Mark stopped as he walked up to it. He reached down and grabbed the door handle. When he yanked upward, the lock wiggled and slammed against the wood.

All five boys were rudely awakened. They had fallen asleep during all the commotion. They had dumped the rags out and used them as blankets and had used brand-new mop heads for pillows. Billy grabbed the striker he had gotten from the toolbox. The Armybrats had felt constructive that morning and designed a plan to protect themselves. As Mr. Fifer leaned against the cellar door, he smelled strong fumes.

Billy lit some rags that were strung together. They ignited and fused upward toward the washbasin. Mr. Fifer saw the flames through the crack and smelled fumes from the gas cans. The cans were resting inside the washbasin that was tipped upward and aimed right at the cellar door. Little did the Armybrats know they were attacking Mr. Fifer.

Fortunately, Mr. Fifer lunged out of the way and tackled Mark. The flaming rags burned like a fuse, and fire crawled inside the washbasin. The cans ignited and blew out the door.

The SWAT guys had no clue what was going on, and they ran up and surrounded the cellar, aiming their rifles at it. The Armybrats watched several men surround the cellar. Mr. Fifer walked out, and they looked up at him.

The boys screamed when they saw the mud man. They had flashbacks of Watches chasing them near the bridge when he was covered in mud years earlier. It was the first time they had met Watches. They screamed even louder this time, but it was only Wesley's grandfather.

"Look at what you nincompoops did to my cellar door," Mr. Fifer said.

Duffy smiled. "It was cold, so we lit a fire."

Then Mark walked up and gazed into the cellar. A blackened washbasin sat on the first step. It was bowed outward. The Armybrats had taken physics into consideration with its blast. The basin had protected them as the blast aimed for the cellar door. If Mr. Fifer hadn't smelled gasoline, they could have ended his life or Mark's.

"Stand down, guys." Mark told the SWAT team.

The officers backed away.

"Dad!" Billy hollered.

"Dad!" Danny echoed. They charged up the steps, shoved the washbasin aside, and slammed into his stomach, hugging him.

Wesley stood up and approached Mr. Fifer. "Grandpa?" he said. His eyes were two different sizes, and his lip arched upward as he tried to confirm if the mud man was indeed his grandfather.

"Yes, boy! Come here, so I can give ya a big kiss." Mr. Fifer smiled and took a knee.

Wesley's eyes widened because he didn't want to hug his muddy grandpa. He held his side in agony as Pete helped him walk. Duffy yawned. Then he lay back down and covered himself with rags. He shut his eyes and tried to rest some more.

Suddenly, Jake Carson poked his head around the cellar door. Pete left Wesley's side and ran to hug him. Coming out of the dark cellar and entering the bright day was murder on their eyes. As the other boys hugged their fathers, the paramedics put Wesley on a stretcher and took him to an EMT vehicle.

The SWAT team assembled in the parking lot. An ambulance drove up the drive carrying Mr. Fallway in the back. His hips, arms, neck, and face were wrapped in gauze. One of his hips was shot out and seemed critical. When they found him in a mud puddle, his body was covered in mud and blood. Mud was all over his clothing. Some was dried to the bandages over his forehead. His one eye was even wrapped.

Billy watched the ambulance drive into the baseball diamond just beneath the hill where the helicopters were. He stopped hugging his father and stared into the back of the ambulance as the paramedics opened the door. Mark turned to Danny and hugged him. The football fields and soccer fields were full of SWAT guys. Injured people lined the edges. A single SWAT team member walked away from the tree line. He was farther up the hill away from the other groups of SWAT team members and headed straight toward the hill where the helicopters were.

Billy stared at the man on the stretcher for a while. All he could see was white gauze. He walked slowly toward the baseball diamond, fixated on the ambulance. He heard his father talking to Mr. Fifer in the background, but he was in a zone. As he approached the backstop near the bleachers, he heard a couple of cops laugh, but he never took his eyes off the stretcher in the back of the ambulance. At that moment, Mark glanced up at his son for a second and realized he was walking away from them.

Billy could see over the man's feet now. The floor of the ambulance was caked in mud and blood. There was blood on the stretcher's frame. The victim was wrapped like Duffy's neighbor's shrubs the night they had toilet papered them. Billy could see the man's nose, but that was about it. He wanted a closer look, but he wasn't sure he wanted to learn the truth. Danny walked toward him and stopped only to shout his name, but he didn't respond.

Mark looked away from Mr. Fifer to check on his boys. Jake was standing behind Pete with his hands on Pete's shoulders. He either felt the need to hold onto his son or was using Pete to prop himself up because he hadn't sleep the night before in detox section B.

Billy stopped and gazed at the bandaged man, then continued toward the ambulance. More bodies were gathered in the baseball diamond. He heard a paramedic shouting that they needed to move the patient back off the truck to get to the breathing apparatus for a victim near the baseball diamond. Billy stopped walking as the body slid out of the ambulance. The paramedics rested him right behind the ambulance. Then the paramedic closest to him jumped back into the vehicle. The patient rolled his head slowly toward Billy. One eye stared back at him.

Billy's eyes widened. The man's muddy arm was half covered in gauze, his shoulder was covered in dried mud, and his bicep was caked with a thick black mud mixed with blood. He raised his fist and gave Billy a thumbs-up. He winked at him, and his teeth showed as he smiled.

It was about 0930 hours as Officers Darcy and Penske headed toward the helicopter to wait for their ride home. Mark was still unhappy with them for the way they had mishandled information. He would have gotten to his sons a hell of a lot sooner than he had, no thanks to those two clowns. Vital information about Jake was not included in their report, and that screwed things up by postponing the truth.

Darcy looked back to see a man on a stretcher. He had the oddest look on his face as he scratched his mustache. Then he strode over to the stretcher and held the blankets over Mr. Fallway. He had seen blood through the gauze where his hips appeared mangled.

"You look pretty messed up, mister," he said. "A man gets wrangled like that and—"

"Am I gonna lose my legs, Derek?" Mr. Fallway asked.

Darcy stopped dead in his tracks as the paramedics unlocked the feet on the stretcher to move Fallway back into the ambulance. He dropped the blanket back over him. How could the man know his first name when Darcy had no clue who the bloody, muddy, bandaged man was? He pulled at his mustache once again. Mr. Fallway held his hand up to the paramedic. "Hold one second, fellas."

Billy approached him. "Is that you, Mr. Fallway?"

He smiled. "In the muddy flesh, William."

Sheriff Dunfri walked up the hill with more SWAT guys. Mark noticed him and then glanced farther up the road toward his squad car. The car faced the entrance to the camp. Mark cocked his head at the car. People were all over the place. Families were leaving the camp left and right. A long line of cars, bumper to bumper, tried to exit. Some people were hounding Mr. Fifer for a refund. Mark looked up ahead at the line of cars leading out of the camp and noticed Officer Penske was walking along the road.

SWAT guys were in the ditches on either side of the dirt road walking back toward the main lot from the river. Penske continued walking toward the helicopter. He realized he was walking side by side with a SWAT guy who was walking on the opposite side of the road. Penske smiled and waved. "Hi!"

The guy looked back at him. "Hi!" It was Bonzo dressed in a SWAT uniform. Somewhere in the forest, one of their men lay naked. Bonzo had stolen his uniform to blend in with the masses.

As Bonzo neared the aircraft, he noticed military personnel working in and around it. He crossed the road toward the aircraft and jogged up to Penske. He glanced back at the ambulance and saw Billy standing with the patient on the baseball field. He wrapped his arm around Penske's shoulders and smiled. "Wow, talk about some exciting shit this morning, huh?"

Penske was a bit startled at his enthusiasm—almost like a reckless thrill seeker. "Yeah, that was something else." He felt a hard object poke into his side, and he glanced down. Bonzo was holding a pistol against his gut. Penske felt the hole of the silencer's barrel.

"Hand me your piece now," Bonzo whispered.

"What is this?"

"Shhh, gun now or bang-bang."

Penske slowed down, but Bonzo kept pushing him along. "Keep walking, copper. No sudden movements, or I end you."

Penske handed him his piece. They walked around the rear of the helicopter. The military guys were sitting along the cabin door track. They were the crew chiefs who maintained the aircraft's readiness. Two pilots had flown the

SWAT guys in the two aircraft. One was a Blackhawk from the Wisconsin Army National Guard out of Madison at Truax Field near the Dane County Regional Airport. The other was an FBI chopper.

Bonzo shot a couple of the crew chiefs and then hopped into the chopper. He pushed Penske forward and shot him through the back. Then he shot the last crew chief left standing outside the aircraft. He crawled into the cabin and fired up the engines. One pilot hollered at him. SWAT guys began shooting at him.

Only one pilot sat up front. The other pilot was in the woods relieving himself. One crew chief was crawling along the floor of the cabin. A blood trail followed his legs. He looked down at his pistol strapped in a holster hanging off the gunner's seat. A Velcro strap held it in place. He played dead on the cabin floor. The main rotor blades whipped around. Bonzo pointed his pistol at the pilot, demanding he take off.

A bullet cracked through the window and grazed Bonzo's cheek. He spun around and jumped into the gunner's seat, where an M60 was mounted. He rotated the weapon downward and shot four SWAT team members as they tried to board the aircraft. The crew chief stood up slowly. He sat in one of the seats and unfastened the Velcro strap. As he pulled out his pistol, Bonzo let go of the M60 and spun around.

He grabbed the man's wrist and held it away from him. Then he kicked him in the groin and knocked the weapon from his hand. The crew chief disassembled a seat frame and beat Bonzo's head with it. Bonzo punched him in the face, and the crew chief dropped the seat frame and flew over the gunner's seat. He stripped the M60 off the mount and spun around, but Bonzo was gone. Then the crew chief felt his ankle split open. He fell over, crying in agony. Bonzo ripped the weapon out of his hand, and the crew chief fell against the cabin door.

Bonzo raised the M60 to his shoulder. The crew chief placed his hands over the latch on the door and threw his leg outward. With his other leg, he spun around and tripped Bonzo. Then he unlatched the door and dropped out. Bonzo walked over to the door and unleashed fury, blasting the M60 toward the ground as the crew chief rolled beneath the helicopter. The pilot flew closer to the group of SWAT guys, allowing them to get shots at the intruder. Bonzo dropped to the floor and shot at them. They rolled behind foothills and fired back. Bonzo slammed the sliding door shut and jumped up to the cockpit. A new bullet hole in his leg forced dribbles of blood toward his ankle. "Take us out of here now!"

The pilot looked up at him. "I'm not the pilot."

"Take us up now."

The pilot was only hovering at that point, trying to buy time. Bonzo sat in the copilot's seat, then turned and shot the pilot. He fell against the window. Blood splattered over the Plexiglass and dripped down as Bonzo took over the controls.

A few men struggled onto the aircraft. One guy fell across the back and cracked through the glass on the other sliding door. His body blew right through it, and he slammed into the ground outside. The aircraft jittered as Bonzo attempted to knock the other guys off. Then he took off over the crowds of people.

Mr. Fallway struggled off the stretcher and shoved Darcy onto the ground after stripping him of his pistol. He tilted to one side on the stretcher and aimed at the helicopter, then fired at the cabin window. Loose strands of gauze lifted up from the sides of the stretcher and flapped outward. Some officers dropped to the ground for cover. Danny grabbed Billy and threw him into the dugout.

The helicopter lifted off and tilted during its ascent. The aircraft's nose tilted over the baseball diamond. Mr. Fallway shot straight in the air as he came face to face with Bonzo, who scowled out the window at him. Mark took a few shots at the aircraft after he noticed what the patient was shooting at.

The helicopter headed west toward the camp's entrance. Mark continued shooting at the helicopter and then redirected his aim at the patient on the stretcher. The other pilot ran out of the woods screaming as he zipped up his flight suit and shook his fist at the aircraft. He noticed Mark firing at his aircraft. Then he turned around, sweltering with confusion.

Hydraulic fluid was leaking from the ceiling in the passenger bay. The crew chief had managed to cut the lines to the fuselage through an access panel above the drip pan in the passenger compartment before falling out of the aircraft. Bonzo jumped to the side of the seat and glanced back to see fluid splashing onto the empty passenger bay's floor.

Mark stopped firing at the aircraft when he noticed flames in the passenger bay. Then he noticed Penske lying on the ground, paramedics hovering over him. He looked back up at the helicopter as it nosedived. Fearing for the safety of the people on the main road, he ran down the asphalt drive. Sheriff Dunfri joined him, trying to clear people away from a possible crash site.

The paramedics dug Mr. Fallway out of another mud puddle after Darcy flipped his stretcher and kicked the daylights out of him. Mr. Fallway dropped Darcy's weapon during all the confusion. The paramedics backed the cop off their patient and returned him to the stretcher. Darcy stopped them just before they hoisted him inside the ambulance and handcuffed him to the stretcher. They hoisted him back up into the ambulance. He no longer had any white gauze showing through the mud. Darcy straightened out his uniform and then jumped into the ambulance with the paramedics. " I'm tagging along, boys," he said. "This guy is mine."

At the end of the driveway, out on the main road, campers who were exiting the camp were lined up down the road. They watched as the helicopter angled toward them. A few people screamed and ran away from their vehicles. One guy was standing on top of his car videotaping the entire thing; he was one of the reasons why traffic was jammed up. Mark waved his hand at the people and screamed for them to evacuate.

An older couple screamed as their Cadillac rocked on its tires. The old man gripped tightly to the steering wheel. The nose of the aircraft scratched the surface of their vehicle's roof. The violent shake of the car eased up. The elderly couple sat still staring out the windshield—dumbstruck.

A flock of people ran out of the campground as the helicopter skimmed the surface of the archery field. The main rotor nearly knocked the cameraman off the roof of his car and skimmed a few trees. The blades chopped through a few branches, shredded hay bales, tossing up target paper, and its underside ripped open as it scraped the ledge and dove into a ravine on the other side of the road. Mark ran toward it. The cameraman ran to the edge and filmed the whole thing. People stood and pointed down into the ravine.

Bonzo looked back at the cliff as the helicopter slammed into a ledge farther down the rock face. He jumped over the gunner's seat and slid the door open. He lunged from the door and rolled up against the rocks. He looked up at the sky as the tail rotor sparked down the cliff toward him. He flipped over and hung from the ledge, nearly losing grip. The blade smashed over the ledge and scraped the rocks as it broke over his back. He stood up slowly and then hoisted himself back onto the flat surface.

After a harsh tailspin, the helicopter dove. The nose pierced the Wisconsin River far below. Water exploded into the air, engulfing the aircraft. Once the nose bottomed out on the riverbed, an explosion whipped backward and blew off what was left of the tail rotor. More water blew upward from the force of the explosion.

Mark ran up to the ledge. He fell to the ground as the rotor took out the cameraman right next to him. A stream of blood burst across the road, and the video camera fell on top of a bloody shoe. The rotor continued on an upward journey and sliced a huge limb off a tree. The limb fell toward a group of people, who scattered to avoid it. A man saved a little girl from nearly being crushed. The limb smashed over a few vehicles, and their windows imploded. Pieces of glass splashed and bounced across the road.

Bonzo rolled over as blood splashed over the rock and sprinkled down his back from the cameraman. Mark rolled onto his side, and blood ran down the rock next to him. He stood up and peeked over the ledge. People backed away from the blood. The cameraman was nowhere to be seen. The rotor had chopped him up and spit him out with no remnants to prove his existence— other than a short blood trail and one shoe.

Mark glanced down the rock face. Blood ran down the side, and a fire burned on top of the river. Pieces of the helicopter were floating downstream. He noticed Bonzo lying on the ledge with blood all around him. "Well, now we know where the cameraman went," Mark whispered to some tourists. When he glanced over his shoulder, an elderly woman gasped, unable to believe what she had just witnessed.

CHAPTER 35
BONZO

As Mark walked back toward the main office, all he could think about was Penske being hauled away in an ambulance. He walked up to his sons and pointed at Danny. "You, you're mowing the lawn all summer. You come with me," he wrapped his arm around Billy's neck and dragged him down toward the beach.

Danny had never seen his father so pissed. If Billy didn't stride as fast as his father, he would have been strangled to death. Billy's face was red as he held his head down to preserve his flow of oxygen. When they were away from the crowds of people, Mark threw Billy onto the sand.

"I'm gonna kick your ass, son. This can't wait for when we get home."

Billy stood up. "No, Dad."

Mark pushed him down again.

Billy crawled away as his dad charged him. Once Mark caught up with him, he slapped his hands over his son's back. Billy flipped around. Sand particles flew through the air as he spun on his back and chopped his legs like a pair of scissors over his dad's leg. He continued to spin in a circle, knocking his father down. Mark stood up and threw a punch at him. Billy blocked it and nudged him back toward the ground. His father went down and landed on his face. He sat up and remained seated on the cold sand, looking up at his son in amazement.

"Where did you learn that?"

"Give me a minute to explain."

"OK!"

"That man on the stretcher, Mr. Fallway, he was training us for a mission to help him capture this psycho. Watches is your old deliveryman, Dad. And Mr. Fallway has been tracking him down for over fifteen years now. He's an investigator."

"I explicitly told you and Danny not to see that man."

"I know, Dad. We were just—"

"Shut up! You should know better. Damn it, Billy!" Mark was scared to think about Stanley Markesan reentering their lives. "You were lucky I didn't find you 'n' your brother in body bags today. You're grounded, and I'm suspending you from your license as well. You're not allowed to drive for a month."

"What? I'm an adult, dad . . . oh hell no!"

His father turned to walk away.

"Mr. Fallway has been more of a father to me than you've ever been. He's spent more time with us than you have in the past fifteen years. You aren't my father. You care more about work than you do about family, so what do you think about that?"

Mark stopped walking. He put his hands over his hips and lowered his head. He shook his head and then looked up. He didn't want to turn around to face his son, who knew certain truths about him.

"You know it's true," Billy said, continuing to slam his father. "It's pathetic, isn't it? You spend more time at work than you do with Danny and me. It's almost like you don't care anymore. Where did you think we were hanging out after school? We spent every night with Mr. Fallway. Do you know what my passion is, Dad? Guns! I know everything you might want to know about the last decade of weapons produced in the United States and a few other countries too. We know over a hundred different ways to kill someone, and Danny knows seven different forms of martial arts. Do you know who taught him, Dad? Duffy can lasso a soda can resting on a fencepost twenty feet away and bring it back without it bursting with fizz. Pete's accuracy with knives—deadly! Wesley could drop you with his pinky and snap your spine if he wanted to. Do you know who trained us to do that?"

Mark turned around and approached Billy, stopping two feet away from him. He pulled his pistol up from his belt. "Can you shoot?"

Billy nodded. "Yes."

"Oh, you think you so, hey?"

"I know so."

"Here." Mark handed the pistol to him. "Prove it."

Billy twirled the gun over his index finger and then, without even looking, pulled the trigger. Mark turned around, and a padlock holding a chain that wrapped through ten different canoes sparked. The lock fell onto the sand along with the unraveling chain. A poof of sand fanned out around the lock. The ten canoes tipped over.

Three canoes slid forward, revealing men hidden inside. They perked up, and one guy fired an Uzi at them. Mark crawled over top of his son. Billy held the pistol up and squeezed the trigger. The man's hands exploded over the Uzi, and the weapon fell to the ground surrounded with blood. Mark backed off his son. He pulled out Mr. Steely, and they aimed at the men.

"Don't move!" Mark hollered. He looked at Billy, who kept his gun trained on them.

They approached the three men, who raised their arms. When they drew near, tension grew tight. They were Watches' men. Suddenly, the men raised their weapons. Billy and Mark rolled through the sand and fired as they tucked their heads beneath themselves and rolled onto one knee. They shot the two men, who fell back into the canoes.

Mark looked at Billy. Three more of Watches' men were taken care of. Then he looked back at the canoes and stood up. He raised his weapon and inched toward the canoes. He couldn't see over the bows, so he couldn't tell if the men were alive or dead.

"Back me up, Billy."

"Got ya covered, Dad."

Suddenly, Mark stopped dead in his tracks. He tucked his pistol into his pants and stared back at Billy, who kept his gun trained on the canoes, still down on one knee, using it to support his weapon. Mark turned back to the bodies. At center mass were perfect holes through the last two men. Mark sat on the bow of the middle canoe, folded his arms over his chest, and stared back at his son.

Suddenly, the man inside that canoe threw his entire body over Mark's shoulders and choked him. Before Mark could react, blood splattered across his cheek. Billy had shot the man right through his forehead (five inches from his dad's face). Mark shoved the man's forehead away using his fingertips. The man fell and hung outside the canoe. Mark got up and walked toward Billy. He stopped in front of him and looked into his eyes.

"Where did you learn that?"

"I told you already," Billy replied, then whipped the weapon around and twirled it so that the pistol grip faced his father.

Mark took it from him. Then Billy turned and walked away. Mark stood there in awe. He looked down at his pistol and then dropped it. He fell to his knees. "I love you, son!"

Billy stopped. He dropped his head and cried. He turned around and looked at his father for moral support. His dad placed his hands over his knees and leaned forward, crying his eyes out. Billy walked over to him and crouched down before him. He threw his arms around him, and they hugged on the sand. "I love you too, Dad. Mr. Fallway taught us evil. There's so much evil in us now."

"No, Mom and I taught you love. This man was wrong. He brainwashed you kids. You have to let go. Love is stronger than evil. Your mom 'n' I love you boys with all our hearts. Where is this Mr. Fallway character?"

With that thought, Mark stood up and ran up the hill. As he neared the main part of camp, he noticed Danny chilling with the other boys. He looked over at the ambulance as it drove out of the campground carrying the mummified victim (Mr. Fallway) away from the crime scene. Mark was too late to question him.

Sheriff Dunfri crawled beneath a squad car out in the field. He was making sure all was okay with his baby. He was also checking for any kind of ordinance. Then Mark remembered the camcorder near the bloody shoe. Critical evidence was on that thing, he thought as he ran toward the main entrance.

A few people were in their vehicles trying to get around a couple that had crashed into each other during all the commotion. It was a simple fender bender, but the cluster blocked the entire road. Mark jumped up on someone's hood and ran across it. The guy leaned out his window and cussed at him. Mark jumped down off the hood and kept going.

He noticed the camcorder lying in the middle of the road. Just then a car turned onto the road, its front-left tire headed right for it. Mark aimed his gun at the driver. "Stop!"

The driver nailed his brakes. The tire crawled over the camcorder's handle. Plastic shot out as the handle snapped. Mark hurried toward the camera. "Stay right there, sir," he said. "Do not move your car."

"What's wrong, officer?" the elderly driver asked as he leaned out the window of his Cadillac. He and his wife had been trying to enjoy a quiet campout together until that day.

Mark yanked the smashed camcorder from under the tire. "Thank you, sir!"

The man stared at it. "What is that contraption?"

Mark smiled, "A bomb that could have been very tragic for you two young birds."

The man's wife leaned out the passenger window and smiled. "Thank you so much! You're a wonderful person. God bless you, son." His wife slapped her husband's shoulder. "Oh Norm, I told you these Indians are crazy."

Mark smiled. "Drive carefully now."

"We will!" Norm replied.

As they drove away, Mark opened the camcorder and removed a VHS cassette. He kissed the mangled plastic scrap that was once a camcorder and then tossed it into a dumpster at the end of the asphalt that led into the camp. He walked over to the cliff and looked down at the burning helicopter spread across the area for about one hundred feet in each direction. National Guard soldiers surrounded the wreck. His sons came to his side, and he wrapped his arms around their shoulders.

"I love you guys. I want you to know that. And if there's anything on your mind, I want you to be open with me. No more secrets."

Danny nodded. "No more secrets, Dad."

"And when we get home tonight, I want to sit down with you boys and Mom and discuss everything."

"Yes, Dad!" they replied in unison.

"OK." Mark hesitated as he noticed the ledge along the face of the cliff. The figure that had been lying there was gone. He gasped and then dropped to his stomach, pulling himself over the edge to look closer at the cliff face to see if anyone was climbing. Bonzo's body had disappeared. Billy and Danny asked what he was doing, but he ignored them as he wiggled around trying to see the entire ledge below. "Well, I'll be damned," he said.

"What, Dad?" Billy asked.

"Earlier, I thought . . ." He cut himself short and stood up. From the pocket of his vest, he withdrew the videotape and snickered at it.

The boys stared over the ledge. Then Danny looked up at his dad. "What's up, Dad?"

Mark didn't reply. Instead, he started jogging toward the office building past crowds of people gathered on the road.

Billy smirked at his brother. "Yeah, no more secrets."

They looked over the ledge. Farther down they noticed blood smeared across the ledge. Danny cringed and looked away. Billy stared at the wreckage in the river. Suddenly, a man walked between the two brothers wearing a camouflaged cap low over his eyes. Billy grabbed Danny for fear of falling off the cliff. People were gathered all around. He peeked up at the man. "Excuse me!"

The man nodded. Billy didn't recognize him because they had never met before. It was Bonzo. He smiled and winked at them. Glancing over the edge, Bonzo shook his head. "Wow, that had to hurt, huh?"

"Yeah," Billy said. "Taxpayers. Say, why is your shoulder all bloody?"

Bonzo looked at his shoulder and smiled. He pointed at the blood puddle in the road. "Call me a klutz, but I slipped and fell right there. Well, boys, I'd love to stay and chat, but I must be on my merry way."

"OK, take it easy, sir," Danny said.

He walked away and waved over his shoulder. He stared at the road and walked with his hands in his pockets. "Yeah! I'll be seein' ya," he whispered.

Danny followed his dad. Billy watched Bonzo walking past the line of vehicles down the road. He glanced over at Danny, who was walking behind Mark. He turned back to Bonzo. He knew something was off with the guy, the way he walked, the way he talked, the way he was dressed. Even the blood on his dirty shirt seemed strange. But he couldn't quite understand what bugged him about the guy. Then he noticed the long line of cars. Bonzo seemed to be the only man walking toward the exit. Where was his car?

Mark ran up to Mr. Fifer. "Gerr, do you have a VCR?"

"I sure do. It's in the office. Why?"

"I need to review this tape."

"Follow me." Mr. Fifer smiled as they entered his office.

As they walked into the foyer, Mark noticed officers taking pictures of Samantha's body on the leather sofa. "What happened here, Gerry?"

Mr. Fifer walked into another small room with three tiers of sofas, chairs on both ends, and an entertainment center at the front. A popcorn machine was near the minibar. A good-quality surround system lined each wall. On the other side, computers captured footage from his security cameras. Mark noticed how extravagant the room was. Mr. Fifer had invested a lot of money in his home theater. The old man sighed. "I shot my counselors!"

Mark stopped and looked around as Mr. Fifer took the tape from him and walked over to a VCR resting inside a gorgeous cherrywood credenza with glass doors. It contained five VCRs, two computers, two monitors, ten twenty-one-inch TV monitors that showed various perspectives on the camp's perimeter, and a printer. Near the flat-screen television, a dimly lit entertainment center held the components inside. Fancy strip lighting ran through and around the entire system. Several components sat up on a shelving unit built around part of the TV. A lighted receiver with different dials and gadgets had turned on. Mark knew how expensive that model was since he knew which stores around town sold them. It was top of the line.

Mark glanced back at the credenza as the TV flashed to digital cable—clear as a whistle. "What's with the security, Gerry?"

Mr. Fifer laughed. "Oh, me likes me protection!"

"Something bothering you, Gerr?"

"Mike, let's watch the tape, huh?"

Mark stared at him wondering what was on his mind. He stood in front of the TV, which was as tall as he was. He had his arms folded as Mr. Fifer rewound the tape. The image on the screen zoomed backwards. Smoke moved into the river, withering downward. It became thicker toward the bottom, and it looked like the river sucked it up. A quick flash over the river made a helicopter jump out of the water and fly backwards up along the cliff. It leaped over the ledge with some movement on the left side of the screen as the helicopter came up over the road and flew right over the man filming. The forest whipped by as the cameraman turned. Then the helicopter was flying away from him, backward into the campground.

"Stop!" Mark shouted. "Play!"

Mr. Fifer played the footage. The speakers kicked on, and Mark jumped and stared up at them. Mr. Fifer fumbled with the remote and turned the volume down. Mark shook his head at the expensive setup. Then he glanced at the screen. "Pause!" Mr. Fifer hit a button, and the screen was crystal clear. An object was flying up at the cameraman. It was the tail rotor just before it sent him into orbit. "Back it up slowly!" Mark said.

Mr. Fifer fumbled around. "Oh, I know how to do this." He hit a button, and the screen backed up frame by frame. Just before the tail rotor flashed in the corner of the screen, a man lunged out of the aircraft onto the ledge. Mr. Fifer paused again, and sure enough, a man was lying on the ledge. The cameraman had continued to film. As Mr. Fifer played the film slower from that point, the helicopter dragged its tail end down the face of the cliff. Bonzo rolled off the ledge and clung to it with his fingertips as he pulled himself back onto the ledge.

At that point, it was a perfect facial shot of Bonzo. The cameraman must have zoomed in on him. Mark had Mr. Fifer pause it. After the helicopter hit the riverbed and exploded, a tail rotor blade detached and shot upward. The man covered his face and the image turned toward the sky.

"Oh no, back that up!" Mark said. Mr. Fifer did as he asked. The tail rotor blade retracted, and Bonzo sank below the rock, so only his fingers were showing.

"Shoot, go forward again!" Mr. Fifer hit a button, and the tail rotor shot up and killed the cameraman. Both of them jumped a foot as the stereo blared. "Damn!" Mark said.

Mr. Fifer went back to the image of Bonzo and caught it just right. Since the TV was thirty-two inches wide, they could see his face well, but it was still cluttered with pixels and fake colors. Mr. Fifer walked over to a computer. He double-clicked an icon in the upper-left corner of the screen as Mark continued to stare at the TV.

A few cops entered the room, and Mark glanced over at them. Among them was Sheriff Dunfri. "What's that footage of?" Dunfri asked.

"The Blackhawk crash," Mark said.

"Oh, no way," one cop eased past the others and plopped onto a sofa.

"OK, chief!" Dunfri shouted, red in the face. "You investigating my crime scene without me?"

Mark unfolded his arms and turned around to look at him. Sheriff Dunfri was a bit perturbed at Mark investigating what had taken place without his authority. Dunfri walked over to the sofa and pointed at the other two cops inside the room. "OK, you two, out." He followed them to the door and slammed it shut. "Now . . ."

Suddenly, the TV screen went blank, and a new image appeared. Mr. Fifer was working on a close-up of Bonzo's face, and it was perfect. Bonzo's face fit the entire screen, and it was crystal clear. Dunfri circled the couch and glared at Mark. Then he walked over to the VCR (the only one lit up) and hit the "eject" button. The tape protruded from the door flap, and the TV went to a blue screen.

"Thanks. I'll mark this in my exhibit."

"Why do ya gotta be like that, Sheriff?" Mark snapped as Dunfri walked toward the door.

"Hey, I thank you a lot for helping me out with this. But nothing was accomplished here, chief. I have tons of tourists at this camp, and tomorrow they may give Little Rapids a bad review, but I have no one arrested to take the blame. So, hopefully this will be my evidence to clear up this mess. I'll take it from here, chief. Thank you for your cooperation. Good day. Bye, Gerry." He glared at Mr. Fifer and then stepped out the door. "I expect you and the other teams will be gone within the hour," Dunfri added without even looking at Mark, though the comment was directed at him.

Mr. Fifer sat back in his chair and stared at the ceiling. Mark plopped onto the sofa, and a moment of silence set in. Mark looked up at the monitors over the credenza and watched Sheriff Dunfri exit the main office building with the other two cops. He reappeared on another monitor as he headed toward his squad car parked in the field near the baseball diamonds.

Mark looked at Mr. Fifer as he stared off into space. "Who's Samantha, Gerry?"

"One of my counselors!"

"Who shot her?"

"I did!"

"Why? What happened here?"

Mr. Fifer stood up and paced around the room. "I've been receiving threats, that's all. Nothing big."

Mark held out his hands and shrugged. "Nothing big?" he said sarcastically. "Look around you, Gerry. Your camp looks like World War Three. You killed one of your counselors, and you have more security here than a police station. So, for some reason, I think it is something big, something very big. You don't want to admit you have problems here, but you do, and you need to tell me, Gerry. I'm your friend. I've known you for a long time, longer than Sheriff Dumbfri. Hell, you cooked for my family every weekend. I love you for that, Gerry, and so much more. So, talk to me, big guy. If anyone's gonna help you, it's me." Mark leaned forward on the sofa with his elbows on his knees and his hands together as if in prayer.

Mr. Fifer looked at him. "OK, ever since my wife died, I've seen her spirit most nights. She came to me last summer. And she came to me again last fall. And just last week, I saw her once again."

Mark raised an eyebrow with anticipation.

"She loves me very much, Mike."

Mark scratched his cheek and rolled his eyes. He wasn't sure where the story was headed, but it was clear Mr. Fifer was going to bare it all.

"She's my saint. She comes to me to warn me. She even warned me about you."

Mark squinted and smiled. "Oh yeah? She was so sweet. What did she have to say, Gerry?" Mark wasn't sure what kind of conversation he was having, a truthful one, a spiritual one, an Indian one, or all of the above.

"There was scorn and hatred within the fire that night your home burned down, Michael. The evil spirit himself was in your house."

"You went to my house, Gerry?"

"Oh yes. I saw it on the news, but the spirits told me to go. So, I went. And I saw your friend Wayne Richards there."

Mark's eyes lit up. "Wayne Richards was at my old house?"

"Yes. He told me that he was a private investigator, and he was after the man who destroyed your home."

"The man who destroyed my home was a drunken truck driver."

"You're correct, Michael. However, the man who ran into your home was not just any truck driver. He was a deliveryman."

"I'm sorry, what?"

Mr. Fifer looked up at him. "Have you ordered anything through UPS lately, *Mark*?"

Mark leaned forward on the sofa, suddenly remembering that Mr. Fifer knew about his name change. "I-I . . . uh, you know about my name change?"

"Yes, I do!"

"But you kept calling me Michael."

Mr. Fifer stood up. "I've grown up in a world where I never needed a government to protect me. You should be proud of your family heritage and your name. Therefore, I wish to call you by your real name because I don't know Mark. Of course, that's the Native American in me speaking. Please forgive me."

"Don't lecture me about do's and don'ts, Gerry. I had a family to protect."

"OK." Mr. Fifer smiled, but Mark's excuse seemed insignificant to his own morals.

"You're my friend, Gerry. I want to help you. But you need to tell me what's going on here."

"I'm a strong believer in self-righteousness. And until you know the true meaning of righteousness, Michael, you can't begin to understand my integrity as a Native American. I'm the owner of this land. If a man crosses it, I let him pass. However, if that man turns around and dwells on it, I question him. And if that man persists in taking any of my possessions from me, I deal with it. Unlike you, Michael, I do not turn to anyone else for help. I don't want that. I don't run from my problems. It's not in my nature."

"Are you calling me a chicken?"

"I didn't say that. Chickens have a strong attitude about them. But how can you protect me when you're in hiding?"

"That's, uh, that's a strong question, Gerry. You're telling me that I can't protect my own family, so how can I protect you?"

"I ask you, Mike, what good is it for me to tell you about my problems when you're hiding from yours?"

Mark sat there for a few minutes, thinking. "As your friend, Gerry, I think you should tell me everything. But before you do, may I use your phone?"

Mr. Fifer picked up the cordless phone from the end table beside him. "By all means, I'm just going to shut my computer down." Mike dialed the phone and nodded to him. "Oh, and before I do," Mr. Fifer said, "did you want me to save this, Mikey?"

Mark glanced up at his computer as Mr. Fifer bumped the mouse, and the screensaver went away. A picture of Bonzo was in his viewfinder program, which had allowed him to capture a still image from the video. Mark sat up and placed the phone on the armrest. "You saved it?" He was a little behind the times with electronics, and he hadn't realized Mr. Fifer could keep the image off the videotape before Sheriff Dunfri nabbed the evidence.

"Not yet, but I can."

"Can you print it?"

"Hell yeah I can print it, brother. I can email it. I can fax it. I can mail it to your mom. In color too." He smiled.

"Oh, beautiful! I knew I loved you for more than one reason, Gerry."

Mr. Fifer laughed and winked over his shoulder. "Don't tell your wife."

"Actually, I'm going to call her right now."

Mr. Fifer snickered. "Oh boy . . ."

Mark grabbed the phone and dialed like a madman. She picked up with a beautiful voice. "Hi Clarice," he said in response to her sweet greeting.

It was the first time in over fifteen years that she had heard that name. She had just returned from a three-mile jog around the neighborhood. So, between her panting and grabbing an apple for some nutrition, she was just as shocked as when the air-conditioning hit her on her way inside the house. She leaned over the kitchen counter with the apple in hand and smiled. "Mark?"

"No, babe, its Michael, your husband."

Her jaw dropped. "Honey, what's wrong?" She was about to cry.

"Nothing. Our sons were kidnapped."

"That's not nothing!" she screamed, dropping the apple. It rolled across the countertop and toppled off the other side. She sank onto one of the barstools near the counter.

Mr. Fifer looked up from his printer when he heard her scream over the phone.

"Don't worry, honey. They're fine. Look, I sat down and talked with an old friend of ours, Gerry Fifer. You remember Gerry and Nadine from Ma and Pa's Diner?"

"Of course."

"Ma is no longer with us. She passed away a few years ago."

"Oh no. What about Danny and Billy? Are they alright?"

"Yes, don't worry. They're with me. I just wanted to let you know what was going on and that I love you."

"I love you too, honey."

"But we need to set things right. After I talked with Gerry for a bit, he made me realize something."

"What's that?"

"We can't go on hiding from our past. We need to overcome this. I think it's time to return to our old lives."

"Oh, honey, you always surprise me," she cried. A tear ran down her cheek, and she fell silent.

"Honey, you there?"

"Yes. Please come home, Michael," she replied. She was bawling her eyes out. She was so happy for him. She wanted her name back. She wanted to return to her old life. She couldn't do anything but cry her brains out. Mike teared up too. They said their goodbyes and then hung up. Mike wiped tears from his eyes.

Just then Billy burst through the door. "Dad . . ."

Mike looked back at him. "Son, I love you."

Mr. Fifer laughed his ass off that Clarice's crying had gotten Mike so worked up that he was being emotional with his son.

"Dad." Billy sighed and squinted. Mike walked up to him and squeezed the living daylights out of him, picking him up off the ground. Danny shook his head at him as if he were nuts.

Danny walked over to the computer screen and noticed Bonzo's face. "Hey, Billy, there's that man we were talking to."

Mike released Billy from the tight squeeze. Billy fell backwards and smashed through a potted tree. The tree tipped over, and soil splashed across the carpet. Soil spilled into the wall, and specks of dirt stuck to it as the wave washed into a pile on the carpet. "Oh, I'm sorry, Billy."

"That was a touching moment," Billy said while sitting in soil. He waved his dad off as he tried to help him stand. Billy struggled to pick up the plant, but it tipped over again and knocked him over. He stood up holding just the plant in his hand with a big wad of roots spitting more soil all over the place.

"Oh boy, I'm sorry, Gerry," Mike said.

"No need." Mr. Fifer laughed and stood up. "I got it, Billy, don't worry. Let me get a new pot for it." Mr. Fifer grabbed the plant, placed a hand beneath the roots, and walked away with it.

Billy brushed himself off and then squinted at the computer screen.

Mike placed his hands over Danny's shoulders. "You kids saw this man?"

"Yeah, just a few minutes ago out on the main road!"

Outside, farther down the road, Sheriff Dunfri was driving back toward Little Rapids. He noticed Bonzo limping peacefully along the road. He slowed down next to him and rolled down the passenger window. Bonzo stopped and glanced into the vehicle. "Heading my way?" Dunfri asked.

Bonzo approached the car and pulled his hands out of his pockets. He rested them over the door and peeked inside. "I'm not sure. Are you?" He smiled.

Back in the office, Mike picked up his handheld radio. Static blasted from it as someone responded. "Go ahead."

"This is 315 of the Verona Police on a civilian-band radio. I need surveillance on the main road north and southbound along the Upham Woods campgrounds. Be advised you're in search of a suspicious middle-aged man . . ."

Mike squinted at the computer monitor. "Between the ages of forty-five and fifty with long brown hair, and it may be tied back in a ponytail. Suspect is wearing," Mike released the button and reviewed the monitor, then looked at the collar of Bonzo's coat. "A gray trench coat. Over."

Bonzo glanced at Sheriff Dunfri after the radio announced his identity. The sheriff looked away from the radio and glanced at Bonzo.

The FBI helicopter started its engines. The boys walked outside with their dad. He was rambunctious as he strove to find his man, pacing in circles. The boys appreciated their father, but sometimes he failed to show simple emotion. Mike was furious. He wanted answers. He wanted to find the men responsible for kidnapping his boys. He almost seemed lost, as if he felt useless.

"Dad, you need to chill!" Billy said.

Mike stopped pacing and smiled. "Billy, you kids were kidnapped, and you're telling me to chill?" He gripped Billy's arms and shook him. "How dare you, son? You left with this Mr. Fallway character, and you're telling me to chill?"

Danny looked over at Billy, who looked scared. The helicopter was picking up. Their hair was blowing all over. Danny was trying to stand still as the wind beat him to death. He could see Billy was about to melt down and hit his father just to knock some sense into him. Danny placed his hand over his dad's arm. "That's what he said, Dad."

Mike looked over at his son.

Billy looked at Danny and then back at his father. "OK, Dad, now is the time for you to come to your senses and quit being a hypocrite."

Mike was astonished at his accusation. "What?"

"You stood out there and told us to be honest with you. Well, look at Danny, and tell him that you have been honest with him."

Mike couldn't look away from Billy. He thought it would devastate Danny to tell him that his grandparents were alive and well. Their relocation was not only vital to protecting the family, they had kept the entire family from them. Therefore, Danny never met his grandparents. Mike swallowed and looked over at Danny, who squinted due to the debris swirling around. He closed his eyes and shook his head. "Danny, there's something I need to tell you!"

Before he could, his radio buzzed. "There's no sign of the suspect," a helicopter pilot said. "There's no sign of anyone who fits the description you just gave. Our fuel is running low, so we're going to call it a day, sir. We'll be bringing another chopper out for the SWAT team. Otherwise, it looks like we may be wrapping this thing up."

"This is 315 to Little Rapids Sheriff Dunfri," Mike said. "You there?"

Down the main road, Dunfri's squad car continued southbound. He looked at Bonzo, who sat in the passenger seat. They were laughing over the conversation they were having until the radio interrupted them. Dunfri glanced down and unclipped the mic from the CB radio. "Go ahead, 315!"

"Hi, Sheriff. Please be advised the suspect on your videotape is still at large. He was last seen twenty minutes ago heading south on Highway 12 on foot toward Little Rapids. Over."

"Thank you, Mark." He glanced at Bonzo and smirked. Bonzo returned a smile. "I specifically told you to stand down from this investigation. I have jurisdiction here, and you and your cronies were ordered to leave. So, with that said, 10-4, good buddy." Dunfri shut the radio off and placed the mic in the plastic holder mounted to the dashboard.

"You're making the right choice, Sheriff," Bonzo said.

Mike nodded. "Ten-four, good buddy," he whispered to himself. He had no idea about the old sheriff being a "good buddy," but he had his suspicions. Apparently, Sheriff Dunfri had a new buddy as well. However, there were demons in Dunfri's closet, and Mike wasn't playing on either one of their sides. The evil side seemed to have multiplied. Everyone seemed to want in on a piece of Mr. Fifer's baked pie, but no one knew where he kept the baking goods except the old man himself.

Down near the boathouse, the herd of local law enforcement and other federal agencies, including the National Guard, were thinning out.

Across the river was the old sawmill, the one that Mr. Fifer had worked at for many years before buying the campground. It rested on a hill, and it was dark inside. Out in front of the mill, a nice white boat rocked on the water near one of the many piers. It was the only boat out there. It seemed out of place, out of mind. On the back, the word "Wake" was nearly scraped off, but "Part III" was still visible. It was the missing boat from bay three in the boathouse that Watches had destroyed. That remained a mystery. Well, that and the bloody handprints on the side of *Wake Menace Part III* as the wake continued to rock the boat. A hand slapped up over the bow, and a body pulled itself upward. It was a man covered in mud. He coughed and wiped his face. He was bloody, in pain, and out of breath.

CHAPTER 36
MEETING THE FAMILY

A big oak door opened, and a sweet, elderly woman stood there and smiled. A moment later, she practically tackled Mike as she hugged him on the stoop. Then she noticed Billy and Danny standing behind him.

Mike sighed. "Hi, Mom."

"Oh my," she gasped. "Are these? Oh my word . . ."

She detached from her son and knelt to hug Danny and Billy at the same time, mashing the boys together.

In the foyer, an elderly man stepped into view and stared at Mike. Mike used all his might to keep from shedding a tear. The man was holding a file and a chainsaw blade. His hands were black from oil. He wore blue pleated pants. His shirt was dark blue with a breast pocket, a pair of glasses hanging from it. They stared at each other as the boys were being mauled by their happy grandmother.

"Hey, Dad."

His dad grew a smile and then nodded with a smirk. "Back from the dead, huh?"

CHAPTER 37
HANDCUFFED

Jake, Pete, Duffy, Danny, and Billy were standing around Julie Carson's hospital bed. The pastor was there saying words of peace and prayer, hoping for a quick recovery from her coma. But there were still no signs of life. The beeping of the machine just past her head was the only sure sign of life.

In another hospital room lay a gauze-wrapped man. His one eye snapped open. A bright-ass fluorescent light forced him to squint. He tried to sit up but felt strain on one arm followed by a jingling sound—metal on metal. A white sheet covered his body. One leg was elevated in a sling. He moved a bit more, and the clanking sound returned. He dropped his chin to his shoulder and noticed a pair of handcuffs attached to the bedrail. He glanced down his body to see his legs in casts as well as his arms. Then he realized he had been handcuffed to the hospital bed.

"What did you think?" Mike's voice caught him off guard as Mike sat in a chair near the foot of his bed, glaring at him. "You could just kinda kidnap my boys and walk away from this?"

"No, sir," the patient said. "I did not."

"Stop right there." Mike said. "You were seen driving a black Dodge Charger registered to Wayne Richards from Granite View, Wisconsin."

The patient sighed. "I can explain that."

"You murdered him. You cut his throat."

"No, sir. I did no such thing."

"Oh yeah, and you thought, dead guy, nice car." Mike said. "There are people who have never heard of you, Ralph P. Fallway."

"Yes, sir!"

Mike grabbed the bed rail and rattled the man's brain along with the handcuffs. "Cut to the chase, *Ron*. I know who you are."

The man in the bed rolled his one eye up at him. "What did you call me?"

"You know who you are. You're the devil's son. When did you kill Wayne? Where's his body?"

"You have this all wrong."

"No, I'm spot on. You killed my handler, and you used my kids as bait. You tormented the locals. You're a fake, Ron, a fraud. You aren't even an investigator. You have no credentials here. You were after my family the entire time."

"No! Watches killed Wayne. I love your kids. Watches is the true monster."

Mike threw his arm back and grabbed a braided cord looped through a pulley. He yanked on it, and the patient's leg rocketed up, kicking a tray. A plate of peas flipped upward. A fork tapped the floor, and a glass of water sprayed into the air. The patient screamed from the agonizing torture.

"Let me set you straight, mister. I love my kids. Got that?"

"You can't arrest me!" the man cried. "I know Watches, and I have to stop him before it gets any worse."

"He's gone, Ron. He's dead."

The man lay there in bewilderment and clenched his teeth. "No, he's not. I don't buy that. Not for one minute."

"He blew himself up. And your mom, she's here. She's upstairs in a coma. Watches put her here. Hell," Mike laughed, "he put you here too. One big, happy family."

"Mike, you can't do this."

"I already have." He dropped the man's leg and turned to exit the room. "Oh, and um, I have my best cops hanging outside your door. If you itch your nose, I'll know about it. If you have visitors, I'll know about it. Even if you get up to take a crap . . ."

"Yeah, yeah, I get it, you'll know about it."

"No. You keep that shit to yourself."

"I have no one!" the man screamed.

Mike spun around and pulled on his leg cord once again. "Ron, Ralph, whoever you are, you and I both know that's not true. Somehow in this sick and twisted plot of yours, my sons learned some things from you that I don't quite understand. And I'm partially to blame. I'm not saying they trust you one hundred percent, but they confided in you, which leads me to believe you have someone. Unfortunately, they're my damn sons."

"Mike, I have to tell you something. It wasn't me."

"What wasn't you?"

"Watches killed poor Wayne Richards. He's been trying to get to you. I've been tracking him ever since. I took your sons and their friends away to train them on how to defend themselves. I wasn't using them as bait. I promise you that."

"A promise is only one that's kept. You may need a good lawyer. Now that's a promise."

The man dropped his head onto the pillow, which made a crunching sound. He didn't say another word. Mike carefully lowered the man's leg and then left the room.

One of the charge nurses stopped him in the hallway. Earlier, when his sons and their friends were admitted to the hospital, they were dehydrated and had minor injuries. Wesley had his own room where they tended to the bullet wound.

"What's up, nurse?" Mike asked.

She examined her clipboard. "Based on the test results, each one of those kids had high doses of Phencyclidine."

Mike's eyes widened. "You mean PCPs? They were drugged?"

"Aside from being badly dehydrated, they probably suffered through some serious hallucinations or bad delusions. They're lucky to be alive, sir."

Mike fell against the wall in shock. The nurse entered the man's room to check on the machines. Mike walked back inside and aimed his gun at the patient. The nurse screamed and backed away from the bed.

"Did you drug those boys?" Mike screamed. The man's eyes were closed. "Ron, Ralph!" Mike approached his bedside and stared at the monitor, then turned to the nurse. "Why isn't he responding?" The man's blood pressure and heart rate read normal, but he appeared to be out cold.

She held her clipboard against her chest, her eyes on Mike's gun. "He's sedated."

Mike slid his pistol back into its holster and stared at the patient. When he turned around, he stopped dead in his tracks. A clown poster was hanging on the wall near the doorway. He approached it slowly.

On the bed, the man opened one eye and glanced at Mike as he stared at the picture. Something was awfully familiar about it. It reminded Mike of the hospital room where old fireman Winston had died years earlier.

Finally, he exited the room. The nurse followed him into the hallway but then walked in a different direction. The door shut behind them.

The man in the bed opened both eyes, and then a mysterious thing happened. One of his eyeballs popped out and rolled down his body cast into the crevice between his side and the railing. "D'oh, I hate it when that happens," he said. Now he had a cavity where an artificial eye used to be. It wasn't Mr. Fallway in that full-body cast. It wasn't Ronald Markesan either. His lips curled, and the gauze on his face bunched up as his one eye narrowed and glowed red. The man chuckled. "Watches, Watches, Watches!"

NOT THE END

ABOUT THE AUTHOR

Richard King hates horrors and thrillers, and yet he's now written two of them. Prior to becoming a writer, he served for over twenty years in the US Army and has always hated the sight of blood, and yet he has just written two books that include pages and pages of blood, violence, and mayhem. However, like many writers, he knows the mind works in mysterious ways. So, rather than flee from the darker side of himself, like he fled from a haunted house on the shoulders of his stepfather as a kid, Richard has decided to embrace it and grapple with some of his fears through fiction.

Richard's novels are inspired by his home state of Wisconsin, where his father, David, lives with him.